Torn
Jacob's Story

Other Books by Ed Dickerson

Grounds for Belief

Torn
Jacob's Story

ED DICKERSON

Pacific Press® Publishing Association
Nampa, Idaho
Oshawa, Ontario, Canada
www.pacificpress.com

Cover design by Gerald Lee Monks
Cover illustration by Lars Justinen
Inside design by Aaron Troia

Copyright © 2009 by
Pacific Press® Publishing Association
Printed in the United States of America

The author assumes full responsibility for the accuracy of all facts and quotations as cited in this book.

Additional copies of this book may be purchased online at www
.adventistbookcenter.com or by calling toll-free 1-800-765-6955.

Library of Congress Cataloging-in-Publication Data:

Dickerson, Ed (Edgar Dean), 1950-
    Torn : Jacob's story / Ed Dickerson.
        p. cm.
    ISBN 13: 978-0-8163-2363-0 (pbk.)
    ISBN 10: 0-8163-2363-1 (pbk.)
    1. Jacob (Biblical patriarch). 2. Bible. O.T.
    Genesis—History of Biblical events. I. Title.
    PS3604.I285T67 2009
    813'.6—dc22

                                                2009032287

09 10 11 12 13 ♦ 5 4 3 2 1

Dedication

For Mavis

Contents

Preface

I never planned to write this book, and now that it's done, it seems to me more that it took root in my soul and wrote itself. It began, although I did not know it at the time, nearly a decade ago, with a review of the book *The David Story: A Translation With Commentary of 1 and 2 Samuel* by Robert Alter. There I first encountered the beauty and depth of biblical Hebrew. Other than a general enchantment with the language of the Old Testament, all I remembered of that review was the revelation that biblical Hebrew has no word for *Yes*. That is why *Yes* never appears in the body of this book, and I hope you will agree that gives a distinctive texture to the dialogue.

Then, several years ago, my wife, Mavis, and daughter, Elise, gave me *The Five Books of Moses: A Translation With Commentary* by Robert Alter. As I began reading, the story of Jacob entranced me. Alter's brilliant commentary exposed a richness and subtlety in the Hebrew text that is often obscured in English translations. The more I read, the more the spare biblical narrative enthralled me. I first wrote a long sketch, most of which is now in the first chapter, and shared it with my wife (after all, she had given me Alter's book). She encouraged me to expand it and then to share it with my writer's group.

They, in turn, kept asking for new installments, and so, month by month, the manuscript grew until Christmastime 2008. By then I had completed twenty-one chapters of what I projected would be a total of forty. A siege of cold weather, furnace problems, and automotive woes followed Christmas. But this book was ready to be born. And like a mother's labor, once the process of birth began, nothing could stop it. By February 15, I had finished the book, writing seventeen chapters, approximately forty-five thousand words, in eight weeks (later revisions expanded the book to its present size).

Anyone presuming to write about such a towering figure in the Bible faces a daunting challenge. While virtually everyone knows the basic story, few have any real picture of the world in which Jacob lived. Much like the medieval pictures of the Nativity, which show Mary, Joseph, and the wise men dressed like European nobility of the time, we tend to see our world in Jacob's story. But Jacob lived in a very different world. The writer's job is to bridge that gap, to take the contemporary reader as far into that world as possible. But every such attempt is by necessity a compromise. Even if I possessed enough knowledge to re-create that world, simply translating it into English, and into concepts readily understood by today's reader, necessarily changes that experience.

For example, when we say that Jacob served God, we mean the God we worship: a divine Trinity served by angels and opposed by the devil. But Jacob's God was one of many. Indeed, centuries later, in the first commandment, God demanded that there should be "no other gods before me" (Exodus 20:3, KJV). In other words, people—*His people*—still worshiped other gods, still believed in the existence of many gods.

It's difficult for us to realize how great a faith it took simply to believe in the God that today we take for granted. In those days, great empires reigned in the name of their own gods, and thousands and hundreds of thousands of subjects of those empires worshiped those gods. But who was this El Shaddai that Jacob worshiped? In the book, Rachel comments concerning this disparity between the gods whose temples dominated cities and were worshiped by thousands, and El Shaddai, who is "the God of but one family, the God of three sheep-and-goatherders"; the God of Abraham, Isaac, and Jacob.

Initially, I used Hebrew chapter titles and transliterations of several names in an effort to convey to the reader the vast otherness of Jacob's world. The reader might feel quite confident in his knowledge of Jacob, but not so much of *Ya'aqôb*. We who do not read Hebrew, and I certainly do not, miss much of the richness of the story. Time and again the language conveys details concealed by translation. It is not obvious to us why *Jacob* means "supplanter," or as I express it, "cheater." But if we understand that the Hebrew *'aqob* means "crooked," then the eye picks up the similarity between *'aqob* and *Ya'aqôb*, and we can imagine a child being tormented by being called 'aqob Ya'aqôb, "crooked Jacob," or "crooked Cheater." But in the editorial process, wiser heads prevailed, restoring familiar spellings of names. Only the Hebrew chapter titles remain.

Language, of course, is an integral part of culture, but there is more to culture than language. Jacob was a nomadic herdsman, and the original account was written for those who understood that life. But we in our largely urban, mechanized culture don't often think about those differences. It's not as though Jacob commuted to the sheepfold, where he punched in at 8:00 A.M., shared news at the watercooler, punched out at 5:00 P.M., and got home in time for the evening news. But the herding culture in which Jacob lived informs every part of the story. For example, Genesis 31 indicates in passing that Jacob escaped from Laban during the time of sheepshearing. Although I read the account many times, I never placed any significance on that bit of information; in fact, I doubt whether I would have recalled that detail. But the Bible author mentioned it because it mattered. Ancient audiences, familiar with what sheepshearing involved, understood why Jacob chose that time and saw the brilliance of Jacob's plan. Until I wrote that chapter, I had missed it altogether.

The further I went, the greater respect I developed for the original account. For I repeatedly discovered that every detail included in the biblical account posed or answered crucial questions. And every detail that we would expect to find, but was excluded—such as Sherlock Holmes's tale of the dog that didn't bark—also posed or answered equally important questions. The longer I worked with the story of Jacob, the more I identified with him and the more wondrous I found the Bible account. I hope readers feel a little of that enchantment as they read this book. It has been my intent to stay as close to biblical narrative as possible. I tried to ensure that every scene and every character were designed to illuminate the biblical account, to answer those questions inherent in that narrative. If questions arise concerning details in my telling of the story, I hope the reader will go to the Bible to verify them and rediscover the richness of that original account.

The first acknowledgment I must make is to accept responsibility for any and all errors in the Hebrew. I used many sources and asked many questions, but in the end, the choices were mine and mine alone. The purpose is to convey atmosphere, not to teach Hebrew. Sometimes I knowingly took small (I hope) liberties; most of the time, I didn't know any better. So I apologize to all those who actually know something about biblical Hebrew.

First, although regrettably I've never met him, I must acknowledge Professor Robert Alter. His masterful translations and commentaries of biblical Hebrew were the initial spark. My writer's group gave valuable input, and even more valuable encouragement, as they kept asking for the next chapter. Although others came and went, Kim Gollnick, Celeste Grossman, Kristin Snodgrass, Michael Goater, and Bryant Haldeman form the nucleus of the Iowa Scribes, who gave me much feedback and constant encouragement. As always, my dear friends Jon Paulien and Jerry Moon took time from their busy schedules to read the manuscript and give me valuable feedback. My daughter-in-law, Erica Dickerson, continually prompted me for "the next chapter," which motivated and encouraged me.

The good folks at Pacific Press®, especially Jerry D. Thomas and Bonnie Tyson-Flyn, always provide valuable help. And my wife, Mavis, without whose unconditional love and support I would not be able to write at all.

When people found out the project I was working on, they almost universally said, "Jacob. I really identify with him." The more I wrote, the more I did too. And I think I know why. Because while we may idealize certain Bible characters, making them untouchable icons, in Jacob we find a man deeply flawed, torn by envy, resorting to deception, betrayal, and treachery; a man chosen by God for great things, but who struggles—and often fails—to understand God and live within the divine will. In other words, someone like ourselves.

Garrison, Iowa

June 2009

פְּקֻדָּה

pĕquddah

Reckoning

No matter what he did, Reuben could not shake the sense of foreboding that had settled on him from the moment he received the summons. The imminent death of his father meant that his time to make amends had run out. He had tried for years but could never find a way to atone for his transgressions. No amount of currying favor could offset the weight of his offenses on the scales of his memory; nothing he could do could tip the balance in his favor.

The grim expressions on the faces of his waiting brothers told him they had come to the same conclusion about themselves. No one spoke, not even Benjamin, who had nothing to fear and was therefore largely oblivious to the dark thoughts that occupied his brothers. When the young boy they called Dishan ran breathlessly past them, the waiting men knew the last of their number would soon arrive. The cloud of dust on the horizon could have meant many things, but the rolling wave of silence heralded the progress of the royal procession more surely than pharaoh's trumpets. In the midst of the harvest, only one thing could stop the songs that paced the farm workers as they cut, stacked, and shocked the grain. Only the passage of the royal guard could silence the weary but joyful workers, cause them to cast down their sickles and their bundles of grain, and prompt them to prostrate themselves toward the road.

"*Ahmose! Ahmose!*" Dishan cried, as he approached the door of the mud-brick house, ignoring the shushing sounds of the veiled women gathered on benches outside the door. No one remembered whether the urchin's name, *Dishan*, which meant "a threshing," described his constant agitation, or the discipline he sometimes earned because of his inability to remain still for any length of time. The sudden appearance in the doorway of the chief steward, with hand upheld, calmed Dishan momentarily, so that he paused and declared in a whisper that would etch glass, "He comes, *Ahmose*. The Great One comes."

Amos—for that was the chief steward's real name, not the pagan *Ahmose* the boy called him—nodded at the boy and glanced over at the waiting men.

"Go tend your goats," one of the women on the benches called out to Dishan. She shook her head in frustration when the boy raced back up the road, and the brothers laughed, a little too hard perhaps.

" 'The Great One,' " snorted Gad. "That says it all, doesn't it?" Joseph, the eleventh of twelve sons, yet favored above all others, he had truly been the "Great One" since birth in his father's eyes. Great dreams, great betrayal, and now—great power. Would the impending death of their father tempt him to wield that power to extract vengeance? Gad spoke what they all were thinking. "We may not outlive Father by much."

"Isn't this an interesting turnabout?" Dan said. "All those years ago, we didn't know he was coming, and he didn't know our plans for him." He gave a bitter laugh. "And here we are. We *do* know he's coming—but as for his plans—you're right, brother Gad, it may not be just our father who is in his last hours."

"What are you talking about? He has assured you, over and over again—" Benjamin began, but Asher cut him short.

"No matter what he may *say*, he has every reason to hate us," Asher said. Benjamin started to speak again, but Asher wouldn't listen. "Look, little brother, you have nothing to worry about. You are his full brother, and you were too young all those years ago."

"Joseph is not stupid, you know. How better to keep us from suspecting anything than keep assuring us we have nothing to fear?" said Simeon. "Would it be mere coincidence, Benjamin, son of Rachel, that you keep trying to convince us not to suspect your brother of anything?"

Levi joined in, "That's right. We will be easier to kill if we listen to those soothing words and suspect nothing. That's the way I would do it."

"That *is* the way *you* would do it," Asher said. "Just ask the women of Shechem."

At the mention of treachery and Shechem, Simeon and Levi, with fury in their eyes, took a step toward where Asher and his full brother, Gad, stood side by side. Dan and Naphtali moved to support Asher and Gad. Seeing this, Simeon snarled, "So the handmaids' sons make common cause against us. At least we are sons of a real wife, not some servant girl!"

"A servant girl wasn't too low for your brother to dishonor!" Dan said, shooting a poisonous look at Reuben. "We all know you three," he said, gesturing toward Reuben, Simeon, and Levi. "Though you may be the sons of the first wife, none of you will receive the birthright."

"That's enough. Stop it, now," Judah said, stepping between the seven angry brothers—three sons of Leah matched against the four sons of Zilpah and Bilhah—forcing them apart with outstretched arms. "Is it not enough that the most powerful man in the kingdom might be planning to kill us? Or should we fight among ourselves and save him the trouble? Our father honored four women with the privilege of bearing his sons, and he would not be pleased if we dishonor any of them." He looked at each of the brothers in turn, and each of them grunted or nodded, agreeing with Judah.

"All right then. The real problem is that ten of us—all except Benjamin—betrayed our brother and sold him into slavery all those years ago. And if he still harbors resentment for that, he may just be waiting for father to die before he takes his revenge. And there is nothing we can do to stop him." He looked from one somber face to another and said, "I do not know what will happen over the next several hours. But I do know that fighting among ourselves only makes us more vulnerable." Again he scanned his brothers' faces. "Do we want to do that? Or would it not be wiser to appeal to Joseph that we should make common cause as brothers?" Judah could feel the fight draining out of them.

"Rather should we not dwell on our common father? Is it not our one father who lies dying in that house?"

"It is our father," they agreed.

"And he is Joseph's father too," Judah said. "If that is not enough to protect us, then no scheming of ours will save us."

Just then, like a rabbit fleeing a wildfire, Dishan scurried into the courtyard, barely in advance of Joseph's obtrusive arrival.

No doubt because of the haste, Joseph arrived with a smallish retinue. Even so, it subdued Dishan, who was for once awed into a tense inactivity.

The young boy stood transfixed by the eight massive Nubian warriors bearing spears, their rippling black bodies clad in leather and leopard skin, who preceded Joseph's sedan chair; four archers followed, and four even larger men carried the chair. Dan and Reuben exchanged knowing looks. Eight warriors, four bearers, also armed, and four archers. Sixteen trained warriors, who could make quick work of the eleven herdsmen, if that was their mission.

When they reached the courtyard in front of Israel's house, at a sharp command from the captain of the guard, the bearers in unison went to one knee, and then bowed their heads, smoothly lowering the gilded sedan chair to the ground. Two guards flanked the side opening at attention, spears at the ready, as Joseph, clad in crisp white linen trimmed in blue and gold, stepped down to the ground. His guards frowned, seeing that the waiting men only bowed slightly rather than prostrating themselves before the viceroy. Even Dishan stood, mouth open, until a sharp look from the captain of the guard sent the boy facedown on the dusty road. Another command, and the sixteen warriors quickly deployed on all sides of the house and the courtyard. *A security perimeter*, Dan thought. *To keep us in or others out?*

"Please forgive me, my brothers," Joseph said, motioning for them to lift their heads. "The Lord of Upper and Lower Egypt," he paused, "my master, refuses to let me go anywhere by myself anymore. Otherwise, I would have mounted a horse and been here earlier, and," he motioned ruefully to his guards, "alone." At this, the captain of his guard looked at Joseph in alarm. Joseph's role in selling grain, although it had saved the lives of countless thousands in Egypt and elsewhere, had earned him the animosity of many of the former aristocracy, who would gladly see Joseph dead. Pharaoh refused to allow a chance that his viceroy's invaluable service might be ended by an assassin, and thus he sent the powerful bodyguard. Joseph said, "It's all right, Captain Kafele. My brothers intend me no harm." Then, in quiet tones, he said, "That's all long behind us," and Joseph laughed.

We intend him harm? The brothers thought, exchanging wary glances. *He arrives with sixteen armed men and jokes about us harming him? Is he taunting us?* Joseph held out his arms to them, and they embraced him stiffly.

Inside the house, Amos heard the commotion as he sat by Israel's bed. Amos remembered well the night, many years in the past, when his master wrestled through the night. The old man stirred, his eyelids fluttered, and he spoke—his words barely audible over the fitful guttering of the olive oil lamps.

Amos nodded and replied, "They are all here, master." Amos paused, "Quarreling, as you predicted." When Israel did not speak for some time, Amos asked, "Do you want them to come in now?"

The old man pondered. "Quarreling, you say?" A deep weariness enveloped Israel. Even though he could not hear Reuben's thoughts, nor those of the others, still he knew what they were thinking.

The approach of his own death had helped Israel realize that, like many fathers, the years had made him a different man now from who he was when these sons were born and when they were growing up. A different man with a different name.

"Tell me, Amos, faithful friend, is there any hope? Can I mend the rent in the fabric of this family? Will Joseph—" He could not finish the thought. He sighed a sigh that resonated through his whole body. "I have so little strength remaining."

"I have learned that with El Shaddai blessing you, there is little you cannot accomplish. But their betrayal was so . . . vile." Amos shook his head. "Few could forgive such treachery."

"These twelve men, they are too much like me? Too stubborn? Is that what you are thinking?" Israel asked.

"Any man would find it difficult to forgive what the ten older sons did. But these are not ordinary men. These twelve men, these sons of yours, they *do* remind me of Old Stonehead, that stubborn old ram. Always spoiling for a fight."

Israel smiled at the memory. "I remember that old ram." He paused. "You are right, my old friend. We have a lot in common—my sons, Old Stonehead, and me." He looked at Amos, his mind drifting to that querulous old ram. While thinking of that buck sheep, his thoughts turned to events long past. Thoughts became dreams, and he drifted along to sleep.

Later, a bird called once in the gathering darkness, and Israel roused himself. "It will soon be over."

Amos started. "Master?"

Israel's eyes opened, then darted around the room.

"Your dreams, master," asked the ever-vigilant Amos, "are they of good or ill?"

Israel rattled out a brittle laugh, like the crackling of dry papyrus. "Dreams and plans, past and future, mere men cannot say which are good and which are ill."

"Master—" Amos began, concern in his voice.

Israel looked at his faithful friend with clear eyes and waved his hand dismissively. "Do not worry, Amos. I am not crazy—no more than usual. Bring my sons, my stubborn sons."

Amos summoned the brothers. "The waiting has ended," he said. "Your father will see you now."

The brothers looked at Joseph, their father's favorite. He shook his head. "My Egyptian rank means nothing here," he said. "Let us go in the order of our birth."

That makes him next to last, the brothers thought. *He will be behind all of us who sold him. Will he make some signal to his men? If Father dies, will we leave here alive?* But they could not tarry without arousing his suspicion, and so, uneasily, they filed inside.

"While you waited, I dreamed of the past," Israel said, surveying the sturdy men his sons had become. "Amos asked me if my dreams were of good or of ill. Perhaps you can tell me?" He looked at his sons.

"What did you dream of?" asked Reuben.

"I dreamed of rams and sheep, of green valleys and wide rivers, of rugged hills and stone-heaped watchtowers, of shearing sheep and burning cities, of drought and famine. Were these dreams of good or ill? I am hoping you can tell me, for the dreams are not ended."

The brothers looked from one to the other, then at Amos. They whispered among themselves, and finally, Joseph spoke up. "My brothers look to me to interpret dreams, Father. But only El Shaddai knows your dreams." A murmur of agreement rumbled through the assembled brothers.

"You speak wisely, Joseph," Israel said. "Perhaps more wisely than you know." He looked again at each attentive face. "Before I sleep with my fathers, I have brought you here to receive your inheritance and my blessing."

Reuben spoke up, "Thank you, Father. We long for your blessing."

"And you shall have it," Israel said. "But first, your inheritance."

"I have no land to give you. El Shaddai promised Abraham, my father's father, a land of abundance and great beauty. But when Abraham's wife, my father's mother, died, he had to purchase a cave for her burial. When he died, his body was placed in that cave also. That is all the land I have to give you."

"Is our inheritance, then, only one of your dreams?" asked Simeon, with an edge that drew shocked looks from most of the brothers and a look of warning from Amos.

"But, Father," Reuben said, trying to make peace, "pharaoh has given us this choice land of Goshen."

"You speak of my dreams, and you trust in the word of a man? Even now masons and builders labor constructing this pharaoh's tomb. He will not rule this land forever," the old man said. "What one pharaoh bestows, another may take away."

"But, Father, pharaoh has set his seal upon the decree. That document will remain, even after he dies," Judah persisted.

"Do you believe so?" Israel gave a low chuckle, "Let us ask Joseph, who waits upon the ruler of Upper and Lower Egypt personally. Do you trust in this fragment of papyrus to safeguard us?"

Joseph shook his head. "So long as this pharaoh lives, we have his goodwill. But when he dies—even if he cut his decree concerning the land of Goshen into the stones for us—" a murmur of disagreement rose from the brothers, but Joseph persisted. "Glyphs chiseled at the order of one pharaoh may be chiseled away at the order of another pharaoh."

"This is not our home, my sons," Israel insisted. "Remember that, and remember the cave where the bones of your ancestors lie. Promise me that."

"We will, Father," Joseph said. His brothers looked skeptical, so Joseph declared, "I have instructed my sons that my bones shall lie there with my ancestors at my journey's end." The others looked from one to another with concern but made no move to speak. *Will our bones be in that cave soon?* they wondered.

"This is not our home, and I have no land to give you," Israel continued. "We lost most of our flocks and herds to the great drought and famine that drove us here. The herds and flocks that have grown from the remnant of those animals, and the servants, you already possess." He looked from one to another.

Judah spoke again. "We know this, Father. Why do you tell us this again?"

And Levi asked, "If this is not our home, where is it? Even if our bones may go to some cave when we die, our families, our flocks, and our herds cannot live there. We are herdsmen. Without land, we will die!"

A weary sadness filled Israel's countenance. "Be careful what you say," the old man said. "I have heard many words like that in my long years of sorrow." He closed his eyes and covered them with his hands, as echoes of the past rang in his ears. " 'Give me food, or I will die.' 'Give me sons, or I will die,' " he said softly. Then turning sharply on Levi, "I warn you, if you insist that 'without land,' you will die, you may someday have to face life without land." At these words, the sons looked at each other in alarm. "Are you so sure you know what life is?" The looks became more alarmed, but he held out a calming hand. "Do not worry, I have not left my senses, yet."

Impatient, Reuben asked, "What inheritance remains, then, for you to give us?"

"The most precious things I possess," he said. "The things my years and my struggles with El Shaddai have taught me. Some of the events you already know. Some parts you may have guessed at. But we were all too busy living it to recognize the great forces at work, in ourselves as well as others."

"Struggles?" Simeon asked. "We know of your wrestling long ago, when you injured your hip." He looked to the others for agreement. "But you are a wealthy man, with many sons, and an honored guest of pharaoh himself. What struggles do you speak of?"

At this, the old man began laughing that dry papyrus laugh again, till it gave way to an even dryer cough. The sons feared for their father's sanity again, and Amos rose in alarm, but Israel motioned him away. "It is not yet my time to die, faithful friend. It will be soon enough, but for now, I must share what life and El Shaddai have taught me." Turning to the brothers, he said, "I did not know it until now, but the greatest of all my struggles lies directly before me. Greater than the struggle with my brother. Greater than the struggle with my father-in-law and his daughters. Greater, even, than my struggle so long ago that you mentioned, Simeon. Upon the outcome of this struggle depends my entire legacy and your individual fates, so listen, my sons. Listen well, for the time of reckoning is upon us." The intensity of the old man's gaze sobered each brother. "And as far as dreams, Simeon, at this point in my life's journey, all my past seems a dream, a series of dreams. Some evil," he said, gazing beyond the brothers into the darkness, "and others of stunning beauty." Blinking away tears, he focused on his sons again. "The dreams—and the struggles—began before I was born."

הַדָּבָר הַקְּלָלָה

hadavar, haq'lalan

The Promise, the Curse

Even in the dark, Rebekah sensed the knife blade poised above her. Panicked, she struggled against the unyielding ropes that bound her to the stones. She tried to cry out, but no sound emerged as the blade flashed downward and struck her belly. She lay paralyzed with terror as her entrails writhed and recoiled from the blow. She felt something cold on her forehead, and a voice demanded, "Quiet, Rebekah. Quiet, child." Through the nausea she swam back to consciousness, to her bed in Isaac's tent, to old Deborah cradling her head. *Not again*, she thought, *not this nightmare and sickness in the dark.* Her spirit cried out, *Adonai, why did You do this to me?* but she kept silent. *And to think how long I waited for this.*

More than twenty years earlier, Rebekah had eagerly accompanied the venerable steward Eliezer back to Isaac's tent. From the moment she saw Isaac, she had not regretted her choice. They looked to a future of happiness together.

But then seemingly endless years of drought and famine came, driving them from their ancestral grazing lands to find sustenance. More painful to them both, Rebekah remained as barren as the rain-starved earth. Isaac sacrificed and prayed, somehow confident that El Shaddai would intervene and give them children. And they waited.

It is easy for Isaac, Rebekah thought. *He has the memory of Mount Moriah, of the Voice from the clouds staying his father's hand, of a ram caught in the brambles.* Isaac, Rebekah realized, *knew* that Adonai had spared him. Isaac somehow knew that the Promise of a multitude of children, made to his father, Abraham, would be fulfilled through him. Isaac *knew*.

Perhaps she, too, had once felt such certainty. But after twenty years of waiting, her certainty had evaporated. She felt herself drying out, her hope withering like the drought-stricken lands they passed through. She wondered if she, too, would be left behind for greener pastures. She could not let that happen. *Whatever some deity might promise, sometimes men and women must act*, she thought. *That's what my family believes.* So she decided to act. She remembered the day, at dusk, just as the evening star announced the coming of night, when she decided to speak those thoughts.

"Isaac, my husband," Rebekah approached him carefully in his tent. "Fifteen years we have been man and wife."

"Fifteen years, my lily," Isaac said, smiling at her in the flickering light of the oil lamp.

"And still Elohim has not blessed me with a child," Rebekah continued.

"Not blessed you *yet*," Isaac interrupted her. "Adonai will not forget His promise."

"As you will, husband." Rebekah paused, wondering how to broach the subject again. "But we must do our part, even depending on Adonai Elohim, we must do what we can do—is it not so?"

"What are you trying to say, dear one?" Isaac asked, genuinely concerned now.

"Perhaps it would be best . . . ," Rebekah hesitated, searching for words. Isaac waited, knowing from experience she could not be rushed. "It is the way of our people . . . ," so long she had pondered this possibility, but even now she found it difficult to face. "It seems the only way I can give you children would be . . . my handmaiden, Hadasseh."

"So that's what you've been thinking." Isaac nodded. He stretched his hands before his eyes, weighing his words. Then he took her hands in both of his and looked into her eyes. "Rebekah. El Shaddai will honor His promise to my father. I am living proof."

Rebekah had vowed not to cry, but the tears began despite her resolution. "You should have *many* sons . . . and Hadasseh is willing. I've spoken to her."

But Isaac was shaking his head. "Dear one, I will not hear of it." He drew her to him, cradling her head on his shoulder. "It seems a remedy to you now. Your handmaiden carries the child in your name, she gives birth in your tent, and your reproach—as some think of it—is removed." She nodded, not speaking. "And so my mother thought. But it did not remove her reproach, far from it."

She started to protest, but he placed two fingers against her lips. "Every time she saw Hagar with Ishmael, she felt her own barrenness more deeply. Even after I was born," he paused, remembering words spoken in whispers, furtive glances exchanged, "especially after I was born, when her joy should have been full, Ishmael and Hagar reminded her, every day, every moment, of her barrenness, of her despair, her failure to trust Elohim."

"You love Hadasseh, do you not?" Isaac asked, and Rebekah nodded. "Have you thought how her carrying my child would affect the two of you?" Rebekah looked puzzled. It appeared she could make no sense at all of what he had asked, so Isaac elaborated. "How do you think you would feel, watching her body swell with my child? How would both of you react if her body provides for me what yours has not?" At this thought, Rebekah began weeping again, averting her gaze, so he cupped her chin in his hand and looked directly into her eyes. "I am sorry to bring you this pain, my beloved. But I must say this, so that you will understand why I deny your request." He shook his head, sorrowing.

"My mother loved Hagar too," he said, now looking past Rebekah into the mists of memory. "Mother never spoke of it, but in such a camp—" he made a sweeping gesture with his left hand. Then he acknowledged, "One hears things. Fragments of whispered stories in the servants' tents when they think none of the family is near." His eyes moved back and forth, probing the past. "An awkward silence when a name is mentioned. Sentences that break off suddenly. Eventually they form a pattern, like a dark shape in the mist." Now he looked at Rebekah again, seeking understanding in her eyes.

"When my father's seed took root in her womb, Hagar made it clear that she no longer felt obligated to act as becomes a servant." Shock stamped Rebekah's face. It had never occurred to her, Isaac saw. "She said little, but her tone of voice, every facial expression—even her posture, so I heard—taunted my mother, flaunted her superiority to my poor mother." He shook his head. "It came to be, that eventually, my mother could not bear Hagar's presence. Friends for twenty years, and then—you do not think it will happen to Hadasseh. But you cannot know."

Again Isaac placed his hand under Rebekah's chin, lifting her face. She dried her tears and looked directly into his eyes. "It did not remove her reproach; the child *became* her reproach. I don't think the bitterness ever left my mother's heart." Now Isaac wept, too, gazing back in time. "Even in times of joy, shadows of sadness haunted her eyes. And my father—" The emotion blocked Isaac's throat. "I knew my father loved *me*, but his father's heart ached for Ishmael. I doubt he ever fully forgave himself."

Holding her by her shoulders at arm's length, he looked into Rebekah's eyes once again. "We can wait, my dove. We can trust Adonai. Do not ask me again. Do not make me choose between causing you pain and banishing my own flesh and blood. I cannot even bear the thought of it." He paused. Night surrounded them now as they sat in a pool of light from the oil lamps.

"Besides," he added, smiling, "El Shaddai will honor his promise to *you*."

"I wish I could be as certain as you are," Rebekah said to him.

Isaac held up his hand. "Wait just a moment," he said, as he went to a corner of the tent. He returned holding an exquisite box of sparkling blue stones called *sappiyr* that just filled his hand. Removing the lid revealed a long, two-pronged thorn.

"I do not understand," Rebekah said.

"This thorn is from the bramble," Isaac said.

At first Rebekah's eyes narrowed as she tried to understand his meaning, then suddenly went wide with recognition. "The bramble in which the ram was caught? The ram sacrificed in your place?"

Isaac nodded and replaced the lid. Then he set the beautiful blue box in Rebekah's open palm, and, taking her other hand, folded them both about it. "I kept it as a reminder of El Shaddai's promise to me. My mother gave me the *sappiyr* box to keep it in, so that both she and I would remember the Promise. And now I give it to you, Rebekah." She could not speak but simply gazed at the box. "Whenever you doubt the Promise," he said, nodding toward the box, "open it and remember how El Shaddai delivered me."

"And be certain that El Shaddai *will* honor His promise to you." Then Isaac tilted his head and looked at her slyly. "Perhaps beginning tonight?" he said and swept her, giggling like a young girl, into his arms.

After that night, she waited silently, never again speaking of her fears. For his part, far from abandoning Rebekah, Isaac never ceased his attentions. Himself living proof that El Shaddai could bless any barren woman at any age, Isaac's faith never wavered. Indeed, his mother had laughed when told that at the age of ninety, she would become pregnant. His name, *Isaac,* meaning "laughter," served as both a reproof to his mother's unbelief and a testimony to her joy at his birth. So he kept praying. And, whenever she had doubts, Rebekah cradled the blue stone box containing the thorn in her hands and clasped it to her heart.

Five years after she offered her handmaiden, twenty years after they married, it happened. The new moon came and went, then another. Before the third new moon came, Rebekah knew for certain from the changes in her body that she was with child. Though personally convinced, she said nothing. She refused to risk disappointing Isaac, who had prayed so long that her barrenness might end. And, truthfully, she feared to speak of it, lest Adonai change His mind and take the child from her. Rebekah wished to share Isaac's certainty in El Shaddai's favor, but could not find the way.

The midwives, especially old Deborah, fussed over Rebekah endlessly, but the expectant mother never felt truly contented. When she finally told Isaac, he danced a little jig and ordered immediate feasting and sacrifices to give thanks. And even at the age of sixty, he moved about his daily tasks humming tunelessly. He couldn't sing, and hearing him the servants could barely hide their amusement. Even stolid, old Eliezer, the reliable chief steward who had served Isaac's father, who had brought Isaac and Rebekah together, now so elderly that he only sat in the sun and talked of days long past, had a twinkle in his eyes when he looked at Rebekah.

At first Rebekah slept deeply and thought in motherhood she might finally find repose for her very soul. But then the problems began.

Rebekah had heard that pregnancy caused some women nausea in the morning, but of all her relatives whose pregnancies she had observed, none suffered from that peculiar malady. Neither did Rebekah herself, at first. As her belly grew and grew, the midwives didn't think she saw their looks of concern or heard the worried tones of their hushed consultations. They thought they had concealed from her their conclusion that she carried twins. None of that worried the mother-to-be or disturbed her sleep, but when the fourth new moon of her pregnancy arrived, the growing life within her brought her increasing discomfort.

As every mother did, she looked forward to the quickening within her with great anticipation. Rebekah expected activity, but she experienced such violent internal turmoil that she could keep down little food in the morning or at any time. And then the dreams began. In the night, her husband's certainty of his own deliverance at El Shaddai's hands and his insistence that He had given her this, this *curse* of battling babies had combined in a recurring nightmare. In the terrors of the night, she took Isaac's place on that altar of so many years past. The hand that would have slain her husband before she met him became the hand that roiled her belly. Only awaking, nauseated and perspiring, delivered her from the fatal blow. *Adonai Elohim*, her spirit cried out again, *why did You do this to me?* But she dared not give it voice, and the necessity of silence only made her plight more bitter.

In the daytime, her fears paralyzed her. Did this internal turmoil presage a miscarriage? Could she be in danger of losing the baby she had wished to conceive for so long? Would she be responsible for breaking the Promise? Would Isaac be forced to find another woman who could conceive and give birth? So much depended upon this pregnancy, the weight of all her hopes and fears fell upon Rebekah and played themselves out in her dreams.

One night, after the passing of the fifth new moon of her confinement, the terrible dream came upon her again: the knife blade poised above her, the panicked struggle against the ropes that bound her. But this time, she did cry out, "Adonai Elohim, why did You do this to me?" just as the blade flashed downward. And this time, the glint of light on the blade expanded and intensified until she sat upright, engulfed in its radiance. Awe replaced the terror of the nightmare, and she began trembling. Again she cried out, "Why, Adonai? Why did You do this to me?"

"*Two nations are in your womb,*" came the answer. "*And two peoples from within you will be separated; one people will be stronger than the other, and the older will serve the younger.*" And then the light vanished, leaving the world around dark, but the earth kept shaking and shaking. She thought she heard the Voice from the light speaking again, but she could not believe her ears. In the distance, she heard another voice, moving closer, calling out her name. And the shaking continued.

"Rebekah!" Deborah shouted, and finally Rebekah's eyes fluttered open.

Deborah was holding her and shaking her, and the twins—for she knew the Voice in the light had spoken truly—the twins within her took up quarreling again. Although in discomfort, she now felt no nausea because she no longer feared the turmoil within her. "I am well," she said. And Deborah cupped her hand to her mouth in amazement and concern. "I am well, Deborah," she said. "Please fetch me some figs and honey." Deborah hesitated, but Rebekah nodded forcefully, and the old serving woman moved to comply.

While Deborah went to fetch the delicacy, Rebekah collected her thoughts. With her eyes open, sitting up in her bed, her certainty about the Voice in the dream began to fade. She needed confirmation and decided that Deborah might be able to tell her something that would reassure her.

When Deborah returned, Rebekah took a handful of figs and asked, "Did you hear anything—you know, when I was—while I slept?"

On hearing the question, the old woman looked as if she had seen an apparition. She turned her head sideways and regarded Rebekah with narrowed eyes. Her voice trembling, she asked, "Wh–What do you mean, child?"

Now concerned, Rebekah said, "Just tell me, Deborah. Did you hear anything or *see* anything unusual?" The old woman, her eyes guarded, nodded once. "What? Tell me, Deborah, what did you see? What did you hear?" But Deborah just shook her head vigorously, rose, and fled the tent.

Deborah never spoke of that night again, at least not to Rebekah. But something *had* happened. Not only did Deborah's behavior and Rebekah's own recollection confirm it, the actions of the rest of the midwives revealed the influence of that fateful event. Deborah smiled and exhibited more assurance, but others of the midwives and serving women looked at Rebekah darkly, speaking in whispers behind their cupped hands and flitting away when Rebekah came toward them like birds at the approach of a cat. Isaac remained apparently oblivious to all the hubbub, smiling at his beloved wife with benign confidence. Most of the menservants mirrored his mood.

And so silently, without announcement or open declaration, the entire camp slowly separated into two factions. Both anticipated the pending birth to their master and mistress: some with joy, the others with dread.

tiqvah

Expectations

"Demon child." None dared speak the curse aloud, yet it swirled through the encampment like the night mist, condensing on every surface, creeping into every tent. Hadasseh had expected that when Mistress Rebekah finally gave birth, all of Isaac's host would rejoice, for the birth betokened approval of the gods and gave hope of continued prosperity. War, pestilence, drought, and famine made life tenuous at best for the herders of Kinahhu, or as some called it, *Canaan*. Even a callow servant girl like Hadasseh, whose memory held only nineteen summers, knew that a son for the master made everyone in the encampment more secure. Now at least they could hope that their way of life, following the herds and flocks, might survive even after Isaac slept with his fathers.

Hadasseh knew only too well that if food and water became scarce, young servant girls might be sold, or worse. During one such drought, one of Isaac's herdsmen had found Hadasseh as an infant in the desert, too weak and parched from the sun even to cry. For many days, Deborah and Rebekah had hovered over the baby until she regained her strength.

As soon as she could toddle about, Hadasseh became Deborah's shadow. In fact, the other servants often called her *Tzel*, meaning "shadow." Because Rebekah relied more on Deborah than any other serving woman, Hadasseh naturally shared her mistress' confidences. So Hadasseh knew for certain that the birth of Esau and Jacob delighted Rebekah and pleased Deborah. And of course, Rebekah's survival in good health and the addition of two sturdy sons all augured well for Isaac's household. So Hadasseh could not understand the fear and suspicion that haunted the faces and conversations of the other serving women.

"Foolish talk from foolish women." But whatever Deborah said to Hadasseh, the wise old woman knew that these rumors had spread through the camp and infiltrated every tent like a sandstorm. No one could stop it. Truthfully, the events of this delivery had unnerved Deborah as well.

After the birth, Hadasseh gave voice to her questions. "What does it all mean, Deborah? Why do they call the younger one 'demon child'?"

"You saw the birth omens yourself, did you not?" Deborah asked.

Hadasseh hesitated. As Rebekah's two most trusted serving women, Deborah and Hadasseh had been at her side the entire time. "I . . . I cannot say. I never saw such a birth before."

Deborah sniffed, "I dare say." She paused and shook her head; her eyes closed, mouth a grim line. "Few have."

Hadasseh waited, eyes wide. She knew that in time Deborah would tell her what she wanted to know, but prodding the old woman to speak only made her more closemouthed. Hadasseh had seen the twins born. The first emerged, after many hours of labor, rough-skinned, ruddy, and covered with hair that partially obscured the purple swelling on the crown of his head. On seeing him, Akira, an aged Nubian from far away in the south, had muttered, "Ape child" under her breath. Hadasseh had never seen an ape, but she had to admit the child looked strange—wild and untamed, she thought.

And then there was the odd business of the tangled limbs. From the time the first baby's head appeared, the delivery went quickly, until it was time for his right foot to come free. Somehow, the first child's foot became entangled with his younger brother's hand and, to a lesser extent, his head. It looked almost as if the two babes had been wrestling in the womb, the second twin grabbing at his older brother's heel.

Deborah had moved quickly, untangling the infants and at the same time screening the other women's view with her considerable girth. The persistent rumors told her she had not moved quickly enough.

On this day, seeing Hadasseh's perplexity, Deborah asked, "What troubles you, Hadasseh?"

Hadasseh knelt beside Deborah, watching the older woman weaving fine linen. She loved to watch the cloth slowly lengthen as the loom shifted and the shuttle drew the thread back and forth. It seemed to Hadasseh that Deborah played the loom as one might pluck a many-stringed harp, with cloth flowing from the instrument like visible music. "I do not understand," said the young serving girl. "Why do they call the young one, 'demon seed' and 'cheater'? How can he cheat anyone? Besides, did the mistress not tell us—" Deborah lifted her hand from the shuttle and held it up for a moment, and Hadasseh realized she had been chattering again. "Sorry," she said. "I am trying to do better. I try not to speak the first time I think of something. But two whole weeks have passed since the birthing, and I hear these things every day."

"Hush, child," Deborah said, shaking her head with amusement, this time not breaking the rhythm of weaving. "I cannot answer your questions unless you give me a chance."

"Forgive me, I—" said Hadasseh, but a cautioning look from Deborah silenced her.

"Do you not remember the stories I have told you?" asked Deborah, who had reached the end of one strand and deftly began splicing on another.

"Stories, I . . . I . . . story?" Hadasseh had a hard time concentrating, distracted by the beginnings of a blue stripe on the white linen in the loom.

"Stories about the old times, stories of long ago," Deborah clarified. But Hadasseh remained confused. "Stories of the beginning."

"Oh, you mean about the Beautiful Garden, where everything was perfect—" Hadasseh began, but Deborah cut her off.

"What happened when they had to leave the Garden? Do you remember the promise they received?" Deborah asked.

"You mean, about the Seed and the serpent?" Hadasseh said, and then she gasped. "Is that the meaning of the bruise on Esau's head?"

Deborah shook her head, explaining, "The first time a woman gives birth often takes longer and is slower than later births. Many times have I seen such bruises on the heads of firstborns," she said. "Besides," Deborah paused in her weaving and faced Hadasseh, "in the Garden story, which one would be bruised on his head?"

Hadasseh frowned, trying to remember. "The serpent would be bruised on the head, and the Seed of the woman on the heel," she said. "But that would make Esau the serpent's seed. Why apply it to Jacob?"

"Just so," agreed Deborah, who now sat turned away from the loom, one hand on her knee toward Hadasseh, the other stroking the cloth she had woven so far, her fingers gauging its smoothness. "But not everyone reasons so carefully," she said and turned back to the loom.

"What do you mean?" asked Hadasseh.

"Fearful people see demons dancing in the firelight," the older woman said, and Hadasseh looked at the floor, her eyes narrowing. "Listen, child, and remember this: people who are afraid often imagine they see what they fear," Deborah continued. "Akira comes from a land where people believe they are constantly under attack from evil spirits. If you believed that, would you not also be fearful?"

Hadasseh felt her scalp begin to prickle, "It frightens me even now."

"When frightened, do you ever hear strange sounds in the night, sounds that you imagine are beasts ready to attack you?" Deborah asked, although she knew the answer. The older woman had often cradled Hadasseh in her arms when nightmares disturbed the young girl's sleep. For her part, a wide-eyed Hadasseh merely nodded.

"And if you believed a lion waited in the darkness in order to attack you unseen, would that make it more likely you would hear lion sounds in the darkness?" Deborah asked, met with the same wide-eyed nod.

"So it is with some foolish women here in Isaac's encampment. They hear something about a bruised head, a heel, a hand, and they turn that into an evil omen."

"But is it not strange that twins would look so different?" asked the younger woman.

"A little," Deborah conceded. "Unusual, but not unheard of. Sometimes twins look alike, sometimes not. You have heard of a boy and a girl as twins, have you not?" asked Deborah. When Hadasseh nodded, Deborah continued. "Can any two boys be more different than a boy is from a girl, hmm?"

Hadasseh had never thought of that. "Then there is nothing to the whole idea of the brothers warring against each other?" she asked.

"Now, when did you ever hear me say that?" asked Deborah, and her tone warned Hadasseh not to press further. "Do not the orphaned kids need to be fed?" Deborah asked, a twinkle in her eye.

Hadasseh almost leaped in delight at this invitation. "But will the herdsmen let me?"

"Tell them Deborah said so." And the old woman smiled to see Tzel, her little shadow, run out to feed the kids. Hadasseh would not spread the foul gossip that poisoned the very air of the encampment. But Akira and the others were another matter.

Deborah did not know what to do. To deny the gossip, she would have to state it explicitly, which would spread it to every ear. And in Deborah's experience, denying gossip only made it more believable to those already inclined to accept it.

Neither could Deborah mention it to Rebekah. Her mistress would either fly into a rage or dismiss it, and publicly at that. And both of those outcomes only gave more force to the perfidious lies, lies too strong already. Besides, the mistress would instruct all the women to pray, not realizing what some would be praying for—or to whom they would be praying.

Rather than uniting the camp in joy over the arrival of an heir, the birth of the twins had divided everyone's loyalties. The manner of their birth and the gossip surrounding it aggravated that division. Isaac already exhibited a marked partiality to Esau. And an unearthly experience during Rebekah's pregnancy gave Rebekah an unshakable allegiance to the younger one, Jacob. And now, these murmurings of "demon child," "cheater," " 'aqob,"—the last meaning "crooked"—and dark rumors of bruised heads and entangled heels, all of these things filled many hearts with dread and filled many minds with expectations, good and bad. *Poor little boys,* Deborah thought. *You're only a few weeks old, and already everyone thinks they know who you will be. People will scrutinize every action, every unguarded moment, looking for evidence that matches their expectations.* She shook her head. She knew people. Whatever they saw in the boys that matched their expectations, they would exaggerate. Whatever contradicted those preconceived notions, they would reject and forget. *Poor boys,* she thought. *You never had a chance.*

mitabkim

Wrestlers

The grazing goats had moved on, leaving Jacob and the kid with the brown splotches perilously distant from the rest of the herd. The usually vigilant Rebekah, distracted by two quarreling servant girls, failed to see the shape moving from the shadow of a rock to the concealment of a desert shrub, from that shrub to a shallow gully—each move coming closer to little Jacob, who was stroking and talking to his companion.

Only when Isaac beckoned to her, a finger to his lips, did she see the shape of the stalker and recognize it as Esau, the older twin.

"What a little hunter he is," Isaac said, watching Esau's movements.

You encourage him too much, thought Rebekah, but being an obedient wife, she said nothing. It had become almost a daily occurrence, this play hunting. Esau would stalk a lamb or a kid, moving with stealth until he could spring and grab the frightened animal by the tail, much to his father's amusement. Jacob and Rebekah protested this needless frightening of the livestock, but nothing could convince Isaac, and thus nothing could deter young Esau. So, although Rebekah wanted to warn Jacob of Esau's impending attack, she dared not. However, unknown to all, another watcher, indifferent to Isaac's desires, also monitored Esau's progress.

By this time, Esau's movements brought him to a small shrub within striking distance. He sprang forward, but a dark blur cut between him and his prey, striking Esau in the side and converting his shout of triumph into a pained grunt. The impact sent him flying, and he landed in a heap to one side.

Startled, Jacob turned in bewilderment toward the sound and movement. The speckled young goat bolted from his grasp and trotted, complaining all the way, to his mother's side. For her part, the doe stood over the prone Esau, daring him to get up, and warning him to leave her kid alone in the future.

Esau sat up, rubbing his sore ribs, angry as a hornet, not so much at the doe, as at the laughter that erupted on all sides, especially from brother Jacob. Dusting himself off, he saw his father laughing and grudgingly joined in.

Rebekah's mouth smiled at Isaac, who was laughing too hard to notice her somber eyes. Then she covered her mouth, as though laughing. But she was not, because she saw the poisonous looks exchanged between her two sons. She had loved Isaac dearly, even desperately, from the first time Eliezer had brought her to Isaac's camp. Rebekah wondered if perhaps because they had just two children, both parents felt such a deep interest in one or the other. She had hoped to give Isaac many children, but Elohim had blessed them only with the twins. Instead of uniting them, the birth of the two boys brought the first hints at division between her and her husband. Not only did the boys look different, sometimes they seemed to have nothing in common.

* * * * *

"And then little Jacob looked at me very gravely and said, 'Animals do not gossip, Father. That's why I like them!' " Isaac told Rebekah weeks later, as they retired for the night.

"He said what?" Rebekah asked incredulously.

" 'Animals do not gossip, Father.' He said those very words. A serious statement," Isaac said, eyes dancing with amusement, "for a boy who has as many fingers as years."

Rebekah shook her head in amazement. "So different." She had said the words under her breath, but Isaac heard her anyway.

"Different? They could not be more different," Isaac agreed. "Esau would never say such a thing. He might talk of how animals hide or hunt," and then he chuckled, "or maybe how they taste!"

"Truly. Esau seems to spend every waking hour hunting," Rebekah said, "while Jacob spends his time with the herds, and the herdsmen. So much time you would think him already the master." Isaac flinched visibly when she said this.

"Esau will grow into his responsibilities," Isaac said, careful of the first-born's prerogatives. "Besides, I think Jacob's far too serious for one so young. Gossip, indeed! What sort of a child worries about gossip? He needs to act more like a little boy."

"He *is* far more serious than Esau," Rebekah said.

"I do not want this argument again," Isaac stormed.

"I agreed with you, Isaac. How can that be an argument?" she asked.

How indeed? Isaac wondered. *Her words agree, but her tone of voice contradicts me.* He sighed. "Rivalry ravaged my father's household." Isaac declared. "I will not allow it!"

"Of course not, husband," Rebekah said. "I meant no challenge to that. I only said—"

"What you always say," Isaac remained adamant. "That Jacob acts responsibly and Esau does not." He waved his hands before him. "Give me peace on this, Rebekah. They are still little boys. Esau is firstborn. That will not change, and I will not change my mind in this matter. I know more than anyone else the damage it would do to both boys. Let the boys be children."

Rebekah opened her mouth to speak, but thought better of it and simply bowed her head in acquiescence and obedience. *So my little Jacob says, "Animals do not gossip,"* Rebekah thought. *And no wonder. Animals do not care who is firstborn. All they know is who cares for them and who abuses them. And Jacob thinks about such things because his whole life he has been the object of gossip.* She sighed. She would let them be little boys, she decided. But even that had limits.

* * * * *

"Look at this!" Rebekah demanded. Jacob squirmed as she held his arm up, exposing the purple bruise on his ribs.

"Tattler!" Esau said, lunging at his brother. Isaac caught and restrained him, hands firmly on the boy's shoulders, but he looked inquiringly at Rebekah.

"Jacob said nothing. In fact, he tried to hide it," Rebekah explained, "but I saw him grimace when he turned, and that gave it away." She fixed an angry gaze on Esau, then on Isaac. "What are you going to do about it?"

Her expression made it clear that she wanted more direct action from him.

"Did you do this?" Isaac asked of Esau.

"I did," Esau said, clearly pleased. "Jacob was an addax," the boy said, referring to the large antelope with the curling horns, "hiding from the mighty hunter. The addax is strong. A hunter must strike hard to bring them down."

"And so you struck him hard with your blunt stick spear?" Isaac asked.

"I did. I saw him hiding by the bank of the wadi, so I crouched low and moved silently like a leopard until I got close, and then I swooped in like a diving falcon—" Isaac smiled in appreciation of Esau's enthusiasm until his eyes met Rebekah's indignant expression. "And—"

Isaac, now grim, said, "I think we understand what you did." Turning to Jacob, Isaac asked, "Did you agree to be an addax?"

Jacob nodded silently, then said, "I chose to be an addax."

"What difference does that make?" Rebekah said, indignant.

Isaac held up his hands, fending off her anger. "Do not overprotect them, Rebekah. Let them be boys." He gestured to the twins, "Go and play now. Your mother wants to talk to me." Esau grinned and raced off to parts unknown. The grateful Jacob broke free and quickly made his way to the nearest goat pens.

"Did you see that bruise?"

Isaac looked stricken, then covered his eyes with his hand, rubbing his temples with thumb and fingers. "I saw it, Rebekah," he said, his voice weary. "Boys play rough. Sometimes they get bruises."

"*They* do not, Isaac," Rebekah said. "When did Esau ever come to you with a bruise?" Isaac shrugged his shoulders, and she continued. "They play that dreadful hunting game. Esau stalks Jacob and strikes him with a stick, like a hunter spearing his prey."

"I know about their little game. Esau wants to be a hunter. Jacob chose to be an addax."

"Are you saying Jacob provoked such treatment by choosing to be a large animal rather than a small one? Esau should not be hunting his brother!" Rebekah said, outraged. "Jacob agrees because he fears looking like a coward. He chose the addax because the beast is powerful. He fears *you* will think him a coward, and he knows you will side with Esau no matter what he does."

Isaac began massaging his temples again, this time with both hands. "I do not want to talk about it, not again."

Unseen, Jacob had drifted around the side of the goat pen. He wondered what his father would say about Esau's bullying.

"Well, I must talk with you about it. I can wait no longer," Rebekah said. "It is my duty as your wife to warn you: you are turning Esau into a monster," she said. "From their earliest days, you have praised Esau and criticized or ignored Jacob."

"And you do the opposite," Isaac began, but the dark fire in Rebekah's eyes stopped him.

"Jacob must have *some* encouragement. You would destroy his spirit. With you it is always Esau, only Esau, the hairy one, so masculine and strong and a hunter by nature. Esau, ruddy of skin, nicknamed *Edom* meaning 'Red.' " She shook her head in disbelief. "If that were not bad enough, you have to keep pointing out that Edom is not just your pet name, a name of parental endearment, but much more. You compare Esau with the first man, the greatest of all men, the man Elohim formed out of clay with His own hands. Elohim named that man 'Adam,' so you call your son 'Edom'—almost exactly the same!"

"Well," Isaac said, defending his choice, "after all, both names mean 'red.' " Isaac's expression bespoke innocence, "You have to admit, the name fits."

"Is that all you can say? 'The name fits'? "

"Red for the earth, red for the clay from which the first man was formed," Isaac shrugged. "*Edom, Adam*; they sound alike." He smiled hopefully.

"But you use it to puff up the boy! You make him think he's a paradigm of manhood—almost as if he were the great Adam himself." Isaac stared at Rebekah. He rarely saw her so agitated. "All anyone hears from you is 'Look at Esau,' 'See what Red did,' 'How manly, how like Adam is Edom.' The servants echo your words and mirror your attitudes.

"But you say nothing so positive about Jacob. And the servants notice that. From the moment of his birth, the midwives and servants whispered, 'Better keep an eye on that one. Do not turn your back on that one. He will trip you up, for sure, like he tried to trip his brother. Demon child!' They say this about your child, Isaac! And you do nothing to stop them!" Rebekah became quieter. "Esau lords it over everyone in the camp, abuses his brother, and all you can say is 'Let them be boys'?"

Tears of anger and frustration filled her eyes. "Do you wonder that Jacob feels angry and resentful? Someday, Isaac—" Rebekah held a hand to her mouth, and after breathing deeply, she fixed Isaac with a pleading glance. "If you do not do something, someday this will cause us all great pain. I plead with you."

Isaac, his face grim, said, "Esau is firstborn. Nothing can change that. The sooner Jacob resigns himself to that, the easier it will be—for *everyone*. You have told me of your dream, 'the older shall serve the younger.'" He paused, shaking his head. "That will bring only more confusion, more grief," he made a slashing motion with his hands. "I know that of which I speak. I sometimes wonder if Ishmael's anger toward me will ever be quenched, or if his children and mine must fight throughout the ages. I cannot be moved on this."

You cannot be moved, Rebekah thought, so she bowed her head in resignation and returned to supervise the serving women as they performed their daily household duties. But Rebekah could not forget the words of the Voice from the light. Whatever others thought, in her heart, Rebekah knew that Jacob would be the greater. "*Two nations,*" the Voice had said. "*The older will serve the younger.*" Rebekah repeated the words again and again in her mind. Some of the words did not make sense to her, but those that did grew in significance. So as she walked, she spoke them aloud to herself. "I will be known as the mother of two nations," she told herself, "but shall the older serve the younger?" On the way, she passed a young boy tending to the goats without noticing him. Jacob had heard everything.

* * * * *

Time passed, and as manhood beckoned, the boys grew taller—and further apart. From the beginning, Esau felt one with the wild, especially the hunting animals. Impatient with the sheep and goats, he always drifted to the edge of the grazing lands, heeding the call of the hunt. Even as a little boy, nothing thrilled him so much as the swooping dive of a falcon, the startling speed of the cheetah, the rippling strength of the lion and the leopard, and the raw power of the bear. Constantly he searched for them, watched them as they hunted, learned the habits of their prey. Then he imitated their methods as best he could, first on his brother and the domestic animals, and later hunting the prey himself.

By contrast, Jacob found refuge and acceptance with domesticated animals. Even when they suffered, and he had to cause them pain, as when removing a thorn, animals seemed to trust him; a stark contrast to the suspicion so many people exhibited toward him. As time passed and both boys grew in stature and experience, Jacob tended to spend time with the flocks and herds, and with the servants.

He also grew more reflective. As one who reckoned himself disfavored by the circumstances of his birth, Jacob empathized with the servants. *They could no more help being born in servitude than I could help being born second,* he reasoned. Of course, he could not speak such thoughts. His father, as the child of the Promise, refused to hear such seditious ideas. But Jacob's actions spoke for him and earned him the goodwill of all but the most haughty and superstitious. It amused him that some of the women still insisted on seeing evil omens in his courtesy and kindness to those less privileged than himself.

Where Esau lived for the hunt and felt at home only on the trail of the wild, Jacob found a sense of peace out among the flocks and herds and the servants who tended them. He found the work challenging. One day might find him and some of the other herdsmen hunting down a lion or other large predator that had been taking lambs, while another day might require them to wrestle a quarrelsome ram into submission. And subduing one stubborn sheep after another for shearing demanded stamina, strength, and patience. Watching young kids caper and butt heads delighted him. One day he realized, *They are preparing for the real battles they will have when they grow up.* He pondered that. *Like Esau and me? Perhaps. Best not to get into the habit of losing.* As the boys grew toward manhood, those play battles continued. For once Isaac had given his permission, nothing could stop Esau from hunting and tormenting his younger twin. Almost nothing, that is.

* * * * *

The laughter began as soon as they saw Esau, trudging into the camp. His face registered puzzlement at first, then suspicion.

"Are you looking for someone?" Jacob asked, and the laughter increased, despite—and because of—Esau's increasingly stormy expression.

Earlier that day, the whole camp had witnessed the argument between the brothers. "Do not stalk me again," Jacob said, with such quiet menace it commanded the attention of all. "I do not have time to waste."

"Truly, it is poor sport to hunt such easy prey," Esau said. "But it is better than being bored. So I will do it when it pleases me."

"Then I will see to it that it no longer pleases you," Jacob said, but Esau shrugged it off with a smirk. Without further argument, Jacob and the young Egyptian serving boy, Gahizi, left to inspect the flocks.

Some distance outside the camp, Jacob had exchanged sandals with Gahizi, whose name meant "hunter," because of his enthusiasm for tracking down missing lambs. "After what I said to him this morning, Esau is certain to come after us." Gesturing toward Gahizi's feet, he said, "He will follow those sandal prints. So lead him a merry chase toward that ridge," Jacob instructed him. "Walk past the flock your brother Seb is watching. He is expecting you, and he will drive the flock across your path. Once you're on the rocks, take off my sandals. You should be able to circle back to the flock along the series of rocky outcrops without leaving a trail. Hide yourself and wait until my brother passes by, then put the sandals back on and return to camp as quickly as you can."

"Gladly, master," he said, eyes sparkling as he started down the path, laying a clear track of Jacob's sandal prints.

Jacob grunted as he walked on tiptoe, so that his toes and heel prints did not show around the sides of Gahizi's smaller sandals. But he had picked the exchange point carefully, so that after only a few steps, his trail disappeared over the edge of a dry wadi. *Intent on proving a point with me, he will focus on my sandal tracks and not care where the others lead.* He smiled at the thought. *And young Gahizi knows all the tricks. Esau should find plenty to keep him busy.*

When he returned to camp, Gahizi grinned and danced, kicking up his feet with Jacob's sandals on them, describing his afternoon's adventure. When the servants saw Jacob smiling, they joined in the merriment. So it was that laughter greeted the dusty and exhausted Esau when he returned.

And, when Jacob asked, "Are you looking for someone?" every servant in or near the encampment knew the answer. The anger in Esau's face only made it funnier. At first.

Then Esau spotted Jacob's sandals on Gahizi, as the gleeful serving boy danced near, and the storm of his indignation broke. He grasped his stick spear in both hands, and, with a sweeping blow at the boy's legs, sent Gahizi sprawling. The crowd held their breath as he brought the stick up for another blow, but with quick strides, Jacob reached his brother and grasped the other end of the stick. Esau wheeled on him, furious. The curious servants moved away from the brothers, forming a rough circle, straining to see what would happen next.

"Do not beat Gahizi, Esau," Jacob said. "He only obeyed my instructions. If you need to beat someone, beat me." Jacob paused, sent Gahizi away, and, tipping his head toward his brother, said quietly, "If you can."

Esau growled and tried to pull his stick free, but Jacob held firm. "No stick, Esau," Jacob said. "Just you and me," he said, gesturing to the circle of servants. "With your bare hands." The first hint of uncertainty clouded Esau's angry face, so Jacob goaded him. "Unless it is your stick that makes the 'mighty hunter' mighty."

It worked. With fire in his eyes, Esau shoved the stick away, daring Jacob to do the same. With a shrug, Jacob flung the stick outside the circle of servants. The brothers faced each other, and once again Jacob thought of the capering goats and their play fights. *Preparing for the real battles they will have when they grow up.* He spread his feet for balance, bent his knees, and extended his arms. *Best not to get into the habit of losing.*

As Jacob settled into his ready stance, Esau's face broke into a bitter smile. "A shepherd is no match for a hunter like me," he said striking his own chest with his open hands, looking around at the crowd, and stepping sideways. Jacob countered his movements, and the boys slowly circled each other.

"I am more lion than *lamb!*" Esau shouted the last word, and, with head down and hands reaching, charged straight at his brother. Just as Esau reached him, Jacob pivoted on one foot, sidestepping Esau, grasped Esau's outstretched arm with both hands, and pulled his brother over his planted leg, tripping him. Esau hit the ground with a thud.

Stunned, he lashed out with his arm, but Jacob danced away. Esau stood up, oblivious to the dust now streaked with sweat that covered his torso. "What is this?" he asked. "Afraid to fight me man to man? You cannot take a blow, can you?"

Jacob said nothing but held his hands out in the universal gesture for "come and get me." Enraged, Esau closed again, but this time he dove toward Jacob's leg, so his brother could not sidestep him again. Jacob stepped back with that foot, and as Esau lunged at the other, Jacob brought his knee up sharply. Esau turned his head at the last moment, so instead of striking his chin, Jacob's kneecap bounced off his cheekbone and gave his eye socket and nose a glancing blow.

Roaring with pain, Esau put his hand to his face as Jacob moved away again. Esau looked at his hand, bloody from a cut over his eye. His eyes glittered with rage as he charged Jacob once again. This time he kept his head and hands high. Everyone watching knew that he intended to choke his brother to death. Jacob did not step away this time. As Esau reached for his throat, Jacob put a hand on each of Esau's shoulders. Not to be denied, Esau kept coming, pressing Jacob backward. Suddenly, Jacob fell, rolling on his back. Esau's momentum, coupled with Jacob's knees in his belly, threw the older boy over in a loop. Esau landed flat on his back and all the air went out of him. While he struggled for breath, Jacob scrambled up and rested a foot on his brother's neck.

"Enough?" Jacob asked. Esau, still gasping for breath, could only close his eyes and nod in submission. Jacob removed his foot from his brother's throat and stepped away. "I told you this morning," Jacob said. "Do not stalk me again."

Turning to the servants, Jacob said, "Bring my brother a basin of water and cloths to wash himself." With the fight over, the servants hurried to appear busy.

"Tell me," Esau said, as one of the women washed the blood and sweat from his face, "how does a shepherd learn to fight like that?"

"If a large addax charges a hunter, the hunter simply kills the beast," Jacob said.

"That is what it means to hunt," Esau said, not understanding.

"But if one of our prize breeding rams becomes unruly, a shepherd has to subdue the beast without killing him," Jacob said. "And shepherds also hunt. We have to protect the flocks from lions and other beasts."

Esau still looked puzzled.

"Next time you come up against an angry addax, tie him up and bring him home alive," Jacob said.

Esau shook his head. "Bring an addax home alive?" he said, puzzled. "Why would I do that?"

"To understand what a shepherd knows about fighting," Jacob said.

"You speak in riddles," Esau said, his anger returning. "I should have expected it from ʿaqob Jacob, my crooked little brother." He pushed the serving woman away. "Spends his time with goats and sheep. Pathetic little animals."

"Those pathetic animals provide you with food and clothing," Jacob said, his temper rising. "If we had to live off of your hunting, everyone would starve. Those animals you so despise make this family wealthy, make you wealthy!"

"They do, little brother," Esau said, smiling wickedly. "And just remember this: When Father dies, custom declares that all his wealth be divided up into three portions. One for each son, and one more besides. And then the first-born gets two of those portions."

"I know this," Jacob said.

"I am glad you understand this," Esau said. "So every time I am out hunting, while you tend these flocks and herds, think about this: everything you do makes me twice as wealthy as you."

The color rose in Jacob's face.

"You do not like that thought, do you, my crooked little brother?" Esau said, smirking. "Well, I do. Every day I spend on the trail, enjoying the glory of the hunt, I think of my pathetic little brother, working so hard with those boring animals, trying to secure his future wealth. And then I laugh. Because no matter how rich you make yourself, you make me twice as rich! And I do not have to even lift a finger!" Esau stood, dusted himself off, and walked toward the camp, laughing.

le'erek 'af^ekha

Patience

The clamor at the edge of camp roused him. Jacob emerged from his mother's tent to see, at the far edge of camp, a moving group of servants, laughing and dancing. And without looking, Jacob knew it had to be him, again. His father's voice soon confirmed Jacob's worst fears.

"Come see what Red has brought me," Isaac said with delight.

Another gazelle? Jacob wondered. Isaac loved venison, but Jacob knew there was more to it than that. Isaac loved everything Esau did. "See what Red brought me." "Red" was on Isaac's lips and in Isaac's thoughts all the time.

It is so unfair, Jacob thought. *I tend the flocks and take care of the chores around the camp, while Esau goes off hunting, sometimes for days at a time.* Esau didn't care for chores, didn't like the herder's life. *At least he does not come after me anymore,* Jacob thought. Years before, the brothers had settled that issue.

All these years later, Jacob thought, *and I still do all the work, and Esau gets all the glory. As it is right now, everybody is celebrating Esau's trophy, while I do the hard work.* Jacob knew that his mother, Rebekah, saw the injustice, but Isaac still reveled in Esau's irresponsible antics. And it was at times like this that the feelings of injustice stung Jacob.

Jacob felt a hand on his shoulder and recognized Rebekah's touch. He turned and she barely shook her head, then fixed a smile as she looked toward the moving commotion.

"Ah, Red," she said, caressing his name with her voice, drawing it out, "what have you brought us?" She had learned long ago not to antagonize Isaac over their sons, so she smiled with greater determination, and called again. "What is it, Red?"

The group of dancing servants and children parted to reveal Isaac clapping his hands and gesturing toward Esau. The hunter had an antelope draped over his shoulders. This was no small doe gazelle, nor even the larger *yachmur* or fallow deer, but a massive white buck of the kind with the twisted horns longer than a man's arm—an addax. Difficult game for a single hunter.

There will be venison for days, Rebekah thought, *and Isaac will be uncommonly pleased with himself, and Jacob will probably pout. Perhaps I can prevent that,* she thought, looking back at Jacob. "Be patient, Jacob," she said quietly. "Try to be happy for your father. If he sees that you alone are unhappy, how will that help you?" She tilted her head and framed the question with her eyes. Then she turned and began directing the servants to prepare for a feast.

Jacob knew his mother was right, knew that his conspicuous unhappiness would exasperate Isaac, but his anger overruled his reason. *Let Father be annoyed,* Jacob thought. *His adoration of my irresponsible brother annoys me.*

That evening they feasted. "Oh, my lovely Rebekah," Isaac said, with sauce leaking from the corner of his mouth, "you make the best roast venison." A ripple of agreement spread through the assembled family and servants gathered around the large fire. Jacob nodded. "Very good, Mother," he mumbled. Jacob held up his bowl in a salute toward Esau, who sat across the fire pit from him, but Jacob could not bring himself to speak. In the flickering firelight, his eyes locked in on Esau's for a moment, and Jacob nodded again. *There,* he thought, *I've done my brotherly duty.*

Isaac, seeing only what he wanted, clapped his hands in glee, then gestured for Esau to stand and address the gathering. "Tell us of the hunt, Esau," Isaac urged him. Esau feigned reluctance, but Isaac persisted, saying with a twinkle in his eye, "Tell us how you stalked our wily supper." Waves of laughter swept through the crowd, and Jacob smiled and nodded, but the watching Rebekah noted the bitterness in his face. She frowned a warning to Jacob as Esau rose to address the gathering.

Jacob groaned inwardly as Esau began his ritual dance. *It's the same every time,* Jacob thought. He could recite the whole tiresome narrative himself. *It all began at the watering hole,* Jacob narrated the tale in his head as he watched Esau's flamboyant reenactment. *I carefully searched around the edges, looking for animal tracks,* went Jacob's mental narration as Esau made a show of searching the ground. Suddenly, Esau looked up and pointed, and Jacob thought, *There! Off to the left, I saw the tracks of a large addax.*

Jacob had heard it a thousand times before. Always the same: the clever, skilled Esau overcame all the wiles of his quarry, which he then brought home in triumph. Esau's voice droned on and on, and the fire danced and flickered, pushing Jacob to the edge of sleep.

Suddenly, something landed on Jacob's back, jarring him to consciousness. "And I sprung out from behind the rock," Esau shouted from directly behind his ear, "and stuck my spear—" here he jabbed his fingers painfully into Jacob's ribs, eliciting a yelp from his younger twin, "straight into his heart." And Esau slapped his brother on the back and roared with laughter, joined by Isaac and all the servants. Jacob smiled as he rubbed his aching ribs, but his eyes glittered with hatred. Rebekah detected Jacob's fury and gave an almost imperceptible shake of her head. *Not now,* her eyes clearly said.

Jacob swallowed his humiliation and laughed with the rest. Isaac was holding his sides, and some of the servants bent double, and others slapped their thighs. *It was not enough that we celebrate your great feats,* Jacob thought, looking at his brother with an icy smile. *You know better than to stalk me as you did when we were boys, but you knew you could get away with it here. You just had to humiliate me, didn't you? You call me "cheater" or "supplanter." Well, you will pay for this, dear brother. You will pay.* And, contemplating the sweetness of revenge, Jacob threw his head back and let go with genuine laughter.

That caused Isaac to look at Jacob warmly, and Esau slapped him on the back with rough affection. *I fooled you,* Jacob thought, laughing with renewed relish at the thought. *I fooled you all.* And Jacob laughed again, so hard his stomach ached. He laughed and he laughed, but his heart filled with thoughts of murder.

I must get away, he decided, *or they will see my hatred.* So he mumbled excuses mingled with laughter and went out to join the sheep and the goats in the far grazing pasture. Once there, he sat with his back against a smooth rock, looking up at the sky. *My brother,* he flung the thoughts at the sky, flung them at Isaac, flung them at Elohim, his father's God. *My lazy, pompous, worthless brother. You all act as if he is so clever, so skilled. Nobody ever mentions the times he comes back from the hunt without game, tired and hungry and whining about his misfortune. Oh, he is brave enough when he has a spear in his hands, stalking an animal. But around camp, he can be childish, helpless, and irresponsible.*

"Patience." Mother keeps telling me, "Be patient, and all will be yours." How can I be patient, he thought, *when I was born second? I'm always trying to catch up, but I can never make up for those first moments. If only I had been born first,* Jacob thought again. *All of my woes spring from those fleeting moments that separated our birth.* "Patience," he heard his mother's voice again. Why should he be patient? Patient for what?

Sitting there, looking up at the stars, he remembered Rebekah telling him, "You can be patient, Jacob. I've seen your patience in waiting for the ewes to bear their lambs." Then she had placed her hand upon his shoulder and looked deeply into his eyes. "Learn to be patient with your brother."

"Patient? If had been more impatient at birth, if I had been born first, Father would favor me!" Jacob said. "Esau can be patient because he has every advantage: firstborn, Father's favor."

"I have told of the Promise I was given before you were born," Rebekah said.

"The Promise! Little good that has done!" Jacob said.

"How can I—" Rebekah said, then her eyes lit up. "Just a moment," she said, and she went inside her tent and returned with a small box of bright blue stone. She opened it to reveal a two-pronged thorn inside.

Jacob shrugged.

"Your father gave me this, when I doubted the Promise," she said. "This thorn came from the bramble where the ram was caught—the ram that was sacrificed in his place."

Jacob was stunned. "Truly? He kept it all these years?"

Rebekah nodded. "One night, years before I conceived you and Esau, I doubted the Promise. I tried to convince Isaac to lie with Hadasseh, to give me children through her."

Jacob could barely credit his ears. "You have never spoken of this before."

"I . . . I was ashamed," Rebekah said, "ashamed of my lack of faith. Especially after, well, after your births." She paused. "Your father gave me this reminder of El Shaddai's faithfulness then. To remind me that He keeps His promise." She paused, replacing the lid on the box and holding it out toward Jacob. "And now I want you to have it," she said. "So that when you doubt the Promise made to me, that your brother would serve you, you will look on this box and remember." She pressed the box into his hands. Then she kissed him once on the forehead and said, "Remember the Promise, and have patience."

Patience. Is Esau patient? I suppose he must be, stalking his prey, Jacob thought. *But how?* He thought back to Esau's reenactment of his most recent hunt at that evening's meal. It all began at the watering hole. It always began with Esau at the watering hole. But why? Why always at the watering hole?

Jacob pondered, then realized that even the most wily game had to drink, had to eat sometime. If it became thirsty enough, even the most cautious animal would risk all for water. If it became hungry enough, because of a scarcity of plant food for the grazing animals or lack of prey for the hunters—lack of prey for the hunter! And suddenly there it was. When Esau returned from an unsuccessful hunt, he was ravenous with hunger. Now Jacob knew how to stalk his brother, how to set a snare that would finally set things right, give Jacob the prestige and status he deserved. *I must be patient. And I must be pleasant and appear content so that Esau suspects nothing until I strike.*

Then he began laughing again. The answer was there all along: *The mighty hunter would starve without these domestic animals he holds in such contempt. I even told him that. And those domestic animals are under my care. Now that I know what I wait for, I can be pleasant. I can be content,* Jacob thought. *Time will pass. Memories will fade. I can wait. I can be patient.* His plan was so perfect that he could not contain his fierce delight, and all his anger and disappointment and bitterness erupted in gales of savage laughter. Jacob pulled his cape around him to ward off the chill of night on the desert. Soothed by contemplating the perfect snare for his brother and warmed by his anger, he slept. That night, for Jacob, the waiting began.

In the days and weeks that followed, Jacob waited on the herds and flocks with a light heart. One afternoon, when Jacob had left for the far grazing area, Isaac remarked on it to Rebekah. "Jacob seems so happy of late. Do you know why?" he asked.

Rebekah did not know why, and it concerned her; but she didn't want Isaac to know, so she replied with a smile, "He does seem quite happy. Even the servants have mentioned it. Perhaps it has something to do with his new record-keeping scheme."

"What is it about?" Isaac asked.

"He does not say," Rebekah explained, "but it has something to do with how many and what kind of young the flocks and herds produce." She shook her head in incomprehension. "Only he understands it."

Isaac sighed. "He certainly spends more time than ever with the animals.

Whatever causes this new attitude, I am grateful," and then he smiled at Rebekah. Maybe peace between their sons would bring healing to husband and wife, as well.

Had Jacob heard that conversation, he would have laughed with delight. But at that moment he sat in the shade of a small twisted tree at the far reaches of the grazing areas, marking on a tanned goat hide with a charcoal stick. It did indeed contain the records of the flocks and herds. But in the upper corner, he kept a different tally; how many days for each of Esau's hunting trips and whether he returned with game after each one. These numbers told Jacob that Esau invariably returned within four days when he found and killed game. An absence longer than four days indicated that the mighty hunter had failed, and Esau would return hungry and careless. The numbers also said that this was the sixth day for this particular hunt.

When he saw a solitary figure on the horizon, moving slowly toward them, Jacob smiled, then called out to the nearest servant. "I will make some of my renowned red lentil stew!"

"What do we celebrate, master?" the servant replied, delighted, for Jacob's red lentil stew was a treat highly regarded by servants out among the flocks, but Jacob just smiled that curious smile of his and motioned the servant to go about his business.

Later, as the hearty lentil stew bubbled over the small fire, Jacob looked up and saw the solitary figure again. Even at this distance, he recognized Esau. He started to laugh out loud, but caught himself. The snare was set; the game approached. *Patience,* Jacob thought. *Only a little longer, and the waiting will be over.*

מארב

ma'arv

Ambush

Esau, bare-chested, burnt by hours in the sun, and caked with dust from the long trail, trudged up to the edge of Jacob's temporary camp at the outermost grazing area. Sniffing the air, he walked to the cooking pot and bent over the bubbling stew. "This red—what do you call it?—red-red stuff smells delicious," he said. "And just in time too. I feel ready to die from hunger." He motioned for the goatherd to fetch him some.

"Fetch my brother some water to wash off the dust of the hunt before he eats," Jacob said. Esau stiffened, and the servant boy, Nir, moved quickly to fetch the water.

"Wash the dust?" Esau said angrily, "What is this, a camp full of women? I am hungry!"

Jacob replied, "It's *my* camp, *Red*." Esau looked up sharply, for Jacob *never* used his nickname, "At least it's *my* fire and *my* red-red stuff. And I don't want you getting any dust in the pot. Or you could walk on to the main camp." By this time, Nir had returned with the water and a large wooden basin, which he placed on the top of a flat stone a few steps from the small wooden camp table. Esau walked over to the stone where the wooden basin sat, leaned his short hunting spear against the stone, then removed the bow and quiver of arrows he carried slung over his shoulders and placed them next to the spear. "Look at you." Jacob said and began to laugh. "Between the sun and the dust, you've never been more red, Red," and he laughed some more.

Esau extended his arms, examined his torso, and gave a short, uneasy laugh. Cupping his hands in the water, he splashed it on his face and then on his shoulders and arms. As the dust washed down in muddy rivulets into the basin, he began to laugh in earnest. He *did* look very red indeed. The servant boy handed him a rough cloth, and he dried off the last of the water. "Now, where's that red-red stuff?" Esau sat down at the camp table. Jacob leaned back against the flattened stone.

"Do not be hasty, Red," Jacob said. "Tell me of the hunt."

"The hunt? The hunt!" Esau fairly growled. "You see I returned with nothing except sunburn and hunger for my efforts."

"You're never shy to speak of your success. I always wondered what happened when you returned without game," Jacob explained.

"Nobody wants to hear about a failed hunt," Esau grumbled. "And I certainly don't want to talk about it."

"But I want to hear about it," Jacob said. "Consider it part of my price for the red-red stew."

"Price? You demand payment for feeding your older brother?"

"Nothing you value. As you say, you don't value the tale of a failed hunt. But I have some questions," Jacob said.

"Ask all you want, after you give me the red-red stew," Esau replied and motioned for Nir to fill a bowl. But Jacob held up a restraining hand, and Nir paused, the bowl tantalizingly close to Esau. The hunter tried to make a grab for it, but Jacob leaned in between them and blocked his way. "Look Brother, I'll pay whatever you ask!" Esau shouted. "I am starving. If you do not give me some of that red-red stew soon, I will die. Then you won't get anything. Ask anything you want; just give me some red-red stew."

Jacob looked him in the eye and said, "I have your solemn oath? Anything I ask?"

"Anything," Esau said. "On my oath! Anything!"

Jacob smiled, then motioned to the servant, who handed Esau the red-red stew.

"So tell me of a failed hunt, Red," Jacob said, as he handed his brother a piece of flat bread.

Esau bolted the first bite of the stew. It tasted as delicious as it smelled. "I went out, the game got away. I came back empty-handed. There, that's the story of a failed hunt." That duty fulfilled, he stuffed his mouth with stew and began chewing with a contented smile.

Unruffled, Jacob leaned forward and asked, "Did you ever have a lion or a bear stalk you?"

Esau frowned in thought for a moment while continuing his rapid chewing, then he shook his head and grunted, "Nah."

"Did you ever corner a game animal and have it turn on you?" Up till now, his hunger and the savory stew had largely occupied Esau's attention, but with this question, he paused his eating and looked warily at Jacob, still leaning casually against the flattened rock. The younger twin's bland expression revealed little except curiosity.

"Why all these questions, Brother?" Esau asked, gesturing with a fragment of bread, suspicion growing.

"You're the mighty hunter, the Nimrod of the family. I do not share your experience with wild animals. I spend my time with tame ones," Jacob answered. "Some even think our occupations mirror our characters," he continued. "You're the wild, exciting one, and I'm the tame, boring one."

"*Some* think that, do they?" asked Esau, all of his hunter's instincts alerted. "And you, Brother? What think you?"

"Oh, I like to think we both benefit the family. You provide wild game and exciting stories; I provide continual care for the flocks and herds. My ordinary life builds wealth and puts food on the table daily," Jacob said, extending his hands, palms up, as he explained. "But sometimes I yearn for excitement too."

As Esau considered this, Jacob continued, "We all do. That's why we gather around the fire and ask you to share the story of your latest triumph."

"So why ask about a failed hunt? Why ask if my prey ever turns on me?" Esau tried to probe beneath his brother's benign facade. He grasped the flat bread with both hands, tearing off another piece.

"Because, watching you walk back empty-handed, it occurred to me that the experience of hunting must include more than just triumphs," Jacob grew expansive. "And, my experience with our flocks and herds tells me any animal will fight if cornered. So I wondered if you had experienced that."

Still wary, Esau replied, "Sometimes." Jacob nodded for him to go on, so Esau sopped the remnants of his stew with a piece of bread and continued talking as he ate. "I pursued this *yachmur* all morning." Esau said. "And it turned into this long, twisting ravine." The hunter paused to chew the stew-soaked bread. He swiped at his mouth absently with the back of his hand as he gazed into the past, the hunt unfolding in his mind's eye. "A game trail led through the ravine and out the other side." He gestured, pointing to the path the trail followed in his mind's eye. Nir sat cross-legged on the ground near Esau, transfixed by the tale. "I began to run, fearing it would escape out the other end. When I came around a particularly sharp corner, I saw that a recent rockslide had blocked the trail solidly. And there, with its head down and its front hoof stamping, a large *yachmur* stag stood with its back to the landslide."

Esau focused on his brother then to be certain Jacob was listening. "Since I was running headlong, I almost ran into it."

Jacob couldn't restrain himself. "How did you get away?"

"If it had charged at that instant, its antlers would have ripped me open. But it didn't. I think my sudden approach startled it. So I started yelling and jumping, throwing pebbles at it, as I slowly backed around the corner. You see," Esau said, now relishing his role as teacher, "sometimes an animal freezes when a hunter surprises it. The key then is to keep the surprises coming, never give it time to think. *Strike!*" Esau jabbed the bread at Nir, causing the servant boy to start. Esau laughed roughly and looked at Jacob. "I came home empty-handed that day too." He slapped Nir on the back, sending the boy scurrying. "Just happy to be in one piece."

"Thank you, Brother." Jacob said quietly. *More than you can imagine, dear brother,* he thought, as he offered Esau another bowl of stew. *Unlike the cornered stag, I won't hesitate.* And moving forward toward Esau, Jacob struck. "Now for the rest of my price."

Esau, tearing off another piece of bread, looked up sharply. "What do you mean, 'the rest of my price'?"

"I said the story was only part of my price, dear brother," Jacob said, his voice heavy with menace. "You gave me your oath."

His initial hunger sated, Esau pushed away the bowl of stew and put down the bread. "What do you want, Brother?"

"Your portion. The older brother's portion."

"The birthright!" Esau roared, jumping to his feet. "You want the birthright?"

"That's my price, Brother. Now pay up, on your solemn oath." Esau lunged forward, but Jacob stepped back to the stone with the water basin, where he grasped and then brandished the spear.

"I won't make the same mistake that *yachmur* made, Esau. Do not test me." With that, Jacob feinted a spear thrust at his brother's heart.

Esau stepped back and held out his arms in submission. "I believe you. You would not hesitate." Esau, holding his hands high, took another step away. "Do you think the birthright can be bought and sold?"

"I intend to find out," Jacob said.

"You think you can buy Father's blessing for a bowl of stew? Does it mean so little to you?"

"Red. Red. *Mighty hunter, Red*. You don't see it, do you?" Jacob's words dripped with contempt.

Esau calmly put his hands forward, waving gently downward. "Put down the spear, Jacob," Esau said, only to have Jacob jab at him again.

"I told you, I am not the *yachmur* stag. I will not hesitate. If necessary, I will rip you open. I will tell Father the story of the stag, only I will say it happened this time. That you returned terribly wounded, told me the story, and died. All I have to do is bring him one of your bloody garments as proof of your death." And Jacob pressed the point of the spear into Esau's abdomen.

"I believe you would," Esau said. A hunter must be able to divine the intent of his quarry, and Esau saw murder glittering in his brother's eyes. Acknowledging defeat, Esau shrugged and put his hands up in surrender. "All right, Jacob, I will sell you the birthright. It will not benefit me if I die . . . from hunger," he added with a bitter grin. "Now what do we do?"

"On your solemn oath before El Elyon?" Jacob pressed on the spear.

"Yes! On my solemn oath before El Elyon." Esau fairly shouted. "Let up on the spear, Jacob. Either let up or finish me. What more do you want, Jacob?"

Jacob suddenly felt weak. He pulled the spear back, gripping it fiercely, lest his hands and arms begin trembling. He would not show Esau any weakness. "Eat your stew, Esau. You paid for it, now eat it."

"I told you, Jacob, you cannot buy the birthright with a bowl of stew," Esau said. While hunting, Esau had learned to eat when food was available. He would not now let circumstances prevent him from keeping up his strength. So with the threat past, Esau returned to his meal.

"Oh, great hunter," Jacob said, practically sneering. "You didn't see it, did you?" Jacob's conquest had made him somewhat giddy, and he couldn't stop talking. "You can't *buy* an animal's life with an arrow or a spear either," Jacob fairly shouted in Esau's face, yet the older brother kept eating impassively.

"The arrow or the spear is just the weapon you use. And you aim it at the animal's vulnerable spot." He began laughing now, nearly out of control. "The bowl of stew was *my* weapon. Your *hunger* was your vulnerable spot."

"But who will know?" Esau asked without rancor. "A hunter returns with a carcass or a pelt. What proof will you produce if I deny it?"

"You will know, and I will know," Jacob said, suddenly concerned. "You would not deny it?" The words were as much a question as a statement.

"Why should I say anything at all?" Esau asked. Jacob had not considered that. Still, Jacob knew he had gained an advantage, despite Esau's apparent nonchalance.

"I shall keep your spear, Red. It will be my trophy of this hunt," Jacob said, suddenly clear.

Esau only shrugged. *I liked that spear, but a hunter cannot grow too attached to his weapons*, he thought. *All right, little brother, you win this round. But what can be taken by stealth can be taken back by stealth. Except a life*, Esau thought grimly. *You should have taken my life, little brother. So long as I live, I can take the birthright back.* "Keep the spear, little brother," Esau said, and Jacob felt a thrill of triumph. But then Esau added, "Having a spear doesn't make you a hunter, little brother." *A real hunter must have a killer instinct*, Esau thought. And he smiled.

quwts

Loathing

It was the same every evening. Isaac stood silently gazing to the north as dusk gathered around the encampment. When no figure emerged from the dusty horizon, Isaac turned without a word and returned to his tent. Concerned by her husband's distress and knowing that Jacob kept track of his brother's absences, she asked, "Has he ever been gone this long before?"

"Never," Jacob replied.

As the days, then weeks of Esau's unexplained absence dragged on, they took a grievous toll on Isaac. He began to look tired, almost frail. He could be heard weeping and praying in his tent almost every night. Even in the daylight, servants moved about the camp almost on tiptoe and spoke in hushed tones. A suffocating sense of dread slowly enveloped the encampment. At midday of the eighty-first day, according to Jacob's records, Esau returned. The cloud of dust undulating just above the horizon announced his coming and caused a stir in Isaac's camp. Runners from the most distant grazing area to the north verified Esau's presence in the group. But they brought little information about the identity of the strangers with him. Nor could they explain the reason for the large retinue.

With time, the dark mass on the horizon moved closer to camp and resolved into individual figures—both people and animals. Isaac looked at Rebekah and Jacob with questions in his eyes, but they knew no more than he did and could only shake their heads. Whatever the import of this arrival, Isaac determined to observe all the proper courtesies, so he commanded the servants to prepare. He and Rebekah washed and put on fresh robes, as did Jacob, before they went to the edge of the camp to greet their incoming party. Servants with towels, basins of water, food, and drink flanked the family on both sides.

As they waited, they watched. Just behind Esau, two veiled women rode on small donkeys. A small cluster of servants followed, some driving a small flock of sheep and a few goats, others carrying small wooden chests. Rebekah viewed the group's approach with growing alarm—and fury. She looked at Isaac, but if he shared her feelings, his face did not show it, so she steeled herself.

Finally, the groups stood face-to-face. The women dismounted and followed directly behind Esau as he stepped forward and bowed before his father. Isaac bowed with stony formality, then he held out his hands in greeting. "Esau, my son, welcome." Gesturing to the strangers with Esau, Isaac added, "And welcome to your friends." Courtesy prevented him from inquiring as to their identity, but Esau quickly confirmed Rebekah's worst fears.

"Father, Mother, meet my wives, Yudith, daughter of Beeri the Hittite, and Basemath, daughter of Elon the Hittite." Isaac remained motionless for a moment, then nodded and greeted each woman with strict courtesy, welcoming them into the family, offering water and privacy to wash the dust of travel away, and food and drink to restore their strength. Then he introduced Jacob and Rebekah to Esau's wives.

The formalities over, Isaac turned abruptly back to his own tent. Before he could make three steps, Esau's angry voice froze him—and everyone in the camp. "What? No feasting? No fatted calf? Is this the greeting Isaac provides for the brides of his oldest son?" Rebekah shot a troubled look at her husband, then at Jacob. Jacob, trembling, started to answer his brother's unbelievable insolence, but Isaac held up a restraining hand toward the younger son. Then Isaac turned slowly to face Esau.

"Of course, Esau," Isaac said, measuring every word. "We will feast in honor of your marriage. We fear that our humble camp does not afford a repast fit for *two* illustrious daughters of the *Hittites*."

Having made his point, Esau took a different tack. "Forgive me, Father, for doubting you. My concern for your good name made me speak rashly. My wives come from notable families among the Hittites, and I would not have them think lightly of you."

Isaac looked suddenly frail and nodded meekly. "You are right, Esau, my son. Forgive me. My concern over your long absence . . . ," his voice trailed off. "We will feast, of course." Turning to Rebekah, he said quietly, "Your mother will see to it." With that, he turned and walked slowly back to the shelter of his tent.

Rebekah showed the women to tents where they could wash and change, arranging to accommodate their servants and other details.

Watching this pitiful spectacle, Jacob felt disgust, revulsion, and despair. Disgust and revulsion at his brother's brazen insolence. Despair, because, no matter how vile or outrageously his brother behaved, Isaac always gave in, always favored Esau. Nothing Jacob could do, it seemed, could ever win him favor. And nothing Esau did, including this latest outrage, could cause him to lose favor.

Once, when they were young boys, Jacob remembered Esau taking a stick and stirring up a papery nest of wasps. Esau's return with his Hittite wives had much the same effect on Isaac's camp, which fairly hummed with talk. Ordinarily, the servants went about their duties stoically. Most of the time, the heat discouraged extraneous activity. But now Jacob heard whispers in the darkness and the low hum of quiet voices during the day. For their part, Isaac and Rebekah said little. Esau pursued the solitary ways of the hunter, even in the camp; and at first, his Hittite wives, Yudith and Basemath, kept to themselves as well. Jacob did not trust himself to speak. So the principal figures in the camp spent every day in an elaborate pantomime, tending to their tasks, observing the courtesies, and speaking almost not at all.

As a result, tension crackled through the camp like lightning in a rainless storm, and soon it became too much for everyone. Esau's absences only heightened the tension when he left camp to hunt alone. Even Isaac, who rarely left camp, began to seek refuge on the far grazing areas, citing the need to "inspect" them as his pretext for fleeing.

This left Jacob and Rebekah, mother and son, in the main camp with the Esau's two wives. One morning, watching from near his mother's tent as Yudith and Basemath performed their daily sacrifices to Asertu, the Hittite goddess of fertility, Jacob could stand it no longer.

"Why have you and my father not rebuked my brother Esau for his disobedience?" Jacob demanded.

Rebekah glanced quickly at the two women and the fleece suspended from the long pole they had erected at the edge of the camp to honor their god Telepinu. Rebekah raised her hand to quiet him, led him to her tent, and closed the curtain at the tent's entrance. "What do you expect us to do?" she asked. "Esau made the bride payments and received their dowries. The ceremonies have been held and the marriages consummated. The deeds can *not* be undone. We cannot afford to make ourselves odious to our neighbors. There is nothing we can do."

"But look at them," Jacob said, pointing in the direction of the women's tent. "They openly worship Telepinu. They honor Asertu with the lion's pelt and the eight-pointed star upon their tent. This dishonors Elohim Abraham. How can Father allow it?" He wanted to ask, How can El Elyon allow it? But he knew he must not voice that thought.

"And after all the grief he caused you. And my father," Jacob said. "I see Father's anguish night after night."

Rebekah shook her head and spoke gravely. "Quiet your spirit, my son. Do not challenge your father on this. Right now he is dreadfully angry with your brother. He may even disinherit Esau and bestow the birthright on you," she said, looking directly into Jacob's eyes. "But if you challenge him, he will transfer his anger to *you*." She gripped him by the shoulders. "Be patient, Jacob, and all may be yours. *But on these matters, you must keep silent!*"

In time, Yudith and Basemath began to make themselves more at home. Unfortunately, that meant they were free with their opinions about everything. They not only worshiped Telepinu and Asertu, they increasingly flaunted their religion. On the rare occasions when the clan feasted together, they spoke endlessly of the superiority of their homeland: its mountains, its customs, its food, and its gods. The two women seemed oblivious to the anger they provoked in nearly everyone else. Esau appeared impassive at such times. But Jacob knew his brother well. He suspected Esau enjoyed it all.

Esau never explained why he had married two women more or less at the same time and had sprung them on the family without warning. With time and reflection, Jacob came to see the brilliance and audacity of Esau's plan. Jacob had learned to study Esau as a hunter studies his quarry. He knew Esau's habits and his techniques; it was almost as if he could read Esau's mind.

As he contemplated the many ways Esau's behavior had shocked and offended his parents, Jacob began to feel a bitter admiration. Jacob now realized that Esau had employed a classic hunter's tactic, one Esau had described to Jacob years earlier, when Jacob had tricked him into selling the birthright.

That day, Esau had described how the hunter used surprise and shock to freeze his prey. "Sometimes an animal freezes when the hunter surprises it," Esau had told him. "The key then is to keep the surprises coming, never giving the animal time to think. *Strike!*"

Jacob began counting the ways Esau had shocked his parents into paralysis. First, there was the matter of the two wives. Before the boys began to sprout beards, Isaac had lectured the boys at least once during every new moon about the follies of having more than one wife.

"An extra wife means extra strife," Isaac liked to tell them. And then he spoke of the conflict between Sarah, his mother, and Hagar, mother of his brother Ishmael. "Even long after she left, my mother still spoke of her with bitterness." Then he would look each of the boys in the eye in turn, shake his finger in their faces, and say, "Marry one woman and stay with her. Your life will be simpler and happier with one wife rather than two." Then he would add, "And that means handmaidens and concubines too. Elohim gave Adam only one wife, and look at the trouble she caused him." He said to them, nodding with his eyebrows raised. "Wedding one wife extends your life," he recited. So, bringing home two wives represented a direct affront to Isaac.

That the women were Hittites made matters worse. Isaac worshiped Elohim, the God of his father, Abraham. Hittite wives brought their Hittite deities with them. This served as an insult to Isaac's God, and as such, it endangered the Promise, the Promise that guided their family, of which Isaac himself was a product.

Not only had Esau married *two* wives against his father's will—two *Hittite* wives against his father's will—Esau had also embarked on his marital journey without so much as *informing* his father of his intentions. Esau's unanticipated long absence nearly drove his father mad with worry.

Any one of these reasons gave Isaac grounds for disowning Esau, for sending him into lifelong exile. But combined, these shocks simply overwhelmed Isaac. Like a game animal, Isaac froze. And, Jacob thought, when his prey froze, Esau *struck!* Feigning shock that his wives were not greeted with elaborate feasting, Esau, who had committed multiple grievous offenses himself, claimed to be the victim of offense. If it had not been so galling, so infuriating, it would have been admirable in a perverse way. Because of his hunter's audacity, Esau had gotten away with violating nearly every precious belief his father held, and yet had retained Isaac's favor.

While Esau remained Isaac's favorite, Esau's shocking insolence and the continual irritation caused by his obnoxious Hittite wives only alienated him further from Rebekah. Every time she saw those haughty heathen women parading around the camp, examining every item as though they already owned it, ordering servants about, infringing on her prerogatives, she felt more deeply the need to make certain Esau never exercised the authority of the firstborn. She remembered the luminous dream that had given her peace during her pregnancy, the dream that had prophesied that authority would flow to Jacob.

Let the idolatrous servants talk of the "devil child" and the "cheater." Let Isaac shun his secondborn as a "supplanter." She knew the Voice in her dream had spoken truly—it *must* be true. The birthright would not pass to the ungrateful renegade hunter she had given birth to—if she could prevent it.

Jacob sat night after night in his own tent, thinking of Esau's spear, which he had taken as a trophy so long before. *And what good did it do me?* he wondered. *Father will never honor our bargain, even if he believes my account of the exchange. He will still give the birthright to Esau,* Jacob thought bitterly. His hopes evaporated like dew on the desert, leaving only despair.

"Cheater," they called Jacob. *'Aqob Jacob,* meaning "crooked Jacob." The irony of the labels enraged him. He was the one cheated! He obeyed his parents and did the dreary, unexciting work of building the family's wealth, while Esau—Esau disobeyed his parents, did little to build the family wealth, and now, this, this outrage of the Hittite wives. As time passed, the vexations occasioned by every word and action of the Hittite women increased. Still, Isaac showed no sign of disowning his rebellious son. It seemed that nothing could shake Isaac's favor away from Esau.

Jacob felt the unfairness of it all eating away at his soul. *I must secure the birthright for myself. But how?*

haphak

Reversals

"She should be flogged!" At these words, the "she" in question, the little servant girl they called *Qesheth*, which meant "rainbow," began visibly trembling.

"She took my . . . my . . . ," Naqiya knew better than to say "amulet," "talisman," or "charm" to describe the tiny bone carving of a bull. Although he would not forbid such possessions, Isaac did not encourage them. For it represented Nanna, the great light that ruled the night, which eternally chased, and then was chased by Utu, the blinding ruler of the day. Every twenty-eight days or so, Utu caught Nanna, and the celestial pair descended to the netherworld, leaving the world in darkness for three dark nights, during which they judged the deeds done on the earth. Then, at dusk on the fourth day, Nanna reappeared as a shining crescent, the shape of a bull's horns. Terah, father of Abraham, had worshiped Nanna and Utu in Ur, the ancestral home; and that worship lingered in the camp to this day, despite Isaac's devotion to Elohim. And because Elohim could not be seen, many clung to the talismans and charms they could touch and carry with them. So all those gathered wondered if Jacob would rebuke the young servant girl.

"Mascot," Jacob supplied, to Naqiya's great relief and to laughter from all the rest. Except the trembling Qesheth. With Esau out hunting, and Isaac cloistered in his tent, Jacob sat as judge of the encampment: arbiter of disputes, dispenser of justice. Except for the few essential herdsmen needed to watch the livestock and personal servants that served every tent, on these occasions all of Isaac's servants circled Jacob, watching him settle the complaints and disputes that regularly arose in such a large group. And Jacob took advantage of that. He worked hard to counter the notion of him as "cheater."

"My—mascot," Naqiya continued, nodding emphatically, then pointing. "She stole it!"

"But I didn't," Qesheth cried. "It came to me," Qesheth said in a halting tremolo. "In my sleep," she said, as Naqiya rolled her eyes.

"Surely you do not believe that," Naqiya said.

"Oh, surely not," Jacob agreed. "After all, a mere 'mascot' made of bone cannot move itself."

Naqiya nodded sharply again but suddenly realized she might be offending Nanna, the god that the little bull carving represented, and said, "But Nanna—" A few sharp gasps from the crowd combined with Jacob's quizzical expression warned the girl that she was straying into dangerous territory. She feared offending Nanna, but Jacob worshiped Elohim, so she threw herself toward the opposite precipice. "Oh, no, of course, . . . I mean to say I . . . I . . . ," thoroughly flustered, she decided to give defiance a try: after all, it had gotten her this far. "It belongs to me, and that is all I have to say." With that, she crossed her arms and lifted her chin.

"Does anyone else confirm that Naqiya owns this 'mascot'?" Jacob asked. Surveying the crowd, he saw several hands raised. "Did anyone see it taken?" He asked again. A hum of inquiry ran through the assembly, accompanied by shaking heads and bewildered expressions. Jacob swept the assembly with a glance, head bobbing; all could tell he had decided. He extended his hand, with the bone carving cradled in his open palm, and spoke with a penetrating voice.

"Clearly, the 'mascot' belonged to Naqiya," Jacob declared, and a murmur of approval—and disappointment—arose, which he quelled by waving his hand and shaking his head. "And clearly, Naqiya lost it." The sound renewed, louder than ever. Turning to Naqiya, he said, "Either you lost it, or it left of its own free will. Do you insist on having it returned?" She started to speak, but he cautioned her, "Think carefully now."

"I do insist," Naqiya said. "It belongs to me."

"As you wish," Jacob said, and then someone gasped as he knelt in front of little Qesheth, putting his eyes level with hers. "It got lost, little one," he said. Qesheth looked at him, serious and unblinking. "Would you want to go home if you were lost?" Qesheth gave a solemn nod. Holding out the tiny carved bull, he asked, "Will you take it home where it belongs?" Her eyes welled, but her head bobbed once again. "Clever girl," he said, as he closed her hand around the small bone treasure and motioned her toward the haughty Naqiya.

Jacob stood and shepherded Qesheth toward her adversary. Qesheth held the disputed carving out to Naqiya. The older girl made as if to speak, but a glance at Jacob convinced her to remain silent, so she snatched the tiny carving and said nothing. He held up his hand, and the attentive crowd grew silent. He knelt again in front of little Qesheth. "And for you, little one," he pulled his left hand from behind him, waved it closed before her, then produced a single copper shekel. "Because you helped a little lost one return home," he said, folding her hand around the precious coin.

Naqiya began to protest, but Jacob silenced her. "Had you not insisted she return the 'mascot,' the shekel would have been yours. You have no cause for complaint. You received what you chose."

The crowd inhaled, the sound like a wave retreating from the shore, which returned as a sudden flow of applause and shouting moved through the assembly.

"How wise is Jacob," the men said.

"Our master is more than just," said the women, "he is merciful and generous."

Their eyes shone and their voices carried to the edge of the camp, where they assaulted the ears of an empty-handed Esau, returning from another unsuccessful hunt. Unseen by the throng of workers, he slipped into his tent. He kicked a napping serving girl awake and ordered her to fetch wash water for him. Yudith and Basemath, alerted by the noise, flitted about, summoning and dispatching servants for food, fresh clothing, wine, and oil—a flurry of activity designed to distract Esau, and he knew it. Although they made a show of wifely devotion, their whining drove him to distraction. Even if Esau had been inclined to stay at the encampment instead of hunt, their constant complaints would have been enough to send him stalking lions with his bare hands.

A servant girl—he didn't know her name or any of the others, for that matter—brought a basin of water. Esau dipped his hands in the water and splashed his hot face. *Jacob has never mentioned that I sold him the birthright,* he thought. Nevertheless, ever since that day, Esau had sought every opportunity to strengthen his claim. He married the two Hittite women, in hopes that being married and receiving the women's considerable dowries would solidify his position and authority. When his father did not immediately order a celebration, Esau thought he saw an opportunity to further establish his authority. Pausing now, his wet face in his hands, he realized he had severely miscalculated. By eroding his father's authority, he had diminished his own.

He held out a hand, and the girl placed a cloth in it, with which he began to dry his face. Esau recognized that since that day, Isaac began to fade. Not just his sight, though Isaac's eyes could barely distinguish day from night. Isaac himself seemed to have drifted into a shadow, waiting in silence to sleep with his fathers. And although Isaac's word still ruled the growing cluster of families, flocks, and herds, he spoke rarely, so more and more the servants looked to the sons, Esau and Jacob, for direction. As firstborn and married, Esau assumed he would carry more authority than his younger twin. But Esau had no patience for the domestic chores of the encampment. His heart and mind always on the hunt, he had left the routine management of the servants, sheep, and goats that comprised the family wealth to Jacob, his younger brother.

As Isaac continued to fade, so did Esau's favor with the encampment. Every episode, like today's resolution of the dispute between the two serving girls, only strengthened Jacob's place in the people's hearts, and Esau knew it. He dropped the wet cloth, which a scurrying servant removed, along with the basin. Other servants proffered platters of olives and figs and bowls of wine.

He downed a bowl of wine, then grabbed a dried fig and began to eat, staring into the distance, still contemplating his problem, as he had so many times recently.

Just the day before, as he lay behind a slight stone ridge, downwind from and overlooking a remote wadi, Esau had contemplated the deteriorating situation in the encampment. *Supplanter, indeed,* he thought. *My little brother spends every moment of every day undermining me in the eyes of the servants. Oh, they still obey me, but sullenly, dragging their feet, daring me to rebuke them.* Movement on the opposing stream bank caught his eye. *Just a bird.* Flies buzzed around him as he sweltered in the heat, but he did not strike at them. The noise and motion necessary to swat them would spook any game cautiously approaching the precious water in the wadi and make his wait longer. As his eyes and ears remained alert, his mind turned again to the problems in the camp.

If things keep going this way, everyone in camp will hate me soon, Esau thought. *I may be firstborn, but Jacob effectively rules as though he holds the birthright.* Memories of the day Jacob extorted the birthright from Esau as the price of survival flooded his mind. The fool had taken his spear as a token of the stolen birthright. *Fortunately, no one will believe Jacob,* he thought. *But wait? Why not?* If they held the two men in equal esteem, Esau's status as firstborn would protect his claim to the birthright. *But if they hate me, they might fix on any excuse to refuse my claim to their obedience.*

As the sun rose ever higher, Esau realized that nothing would come to the muddy stream for water until evening. Waiting longer in the heat would only tire him and make him weaker. To find game now, he needed to force the action, drive his prey out of its midday shelter and into the sun. So he rose quietly and circled to the north, toward the other side of the wadi, staying downwind of any likely game.

When no signs betrayed the hiding places of his prey, he moved into the shadow of a great boulder. *No luck till dusk,* he thought. *You can't force the action if you don't know where your prey is.* He took a drink from his goatskin canteen and leaned back against the cool stone, and his mind returned to the problems of Jacob, the birthright, and the hostile encampment. Then it hit him. *Force the action with Jacob.* But how? Any attempt to force Jacob would only provoke him to make his claim aloud, and the servants would support him. *Stop. Think. What or who is your prey? The birthright, that is my prey. But how can I force that?*

Weary, he moved so that the slanting shadow would move away from him as he rested, and the late afternoon rays of the sun would wake him early enough so he could hide near the wadi again before dusk. He rested, saving his energy for the evening hunt.

When evening came, he had barely settled himself in position above the wadi before he heard the sounds of a cautious approach. A *yachmur* picked its way down the sloping verge of the wadi. The animal moved to the edge of the stream, stooped and sniffed at the water; its wary eyes darting left and right. Without rising, Esau gripped his spear, his shoulders tensing to lift him up and charge the animal as soon as it bent to drink. But just then, a rustle of wind and a shifting shadow alerted both Esau and his prey, a mere instant before a leopard sprang at the fallow deer from behind the dappled shadow of a small shrub that had camouflaged the cat's vivid spots. But the wary fallow deer leaped the wadi and ran directly at Esau. As soon as the deer bolted toward him, time slowed for Esau. His vision became almost painfully acute, sounds seemed muffled and low, and every muscle came alive, instantly transmitting the position of each joint, the flex of each limb. His gaze swept the charging deer from its flaring nose to its rump, taking in each rippling muscle, and then the pursuing leopard. Esau rose, focusing on the golden eyes of the leopard, bringing his spear to the front, spreading his feet to absorb the shock of the charging leopard striking the stone spearpoint. Seeing Esau braced for the collision, the startled leopard darted in one liquid motion to Esau's left and then back across the wadi. There, the big cat paused for a moment, and then, its golden eyes locked on Esau's face, it slunk back to its hiding place behind the shrub.

Esau realized that the leopard held every advantage now. The big cat would claim—and take—any prey captured at this spot on this evening. And Esau didn't want to find out if the hungry cat might consider him a possible meal. Spear or no spear, Esau felt no certainty that he would survive such an encounter. In other circumstances, he might welcome such a challenge. But in his present condition, and with his present weaponry, the savvy hunter recognized his only option lay in retreat. So Esau slowly circled downwind of the leopard, walking sideways to keep his eyes on the predator's hiding place, making it clear that he was ceding the wadi ambush to the big cat.

In the lingering daylight, he made his way home, still thinking about Jacob. He walked all night and arrived in midmorning, already in a foul mood, to the chorus of praise for his brother. Hearing the universal adulation for Jacob only hardened his resolve.

He swallowed the last of the fig he had been chewing and reached for another bowl of wine. *If I don't act soon,* thought Esau, *my brother will have stolen the allegiance of all the servants. And when Father Isaac dies, Jacob, the cheater, will rule. The birthright will be taken from me.* He must force the action, and soon, he knew. Esau drank from the bowl of wine and held the rest under his nose, breathing in its fruity fragrance.

Relaxing now, Esau realized that he could not simply demand that his rights be honored. He could not, like the leopard, simply pounce on the birthright. That would only incite his father. Esau knew that, even in his weakened condition, Isaac would resist with every fiber of his being any attempt to take his authority. *I am not the leopard here; Father is.* And then it hit him: *But I could alert the leopard.* Washed, fed, and with a plan for stalking his prey, he sprawled on his pallet. A patient hunter, he settled in to wait. Hunters must rest when they can. And so he drifted off to sleep.

In less than a week, the opportunity presented itself. In so large a group, grievances and disputes arose almost daily. Esau simply waited until Jacob assembled the servants to deal with them. No one asked Esau if he desired to preside. They had not seen him around his tents and assumed he was away hunting, an assumption that he welcomed. It was half true. *I am hunting all right*, he thought, *but not away.*

Once the assembly began hearing disputants, Esau stole into his father's tent. Isaac's personal servant stirred with surprise, but a motion from Esau kept the aged attendant from announcing him. Reaching the dark inner chamber, Esau started to speak, but his father spoke first.

"Esau! My son," Isaac said, his voice brittle with age. "What is it that brings you to your father's tent?"

"How did you know it was me?" Esau asked. "Can you see again?"

"I cannot," Isaac said without sadness. "How does the *yachmur* know you without seeing you?"

"By my sound and scent," Esau said.

"So it is with me," Isaac replied. "What brings you to your father's tent?"

"Do I need a reason?" Esau asked, startled.

"You do not, my son, but it has been some—that is—so often you are hunting," Isaac said.

"I hunt, Father, but without much success of late," Esau said.

"I wondered," Isaac said. "I so much enjoy the venison you bring me. Have you seen many deer lately?"

"On my last hunt," Esau admitted.

"Did I miss the feast?" Isaac said, gently chiding his son.

"You did, Father," Esau said and sensed his father's disappointment. "I missed it too. The leopard was in no mood to share."

Isaac threw his head back, his throat rattling with dry laughter. Esau joined in. They sat in silence for a moment, father and son sharing a rare moment of intimacy.

After a time, Isaac spoke. "What does bring you to my tent, Esau?" When only silence answered, he inquired further, "Is there a problem?"

"I have no smooth tongue, Father," Esau said. "You know that well enough."

"I do," said Isaac. "Have you a need of soothing words?"

"I have none, whether needed or not," Esau replied. Just then, a wave of sound, muffled by distance and layers of tenting, washed through the darkened space. "Not like some," he said.

"You speak of your brother, Jacob?" Isaac asked.

"I speak of him. I . . . I know not how to say it except roughly," Esau continued.

"Speak roughly, then," Isaac said, "but speak."

"He is well named 'supplanter,' " Esau said. "He curries favor with the servants, Father."

"A wise master does not anger those who serve him," Isaac said.

"You heard that sound, Father. He is judging disputes again. Surely that is your place—or mine." Isaac's eyebrows rose. Esau knew he had his father's attention now.

"He curries favor to undermine me," Esau said. "The servants become increasingly rebellious against me." He saw his father stiffen. "They want Jacob to receive the birthright."

"You have heard them say this?" Isaac demanded.

"No, of course not. But they obey me grudgingly, muttering and dragging their feet. At the same time, they praise Jacob, only Jacob, as if he were the firstborn and their future master."

Isaac cupped his chin in his hand and began absently stroking his thinning white beard, working his jaw slowly. "It is time. I am old. Only El Elyon knows how much longer I will live. So it is time," he finally said, and Esau felt a prickle of excitement.

"We will do it this way, my son. You must do something that only you can do," Isaac continued. "Get me some venison."

"Hunting has not been good lately," Esau protested.

"All the better," Isaac said. "Then only a skilled hunter, such as you, could do it."

"Even I cannot do it for at least two weeks," Esau said.

"But why, my son?" Isaac inquired. "You are a great hunter."

"Game has been scarce of late," Esau responded. "I will not find any while Nanna rides high and shines so brightly."

"The moon?" Isaac said. "Do you hunt at night?"

"No, I do not," Esau replied. "Deer can be difficult enough to see in the daytime. At night, they become just another shadow. When Nanna shines full, the deer can graze at night, and then they hide during the day, giving me almost no chance to see them. When Utu takes Nanna to the underworld, deer must seek food in the daylight. That is when chance favors the hunter."

Isaac pondered then spoke. "At the next new moon, then. In the meantime, we will announce to the camp that I summoned you because I am getting old. That you will bring me a deer as an offering and feast to the passing of the birthright. Prepare the venison the way I like it. Then I will give you my blessing, and we will announce it to everyone." Holding out his hands, Isaac said, "Come closer."

Esau stepped forward, kneeling before his father, Isaac's hands on his shoulders. "Do not be troubled, my son," Isaac said. "The birthright shall be yours. Now, do as I say."

Esau thanked his father, then rose quickly and slipped out of the tent, taking care to be unnoticed, a grim smile on his face. *I roused the leopard,* he thought.

chatat

Shattered

"Send him away," Rebekah said, and though she continued talking, Isaac suddenly heard a woman's voice—*my mother's voice!* he realized—saying, *"Send him away, and his mother too."* The words transported him to his childhood.

"Please!" echoed through Isaac's mind as he looked, bewildered, at his father. He saw deep sadness in Abraham's eyes. *Do not send him away,* thought Isaac. *They will all hate me!*

But watching Abraham wrestle with the decision whether to banish Ishmael, Isaac could not speak because he had too much to say and lacked words strong enough to express his agony. Despite his status as the son of the Promise, Isaac had grown up in a shadow, a shadow cast by Ishmael. Though none dared speak it, many in Abraham's camp resented the banishment of Ishmael and Hagar, and held Isaac responsible. Even as a child, Isaac could sense that some cursed his existence and wished he had never been born. After all, if Isaac had not been born, Ishmael, as Abraham's firstborn, would have remained unchallenged. But Isaac's birth to Sarah in her old age, clearly miraculous, changed all that. And when Sarah had told Abraham about Hagar's taunting and haughty behavior, something had to be done. Despite that, Hagar had her defenders who felt that the severity of her punishment far outweighed her offenses.

What do you want of me? Isaac's young heart had cried out, both to those who hated him and to Elohim, who had brought him life. *I would gladly repent of any deed, no matter how terrible,* he thought, *but how do I make amends for my very existence? Do you not see?* His spirit cried out, *Do you not understand? That day on Mount Moriah, when I thought I was to be sacrificed, that was the first time my existence made sense! It is true I was obedient,* he thought. *It is true I trusted Elohim. But does no one see? Dying on that altar, I could have atoned once and for all for being born, for displacing Ishmael!* But then, Isaac witnessed Elohim intervening, staying Abraham's hand. And, it was clear to Isaac, Elohim had intervened again, when they improbably found the ram, his horns entangled in thorns, a ram suitable for sacrifice. That day on Moriah, for the first time, Isaac understood his destiny. He realized that he could no more be faulted for his birth than for his survival on Moriah: Elohim had willed them both. For ever after that, he knew that all the resentment and anger others directed at him really belonged to Elohim, for Isaac's birth and continued existence both depended upon Elohim's will. And that sustained him.

Having lived all his early years in a community divided by loyalties to different heirs, he vowed that it would never happen in his camp. And then, with the birth of the twins, the very same rivalry entered his own household. He had hoped to blunt it by making it clear that he planned to confer the birthright on the elder of the two twins, on Esau. Yet Rebekah insisted on favoring Jacob. That, along with the great differences between the two sons, heightened the natural rivalry between the children and spread to nearly everyone in the camp, from the chief steward to the lowliest goatherd. That division between his sons, between Rebekah and himself, had afflicted him like an open wound. And now this. Deceit, intrigue, manipulation, violence barely averted, his sons openly at war, and, worst of all, one son now destined for exile. Isaac's one hope had been for a united household. Now it lay shattered like discarded pottery, never to be whole again.

"Isaac? *Isaac!*" his sightless eyes revealed nothing, yet Rebekah sensed he was no longer with her.

"Are you listening to me, Isaac?" Rebekah asked.

"Forgive me, Rebekah. You were saying?"

"I was saying now that Jacob has the birthright, he should be married," he heard Rebekah saying. "Jacob should have a proper wife. Not like Esau's Hittite women." She fairly hissed the word *Hittite*. "I cannot abide those obnoxious heathen women Esau married." She waited for Isaac to react, and when he did not, she continued. "But there are no suitable women nearby. So I thought we should send him away—Isaac?"

Finally, after a silence, Isaac spoke, but he heard his father's voice and saw Abraham bow his head in resignation. "It will be as you say. I will send . . . ," and here he faltered, but he licked his lips and regained his voice, "will send Jacob to your brother in Haran to obtain a wife. See to it."

Something in his tone cut her short, so she rose and left his tent without another word. Despite some serious complications, her plan still seemed ready to succeed. Deceiving Isaac had proved easy because his trust in her had been so complete. In her desperation to secure the birthright for Jacob, she lost sight of how much Isaac trusted her and how much this deception would cost her. It seemed so simple. She knew how Isaac liked his venison, and she could easily make the bland meat of a young kid taste like anything she wanted. So she prepared the meat in secret and gave it to Jacob. Covering Jacob's arms with goatskin to simulate Esau's hairy body had likewise been easy. Disguising Jacob's scent had been his idea, and, as it turned out, had been crucial. In the event, it worked flawlessly, and Isaac conferred the birthright on Jacob.

Jacob had returned from receiving the blessing virtually dancing, she thought. He began telling her every detail of his interview with Isaac. But then, virtually on Jacob's heels, Esau had returned. Jacob looked at his mother with alarm, and Rebekah held her breath as her volatile older son entered his father's tent.

"Go," she hissed at Jacob, "go to the farthest grazing land. I'll send word with a servant what you are to do."

Outraged, Jacob started to protest, but Rebekah raised her hand, palm toward him. That gesture and her blazing eyes silenced him and sent him on his way. Rebekah composed herself and waited for the storm she knew must come.

Moments later, Esau flung the tent flap aside and stomped into his mother's tent. Rebekah sat serenely on a cushion, appearing not to note her angry son's presence. She had anticipated this scene for some time and resolved not to break. "What have you done to me, Mother?" Esau demanded.

"Done to you, my son?" Rebekah asked in a puzzled tone. She looked distracted, almost bored, which confused Esau, but her next flinty words cut through his wonderment. "What have I done to you? I should have thought you would remember." Rebekah spoke quietly, distinctly, so that each word struck Esau like a stone from a slingshot. Surprise blocked the angry words ready to spill from his tongue.

"I carried you in my own body for nine months," Rebekah said. "I suckled you at my breast," she continued. "I cleaned you when you soiled yourself, sat awake when you were ill, and comforted you when you were teething. I kissed your bruises, put salve on your scratches, and soothed your disappointments. Or have you forgotten?"

Still angry and now irritated at her cool tone, her words made him feel off balance. The obligatory reply stuck on his tongue like bitter herbs, but she was his mother, and somehow he felt he had to say them. "I have not forgotten, Mother—" And now he saw her furious tears and felt a chill deep in his core. Never had it occurred to him that his mother might be angry with him. Truly, he seldom thought of her feelings—or anyone's—at all. But he now saw a bitterness within Rebekah that bordered on hate. As clumsy with words as he was skilled with weapons, Esau could only say, "You are angry, Mother."

She turned the full fury of her face on him then and nodded, her head moving so slowly it transfixed Esau, so that he could only stare. "Perhaps," and now her words came, each syllable shaking her tiny frame, "you should ask what *you* have done."

Astonished and flustered, Esau asked, "What I have done?"

"You brought those Hittite females into our camp!" she said. And now the words tumbled out, a landslide of verbiage that pounded Esau. "You disgraced your father, showed contempt for him and Elohim. You did not *deign*," she said, the word almost a snarl, "to seek your father's counsel about a wife, did not even inform him of your plans. You brought those heathen females and their haughty attitudes and their filthy deities here. They act as if they already own everything in camp," she said. "They flaunt their worship of the disgusting Asertu with the lion's pelt and the eight-pointed star upon their tent. At the edge of the camp, they suspend a fleece from a long pole to honor the filthy Telepinu, they boast of their homeland, and they dishonor me." She paused, now sobbing, "You brought them here, and you have the *insolence* to ask what I have done to you?"

Esau stood, shocked and silent. *How can this be?* he wondered. *I am the one who is wronged*, he thought, stirring the coals of his anger, which burst into flame. "*I* disgraced my father?" he asked. "You and your favored brat *deceived* my father, stole my blessing, and took from me the birthright that was rightfully mine!" The rage had returned, the first eruption leading to another. "You think I have done terrible things? I will do things more terrible than these. I will *kill* that cheater, that liar, that deceiving whelp you treasure so much." His voice rising, he knew others could hear, but the rage that held him was speaking through him. "I will kill Jacob," he declared. "I will have what is mine. *I will have the birthright!*"

Rebekah laughed, and the scorn in that laughter seemed to stiffen every hair on Esau's body. "You will not," she said, as Esau stood, slack-jawed. "When you were still in my womb, El Elyon spoke to me," she continued. "Elohim told me that 'the older will serve the younger,' that Jacob would receive the birthright, not you." And she laughed again, a cold, bitter sound. "And when you brought those, those heathen women and their disgusting practices into my camp," her voice was rising, venting a rage long restrained, "you forfeited whatever claim you might have had to be the leader of this clan. Jacob has the birthright now. Killing him will bring upon you nothing but the mark of Cain, a firstborn who kills his brother." She leaned forward, reaching toward him with both hands, as if holding an invisible sphere, and now she began shaking her head, as slowly as she had nodded before. "It is *not* your birthright. It never was, and now it never will be."

Esau lunged forward, but Rebekah flexed her fingers, as if flicking water from her fingertips, and it seemed to Esau as if a strong rope held him back from her. "You should never have fouled your father's camp with those women and their loathsome deities," she said, her nose almost touching his. "You offended Elohim, the Giver of the Promise, the Promise that gave your father life, the Promise that gave you life. And you think that killing Jacob will convince your father to confer upon you his blessing, authority, and all his worldly goods? Foolish boy," she said.

"Do you not know that to this very day he mourns the exile of Ishmael? Ishmael, *his* rival for the birthright?" She rocked back, her mouth a grim line. "He will not honor one who kills his own brother. Your father has many faults." Rebekah smiled grimly. "I know them as well as anyone. But he will not go back on his word, and he will not reward one who commits the crime of Cain. So rid yourself of the idea of killing Jacob, Esau."

"All right," Esau said, biting off each word. "I will not be found killing my brother while Father lives." He turned to leave, then turned back to say, "But Jacob has to visit the far grazing areas sometimes. Who knows what might befall him there? Lions and bears do not care whether they eat sheep or shepherd. You and your El Elyon had best watch over your precious Jacob."

She recoiled now, head turned as if he had slapped her, eyes ablaze. Suddenly, she raised her hand to her mouth. "Now I understand! I heard words that night, words that then made no sense to me. El Elyon Himself declared it to me, 'Jacob have I loved'—do you hear that, hateful boy?—'Jacob have I loved, *but Esau have I hated.*'"

"But why should El Elyon hate me?" Esau demanded in disbelief.

"Because," she spoke quietly, comprehending at last; her anger transformed to wonder. She looked past him and said, "Because He sees the future." Now she looked directly into Esau's eyes, and he saw her eyes filled with pity, not anger, as she concluded, "He knew you would treat Him with contempt."

Fury, astonishment, exasperation, and impotence surged chaotically through Esau's body. He turned, growling savagely, and bolted out into the night.

But Rebekah knew her son. A hunter through and through, Esau would calculate his risks. He knew that Isaac would not live forever. So Rebekah knew that, whatever he might say, at best Esau had resolved merely to wait for Isaac's death before he killed Jacob and claimed Isaac's remaining wealth for himself. And so she had come up with a plan for safeguarding Jacob, while cementing Isaac's blessing at the same time. Isaac hated conflict, avoided it whenever possible, and so she asked his blessing on her plan to send Jacob to her brother Laban in search of a wife. Isaac seized upon this opportunity and quickly agreed. And by consenting to her plan, Isaac had tacitly endorsed the birthright he had already explicitly conferred upon Jacob. But it carried one serious risk.

I may never see Jacob again, Rebekah thought, *but I will not cry. When Isaac insisted on favoring Esau, I knew that I would have to choose.* Even if the Voice had not assured her that Jacob should receive the birthright, Esau's Hittite women made up her mind. *They have no regard for me*, the bitter thoughts echoed through her mind. *When I am gone, they will erase any memory of me. But now that Jacob has the birthright, he will honor me*, she thought. And marrying one of her relatives would be the final assurance. She closed her eyes, pressing her hands against them. *One son hates me and threatens to kill the other. I betrayed Isaac's trust, and I may never see Jacob again; but I have done the will of Elohim, and my memory will be honored. I will not cry!* And then she wept.

After leaving Rebekah's tent, Esau stormed about his tent at the far edge of the camp for several days, violence in every movement, venom in every utterance, while Yudith and Basemath cowered inside. Servants learn early how to blend into the background; and when their master raged, Esau's servants became shadows, instantly available to blunt his wrath, but otherwise invisible, hoping to avoid abuse.

Instead of relief, when Esau left the camp, a feeling of dread settled in on everyone like a killing frost. Esau had vowed to kill Jacob and regain the birthright, and now the seasoned hunter stalked his own brother.

Esau's departure freed Yudith and Basemath, who emerged from their tent, abusing servants, cursing Jacob and bewailing his treachery, and masking their concern over what Esau might do when he caught up with his brother. Everyone, including the Hittite women, awaited Esau's return with nerves as tight as tent ropes in a windstorm.

radaph

Pursuit

Esau woke suddenly, every sense alert. He sniffed the air and cocked his head to listen. *Did a sound wake me? Was there movement on that ridge?* Silently, he grasped his spear in his right hand as he rolled onto his left elbow and scanned the landscape upwind for any evidence that he was being stalked. *My anger has made me careless,* he thought. His anger, at first sharper than a flint skinning-knife, had driven him forward, desperate to catch his fleeing twin. But four days of pursuit had dulled his appetite for Jacob's blood.

The night before, exhausted at the end of those four days of tracking, he had paused to rest. Sheltered by this twisted myrtle tree, he fell asleep within moments, waking up only with the dawn—and with a noise or motion of something unseen. He shook his head, shuddering slightly. *First anger and now fatigue have made me careless,* he thought, *and careless hunters end up hunted themselves.*

With that on his mind, he scouted his surroundings. He rose to a crouch, every sense now focused downwind, where a predator catching his scent might come from. Seeing none, he moved around the tree and looked forward where the faint trail led. Still nothing. Despite that, he couldn't shake the feeling that he had missed something, somewhere.

Detecting nothing, he gathered up his belongings from where he had dropped them the night before. He took a long drink from his goatskin water bag and then fingered his food pouch, seeking a piece of dried goat meat or a chunk of hard bread. He found a small fibrous piece of meat and began chewing slowly. Hefting his goatskin water bag a second time, he thought, *I need more water today.* He evaluated the site where he had slept. *This was far too exposed a position for me to risk spending the night. I must be more careful.*

As he chewed the salty meat, he realized that with each passing hour, trailing his brother had grown more arduous and less rewarding. All those years of playing hunter and hunted had sharpened them both, and Jacob was putting the skills he had learned to good use.

At every opportunity, Jacob found ways to confuse or obscure his trail. Just the day before, the fourth day of the chase, Jacob's tracks disappeared in the spoor left by a pack of hyenas feasting on the remains of a gazelle—probably killed by a lion. It appeared that in their quarreling over the remains, the scavengers had dragged the remains about, including over several small rocky patches. All their tracks and the drag marks from the carcass obscured Jacob's trail. *That was clever, my deceitful brother,* he thought.

Then Esau spotted his brother's sandal marks at the far end of a rocky outcropping, which then led quickly to another rocky stretch of ground. The whole process had slowed Esau's progress and forced him to follow the faintest of trails until dusk, when he stopped to rest at the twisted myrtle and fell asleep.

Esau knew his brother was going to Haran, and that made his chase somewhat easier. Still, he needed to find Jacob in some isolated spot, where no one would witness or interfere with Esau's intentions. But this morning, still not certain what noise or movement had awakened him, he no longer felt certain of his intentions or of the best path to take. *What am I missing?* Every time he thought of catching and killing his usurping brother, his mother's words echoed through his mind: *"Would you pollute your claims even further with the crime of Cain, by spilling your own brother's blood?"*

With Utu, the blinding light that ruled the day, well up in the sky on his daily journey through the heavens, Esau knew he should be on the trail. *Will killing my brother secure the birthright?* Esau pursued the answer to this question back to the events that had set him on this trail.

* * * * *

As they had discussed, Isaac had announced to the entire assembly that he would confer the birthright on Esau when Esau returned with an appropriate gift, in this case a special venison meal for his father. The scarcity of game at the time seemed enough to guarantee that only a hunter as skilled as Esau could secure a deer, even if they had considered betrayal likely; but inexplicably, at the time, neither father nor son had given a thought to the possibility of treachery.

As it happened, Esau found and killed his fallow deer on the very first day after Utu had taken Nanna to the underworld. Without Nanna's light after dark, the deer had been forced to graze in daylight, where Esau easily found it. The successful hunter quickly field dressed the carcass for easier carrying, and, eager to secure the birthright, he set off for the camp without pausing to sleep, the fresh meat over his shoulder. Once in his tent, he slept only for the few hours it took for his wives to cook the venison according to his instructions.

Almost giddy from lack of sleep and growing anticipation, Esau rushed to his father's tent in the evening, bearing a generous tray of roast venison and other delights. Entering the tent, he immediately sensed something was amiss.

"Who comes to my tent?" Isaac inquired.

"Your firstborn, Esau. Prepare to eat my venison and pronounce your blessing upon me."

"Then who was here only moments ago?" asked Isaac, perplexity revealed in his voice. Esau paused, taken aback. He was about to speak when his father added the words that settled in his belly like an ice-covered stone. "He gave me game to eat, and I pronounced the birthright blessing upon him."

Esau dropped suddenly to one knee, almost spilling the tray of delicacies. His head swam, his heart rose in his throat. Every joint trembled. Esau's lips formed the word *Jacob*, but there emerged a sound like the dying rage of a wounded leopard.

Sleeping animals at the edge of the camp bolted awake, and cringing servants hid themselves. Sephret, Isaac's body servant, ran into the tent. And there he saw Esau on his knees, with a tray of delicacies before him, sobbing. Amazed, Sephret quickly withdrew.

Recovering his voice, Esau pleaded, "Bless me, too, Father. The birthright is mine!"

"Alas, Jacob came in and deceived me. He received the blessing and the birthright," Isaac said. "I pronounced the birthright blessing upon him. I cannot unspeak the words; I cannot take back the blessing."

"Jacob!" Esau spat the name, and then said, "He's *'aqob,* 'crooked,' all right. You named him well. *'Aqob* Jacob, crooked cheat, he has tripped me by the heels twice. He took my birthright and now my blessing." Quiet and broken now, Esau inquired, "Do you have but one blessing? Have you no blessing for me, Father?" Esau's voice alarmed Isaac. No one had heard the great hunter weep since childhood.

Isaac reached out and embraced his grieving son. Esau could not remember the rest of his father's words, only that, no matter what, he had lost.

* * * * *

Remembering, Esau clamped his jaw down on the last bit of goat meat, took a deep breath, swallowed, and reached for his water carrier. *What am I missing?* After leaving his father, Esau's fury had driven him to his mother, protesting her betrayal. Drinking from the goatskin, Esau frowned in concentration as he swallowed. That encounter remained a haze of bitterness and confusion in his mind. *But . . . something she said,* he thought. His mind reached for it but could not grasp the words. *I can read the trail of a gazelle,* he thought, *and in dusty hoofprints can tell if it was anxious or carefree. But I do not understand people, especially women!*

He sighed.

At least the gazelle leaves a distinct and single trail leading from one point to the next. But women and their words weave and bob, sidetrack and backtrack. I never know where they're going or when they arrive. Even thinking of it gave Esau a headache. *I wish I could remember Mother's words.*

Utu rode high in the sky, so the best morning hours were spent. *Jacob can only get so far ahead of me,* thought Esau, as he resumed the trail. *Like a fallow deer heading for water, I know where Jacob is headed—to Haran to find a wife!*

Esau stopped walking as the realization hit him. His heel slipped on some loose stones that clattered down the gentle slope to the right of the trail, answered by an echo somewhere behind him.

My wives! Mother hates my Hittite wives! He crouched now, chin in his hand as if studying the movements of some small game animal. *Of course, I knew there was irritation, but,* and now he slapped his forehead. *Fool!* he thought. *She told you, and you didn't listen.* Now he stood and began pacing back and forth. *Killing Jacob won't make anyone love Yudith and Basemath—or me, for that matter! It will be just one more reason to hate me.*

Esau paused in his pacing and crouched again, staring at the ground, but oblivious to his surroundings, his eyes registered nothing. He couldn't just divorce the Hittites, as much as he might desire to. Even he found the women annoying. But their fathers, men of influence and wealth, would not take such an affront to their honor lightly. No, divorcing the two would only bring more troubles, and he needed no more troubles. He looked at Jacob's faint trail, heading in the general direction of Haran.

'Aqob Jacob, crooked schemer, Esau thought bitterly. *He seeks a wife Mother will approve, from her brother's household. Too bad it did not occur to me. Maybe I should have sought a wife from my mother's brother. Or my father's!* Esau leaped to his feet, shouted *"Ayah,"* and smacked a fist into the other palm, startling the birds and small animals within earshot. *Paran!* he thought. *Not Haran, but Paran for me!* He began laughing aloud. Pausing for a moment, he bent over and picked up a stone. Hefting it in his right hand, he shouted, "Run, little brother, run to Haran!" Laughing so hard he could barely form the words, he boomed, "Run along and get your wife from Laban. I seek bigger game." He threw the stone down his brother's trail; and then, laughing harder with every stride, he set off for Paran.

* * * * *

Esau's laughter chilled Jacob to his very core. His clever maneuver with the gazelle carcass the day before had allowed him to come around behind Esau undetected and trail his brother.

Knowing Esau was trailing him, when Jacob had come upon the hyenas tearing at the gazelle carcass, he saw an opportunity. Brandishing his shepherd's staff, he drove the snarling hyenas away from their prize. Working quickly, he sawed off gobbets of meat and skin from the gazelle and hacked what was left of the carcass into two great bony chunks. Then he backed across the sands, pulling the carcass in great arcs along behind him, obscuring his tracks. Finally he threw the remaining scraps along his latest path, counting on the hyenas to finish the job of obscuring his tracks.

They did, slinking back from all directions to fight over the carcass until the only human tracks left were the ones he had planted at the far end of the rock outcroppings where they appeared to lead onto a sketchy game trail.

Concealing himself just below the edge of a wadi, he waited for his pursuer.

A few hours later, Esau obligingly came down the trail, and, as Jacob expected, the very faintness of the trail lured Esau on, allowing Jacob to come up behind his brother undetected. For the first time since he had left his father's camp, Jacob enjoyed the advantage in this deadly game and began to feel a measure of safety.

Careful to keep himself concealed and far enough behind to be safe from detection, Jacob could now trail Esau. Eventually, the hunter would realize that Jacob had eluded him, and he would have to give up. When that happened, the watching Jacob would know and could then finish his journey with less concern. So Jacob had trailed Esau for much of the previous day and saw his exhausted brother lie down by the twisted myrtle tree and fall asleep. Finding a secure vantage point, Jacob settled down to sleep himself. That's when the troubles began.

Suddenly Jacob heard his father's voice, felt hands clawing at his skin. *"You are not Esau! You are the cheat, you are Jacob."*

And then the voice became Esau's. *"You lying little brat. You crooked, betraying brother!"*

Jacob awoke with a start and gasped sharply. The sudden motion sent a lizard scurrying into a thornbush. Silently, Jacob rose to one elbow and peered down to Esau's resting place by the twisted tree, to see his brother also startle awake. His heart pounding, Jacob's breath rasped in and out of his chest so sharply that he felt Esau surely must hear it. But instead of spotting Jacob, Esau began behaving very strangely. After eating and drinking, Esau took to the trail.

Once Esau began moving again following the false trail, Jacob followed at a discreet distance, breathing easier. But then Esau's sudden stop had caught Jacob off guard, had caused him to slip and send the stones clattering, sending Jacob to the ground, his heart hammering again. Yet, for reasons Jacob could not understand, Esau did not seem to hear his noisy tracker. Crawling, Jacob concealed himself behind a slight rise topped with some spindly shrubs. Not much cover, but enough at this distance as Esau crouched and looked out far ahead.

Watching Esau pace back and forth, Jacob felt both puzzlement and growing alarm. *What is he doing?* Jacob wondered. Then, when Esau jumped, shouted, and pounded one fist into the other palm, every hair on Jacob's body stood up, and only with difficulty did he stifle his own startled cry. And when he heard Esau shout, "Run, little brother, run to Haran!" and then laugh, Jacob panicked momentarily. But when Esau turned around and headed away from the trail to Haran, Jacob could only wonder. *Is Esau intoxicated? And what did Esau mean about seeking "bigger game"?*

As soon as Esau disappeared in the distance, Jacob arose and set off for Haran at top speed. Jacob could not be certain whether Esau had given up the chase. If he had given up the chase, Jacob could move safely. If Esau had spotted him, his only safety lay in flight. In any case, every moment they moved in opposite directions made Jacob safer. With that in mind, he made all haste toward his destination. Well stocked with food and water himself, Jacob walked through the day, pausing only for a short time when Utu stood at the top of the heavens, his bright rays burning anything that moved. And when night fell and the curved sliver of Nanna rode the sky, Jacob pressed on.

Tracking proved hard enough in daylight, Jacob knew; tracking at night, with Nanna still small, would be nearly impossible. Troubling thoughts of his brother's vow to kill him, then his brother's strange behavior on the trail, and uncertainty whether even now, Esau might be pursuing him with murderous intent drove him forward. Even with the dangers of night travel, Jacob pressed on with his remaining strength.

But by the time Nanna rode at the apex of heaven's dome, Jacob's legs became as lead, and his pack more than could be borne. When he came to a field of boulders atop a slight rise, he found a great flat slab of stone coming out of the ground at a gentle angle. It looked promising, sheltered from most hazards, and, in his state of fatigue, comfortable. With a grunt, he lowered his pack to the ground and sat at the base of the great stone. *Well, I got the birthright*, he thought. *But what good did it do me? What kind of blessing drives me out to a place like this*, he wondered, his eyes taking in the rugged boulders all around him, *far from home and pursued by my own brother? Mother*, he asked silently, *is this what you intended? Is this the blessing Elohim wanted me to have? Did we show ourselves worthy by deceiving Father and splintering our family? I do not feel worthy*, he thought, shaking his head in sorrow. *I feel ashamed.* He took a quick drink from his goatskin canteen and then placed it by his feet. He took in the alien landscape once again and wondered, *Is Elohim even here? This is far from the tents of my father, Isaac. Far from the cave where Abraham sleeps. Who is the god of this place?* With his stout shepherd's staff beside him and questions spiraling through his mind, he reclined on the rock's welcoming surface and quickly fell into a troubled slumber.

Suddenly, Jacob became aware of unceasing activity. He saw the slanting start of a brick-paved ramp near his feet on the ground. The ramp spiraled upward around a tower of dizzying height, and fleet-footed messengers sped all along its length. Some moved upward, and some downward. Although he saw no torches, the speeding couriers themselves somehow glowed and made the great tower appear like a weaver's loom, with gleaming threads winding their way back and forth, producing a great, glorious spiraling fabric of light cascading from heaven to earth.

A cataract of sound accompanied the cascade of light, a Voice like roaring water that Jacob felt more than heard, saying, *"I, Yahweh, am Elohim Abraham and Elohim Isaac."* Every part of Jacob tingled, both at the assault of sight and sound and at the realization of who spoke. *"The land where you lie, I will give to you and your seed. And your seed shall be numerous like the dust of the earth, and shall burst outward in every direction: to the east and the west, the north and the south. And all the families of the earth shall be blessed through you and through your seed."* Jacob could not see who spoke, only that the Voice came from the great light atop the tower, at the highest point on heaven's dome.

"And look now, I am with you, and I will guard you wherever you go, and I will bring you back to this land; for I will not leave you until I have done that which I have spoken to you."

The sudden darkness and the silence wakened the stunned Jacob. *So Elohim is not just the God of the desert or of our traditional grazing lands, for surely El Elyon, El Shaddai, is here in this place. In my hour of deepest shame, He came to renew His promise. When I came to rest here, I did not know, but there can be no doubt now. I am not worthy of His promise, nor can I ever be. I can only be grateful.* Shivering now, not from the cold but from awareness, he looked around him, remembering the tower, the ramp, the shimmering messengers. *This is a fearsome place,* he realized. *What else can this be but the house of Elohim, the very doorway and path to the heavens?*

Rising early the next morning, he cleared an area directly around the slanting boulder on which he had spent the night, from which he had seen the mighty tower, and where he had heard the voice of Elohim. He took a vessel of oil from his pack and poured some on the highest point of the stone. Then he knelt by the stone and lifting his hands heavenward, he said, "If Adonai

Elohim accompanies me, guards me on the path I am taking, and gives me bread to eat and clothing to wear, and I return safely to my father's house, then Elohim will be my God. And this stone I set as a pillar will be a house of Elohim, and everything that You give to me, I will give a tithe to You."

And Jacob called that place *Beth-El:* the house of God.

עצם ובשר

'etsem v^ebasar

Bone and Flesh

Suddenly, he felt homesick. Since leaving home three weeks before, Jacob had felt fear, fatigue, caution, panic, even exultation at Beth-El, but this was the first time he had felt melancholy, alone, and disconnected. He contemplated this new sorrow as he trudged along the road, with head bowed. The trade route he had followed for several days ran through an increasingly verdant plain, bounded to the east by a series of ridges. He looked up to see that ahead the route turned to the east, toward a break in the ridgeline. Through that opening flowed a welcoming breeze, laden with the scent of grass and sheep, smells of home. Sheep! *To smell them at this distance, there must be many sheep.* He paused and shaded his eyes, seeking the source of those domestic aromas, but he saw nothing. Picking up the pace now, he strode up the traders' roadway, following as it curved and climbed.

As the road reached the top of the ridge, the valley below seemed to open before him like a great drinking bowl. His breath caught as he took in the vast expanse of green and three separate flocks of sheep surrounding some sort of stone structure at the opposite end of the valley. He felt like weeping for joy at the beauty of the sight. Not only did his shepherd's heart swell at the sight and sound—and even the smell—of beautiful grazing, healthy flocks, but the size of the gathering kindled hopes that he might finally be near his destination.

He made a show of leaning on his shepherd's staff as he walked toward the stone structure, which he thought was most likely a well, so as to put the shepherds tending the flocks at ease. He wanted to make it clear that he posed no threat to them or their sheep. Some distance away from the stone enclosure, he paused, put down his pack, and took a drink from his goatskin water bag. "My brothers," he called, his arm sweeping from one shepherd to another, "where are you from?"

Even at a distance, Jacob saw them exchanging glances, calculating the proper response. Finally, one spoke. "From Haran," he said flatly.

Jacob grinned expansively, both to assure them of his good intentions and because he felt such relief. "Haran, you say. Tell me, do you know Laban, Nahor's grandson?"

Another exchange of glances, then all three nodded. And the one who had spoken before said, "We know him." Jacob noticed the speaker's face, weathered like driftwood, beard flecked with gray. *The eldest, most experienced one*, Jacob thought. *The others defer to him.* So he walked a few steps closer, turning his back to the well. "Is Laban well?" Jacob asked.

The old fellow said, "He is well."

Behind Jacob, the subtle sounds of moving sheep grew louder. He turned to see yet another flock moving in, this one led by a mere slip of a girl.

The old shepherd spoke again, "There comes his daughter Rachel with the sheep."

His daughter! Jacob thought. *Can it be? I come to marry Laban's daughter, and she comes to meet me?* He looked at the girl again, still some distance away. *A young thing*, he thought, *but that will be to my advantage. It will take me some time to earn enough to pay the bride-price.*

He glanced around. Everyone stood as though waiting for something to happen. *I must talk to her. Privately. What are they waiting for?*

"Look," he said, "the sun is still high; it is not time for the flocks to be gathered. Why do you not water the sheep and take them back to pasture?"

"We cannot," the old shepherd replied (*Is that a sly smile?*), "until all the flocks are gathered. Then, *together* we can roll the stone away from the mouth of the well. After that, we will water the sheep, and once their thirst is satisfied, we can take them out to pasture again."

While they waited, Rachel and her flock drew nearer. *They will not leave until they water their flocks, is that it?* So Jacob picked up his pack and strode to the well. As he drew closer, Jacob began to appreciate why they waited for more help. A single round stone, a full two cubits in diameter and half a cubit thick, covered the well. But Jacob would not be denied. Having come this far, and Laban's daughter literally almost within reach energized him. The three shepherds drew near to watch as he took a length of braided rawhide from his pack and looped it around the stone. He tied the ends of the rawhide to his shepherd's staff, which he turned, twisting the rawhide and tightening its grip around the stone covering the well. The rawhide still attached, Jacob dug one end of the staff into the ground and pulled the other end toward him with both hands. The stone moved back with a grating sound, accompanied by grunts of surprise from the other three shepherds. Repositioning his staff on the ground, he repeated the procedure, and the stone moved again. A third time and it tipped one edge onto the ground. Quickly he loosened and removed the rawhide. Bowing toward the shepherds, he made a sweeping gesture toward the well. "At your service, brothers."

* * * * *

"Slow down, child," Laban said. "Stand still. Take a deep breath. Tell me why you left the sheep alone in the middle of the day. Slow down, girl. You speak so quickly I cannot understand your words. At first I thought you said this stranger moved the stone off the well by himself. But that could not be."

"But he did! All by himself. It was *amazing!*" Rachel said, her feet moving again, her head bobbing from side to side, looking into her father's eyes for belief. "And then he picked me up—so strong he is, Father, I felt like a feather." She closed her eyes for a moment, relishing that delicious sensation. "He picked me up, and he kissed me on both cheeks," she felt her face flushing and saw her father's frown so she hurried on, but he interrupted her.

"He did *what?* Who does this fellow think he is?" Laban asked, offended.

"I am trying to tell you, Father," Rachel said, putting her hands together, "Let me speak and I will tell you."

Laban attempted to be patient.

"His name is Jacob, the son of Isaac, the son of Abraham." When her father failed to react, she said, "Isaac, who married your sister, Rebekah!"

"Rebekah?" Laban asked, and Rachel nodded. "My sister Rebekah's son? Why did you not tell me sooner?" Rachel opened her mouth to protest, but Laban rose to his feet and said, "I must go and greet him." Turning to his wife, Laban said, "This could be a day of great fortune, Adinah." To his wife's inquiring look, he replied, "I remember well when last a visitor came from the clan of Abraham," he said, eyes fixed on a vivid memory.

"Eliezer, chief steward of Abraham, came here with ten camels, each one loaded with treasure, seeking a wife for Abraham's son Isaac," Laban recalled.

"A wife!" said Adinah. "Treasure?"

"He purchased my sister Rebekah with the treasure," Laban said. Turning to Rachel, he asked, "What did this Jacob bring with him?"

Rachel, wide-eyed, shook her head. "Bring with him?"

"Think, girl," Laban demanded.

"Nothing, Father," she said, "except a large bundle."

"*Hmm.* That surprises me. Still, take me to him," he said, and Rachel felt a flutter in her stomach. "And then get back to those sheep!"

Sheep? Rachel thought. *You greet my Jacob*—for she already thought of the powerful stranger as her own—*and I go to your smelly sheep?* She set her mouth in a firm line. But Laban, occupied with the coming of his nephew, failed to see his daughter's expression.

Laban strode about the camp, summoning servants, organizing preparations to receive the distinguished visitor. "I should go with you, Abba," said Leah, arms folded. As the older sister, of marriageable age at thirteen, Leah considered it only proper that she should meet any eligible men.

"You will not," the distracted Laban said. "You will stay home and help your mother prepare to entertain our guest. Come, Rachel. Stop daydreaming and take me to Jacob." Leah stamped her foot in protest, but Laban, his mind already preparing to meet his nephew, took no notice. Rachel pretended not to.

"Follow me, Father," Rachel called out. She did not look back because she knew Leah would have detected the smile their father did not see.

"Oh, I do wonder what he looks like," Leah said, when they had left.

"You will know soon, my daughter." Adinah said it without emotion. Leah's constant moaning and sighing about becoming a spinster no longer elicited much of a reaction from her mother.

"What shall I wear? Do you suppose he's already married? I don't want to be anyone's second wife—"

"Leah, tend to the cooking!" Adinah said.

"But we have servants to do that."

"And servants need to be supervised," Adinah said, despite Leah's pouty expression, "and if you are so keen to be a wife, you need to get in the habit of supervising them. Off with you!" And Leah left, muttering all the way. *I pity the man she marries*, Adinah thought, and then shook her head to clear it of such thoughts and turned to her own preparations for the visitor.

* * * * *

"Did he tell you?" Adinah asked Laban in a low voice. After a long evening of formal greetings and introductions and obligatory feasting, Laban summoned his wife and two daughters.

"He did not," said Laban.

"If he seeks a bride, what price does he offer?" Adinah inquired. "His pack contained only basic necessities and shepherd's tools."

Laban just shook his head. "I cannot tell." Looking in her eyes, he confessed, "I embraced him closely upon meeting him, thinking he might secretly be carrying gold."

"Father, how could you?" asked Rachel and immediately repented of her presumption. "I am sorry, Father."

"It is my responsibility to provide for all: family, servants, and livestock in this clan," Laban said. "If he seeks my daughter as a wife," Laban said, looking at both girls, "then it is my duty—and in your best interests—to make certain he has the resources to take on such a responsibility."

"So what is he doing here?" Adinah asked.

"He has come for me," said Leah, her chin raised, eyes closed. "I am to be his wife!"

"And how do you know that?" Laban asked.

"Why else would he come?" Leah replied.

"But why did *he* come?" asked Adinah, shaking her head. "Why did not his father, Isaac, send his chief steward and a train of camels bearing gifts, as Abraham did before him?" She pursed her lips. "I do not like it," she said. "He is hiding something, this Jacob. I can feel it."

"Perhaps," Laban said. "Whatever brought him here, it must be important to come so far a distance." He came to a decision. "We will wait." He paused, rubbing his chin. "Wait and see."

Rachel held her tongue, but one thought filled her mind: *He kissed* me.

* * * * *

"Leah!" Adinah called. "Stop daydreaming and tend to your sewing!" Leah knew a good wife needed to be able to sew, and usually her flying fingers drew the bone needle through the fabric at a rapid pace, leaving behind an orderly trail of even stitches. But today, no matter how she tried, her thoughts wandered, and once again she found her hands poised in midstitch. *He has been with us for a month*, she thought, *and Father says he will ask Jacob's intentions tonight*. She could barely contain her excitement at the thought. *That first day when he arrived, he all but said he had come for a wife. That would have to be me. Not only am I older, but Rachel is still such a child. A grown man like Jacob will want someone more mature.* Leah actually nodded her head at the thought. Becoming conscious of the needle in her hand again, she took a thoughtful stitch. *I can run a household better than Mother*, Leah sniffed, *if she would only let me. Mother has become so irritable with me lately. Old women often grow irritable with age*, she thought.

"Leah! Have you finished that yet?" Adinah called.

Leah snorted. "In a moment," she replied and bent to her work again. A serving girl scurried by, giggling as she moved. "Tend to your duties, girl," Leah called out sternly. Too late, she saw her mother walking toward her.

"You could use that advice yourself, Leah," said Adinah. "Look at this!" she said, taking the sewing in both hands. "You should be finished with this already. Not mooning about Jacob." A giggle filtered in through the walls of the tent. "And I do not need you riding the servants. It makes them resentful and slow."

"They make fun of me!" Leah whispered fiercely. "They say I make 'doe eyes' at Jacob," she said, "and then they cross their eyes, as though I would do such a silly thing. They call me 'Leah, cross-eyed over Jacob.' I will not tolerate it."

"Girl, you give them more power than they deserve. Pay no mind to their silly gossip. And keep your voice down."

"But Mother, they are always gossiping about something. And now they make fun of me behind my back," Leah said, full of dignity. " 'Cross-eyed Leah,' they call me, 'cross-eyed Leah'! Just because I love Jacob. They do not know I hear them," and here she turned to where the serving girl had disappeared and shouted, "*but I do!*"

Adinah put her hand to her mouth and cleared her throat. Adinah knew that servants had their ways of mocking a pompous mistress. But, as mistress of the camp and mother to the girls, Adinah could not afford for either girls or servants to realize how funny she thought it was. Leah would be impossible and even more imperious, and the servants would goad the girl even more. Adinah could not permit that. "Ignore them, girl," she said when she had regained her composure. "Ignore them, and they will cease. Retaliate, and it will only get worse." She placed her hand on Leah's cheek. "Real dignity allows one to ignore small slights," Adinah said. But Leah only sniffed, so Adinah left with a silent sigh.

Shaking her head, she thought, *If Jacob does not ask to marry Leah, she will make us all miserable.* And despite herself, she also realized, *And if he does, Leah will make* him *miserable.*

* * * * *

"You have been with us a month," Laban said, as they sat around the fire after the evening meal, "and all the servants admire your strength and your skill with the flocks."

Jacob modestly lowered his gaze. "I am your guest. It is well I should earn my keep—"

"You are my flesh and blood," Laban objected. "Just because you are a relative of mine, should you work for me for nothing? Nonsense!"

Jacob bowed his head. "Thank you for your generosity, Uncle."

"Not at all," Laban said, feeling expansive. "One who works so well as you deserves to be paid. Tell me, Jacob, son of my sister Rebekah, tell me what your wages should be."

Jacob sat, pondering. The fire crackled, and a wolf howled in the distance. Adinah and her daughters sat behind and slightly to the left of Laban. Stealing a glance at her daughters, Adinah noted with satisfaction that they sat modestly, eyes downcast. Rachel's eyes glowed with anticipation. Leah leaned forward, ever so slightly. Neither girl breathed.

Finally, Jacob spoke. "Your generosity encourages me to ask for what otherwise I would not," he said, looking to where the girls sat. Only Adinah noticed both girls take a sudden breath.

Laban nodded, admiring his nephew's tact and bargaining skill.

"I propose to work for you for seven years," Jacob said, letting the value of his offer sink in.

Laban's eyebrows rose at the prospect. Seven years of Jacob's management would greatly increase his flocks. "In return for?" Laban prompted.

"In return for your younger daughter, Rachel."

Neither girl reacted. Leah, stunned, thought, *There must be some mistake. My ears deceive me.* She turned her head slowly toward Rachel. The younger girl sat, the slightest flush on her cheeks, gaze modestly on the floor, knowing she must not reveal her delight. Leah looked again at Jacob, disbelieving. *Father will never allow this!* she thought. *He will correct this mistake.*

Laban looked at his daughter and nodded, saying, "It's better that I give her to you than to some other man. Stay here with me."

Rachel's heart leaped; she felt her face grow warm. She stole a glance at her sister. Leah appeared unmoved. *Jacob will be mine*, Rachel thought. *Leah cannot change this bargain. Jacob will be mine!* Rachel closed her eyes and tilted her head back in ecstasy, listening to the voice of her beloved.

Adinah looked at the two girls. Rachel quietly radiated joy, but what about Leah? Leah did not seem to react at all. *I do not like this*, Adinah thought. *Leah does not take disappointment so quietly.*

Leah did not hear the rest of the talk: the planning, the promises, and the hopes. She did not cry, nor did her face reveal anything other than an eerie serenity. She had come to a realization. *Why, of course. He came here empty-handed, with only his labor to offer, and because of that, Jacob feared that Father would refuse him if he asked for me*, she reasoned. *He thought Father would demand more than seven years of labor for me, but he could not wait! Well, I am worth more—the first daughter, the more womanly daughter. Still, a respectable price. Seven years. Plenty of time to correct this mistake.*

charan, paran

Haran, Paran

The courier traveled through the night, reaching the great green valley on the Plain of Haran while Utu still struggled upward in the sky. Dew lay heavy on the grass, and the first flocks began to make their appearance. Three shepherds stood near a stone structure at the opposite end of the valley. Perhaps they could help him. Mistress Rebekah had given him strict instructions about his mission.

"Under no circumstances should you ask after Master Jacob," she had said. "Do you understand me? This is important!"

"I understand," Elam replied.

"You must speak of Jacob only to my brother, Laban," she continued. "I want no loose talk leading Esau to his brother, you understand?"

More than a year had elapsed since Jacob had left Beersheba pursued by his angry brother. Neither had returned home in that time. And although neither Isaac nor Rebekah spoke openly, they both fretted about the continued absences. They had enough servants to easily care for their flocks and herds, but that did not ease a father's or a mother's heart at the absence of their only sons. And so they decided to send Elam to Haran, to Laban's house, to seek news of Jacob. Not knowing Esau's location or his intentions, they wanted to be certain he knew nothing of Elam's mission.

Seeing the shepherds standing near the stone structure, Elam advanced toward them. "Brothers," he called, opening his arms wide, "where are you from?"

They looked at one another in silence. Finally an old man, with a weathered face and graying beard, said, "We are from Haran." All three folded their arms.

"Excellent tidings," Elam said, "for I seek Laban, who lives near Haran." When they did not volunteer anything, he inquired, "Do you know him?"

"We know him," the older shepherd spoke once again.

"Is he well?" Elam asked. He did not intend to talk of his business with these men, but if he did not engage in the usual courtesies, they would become suspicious.

"He is well, so far as we know," the old shepherd said. "But why not ask him yourself?"

"Good counsel," Elam agreed. "Can you direct me to his camp?"

"We can," the old shepherd said again. "It's just down that path there—" He gestured, and Elam started walking. "But if you wait a few moments," he continued, "his shepherd should be here, leading his flocks. Big, strapping young man."

Another flock had begun surging over a ridge near the path the shepherd had pointed out. *The last thing I want to do is start servants' tongues wagging,* Elam thought. "My business is with Laban himself," Elam said, departing. "I'll just go on my way. Thank you, brothers." With a departing wave, he maneuvered around the oncoming sheep. In the distance, Laban's servant knelt over a lamb tangled in a briar. *Good,* thought Elam, *he didn't notice me. The less notice I receive, the better.* And he sped on down the path in the direction of Laban's camp, leaving the shepherds and the stone structure behind him.

After freeing the sheep from the briar, Jacob strode to the stone well. "Who was that?" he asked.

The other three shrugged their shoulders. "Just some traveler," they said, "seeking your uncle Laban."

Jacob did not comment, nor did he think much more about the man. Laban was a well-known man of substance. Strangers came through looking for him all the time. Looking around, he said, "After I water the sheep, I'm going to take them beyond the south ridge, there." He said, pointing, "Give this area some rest." The men nodded. Jacob was wise in the ways of sheep.

At Laban's camp, Elam insisted on speaking with Laban.

"His actions are very strange," said Adinah. "I do not trust him. Be careful what you tell him."

"I do not trust him either," Laban said, as he went to greet the visitor.

"My apologies, sir, but I am bound by an oath to speak only to Laban, brother of my mistress, Rebekah," Elam said.

"I am Laban," he said. "What is so important that you will not speak in the presence of my servants?"

"My master, Isaac of Beersheba, inquires about his son Jacob," Elam said.

"I do not understand," said Laban, suddenly alert. "Why the secrecy?"

Elam thought for a moment. *How much do I reveal?* he wondered. *Isaac and Rebekah trusted Jacob to Laban, and they insisted I speak only with him. That must mean they trust him.* He reached a decision. "Esau, his brother, vowed to kill Jacob. My master sent Jacob here to seek a wife and to find refuge from his brother's anger. But my master has not heard from either son for . . . for some time now." Elam felt uneasy being too specific.

Laban's thoughts raced. *His brother wants to kill him? And Isaac sent him here! No wonder he arrived without treasure.* Laban sensed an opportunity. "You were wise to speak to no one of this," Laban said. "Remain here, while I inquire of my servants. I may be some time. A serving girl will bring you water for washing and food and drink. Rest and refresh yourself in my absence." Elam nodded, and Laban left the tent. After washing and eating, Elam slept.

I don't want Isaac meddling with my household, Laban thought. *Jacob is too valuable for me to lose.* Walking through the camp, he decided, *The only way to make sure they leave us alone is to convince them that Jacob is dead. Even better, that he died before reaching us.* He nodded grimly to himself. *Finding some rags, making it look like an animal had devoured someone will be easy enough,* he thought. *But how to convince them it was Jacob?*

He had walked across the camp to Leah's and Rachel's tent. Seeing the tent reminded him that Rachel had shown him a small *sappiyr* box that Jacob had given her as a token of their betrothal. With their tent empty, he stole inside to search for it, but without turning everything upside down, he could not find it. Then he realized, *It doesn't matter whether I have the box—only that I know of it. Surely something as valuable as that would be an identifying possession.*

Laban returned as darkness fell. He roused Elam and said, "I have troubling news. My servants have heard rumors of this Jacob—some time past. But he is not in our camp." Elam looked worried. "I fear there is more," said Laban.

"What do you mean?"

Laban produced some old, stained rags. "One of my herdsmen found this, far to the south of here."

Elam looked at the tattered remnants. "When?"

Laban looked very sober. "He could not say. Some time ago."

"Does he know anything more about them?" Elam asked.

Laban sighed. "He showed them around to the other herdsmen. One of them nodded and kept saying, 'Crooked, crooked,' over and over. At least that's what my herdsman thought he said."

"But instead of *'aqob*, 'crooked,' it might have been 'Jacob.' Is that what you are saying?" Elam asked.

"I am saying that I do not know," Laban replied, face grim. "But there is no Jacob here." Laban paused, as if thinking, then said, "There was one more thing; it might just be some old man's rambling. Something about a small *sappiyr* box," said Laban. *Not too much detail,* Laban thought. *They'll be more likely to believe it if they have to put the pieces together themselves.*

"Do you have this box?" Elam inquired.

"I am sorry; I do not. My servant was told of it but did not see it himself."

"Then I must report this to my master." Elam gestured at the rags. "May I take these with me?"

"You may," Laban said, "and we will supply you with whatever else you need for your return journey."

"My master is in your debt," said Elam.

"How long can you stay with us?" Laban asked. "To do honor to your master."

"Stay?" Elam said. "I cannot stay. My master is aged, and his heart yearns for news, even bad news is better than none. I must leave at first light," Elam said.

"I understand," Laban said.

The next morning, as Elam disappeared down the path, Adinah turned to Laban and said, "Now that there is no chance for him to hear, why did you lie to him?"

"Lie to him?" Laban said, feigning injury. "How did I lie to him?"

"You told him Jacob is not in this camp," Adinah said.

"Well, where is he? Right now?" Laban demanded.

"Right now? I do not know. He said he would take the flocks south for a few days," Adinah said, flustered.

"You mean he is not in this camp?"

"Well, not at this moment," Adinah said, awareness growing.

"And where was he last night and since early yesterday morning?"

"I see," said Adinah. "But why lead him to think Jacob had never been here and might be dead?"

"How long did Jacob agree to work for us?" Laban asked.

"Seven years."

"And have our flocks ever prospered so well as under his care?"

"Never," Adinah had to admit.

"What if his father wants him back?" Laban asked. "Did you consider that?"

"He might pay the bride-price," Adinah said.

"And what could he pay us that would be equal to another six years of Jacob's management of our flocks?" Laban asked.

"I see what you mean." Adinah had to agree. No flock so large could travel so great a distance, and Isaac almost certainly did not possess so great a quantity of silver, even if he was willing to pay such a staggering sum.

"If he thinks Jacob may be dead, we will not have to worry about any . . . complications with our . . . arrangement." Laban smiled. "And we might be able to secure his services even longer."

"How will you do that?" Adinah asked.

"I do not know," Laban replied. "But, if Isaac concludes his son is dead, he will inquire no more, and we shall have the benefit of six more years of Jacob's service—and the same amount of time to think of a way to persuade him to continue."

* * * * *

"The herdsmen sent a runner," Rebekah told Isaac. "A small party advances on our camp from the south."

"From the south? Are you certain?" Isaac said.

With his eyesight so poor, Isaac questions everyone else's, thought Rebekah, but she put the irritation aside. Since the disappearance of their two sons, the old couple had only each other for comfort. Esau's wives provided enough irritation for the whole camp, and so Isaac and Rebekah determined to put their own anger and recriminations aside to find what little contentment age and circumstances allowed them.

"Who would be coming from the south?" Isaac asked. "We sent Elam off to the north. Could it not be Elam returning with Jacob from the north?"

"How could Elam be back so soon?" Rebekah asked.

"But who could it be?" Isaac wondered. Rebekah did not answer, except to place a comforting hand on his arm. She felt him relax. They would await word together.

Before long, the whispers began outside the tent, and the swirling currents of servant communication brought them inside. "Esau! It's Esau!"

After so long a time, Rebekah hardly knew what to think. The last time she and her older son had spoken, they exchanged bitter, scalding words. *And now, as we await word of Jacob, Esau returns? And not alone?*

The camp sprang to life. Yudith and Basemath scurried about, preparing to welcome their husband. Isaac and Rebekah donned formal robes to greet their older son. As the travelers approached, the camp assembled, and Isaac and Rebekah walked arm in arm to their place in the front.

Rebekah, serving as Isaac's eyes, spoke quietly in his ear. "Esau is on foot, followed by a veiled woman mounted on a donkey and three servants: a man and two women." Isaac snorted. *He's thinking the same thing I am,* Rebekah thought. *The last time this happened, Esau introduced us to his wives. Did he learn nothing?*

"We have missed you, my son," Isaac said.

Esau looked at the ground. "I am sorry to have caused you anxiety, Father," he said.

A sharp intake of breath somewhere behind them reflected the surprise everyone felt. *Do my ears deceive me? Is Esau apologizing?* Rebekah wondered, eyes open wide. Isaac's grip on her arm tightened; clearly Esau's newly acquired humility had literally shaken her husband. "Wel–Welcome, Esau." Isaac labored over each word. "And you have others in your party."

Esau extended his hand to the veiled woman on the donkey, and she dismounted. Bringing her face-to-face with his parents, Esau said, "This is my wife, Mahalath, daughter of your brother, Ishmael." Yudith and Basemath exchanged fearful glances, then each stared at the new rival, taking her measure.

"Ishmael's daughter?" Isaac asked.

That explains it, Rebekah thought. *Ishmael dwells near Paran, to the south, while Laban lives in Haran, far to the north.*

"The very same," said Mahalath, kneeling demurely, eyes averted. "I bring greetings from my father to you and your household."

Rebekah felt more tremors coursing through Isaac's body. Esau's return, coupled with renewed news of Isaac's long-estranged brother, clearly had evoked deep emotions in her husband. "My . . . my brother . . . is he well?" Isaac asked, his voice barely audible.

Mahalath looked up at Rebekah, who merely nodded. "He is well."

"I . . . I am gladdened by the news," Isaac said, "after all . . . the time that has passed." Isaac took a deep breath, straightened, and said, "Welcome, Mahalath. May your days with us be happy ones."

That does not seem likely, thought Rebekah. *Poor girl, to be third in a household ruled by those Hittite women.* Rebekah glanced over at Yudith and Basemath. *Is it my imagination, or do I see them already plotting to make this girl's life miserable?*

After the obligatory welcoming feast, everyone expected Esau to go hunting, to bring back some delicacy for the celebration. But Esau remained at home.

"When I married the two of you," he said, directing his words to Yudith and Basemath, "I thought to strengthen my position as firstborn, both by establishing a large household of my own and by alliance with influential families in the mighty Hittite Empire." He nodded in the direction of Yudith and Basemath, who simply stared in return. "But my plan failed," he said, still looking at them, "and not only failed, but made my position worse."

He rose and began pacing. "Whatever interest my parents had in obtaining connections with the Hittite empire paled in comparison with their concern about their God," Esau said. "Your open devotion to Telepinu and Asertu—among other things—deeply offends my parents, especially my mother." Yudith and Basemath moved to speak, but Esau cut them off with an angry look. "Whatever chance I have to regain my parents' favor depends upon respecting my mother's desires, and I am determined to do that, whatever the cost." Yudith and Basemath understood the cost might well be theirs.

"My parents sent my brother to find a wife in the house of my mother's brother," he went on. "Realizing at last how important that was to my mother, I went to the house of my father's brother." He stopped pacing and looked directly at his Hittite wives. "Mahalath understands my parents and will please them, rather than antagonize them. That is why I married her." Esau took a deep breath and said in a voice harder than bronze, "From this day forward, Mahalath will be the mistress and ruler of my tents." Shocked, Yudith and Basemath could only stare back. "I will not hear any arguments about who is first wife. You will obey Mahalath without question. If you accept your new place without rancor, you will retain your wifely privileges. On the other hand, if you quarrel or in any way upset my parents, you will incur my wrath, and your best hope will be that I banish you to the farthest grazing area, without serving women. I will not hesitate," Esau looked at each in turn. "Understood?"

Yudith and Basemath read real fear in each other's eyes. They had seen Esau angry; they had seen him determined. But never had they been the objects of such focused anger. As a result, they nodded quickly, mumbling their assent. Neither Yudith nor Basemath had any desire to live in a tent at the edge of the grazing land, without servants to ease her labor.

With Mahalath as mistress of Esau's household, a new sense of—if not peace, at least, order—settled into the camp. For a few days, Esau refrained from hunting and remained in camp, apparently to personally oversee the transition. Naturally, Yudith and Basemath rankled at their change in status, but they feared Esau more than they loved their Hittite gods. For her part, Mahalath had a soothing effect on Rebekah, and Isaac welcomed the return of his favored son. And so, with a sense of accomplishment, Esau departed for a long-delayed hunt.

Returning with a fallow deer slung over his shoulders, he thought, *Mahalath knows how to keep Mother happy, and Father will love the venison. Now I can regain their favor.* He should have been right.

הַמָם

hamam

Troubled

With every day that passed after the departure of Jacob, the ache in Rebekah's heart increased. She and Isaac did not speak of their grief and found what comfort they could in each other. Night after night, she poured out her heart to Elohim. *It is not the exchange of harsh words that pains us,* she thought. *We each have our regrets, but we do not indulge in accusations and blame. I am grateful for that.* She clasped her hands in thanksgiving and then raised them heavenward.

Adonai Elohim, she prayed, *it is not angry sounds that keep our wounds fresh, but the silence.* Now hot tears spilled from her eyes. *I have not heard my Jacob's voice for month after quiet month. No grandchildren shout and giggle with the vigor of young life, nor do childish voices ask Isaac or me to share stories of times long past.*

Only hope sustains us through the silence. Hope that Jacob and Esau will be at peace and that they will return. The weight of sorrow bent Rebekah almost to the ground. *I knew I ran this risk, Elohim,* her spirit cried, *when I helped Jacob secure the birthright. But I did so because of Your promise to me. You promised that the older would serve the younger. I did my part. Please, please do Yours.*

She took a deep breath and straightened herself. *Esau's return has given that hope new life, Adonai. Hope that Isaac and I will once again hear the boisterous sounds of a thriving family. Our family. Children and grandchildren who will brighten our remaining days, mourn our loss, and honor our memory.*

Oh, please, Adonai Elohim. Please let Elam return with good news of Jacob. Turn my hopes into reality.

Rebekah dried her tears. Perhaps her hope *would* be realized. Esau's return and his apparent new attitude gave her hope new life. If only Elam would return soon.

* * * * *

Walking into the camp, Esau was met with almost total silence. The few servants moving about scarcely nodded to recognize his arrival. Even Mahalath was more subdued than usual as she greeted him. She quickly directed servants to prepare the venison from the fallow deer Esau had brought.

"A courier returned while you were gone," Mahalath informed him.

"Courier?" Esau said. "What courier do you speak of?"

"Your parents sent a courier to Haran, to inquire concerning your brother Jacob," Mahalath said.

"How is my brother?" asked Esau, still puzzled.

"Then you do not know?" Mahalath asked.

"How would I know?" Esau replied. "I have not seen him for more than a year."

Mahalath breathed a sigh of relief. "Then all you have to do is tell your parents."

"I do not understand," said Esau. "Why do I need to tell my parents when I saw my brother last?"

"I can say no more, husband," said Mahalath, "but speak with your parents—and soon." Esau moved toward the opening of the tent, but Mahalath stopped him. "Wash and change your clothing first," she said, "and I will prepare some of the venison as a gift of greeting. It will show your respect."

Esau nodded. This was another reason he had married Mahalath. She knew all the social courtesies that he lacked and could tell him what to do in such a way that he wanted to do it. Whereas Esau's Hittite wives antagonized others and exacerbated his own lack of social skills, Mahalath's skills with people complemented Esau's skills as a hunter. Yudith and Basemath had made Esau less; Mahalath made him much, much more. Recognizing his new wife's wisdom, Esau nodded. Mahalath summoned a serving girl. "Fetch Master Esau water for bathing."

By the time Esau washed and dressed in his finest robe, the ever-efficient Mahalath had prepared a tray of roast venison and other delicacies. As if she could read his thoughts, Mahalath spoke to him as he departed for his father's tent. "Whatever happens, try to control your temper. When you get angry, you look guilty, even if you are innocent."

Esau moved quickly to his father's tent, bearing the tray with the roast venison and other offerings. But upon entering the tent, he immediately sensed something amiss.

"Who is this that comes to my tent, and what is it that he brings?" Isaac asked, his bearing stiff and formal.

"It is I, Esau, your firstborn—" Only then did Esau realize what he had done. The last time he had come to his father's tent with venison had been the night of his betrayal, the night of his angry confrontation with his mother, *the night he had threatened to kill his brother.* Rebekah's stern expression made it clear that she remembered, and his father's icy reception left no doubt that he remembered also. Suddenly Esau's mouth went dry and he looked for somewhere, anywhere to put down the food he had brought. Seeing Elam, one of the servants, he moved to hand the tray to him, but a sharp gesture from his mother stopped him.

"Put the food down yourself. Elam is here for another reason," Rebekah said.

"You reject my gift?" Esau said, his temper rising. Mahalath had warned him to keep a rein on his temper, but this encounter seemed to be spiraling out of control, and his emotions with it.

Rebekah ignored his question and asked one of her own. "What do you know of Jacob?"

Even though Mahalath had asked him the same thing, in this setting, his mother's question surprised him. "Know? I know nothing. I have not seen him for more than a year," Esau replied.

"Since you left here?" Isaac inquired.

Esau pondered a moment. "Since he left," Esau said.

"Do you deny you went after him? That you intended to kill him?" Rebekah probed further, and the implied accusation stung Esau.

But Mahalath warned me to control my anger, Esau thought. So he spoke truthfully, in a calm voice, "I did track him. And when I left here, I did intend to kill him, but—"

"Show him," Rebekah said, gesturing to Elam, who produced a small bundle of rags, threadbare and stained. Esau looked at the rags and shrugged his shoulders. "Do you recognize these?" his mother asked.

"Rags?" Esau replied. "Should I recognize them?"

"Jacob never arrived in Haran," Rebekah said. "He is not at my brother's house." She let these words sink in. "Jacob left here, pursued by you, who had threatened to kill him. No one has seen him since. What happened, Esau?"

Esau frowned and began shaking his head. "I do not know."

"A hunter, skilled as yourself," Rebekah said, "and you want us to believe you did not track him down?"

Esau looked from his angry mother to his father. "But I did not! I never saw him after he left here," he said, desperation setting in. "I tracked him four days. Four hard days. That little brother of mine, he learned a lot during our childhood play hunts." Esau smiled in spite of himself and nodded his head in admiration. "He made the pursuit very difficult."

"What happened when you caught up to him?" this from Isaac.

Esau snorted. "I told you. I never did."

"You ask us to believe you just gave up?" Clearly, Rebekah did not believe that.

Esau sank to his knees. *No matter what I do*, he thought, *I cannot seem to regain my parents' favor.* He felt as though a great stone sat upon his shoulders. When he spoke, the words came softly, and his eyes focused on a distant past, as though he was reminding himself. "The trail was very faint and difficult to follow. Jacob used every trick he had learned when we were boys."

Esau settled back on his haunches, his hands on his knees, and resumed his quiet recitation. "At first, my anger at Jacob's treachery drove me on." He looked down at the ground. "Four days of hard tracking left me tired and careless. I woke up the next morning not remembering how I came to sleep where I did in a badly exposed position."

Esau looked at his mother, his eyes searching hers for some sign of understanding. "I began thinking of the things you said to me, Mother, when last we spoke. I realized for the first time how my marriage to Yudith and Basemath—without your counsel and without considering how their worship of their gods would offend you—I realized how deeply those actions wounded you." Esau continued to search his mother's eyes for understanding, but he found none there.

"Where is your brother?" asked Rebekah, unflinching, and the sound chilled Esau to his core.

With a deep sigh, Esau continued. "I know nothing of Jacob's whereabouts. Whether you believe me or not, this is what happened. When you sent Jacob to your brother Laban to find a wife, I thought that was just an excuse to protect him from my anger. But on the trail, on that fourth day, I realized that you also sent him to find a wife who would understand your ways, who would honor you as my wives had not."

"Is that why you married Mahalath?" Isaac spoke up.

"That is why. As your brother's daughter, I believed she would honor you—both of you." Esau said, slowly rising to his feet.

"Where is your brother?" Rebekah asked again.

There is that question again, thought Esau. *I know I have not committed the crime of killing my bother. But until I can answer that question, in their minds, I will bear the guilt of Cain.* "I have told you what I did, and what I know," Esau said, resignation in his voice, arms outspread. "I did track my brother, intending him harm. I changed my mind, and decided to . . . to . . ." He shook his head. *If they cannot see that I am trying to reconcile*, but even Esau's thoughts ended in a sense of hopelessness. Sorrowing, he turned to leave. He paused a moment, picked up the tray of food, now cold, and left.

Isaac and Rebekah dismissed Elam, and, for a time, sat without speaking. Finally, Isaac broke the silence. "He could be telling us the truth," he said, trying to sound hopeful.

"He could be," Rebekah agreed. "Do you believe him?"

"I want to," said Isaac, his voice trembling.

"As do I," said Rebekah. Another silence followed. She would not risk an argument. Neither of them had the strength to suffer harsh words.

"But you do not," said Isaac, the words heavy, dull, and final.

Rebekah hesitated. She well knew that words once said could never be recalled. She searched her heart for hope.

"The rags are just rags," Isaac said.

"And the *sappiyr* box Elam was told about?" Rebekah asked. Isaac did not reply. They both knew that *sappiyr* boxes were not unheard of, even among nomads. Rags and a blue stone box did not prove anything about Jacob. "But where is Jacob?" she finally said. They both knew there was no answer.

For a time, Esau and his wives stayed in Isaac's camp. Mahalath did her best to ease Rebekah's burdens and bring healing to Esau and his parents. But no matter what she did, three words intruded between Esau and his parents. *Where is Jacob?*

Weeks, then months passed. Esau went hunting and gave feasts of venison for all. But every bite of venison brought back the bitter events that had led to Jacob's leaving, and the unspoken question haunted the feasts. Shearing time came, and the herdsmen thought of, but did not speak of, Jacob's joy in that great festival. But the great pile of wool seemed to be missing something—*someone*. And the question rose again. At lambing time, when ewes experienced difficulty, when special skill and gentleness would have saved more lambs, the herdsmen sometimes mumbled, "If only *he* were here," without mentioning who "he" might be. And the question could almost be heard echoing back in the muffled bleating of the lambs.

Eventually, the time came when Esau said, "Mahalath, I think it is time we put some distance between ourselves and my parents."

"If that is your decision," Mahalath replied. "Is there . . . has there been some difficulty I am not aware of?"

"It is not you, my wise wife," Esau said. "Time and again your soothing ways have confirmed my decision to marry you. If anything, my parents would like for you to stay and me to—well, it is clear to me that they are no longer comfortable with my presence."

"Do they still blame you for your brother's disappearance?" Mahalath asked.

Esau grunted. "No one ever says anything about it. They never accuse me of . . . anything with their words." He paused. "But every day, I see the question in everyone's eyes. No one ever accuses me. But no one trusts me, either."

He shook his head. "I join a group, and the conversation stops abruptly. People either suddenly can't stop talking or can't speak." He held out his hands. "Every face looks back at me with the question, a question they will not ask, a question I have answered many times, but obviously, no one believes, Where is your brother?"

"Perhaps . . . in time, it will heal," Mahalath offered.

"I do not think so," Esau said. "Our presence—my presence—here does not heal. It chafes. The longer I am here, the more it rubs raw." Another sigh, and he said, "We must leave. Nothing sudden, and nothing abrupt. But next time we all need to move camp for better grazing, we will put a little distance between our tents and theirs. Eventually, we will be nearby so that we can be of assistance quickly when needed—but not in each other's way. Not in contact every day."

"Will that make the doubts and questions go away?" Mahalath asked.

"How can it?" Esau replied, "For I wonder, too, where *is* my brother?" He pondered another moment and said, "My absence will not make the question go away but may remove me as the focus of those doubts."

Esau did as he said. As time passed, the physical distance between his tents and the tents of his parents grew, until the camps were out of sight, although sounds and scents sometimes still drifted in on the breeze. Eventually, distance silenced even those subtle reminders.

One evening, as they sat quietly together, Isaac seemed sadder than usual. "What are you thinking of, my husband?" Rebekah asked.

"My failing sight gives me much time to think," he said, "and recently I have been thinking of the past, pondering how things might have been different."

Rebekah squeezed his hand. "I have my own darkness, husband, and think sometimes of the same things."

"Odd, how as I age, my mind often returns to my childhood," Isaac said, "the stories my parents told me. I have been thinking of—"

Again Rebekah squeezed his hand and said in a quiet voice, "Of the first brothers and their quarrel."

Isaac turned his sightless eyes toward her, as if seeing her for the first time. "You also?" he said.

"I too," she said, her voice trembling.

"Cain was banished for his crime," said Isaac.

"I remember," said Rebekah.

"And Esau," he said, struggling, "Esau . . . ," Isaac could not finish.

"I know," she said. "Our *suspicion* has banished him." And they wept in silence.

שׁוֹעַ

showa'

Generous

"Silence, woman!" Laban said. Her mouth set in a thin angry line, Adinah's eyes tracked Laban's steps as he paced back and forth. For many months, a single event had hung over them like a great stone at the edge of a precipice. Soon, perhaps within the next week, Jacob would return from the farthest grazing area to celebrate the end of his seven years of service—and to claim his bride. Both events promised disaster.

Laban scanned his surroundings and hissed, "Jacob's leaving gives me enough trouble. No one handles the flocks and herds so shrewdly. The servants show him more loyalty than they do to my own sons. After he marries, he will have no need to stay!" He spread his hands, "And you bring a quarrel between my daughters to me? You are their mother; take care of it!"

Adinah waited, measuring her words. "They are not little girls, Laban; they are young women."

"What does that mean? Do they defy your authority?" Laban demanded. "Do they defy my authority?"

Adinah closed her eyes and shook her head slowly. "They do not, my husband."

"Then handle it! How bad can it be?" Laban asked.

"Did you ask me, 'How bad can it be?'" Adinah said, her voice flat.

"Are you not listening, woman?" Laban repeated, frustration rising. "I said I want to know how bad can it be?"

Eyes brightening, Adinah replied, "As you wish, my husband." She turned and clapped her hands sharply, and a servant Laban had not noticed earlier sprang into action. Moments later, Leah and Rachel appeared, both demurely averting their glances.

"Girls, your father will hear you now," Adinah said. Laban started to protest, but Adinah's next words silenced him. She looked at him directly as she said, "You wanted to know how bad it could be," and then slowly bowed her head as she continued, "I am obedient to your request." Laban wondered, not for the first time, how a woman could be at once both submissive and rebellious.

While he pondered this, Adinah spoke again. "Leah, you are the elder. Speak first."

Leah knelt before her father, nodded her head in a short bow, then looked into her father's eyes, pleading. "I am the elder daughter, my father. It is only right that I should be married first."

"But Jacob asked for Rachel," Laban replied. For seven years, this had silenced his elder daughter. "We struck a bargain. I cannot go back on my word."

Leah looked ready to cry. This unnerved Laban, for Leah rarely shed a tear over anything. "Do you value me less than Rachel?" Leah said, pressing her face into her hands.

Why do they have to cry? Laban wondered. *I never know what to do when they cry.* Laban took her hands and looked into her eyes. "Oh, princess, that is not true."

"Then why do you let Jacob treat me so? He does not value me as much as Rachel." She began sobbing now. "Everyone loves Rachel more than me."

Rachel rolled her eyes and began to fidget, but a slight, sharp gesture from Adinah quieted her. Laban did not see this. As she intended, Leah's distress commanded his attention.

"It is not like that," Laban said, glancing at Adinah for aid, but she did not meet his gaze.

"You mean," here Leah brightened, "is it possible he values me more?"

"I . . . I . . . ," said Laban, and his mouth kept moving, but no sound emerged. Holding his hands wide, he moved his head slowly sideways, searching for help, but Adinah gave only the slightest shake of her head. No help there.

"Maybe," Leah said, drying her tears, "maybe he believes me more valuable than seven years of his labor, could that be it?" She looked at her father for confirmation.

Seeing a way of escape, Laban grasped it. "That must be it, my princess!" Leah's eyes now radiated hope, and Laban began babbling. "He considers you far more valuable than seven years' labor. So he asked for your sister instead!" Laban saw signs of warning in both Adinah's and Rachel's eyes, but he would not let that smother his relief. "That is it," he said, oblivious to the warning signs.

"Then that is the answer!" said Leah, all focus, all business now.

"The answer?"

"If you give Jacob *more* value for his labor than he asked, would that not be generous?" Leah asked.

"It would," Laban said, not yet seeing the trap.

"Then give him *me* for his bride. Or did you not mean what you said about me being more valuable?" Leah ended the sentence in a pout.

"I meant it," he said.

"Then giving me instead of Rachel would be generous, would it not?"

"I suppose it would," said Laban, and everyone moved at once. Laban stood, and Leah leaped up, throwing her arms around his neck. "Thank you, Father. Oh, generous Father. Thank you."

Rachel stood also, keening in fury, but Adinah moved between her and her father.

Then, taking Leah's arms from around his neck, he said, "You have given me a plan, my daughter. One that will satisfy everyone." *Especially me,* he thought. *Most ewes give birth to a single lamb. This little ewe gave birth to triplets. After six years of scheming and failing, Leah gives me the solution at the last moment! Three problems solved with one plan.*

Brightening even more, spreading his arms expansively, "Generous," he said, savoring the word, anticipating the praise of the old men. "I will be *generous.* But say nothing of this to anyone." He looked at each one in turn. "It will be our surprise. I will give Jacob *more* than he bargained for."

Ignoring the furious Rachel, Laban said, "Now, Leah, take some servants and go to your brother Adnan's camp." Reading the questions in her eyes, he said, "I will send you both away to prepare for the wedding. When you return," he said, nodding at Leah, "you will be heavily veiled, according to the custom. You are nearly the same size. The wedding feast will last until late and the wedding tent will be dark; Jacob will not be able to tell you apart until it is too late. Now go, and take your servants and a seamstress with you. Your mother will be along to help, but I have another matter to take up with her."

After Leah danced out of the tent, Rachel could contain herself no longer. "But he asked for *me*, Father! He wants *me*!"

Hearing the commotion from nearby tents as Leah summoned her entourage, Laban spoke again. "And he shall have you, little one. You will be his bride. You will go to your brother Jascher's camp, taking your servants and a seamstress with you. Prepare to be Jacob's bride."

"But you told—" Rachel began, but Laban held a finger to his lips.

"I told her Jacob would not be able to tell you apart. I promised no more than that." As Rachel's face revealed dawning realization, he said, "You know Leah. As long as she remained in camp, she would give no one peace. Even if she did not have a tantrum at your wedding, she would sulk around and make us all miserable." Rachel nodded. "After the wedding, it will be too late to change anything. Wait till Leah has gone; then go in the assurance that you will be Jacob's bride. Mother will go to Leah first to allay any fears, and then she will come to you."

With both girls gone, Adinah turned to Laban. "You play a dangerous game, my husband. You risk angering all three. And how does this solve the problem of losing Jacob's labor and his shrewd management of the flocks and herds?"

As Laban explained, Adinah marveled at the cleverness of his plan. "But they will be angry because you told them—" she said, but Laban's innocent expression stopped her.

"And what did I tell them?"

"You told Leah—"

"I told her that, dressed and veiled as a bride, Jacob would not be able to tell them apart. I am depending on that," he said, smiling. "And I told Rachel that she should go with the assurance that she will be Jacob's bride. I am depending on that, as well."

"And what about Jacob? He expects Rachel for his bride," Adinah reminded him.

"And he will have her," Laban said, "*if* he chooses to." Obviously pleased with himself, he said, "And how can he complain at my generosity? I will have given him even more than he bargained for."

Adinah nodded, thinking, *We all may be getting more than we bargained for.*

* * * * *

How quickly the time has passed, Jacob thought, as he awakened the morning after the wedding. He had never felt so happy. Eyes closed, he took in the scents of jasmine, myrrh, and his bride. His fingers caressed the smooth skin on the back of her shoulder as she slept on her side, facing away from him. *What bliss!*

Seven long years of labor behind him, he had returned to Laban's camp and claimed his reward. "My seven years of labor is up, so where is my wife? It is time for her to come to my tent, to share my bed."

"Jacob, my own flesh and blood, patience! You shall have a wife!" Laban said, laughing. "Do not be so impatient. A wedding of such importance must be celebrated with all my friends! Is it not so in your land?"

Jacob recalled the festivities put on for Esau and his two wives. *Why not?* he thought. *I labored seven years for one wife, while Esau brought home two without asking.* "It is so. Let us celebrate!" Jacob said. *After all, Esau's two wives made everybody miserable, while my one wife brings delight to me. That alone would be worth celebrating.*

So Jacob bathed in scented water, and they arrayed him in beautiful linen. All the men of nearby clans attended the wedding. The tables, bowls, and cups overflowed with food. Lamb and kid, olives, dates, raisins, apricots—Laban had spared no expense for this marriage feast, and it showed.

Men told stories, maidens danced, and laughter filled the air. When the hour drew late, a hush fell on the gathering as Adinah appeared at the doorway with her daughter. Sweet incense filled the air. *What a vision of beauty,* Jacob had thought. His bride had been arrayed in a cloud of white fabric. A slender silver chain circled her waist, with the sparkling blue *sappiyr* box hanging from the bronze clasp. A cap of gold discs covered her head, and strings of golden pomegranates and jewels cascaded from the top of the veil. Only her luminous eyes could be seen.

Jacob had been dizzy, his senses saturated with sight and sound and taste and scent and touch. Jacob could barely remember Laban and Adinah escorting the couple from the wedding party to the carefully prepared marriage tent. After that, he could recall only a jumble of sensations, of touch and taste and small sounds in the darkness.

Ah, Rachel, he thought, pressing his face into his bride's neck. She sighed with happiness and rolled toward him. And his blood froze.

"Good morning, husband," said Leah. *Leah!* Jacob sat up, blinked, and shook his head to clear his vision.

"Leah?" he said, and she nodded languidly, reaching for his shoulder. "What . . . how?"

"Have you forgotten so soon?" she purred, pulling toward him.

He had forgotten nothing. Not the bargain struck seven years before, not the vision of his bride, not the embraces in the night. But this was not Rachel!

"Did I displease you?" she said, pouting coyly as she lay back and hugged the sheet to her chest.

Jacob swallowed. *Whatever else happens, you made her your wife last night,* he thought. "You did not displease me," he said, repenting, and she smiled. "But . . . I must . . ." Confused, he rose and dressed quickly.

"All right," Leah said, patting the bed beside her. "But return to me soon." He nodded, and she giggled at his distracted expression.

I knew he would be pleased to find me instead of Rachel, she thought. *He needed more of a woman than my little sister. Poor girl, she will probably have to settle for being some rich man's second wife—or worse.*

When Laban saw Jacob returning to the main celebration tent, he was prepared. He called out, "We did not expect to see you so soon, my son," and the various servants and remaining guests within earshot greeted the remark with knowing laughter.

"What is this you have done to me?" Jacob demanded, to a chorus of *ooooh* followed by laughter.

"What have I done?" Laban said. "I should think the question is, What have you been doing?" More laughter.

Jacob could see this would result only in more humiliation, so, taking Laban aside, he hissed, "I served you for Rachel! That was our bargain! Why have you deceived me?" Necks craned, but the sound did not carry, so this display only heightened everyone's curiosity.

"Oh, ho," said Laban, loudly for the crowd. "Greedy fellow, are you?" He laughed roughly, and it spread through the crowd. While the laughter continued, he turned and spoke in a low tone. "It is not our custom to give the younger daughter first. Leah is firstborn. No bargain could cancel the rights of the firstborn. Surely you understand that?" Laban turned and smiled at the crowd, saying quietly, "Laugh as though I told a joke. That will keep them busy."

So Jacob laughed, a little woodenly, and Laban joined in, putting his arm around his son-in-law's shoulder, laughing uproariously. Laban had played the crowd just right, and now every gesture and expression he made set them off. As the laughter grew and spread, Laban looked Jacob in the eye. "Finish the week with Leah. Give the firstborn her due. Then I will give you Rachel also." He let this sink in. "And you work seven more years for her?"

Words from the past battered Jacob. His father's voice: *"An extra wife means extra strife."* Then Esau's voice: *"I told you, Jacob, you cannot buy the birthright with a bowl of stew."* And again: *"Sometimes an animal freezes when a hunter surprises it. The key then is to keep the surprises coming, never give it time to think. Strike!" I struck you when you came home hungry, Brother. Well, now it happened to me,* he thought. *That day you said, "If you do not give me some of that red-red stew soon, I will die." Now I know how you felt. All my labors seemed as nothing because I wanted Rachel. Without Rachel, I will die.*

As if reading his mind, Laban whispered once again. "Rachel can be yours. Just a few days from now. Just seven more years." Jacob nodded, then clasped hands to seal the bargain, and he walked back to the marriage tent, accompanied by a chorus of knowing hoots. *I should be happy,* he thought. Inside the tent, a smiling Leah beckoned him. With a little effort, Jacob returned the smile. *A few more days,* he thought. *I can last that long.* And then he lay down beside yesterday's bride.

tanchuwm

Consolation

"Leah 'took it well'?" Adinah said, disbelieving. "She accepted that Rachel would become Jacob's wife—so soon?" In fact, Laban had given Rachel to Jacob as soon as the initial matrimonial week with Leah concluded.

"She took it well," said Laban, shrugging. "I am as surprised as anyone else." He paused, rubbing his beard in slow motion. "I had a lengthy explanation for her," Laban continued, "but she did not need one. Perhaps now that she has a husband, she is contented."

Adinah held her tongue, but in all the years that she had lived, with all the women she had known, and even with all the tales that she had heard, she recalled few contented wives. Resigned perhaps. Temporarily mollified. *But Leah? Can the words* content *and Leah* even occur in the same sentence? Can they fit in the same mouth? Adinah felt a chill. *This will bear watching.*

* * * * *

Zilpah moved quietly through Leah's tent. Zilpah, only ten years old, still did not know her new mistress very well. Only a few weeks earlier, she had been just another servant girl. Then, when Leah departed for her brother Adnan's camp, Zilpah had been surprised, and a little frightened, when Master Laban had singled her out to be Leah's servant, thus designating her as one of his wedding gifts to his older daughter. Exactly why Laban had chosen the little girl with the big eyes, no one knew, least of all Zilpah.

After the wedding, the other servants offered both sympathy and congratulations. Congratulations, because, as Leah's personal servant, in time Zilpah could expect to become a figure of influence and no little power. Sympathy, because, well, she was to be in continual contact with Leah. Leah, who became disappointed easily and did not take disappointment well.

"What do the servants say about me, Zilpah?" Leah asked, lounging in her bed. Although she spoke evenly, Zilpah detected menace in the words. She had better answer, and promptly.

"Nothing to me, mistress," Zilpah said with all the earnestness she could muster.

"Nothing to you," Leah repeated, sitting up, hugging her knees. "But that is not what I asked, is it?"

"Truly, mistress, the other servants no longer talk to me about you," Zilpah said, sensing the anger in her mistress. "And they do not speak of you in my hearing, either," the serving girl added, growing desperate.

"Do they not wonder about me? About why I say nothing concerning Jacob acquiring a second wife? About his marriage to my sister, and so quickly?"

"I suppose they must, mistress," Zilpah admitted. "I wonder too," the girl said, then covered her mouth suddenly, her eyes lighting up in alarm.

Before Zilpah could ask pardon, Leah smiled. "Of course you do." Then, patting the bed beside her, she said, "Come. Sit with me, Zilpah." When the girl hesitated, Leah spoke again. "If you are to be my personal servant, then we two will share many confidences. Is that not so?" Zilpah sat lightly on the bed, ready to spring up in an instant.

Zilpah tried not to cringe as Leah placed an arm confidentially around the serving girl's shoulders. "Can I trust you to keep my secrets, Zilpah?" Leah asked, looking directly into her servant's eyes. Zilpah did not reply, except to nod once, slowly, eyes locked with Leah's. "Wonderful!" Leah said, patting Zilpah's knee. "And can I trust you to carry messages for me?" Zilpah responded with another slow nod. Leah now looked away, off in the distance, pondering her next words.

"Many men of substance, such as my Jacob, take more than one wife. Is that not so?" At this, Leah looked into Zilpah's eyes again, and Zilpah rewarded her with another nod. "Tell me, then, Zilpah, which wife is more important: the first wife or the second?"

Zilpah licked her lips, her eyes still fixed on Leah's. "The first wife, mistress?"

"Just so, little one. And a wealthy man may have many wives, is that not true also?"

"It is true, mistress," Zilpah said.

"And among the women, who rules over all?" Leah asked.

"The first wife," Zilpah said more firmly, gaining confidence.

"Excellent!" Leah declared, squeezing Zilpah's shoulders with both hands. "The first wife rules." She let this sink in. "So why should it trouble me that my husband brings in another woman to serve me?"

"But she also serves him—" Zilpah ventured, but Leah cut her off.

"She serves us both," Leah said, a little too sharply. They sat in silence for a moment. "I am the first wife," Leah said suddenly. "No matter whom Jacob chooses to serve his . . . masculine appetites, I am the first wife. Do you understand?"

Zilpah nodded.

"*Do you understand?*" Leah almost whispered the words, but they cut through the air like the crack of a whip.

Alarmed, Zilpah nodded and said, "You are the first wife. You rule the women. I understand."

Leah smiled, but the sight reminded Zilpah of a cat cleaning its whiskers. "Good. And you will see to it that the rest of the servants understand too?"

Zilpah's eyebrows shot up in recognition, and she quickly said, "I will. I . . . I will see to it. They will understand. You rule all the women, including Rachel—"

"*I do not want to hear that name ever again, do you understand?*"

Zilpah blinked at the sudden fury. "I understand," she said. When Leah cocked her head, waiting, Zilpah continued, "And I will make certain the other servants understand that Ra—that her name is not to be spoken." Leah nodded her head in approval. Zilpah pondered, then asked, "But what shall we call her?"

It was Leah's turn to ponder. After a moment, her mouth twisted into that feline smile again, and she said, "*Second* wife. You will refer to her as Jacob's second wife." She turned sharply to Zilpah, but this time the servant girl anticipated her.

"I understand," she said. "All of the servants will understand."

Contented, Leah threw herself against her pillow, dismissing Zilpah with a wave of her hand. *He might be with his second wife this very moment,* Leah thought, *but I will always be the first wife. And we shall see who has the first son,* she thought. *My little sister is still such a girl. Jacob will need me to give him sons. I know it.* Placing her hands on her belly, she thought, *I feel it.*

Zilpah had lingered at the opening to the tent, witnessing her mistress place her hands over her womb and drift off to sleep with that predatory smile on her face. Zilpah had not chosen to be Leah's personal servant. But having been chosen, she understood that her only safety lay in serving Leah faithfully. Her mistress was not someone to displease. With these thoughts in her head, Zilpah went out to the larger camp, to speak with her fellow servants. *They need to understand.*

* * * * *

As soon as they were alone, Rachel flung herself on Jacob and covered his face and shoulders with feathery kisses. Amazed, Jacob embraced his new wife. "I thought—I feared—you would be angry," he said.

Rachel drew back, tears welling in her eyes, and regarded her bridegroom. "I am angry," she said suddenly. "Angry at Father, angry at . . . at . . . my scheming sister, angry at my mother!"

"Not at me?" Jacob asked, weeping.

"Not at you, my beloved. They deceived us! They lied to us!" she said, her voice fierce. "The servants told me," she said. "Everyone thought I was the bride. Is that not so?"

"It is so," said Jacob. "At the wedding, she moved in a cloud of white cloth. And when I saw the *sappiyr* box I had given you on the silver chain around her waist—"

"She took the *sappiyr* box you gave me?" Rachel demanded.

"I only know she wore it that night," said Jacob, shaking his head. "I thought no one knew of it except us," he said, "so it never occurred to me that someone else could be behind that veil."

"This was my father's work," Rachel said. "Only he knew that you had given that precious *sappiyr* box to me."

"After the ceremony, they took us to . . . to a darkened tent," he went on, kneeling before her, shaking his head and weeping with shame. "I called out, 'Rachel, my beloved,' in the dark." He looked into Rachel's eyes, seeking belief before continuing. "And she answered, 'My beloved.' " He took both of Rachel's hands in his and buried his face there.

"Such deceivers!" Rachel said. "To take advantage of your trust. Hiding in the darkness so you could not see. Using smooth words to trick your ears." She thought for a moment and said, "I must have the *sappiyr* box back. You gave it to me."

Jacob nodded. "You shall have it."

Her gaze softened. "You called out my name?"

He looked up at her, hope illuminating his eyes. "I called out your name. Only yours," he said, and saw her lips curved in a gentle smile. "You do not hate me?" he asked.

Looking into his eyes, Rachel said, "I could not hate you. I have loved you since that day when you moved the stone off the well." She kissed his forehead and smiled a benediction into his wondering face. A benediction that absolved him of all guilt and banished all doubt. He sighed in relief, and she pulled his face into her bosom. And they were one.

* * * * *

"*Second* wife, am I," Rachel fumed.

"I do not understand," Jacob said. Despite the deception and his prior marriage to Leah, the first weeks with Rachel seemed to Jacob a foretaste of paradise. But now she was angry.

"Tell him, Bilhah!" Rachel commanded the young serving girl.

Bilhah looked nervously at her mistress, but Rachel's gaze pressed her on. "The servants have been told that, that . . . we are to call my mistress 'second wife.'"

Jacob looked, uncomprehending from serving girl to Rachel and back again. Clearly, something had Rachel's anger flowing hot. What, exactly, he could not see. "You are my sec—" he started to say, but the look in Rachel's eyes struck him dumb.

"Go on," Rachel said, prompting the serving girl.

"Your first wife—"

"The scheming Leah!" Rachel interjected.

Bilhah swallowed hard, looking for a safe means of retreat. "Mistress Leah sends word that the servants are not to say my mistress' name in her presence," Bilhah said, her eyes downcast.

Rachel looked pointedly at Jacob, who still had not identified a promising response. "What do you intend to do?" Rachel demanded.

"Do?" escaped Jacob's mouth, though he cringed, awaiting Rachel's retort even as the word left his lips.

"What will you do?" Rachel repeated. "Leah was always adamant about not being someone's 'second wife.' This is her way of spiting me."

Jacob's mind raced. "If the servants do not obey Leah, she will find ways to punish them, no matter what I desire." Rachel's eyes softened, seeing the truth of it. "Look at this little one," he said, pointing to the miserable Bilhah. "She is terrified," he said.

"With servants as with animals," Jacob muttered. When Rachel seemed confused, he went on. "Your father treats his animals poorly," Jacob said. "Have you never wondered why his flocks prosper under my care, far more than under his, or under the care of your brothers?" At this, Rachel nodded.

"He treats them like . . . like mere objects," his eyes searched the room and settled on an oil lamp, which he seized and held before her. "Like this lamp," he said. "He moves them here and there, paying little attention to the heat of the day or whether they have rested from being moved. He ignores their needs, and they do not thrive." He looked in Rachel's eyes, and saw puzzlement there.

"He treats his servants the same way," Jacob said. "He treated you and Leah and me as . . . well, as mere objects—to be moved, used, sold, and discarded." He threw the lamp against a table and smashed it to illustrate his point. "According to his whim."

"He says it is his right as master, as father," Rachel said.

"It may be his right," Jacob said with quiet passion, "but living things," he searched for the word, "living things may either assist us or resist us. When we treat them badly, they resist us," he said. "If we make their lives miserable, they find ways to make our lives less easy. If we lighten their burdens, they lighten ours.

"Leah has already made them feel wary, with this petty demand of hers. If we fight her through the servants, we will all lose," Jacob said, stroking his beard and thinking aloud.

Rachel's heart warmed. Jacob's demonstration of gentle wisdom melted her anger, and soothed her anxious thoughts.

"I know," he said, holding up his index finger. The corners of his mouth twisted into a mischievous smile. "Bilhah!" he said, and the servant girl started violently at the sound of his voice. He turned to her, bent over, and, placing a hand on each shoulder, he smiled into her face. "Bilhah, one who serves my beloved. Make sure the servants obey Mistress Leah," he said, chuckling at her consternation and at Rachel's puzzled expression. "Whenever they refer to your mistress, Rachel, they shall say, 'second wife,' aloud. And then, silently, in their minds, they shall add, 'But first in his heart.' "

With that, he stood, and Bilhah's eyes sparkled with laughter as he turned to Rachel. Taking his second wife in his arms, he said, "Always, Rachel. Always first in my heart."

Later, as they lounged upon the marital bed, Jacob cradled Rachel's head on his shoulder and asked, "Bilhah and Zilpah, how did your father come to choose them as serving girls for you and Leah?"

"He did not say," Rachel replied, running her hand across his chest, "but I think I know."

"After the way he deceived me, I question every move he makes," Jacob replied. "Their names sound alike; are they sisters?"

"Not only sisters, but twins."

"Twins? No wonder they look so much alike!"

"Twins do not always look alike, my husband," Rachel said, giggling.

"That is true," Jacob said. *My twin and I look nothing alike*, he thought.

"That is one reason he chose them, I think," Rachel explained.

Jacob frowned. "I do not understand."

"Twins to serve twins," she said. "My father thinks like that."

"To serve twins?" Jacob said, still frowning.

Rachel lifted herself up on her elbow so she could look into Jacob's face as he lay with his head on a large pillow. "You do not know?" she placed a hand on her mouth and began laughing silently. Jacob's expression made his puzzlement clear, so she continued. "We do not speak of it because we are so different."

"Do not speak of what?"

"Leah makes so much of being the older, more mature sister, while I am but a child compared to her," Rachel said, her eyes dancing.

"She is older, you younger. I know this," Jacob said, still bewildered.

"She is older, but only by a few moments," she said, and watched the surprise sweep over Jacob's face. "We are twins, my husband. Leah and I are twins."

Jacob lay, too stunned for speech.

"She never speaks of it because she wants only to speak of her seniority, of being firstborn," Rachel said, rolling her eyes. Then, thoughtful, she said more quietly, "I never speak of it because . . . because I do not look like her, do not act like her because I want to be as separate from her as possible." She put her head back on Jacob's shoulder and began weeping softly. "And now, because of her scheming and my father's greed, she and I are married to the same man, and I can never be rid of her." Minutes passed in silence, until Rachel said in a small voice, "She and my father connived to take from me the one thing I wanted most. To be your *one* wife."

Jacob pressed his lips to the top of her head and held her close. He could not stop his thoughts. *Your twin sister and your father deceived me and cheated you. What bitter symmetry is this?* In the silence, his spirit cried out to Elohim, *Do You punish me, Elohim? My mother and I deceived my father and cheated my twin. Adonai, how long will You punish me for my sin against my father? And why do You punish Rachel?* And then he could not stop his tears.

* * * * *

"Where is he?" Leah demanded.

Zilpah blanched. "Of whom do you speak?" she asked.

"My husband," Leah said. She had been patient. She had given Jacob one week for the second wedding, one week for his second wife, another week for traveling to the various grazing areas and encampments to instruct the servants concerning circumstances that arose during his absence. But now, two more weeks had passed without his attentions.

"Is he with . . . with the second wife?" Leah asked. But before the serving girl could reply, she demanded, "And why do all the servants drop their heads and smile whenever they say that?"

"Mistress!" Zilpah protested, but Leah did not relent.

"Do not pretend with me, girl," Leah snapped, and Zilpah flinched as Leah reached out and placed a hand on her shoulder. "Now, now, Zilpah, we are friends, you and I, are we not?" Leah fairly purred.

"I am your servant—"

"And I, your mistress. But can you not be my friend too? My faithful servant and friend?" Leah asked, while she stroked Zilpah's hair, then grasped a lock firmly.

Zilpah, feeling the slight pressure, nodded timidly in assent.

"Good girl," Leah said. "Tell me, my faithful friend. Tell me!" she said, tightening her grip.

"I do not wish to offend my mistress," Zilpah said, almost crying.

"There, there, my friend," Leah said. "No need to be afraid of me," she said, letting go of Zilpah's hair, placing her hands on the girl's shoulders and smiling her feline smile. "But you will tell me."

"Master Jacob instructed all the servants to obey Mistress Leah about calling Mistress Ra—about calling your sister his 'second wife.' " Zilpah paused, till Leah raised her eyebrows, prompting her to continue. "And that they shall then say, silently, in their minds, 'But first in his heart.' " Zilpah bit her lip and closed her eyes in anticipation of Leah's rage. When only silence ensued, she opened her eyes to see her mistress gazing off into the distance.

In reply to Zilpah's inquiring expression, Leah said, "Men's hearts are fickle, Zilpah. Remember that. A man may fancy a slave girl one day and sell her away the next." Leah pulled at a fine gold chain around her neck and fingered the small bone carving of a crescent it held. "But men like my father and like Jacob, their hearts are constant about two things. Do you know what those are?"

The wide-eyed Zilpah shook her head slowly, once.

"I do," Leah said, glancing at the tiny carved pendant on her necklace. "I do."

אלהים רחמך

elohim, rechem

Gods, Wombs

Please, Adonai, Rachel prayed, weeping silently into her pillow. *Do not let this child be a son! El Elyon, El Shaddai, whoever You are, have I displeased You? Jacob says You are his God. Why do You bless Leah and not me with a child? But if she must have the first child, at least let me have the first son!*

Beside her, Jacob heard the quiet tears, felt the tremors that racked her body. He also prayed, asking El Shaddai the question he had posed to Laban when he discovered Leah in his marriage bed. *What is this You have done to me?* But all he heard in return was Laban's mocking question: "*What have you been doing?*"

At first, after Rachel's marriage to Jacob, an uneasy truce pervaded the tents of Jacob's encampment. So long as Rachel openly deferred to Leah, confirming her status as first wife, the older sister remained civil, if aloof. In return, Leah did not complain that she spent more nights alone than did her sister. In his man's way, Jacob did not concern himself with why this might be so; he only felt relief at the lack of open conflict.

As time passed and the volatile Leah remained quiescent, Rachel, who knew her sister far better than her husband did, grew more apprehensive with each day. Then, one day, the source of Leah's equanimity became clear.

"When did you plan to tell me?" Rachel demanded that evening.

Jacob sighed. "I thought you would know already."

"I did know," Rachel said, "but you *still* should have told me." For some time, everyone in the camp had suspected that Leah was with child. Just this morning, she had decided to flaunt her expanding figure, silently, but definitely, announcing her pregnancy to the camp. "How long have you known?" Rachel demanded again.

"Known?" Jacob reflected. *She did not announce it to me until recently,* he thought, *though I suspected it for some time.*

"Why did you give her a child, and not me?"

He reached out to embrace her, but she put her hands up in warning. So he crossed his arms. "Who knows how such things happen?" Jacob said, but Rachel's rolling eyes told him she rejected that idea, and so he added, "I mean, I spend the nights with you, beloved, except when—when the way of women is upon you."

Suddenly, Rachel began weeping and threw her arms around him. "I know, Jacob. I *do* know." Bewildered by her sudden change, Jacob returned her embrace, his chin resting on her head. Then, pushing away, Rachel looked up into his face, her eyes blazing. "The marriage week," she said, and burying her head once again in his shoulder, her body shook with sobs. Jacob held her, cradling the back of her head with his hand. "They did it again!" she said, the sound muffled because she spoke into his chest.

"They? They did what again?" Jacob asked.

"My scheming, conniving, betraying father and sister. Because of their betrayal, she is with child!" Rachel said, wiping her eyes.

"Your father made Leah pregnant?" Jacob asked, bewildered.

Lashing out at Jacob, she said, "They are not filthy Kinahhu!" using the Akkadian name for the people who lived around them, instead of the local name: Canaanites. Even faraway Akkad, the city that ruled over Chaldea, the land of Laban's family, knew of the Kinahhu and coveted the distinctive purple cloth the Kinahhu made and for which they were named—*kinahhu* means "reed cloth." But Laban's family still worshiped the gods of Akkad and held the Kinahhu and their deities in contempt.

"Dishonest and manipulative they may be, but fathers do not breed their daughters, not like the noisome Kinahhu!"

"I did not mean to say that they were, but you said—"

"By tricking you—tricking us—so that Leah came into your bed first," Rachel said. Seeing he still did not understand, she went on. "Leah must have become pregnant during that very first week," she paused, calculating. "The timing works out perfectly."

"It does not matter," Jacob said. "You are the one in my heart."

"Does it not matter?" Rachel asked, bitterness in her voice. "What if the child she carries is a son?" She let that sink in, saw his expression change.

"I will still love you," he said, and she knew he meant it.

"I know you will," she said softly. *But a man wants sons,* she thought.

In another tent, the woman who carried his child flung her thoughts into the night. *You may spend whatever time you wish with the girl,* Leah thought, *but the Kathirat look down with favor on me.* Every night she prayed to the Kathirat, the seven-sister goddesses of conception and childbirth. Every day she wore the bone carving of seven flying swallows, intertwined into the shape of a crescent, the same crescent shape the victorious Nanna took every month after emerging from the darkness of the underworld, and thus the sign of emerging life. *The Kathirat will give me sons!* her thoughts almost shouted.

* * * * *

"Master Jacob sends you dates and honey," Zilpah said, placing the delicacies on the small table next to Leah's pallet, and to Leah's inquiring look, she added, "For the baby."

Leah smiled. "Men like Jacob are constant about two things, Zilpah," she said. "Do you remember I said that?"

"I remember, mistress," the serving girl replied.

"Do you know what those two things are, Zilpah?"

"I do not. You did not tell me."

"I did not tell you," Leah said. Closing her eyes, she ran her hands across her expanding abdomen. "Can you tell me? Come now, you must have some idea."

Seeing no alternative, the girl spoke. "Master Jacob values his flocks and herds," she said.

"He does," Leah agreed. "And he is constant in that. Do you know the other thing?" Her eyes moved to the honey and dates next to her. "Do you still not know?"

This only confused Zilpah. "I . . . I . . . Master Jacob seems constant about his God, about Elohim, Elyon?" she said. When Leah did not confirm her answer, she said, "Or is it El Shaddai? He seems to have many names for being only one God."

Leah sniffed. "Foolish girl," she said. "Men are as fickle about their gods as they are about women. They serve gods for what the gods give them in return. Besides, what God does Jacob serve? Have you ever seen this God of his?"

Zilpah shook her head. "I have not seen his God. But Master Jacob sacrifices—"

"He says he feeds his God lambs at his stone altar, but where is the God?" Leah spread her arms and looked toward the sky. Grasping the bone carving on her necklace, she held it toward the servant. "This is the most important god for a woman, Zilpah." She held up the exquisite carving of seven swallows in flight.

"It looks like the symbol of Nanna," Zilpah said, "the bright bull who lights the sky at night and whose crescent-shaped horns I see in the sky every month." Zilpah paused, troubled. "But Master Jacob does not worship Nanna. He does not approve—"

"Approve?" Leah snorted. "Jacob will approve when this son is born, Zilpah," she said, once again caressing her swelling form. "All men want sons. Sons carry on their father's name, sons manage and protect the flocks and herds, sons provide for their fathers in old age." *And for their mothers.* Leah touched her lips to the bone carving. "Besides, this is not Nanna. Look closer. Do you not see the seven swallows in flight?"

"I see them," Zilpah said. "Oh!" the girl said, shocked.

"Ah! So you *do* recognize them," Leah said.

"The *Kathirat?*" Zilpah asked, alarmed. "Kinahhu goddesses! Master Jacob—"

"These Kathirat, these seven sweet birds, have given me a son, girl," the words came out fiercely, and Leah's eyes had become slits. "You will see. And they will give me more. Sons."

"Sons, mistress," Zilpah repeated, entranced with her mistress' intensity.

"And when I bear a son for Jacob, he will worship me," Leah said, tipping her head back and closing her eyes. "When I give Jacob a son," she said, her burning gaze targeting Rachel's tent, "he will spend his nights in my tent. My tent, Zilpah, *my bed!*"

Leah's mouth twisted with contempt, and Zilpah shivered. "Not with that spoiled little . . . little—"

"Second wife?" Zilpah supplied.

"Second wife, indeed," Leah agreed. *"But no longer first in his heart, do you understand?"* Before the serving girl could speak, she added, "You will see, girl. Sons and wealth are first in a man's heart. *And when I give him sons, I shall be first in his heart, I shall be first!"*

* * * * *

The camp settled into a routine. During the days, when Utu followed his fiery path across the sky, Jacob tended the flocks and herds and felt a growing sense of anticipation and hope. His first child would soon be born, and such events usually called for rejoicing; but darkness found Leah alone with her maidservant, and Jacob mostly with Rachel. Jacob's absence fueled Leah's quiet anger and fed her determination to demonstrate her superiority and reap her reward when she gave birth to the son she knew she carried. And despite Jacob's and Rachel's love for each other, sadness cast a shadow over their time together.

"Come to bed, Jacob," Rachel said. "Stop scribbling on that hide and come to bed. What fascinates you so about those marks you make, anyway? Are they prayers to Nanna?"

"They are not prayers to any god, certainly not to Nanna. They tell the stories of my flocks and herds," Jacob said. "I have told you that." Still hunched over the marks on the skins, he added, "I have kept such accounts since I was young. They tell me which ewes and which rams give me the most lambs, the strongest lambs. They help me manage the flocks more wisely."

"Does not Dumuzi, the shepherd god, bring fertility to the ewes and rams? And Bilhah tells me that Leah worships the Kathirat, that they . . . ," she stopped, her voice giving way.

Jacob looked up into his wife's pleading gaze. "My family trusts in El Shaddai," Jacob said. "He is the God of my father, Isaac, and of his father, Abraham." He spoke deliberately. "And on my journey here, I witnessed His power and received His protection," Jacob concluded, "and He became my God too."

"But if the Kathirat—"

"Would you stoop to worshiping the gods of the Kinahhu?" Jacob asked.

"My father, Laban, says they are but the local names for the *real* gods, the gods of Akkad, where our father's fathers came from."

"The gods of Akkad? What would they be doing so far from home?" he asked, shaking his head.

"Is this not also far from El Shaddai's home?" Rachel asked. "You told me that His house, Beth-El, is a long journey from here. Surely He is not the God of this place."

"About that, I cannot say," Jacob answered, staring into the distance. "But El Shaddai made Himself known to me at Beth-El, a long journey from my father's tents." He looked at Rachel, his face showing confusion. "Perhaps El Shaddai is not the God of any one place. There may be other gods, but only El Shaddai, El Elyon made Himself known to me, and only Him do I serve."

But the Kathirat are among the gods of this place, Rachel thought. *Can it be that they* did *give Leah a son?* But she did not give voice to these thoughts. Instead, she lay her head on her pillow, and said, "Sometimes you are so strange, Jacob. There are the gods of Egypt, of the Hittites, the Kinahhu, and the gods—so my father Laban tells us—of the great and ancient empire of Akkad, whom my parents worship. Terah, our forefather, one of the great men of Ur, worshiped the great gods of Akkad. Gods whose images and temples, so Father told us, make a man look like a fly. Gods worshiped by so many that the worshipers look like vast flocks of sheep. And then there is your God," she said, looking at him. "Only one God, but with many names. And this one God of many names is the God of but one family, the God of three sheep-and-goatherders." She shook her head. "It almost makes me laugh; we have Ra the great god of the pharaohs and all of imperial Egypt; Telepinu and Asertu, gods of the Hittites; Nanna, Utu, Dumuzi—all the great gods of the powerful Akkad; and then we have El Shaddai, or is it El Elyon? And who is He? Why, the God of Abraham, Isaac, and Jacob." She chuckled, eyes closed. "Whoever heard of such a God?" *And if He is so powerful, why does He not give me a son?*

* * * * *

"Mistress?" Zilpah asked.

"You have a question?" Leah asked. She rested on her bed, her belly swollen with a child soon to be delivered. Servants fanned her and placed cooling wet cloths on her forehead and shoulders. Despite the discomfort, seemingly contrary to her temperament, Leah had become less demanding of her servants as the time of her delivery neared. Her speech and demeanor became almost pleasant.

"I have a question, mistress."

"Out with it, girl! Ask me." Leah replied.

"You do not appear—pardon me for being so bold—to be apprehensive about giving birth," Zilpah said, placing a hand over her mouth in shock at her own words. "Forgive me, mistress. I meant no impertinence."

"Silly girl," said Leah, "You need not fear me, Zilpah." Leah wiped her brow with a cool cloth. "We are friends, Zilpah. You may ask anything." Closing her eyes for a moment, Leah contemplated the question. "You see truly, my Zilpah. Childbirth holds no fear for me."

Opening her eyes, she looked directly at her serving girl. "I am a strong woman, Zilpah," she said, "not a delicate little girl like my sister. The Kathirat gave me this child, gave me this *son*, and these seven sisters will give me strength to nurse and raise this son."

* * * * *

After waiting so long, it happened. Leah's birth pangs began, and she made sure the entire camp knew of it. Midwives and serving women gathered around her and began the vigil. Some prayed for a safe delivery; others prayed for a son; still others prayed only that this child would bring peace to the camp.

And in Rachel's tent, she wept and prayed yet again, *Please, Adonai, Do not let this child be a son!* And yet again, Jacob held her tightly, his own tears silently joining hers. *What is this You have done to me?* he asked the night. And the night turned Laban's jesting question into an accusation: *What you have been doing!*

Please, not a son, Rachel prayed again.

And in the darkness, a baby cried.

שנה על שנה

shanal 'al shanah

Cycles

"Did you see her face, Zilpah, when I announced my son's name? Did you *see* her?" Leah asked, her eyes on fire, as she danced—gently, for she had still not fully recovered from giving birth, but danced nonetheless—around the tent. "Did you see her?"

Paralyzed by Leah's ferocious demeanor, Zilpah could not speak. Of course, Zilpah had seen Rachel's face.

The younger, and still childless, sister of Leah and wife of Jacob had turned white, and her knees buckled so that Bilhah had to brace her up and keep her from falling. And no wonder. *"Re'u, ben!"* Leah had shouted. "See! A son!" And the servants around the fire echoed "Reuben! Reuben! Reuben!"

"She looked as if someone had slapped her in the face, did she not?" Leah giggled at the memory. Zilpah nodded, transfixed by her mistress' fierce delight.

The sisters' conflict caught servants in a desperate position. If they did not shout the new son's name, they would offend the vengeful Leah. But with every repetition of the baby's name, Rachel appeared as if struck with the back of an open hand. So each repetition became more strained.

"And did you see the pride in Jacob's eyes?" Leah grasped the bone carving of the seven swallows, kissed it, and held it up toward the sky. "Thank you, blessed sisters; thank you, Kathirat!" Turning to Zilpah she said, "Now that he has an heir, a son to carry on his name, Jacob will come to truly value me! He will love me, Zilpah. He will spend more nights with me than—tell your

133

sister to prepare herself. The second wife will need her more than ever."

"I will tell her, mistress," Zilpah managed to say.

"And you might as well tell the rest of the servants something, as well."

"Tell them?"

"As mother of the heir, I am entitled to even greater respect. Do you understand?" Leah raised her eyebrows, driving home the message.

"I understand, mistress," Zilpah replied. *So she will be even more difficult than before!* Zilpah thought. *They have to be warned!* But she said, "I will inform the servants, mistress."

Leah, reaching into the cradle, did not hear Zilpah's reply. She held her babe toward the sky like an offering. *Thank you, sweet sisters,* she prayed, silently. *Thank you for giving me this strong son. And giving me back my husband's love.*

"Prepare my bed, Zilpah," Leah said. "And summon a nurse for Reuben. This has been an eventful day, I need rest, and I do not want a noisy whelp keeping me awake. Hurry up, girl." Moments later, as she lay down and closed her eyes, she said, "I am a new mother of the master's firstborn son. See to it that no one disturbs my rest. No one."

"No one, mistress," Zilpah said, as she extinguished the oil lamp, plunging the tent into darkness. *May the gods protect us,* Zilpah thought, as she reclined on her pallet at Leah's feet.

* * * * *

"Why did I hear this first from my serving girl?" Rachel demanded. "And why did you keep this secret from us?"

"We—my brother and I—we did not part on good terms," Jacob said. "Pain surrounds those memories, so I avoid them."

"So I have to hear from Bilhah, who heard it from Zilpah, who heard you telling Leah, that you have a brother?"

"I did not intend to tell Leah. It . . . it just came out," Jacob admitted. So he explained.

It all came about because Leah had summoned Jacob to her tent. She saw that he was seated comfortably, and then she presented her case.

"I have given you a son, Jacob. The servants wonder why you do not show me more honor, why you do not spend more time with your firstborn son,"

Leah said, with an air of deep concern and sorrow.

"Do the servants wonder? I did not know you valued their opinions so," Jacob said.

"It is unseemly!" Leah said, her anger flashing momentarily. Then, in a conciliatory tone, she said, "I have heard you say that we should not treat the servants badly."

"I would not have known," he said.

Ignoring his sharp tone, she caressed his shoulder with her hand. Jacob looked skeptically at the hand, then at her, but she appeared not to notice. "Reuben is your firstborn. The servants will respect him more if you show him special favor."

"My servants will respect him if he grows to be a respectable man!" Jacob said, suddenly angry himself. "Special favor to the firstborn!" he stood, swatting her hand from his shoulder. "I have heard that all my life." His sudden fury unnerved Leah.

"Do you know what all that 'special favor' for the firstborn produces? Do you?" He made a dismissive gesture. "Of course not. You were the firstborn daughter. And look at you!"

Leah, for once speechless, sat entranced by Jacob's rage.

"You do not even realize how demanding you are, how ungrateful. 'Not treat the servants badly.' Do not make me laugh," he said, leaning forward, slinging his words like stones. Leah instinctively put up her hands in defense, but he misinterpreted her gesture as an attempt to strike him. Grasping her wrist with a grip of iron, he said, "You treat everyone like dogs. You pet them when you want something, and you kick them when they get in the way."

He pushed her hand away, and she began to rub the sore wrist with her other hand. "That's what comes from 'special' treatment, from showing favoritism," he said, staring into the distance. He seemed unaware of Leah's presence. "The one receiving the special treatment comes to believe the world belongs to him, that he can do no wrong, that everyone should bow to his every whim, just like my brother." He looked at Leah suddenly, his fury extinguished by alarm at his unintended disclosure.

"You have a brother?" Leah croaked, but Jacob had already left.

Now, in Rachel's tent, he said, "Zilpah must have overheard." He shrugged.

Rachel, who had listened silently, asked, "This talk of special treatment for the firstborn, does that mean that your brother is older?"

"In the same way as Leah is older than you," Jacob said.

"Except that Leah and I are twins, so she is only—" Jacob's expression stopped Rachel short. "You and your brother are twins?"

"We are twins. He was born only moments before me."

"But that makes him the firstborn. I thought you said you would inherit your father's wealth," Rachel said.

"That is why we did not part well. My father, Isaac, gave me the blessing of the firstborn. It made my brother angry."

"I suppose it would make him angry. But why would your father give you the blessing of the firstborn?" Rachel was clearly puzzled.

Jacob sighed, his face reflecting inner pain. "Because he thought I was Esau, that I was my brother." And to her questioning look, he confessed, "He was old. His sight was failing. I knew he could not tell us apart, so I deceived him."

Rachel's expression revealed her horror. "Could not tell you apart!" she said. "Do you realize what you said? What you did? To us?" And she began sobbing uncontrollably. Jacob reached out to hold her, but she pushed his hands away. "Do not touch me!" she said, and she wept, whether more from sorrow or from anger, she could not tell.

Now she knows too, he thought. He moved to take her in his arms, but she warded him off. So he stood, helpless, listening to her bitter tears. *Once again Rachel pays the price of my deception. In their bridal finery, I could not tell the sisters apart and married the other one; so my father in his blindness could not tell his sons apart, and he blessed—the other one. But why, Elohim, do You make my beloved Rachel pay the penalty for my wrongdoing?* Looking at Rachel, he whispered, "Oh that I could pay the price instead of you, my beloved." And then he realized, *Watching Rachel suffer is how I am paying it.*

* * * * *

Before Reuben, everyone in the camp hoped and anticipated that the birth of the first son would change everything. It changed nothing. Reuben grew strong and soon began to walk, but otherwise, the days passed as they always had. Nanna and Utu continued their endless race through the skies. The wool grew long on the sheep, and they were sheared. Lambs and kids were born and grew strong. Women sang their songs as they wove cloth or ground meal. Caravans passed along the trade routes, peddling pottery, metal implements, wine, and cloth in exchange for mutton and cheese, wool and leather. The servants scurried to avoid Leah's displeasure on days when Jacob awakened in Rachel's tent—which meant most days. And they tended to Rachel's needs with care on the other days. Everyone prayed. Leah to the Kathirat, Jacob and Rachel to El Shaddai, and the servants to various gods. Leah became pregnant again, and when the news spread, it seemed as if the rest of the encampment, from Jacob the master to the youngest serving girl, let out a collective sigh, as if they had been holding their breath. Only little Reuben seemed unaffected.

At the appointed time, Leah gave birth to another son. "The gods have heard me," Leah told her serving girl. "*Shama,*" she said, which means "have heard." "So I will name him Simeon." Rachel had steeled herself for the naming ceremony, so she did not faint this time.

As to Jacob and his God, Rachel asked only one question. "Why did your God hear Leah's prayers but not mine?"

Jacob had no answer, so Rachel asked herself, *Are the Kathirat more powerful than El Shaddai? Are His ears heavy from so many prayers?* She knew Jacob would not listen to such thoughts, so she did not give them voice. But in the night, they still came to her. *Perhaps we are too far from El Shaddai's dwelling, from the rocks at Beth-El.* She thought this might be so. *Perhaps He cannot reach so far.*

Reuben's birth had changed nothing in the camp. Neither did the birth of Simeon. Reuben began to babble and then to speak. Simeon crawled and then took careful steps. But Nanna and Utu raced on, the flocks grew woolly until shearing, lambs and kids grew, women sang at their tasks, and caravans plied the trade routes. The two boys kept Leah busy, and Rachel received most of Jacob's attentions. But once again, Leah swelled with child.

She named the child, another son, Levi. "You will see, Zilpah," she said. "With this son, finally Jacob will *lavah*—Jacob will be joined to me." She smiled, certain her exile would end. "Levi will cause my husband to *lava*, to be joined to me." The sound of the word delighted her. "Levi *lava*; Levi *lava*," she said, again and again.

"Do not worry, beloved," Jacob said to Rachel. "My heart will always be joined to yours. She may name the child whatever she wants, but you are still first in my heart."

"But I want to give you sons, Jacob," Rachel said. "Why does your God not hear my prayers? Is He too far away in Beth-El?" Desperation had finally made her bold enough to voice the question.

"I do not know why El Elyon has done this," Jacob said. "His ways are too high for me to understand."

"Well, understand this!" Rachel said, placing his hands against her flat belly. "El Elyon has left me empty, lifeless, and barren!" She began weeping. In a small voice, she said, "My sister prays to the Kathirat, and she has been given three strong sons!"

"Do not accuse El Elyon. His timing is beyond our understanding," Jacob responded. "My mother had no children for twenty years," he reminded her, "but then I was born, as El Elyon had promised." He kissed her cheeks, catching each tear with his lips. "You are not barren!" he said, with such force the shock dried her tears. She looked at him in wonder, eyes wide. "You have not had any children *yet*, but, if El Shaddai wills, you will have children. My grandmother gave birth to my father, Isaac, at the age of ninety-one!" he said.

"I cannot wait so long," she said. "Besides, it seems so clear to me!"

"Clear? What seems clear?"

"My sister worships the Kathirat, goddesses of the Kinahhu. We live in the land of the Kinahhu. She has been give three strong sons!"

"I do not serve the gods of the Kinahhu!" Jacob said. "El Shaddai is the Creator, the Maker of everything."

"And this creation?" Rachel let the question hang.

"It was long ago. Many generations in the past."

"But Ba'al, the god of the Kinahhu, remakes the world every year!" Rachel declared.

"I do not serve Ba'al!" Jacob said.

"Do you not see? Wherever El Shaddai may be, we live in Ba'al's world of cycles. Round and round, Utu and Nanna go. The sheep grow their wool, then we shear them; they grow it out again. The caravans come and go, and come again," Rachel said, pleading. "And in every cycle, Leah has a son, and I—"

"I will hear no more of this," Jacob said. "These wheels within wheels. The loathsome Ba'al." He looked at Rachel. "This will change. You will have sons."

But the land of Ba'al is a land of unchanging cycles, Rachel thought. *Year on year, nothing changes, except I grow older.* But she said no more.

And the birth of Levi, like the births of Reuben and Simeon before him, changed nothing. The race through the heavens continued, and on the earth below, the flocks, the women, and the caravans continued their cycles. Reuben shadowed the shepherds on their rounds. Simeon babbled and then spoke, and a newly weaned Levi took his first step. And Leah conceived again. Another son.

Leah rejoiced that the goddesses had blessed her yet again. "*Odeh!*" she declared. "I rejoice! And so the boy's name shall be Judah!" She felt her triumph was complete. *I have given Jacob four stout sons,* she told herself, *and little sister remains barren.* "*Odeh!* Judah!" she declared, "Rejoice over Judah!"

And despite their allegiance to Rachel, the servants did rejoice. Only the gods knew the future, but four strong sons gave as much assurance as this short life afforded that Master Jacob's household would go on. There would be flocks and herds, food and shelter for many servants, for many more cycles, many more days to come. *Odeh!* Judah, indeed!

The births of Reuben, Simeon, and Levi had changed nothing. The birth of Judah changed everything.

שפחות

shifᵉchot

Handmaids

She walked silently, not realizing that someone watched, illuminated by the cold light from Nanna. At the edge of the camp, she flung herself to the ground, her anguish beyond tears, her despair beyond words. She wanted to cry out to the gods, but the depth of her pain defied articulation. She could only lie prostrate, moaning, yet without sound. *It is the only way!* she thought. *It is the only way. I cannot hold it against them. It is the only way.*

She had accepted it. But she could not remain in her tent, hearing, knowing.

Why? El Elyon, El Shaddai, whoever You are, wherever You are! Why did You put me in this position? Why do You not answer my prayers? She wept herself to sleep, lying on the ground until the cold roused her. Then she walked stiffly back to her tent and fell onto her bed, exhausted and chilled.

And so it went. Every evening the sounds in the night drove her from her bed, but the next morning, she remembered why and how this ordeal had begun.

"Leah has four strong sons," Rachel had said. "I have nothing."

"You have my love, Rachel," Jacob said, smarting, "is that enough?"

"What do you know of *enough*?" Rachel demanded. "They are your sons too. But not mine. If anything should happen to you, I would have no one to defend me from my sister. As first wife, she could reduce me to poverty, reduce me to begging her and *her* sons, for my basic needs."

Jacob did not know what to say, so he just shook his head sadly. Through

140

all the years, all the disappointments, all the trials, their love had remained constant. Now he began to feel it slipping away, and it frightened him.

Once, as a boy, he had seen and felt the very ground beneath his feet move. He had heard a deep rumbling sound and had stood transfixed as the undulating ground moved slowly toward him until the wave reached him and knocked him off his feet. Rachel's anger at this moment stirred the same sense of helplessness and fear.

"I must have sons," she said. And when Jacob only sighed in reply, she exploded. "Give me sons, or I am as good as dead! Do you hear me? I must have sons!"

Her angry words ignited Jacob's smoldering temper, and he replied, "And am I to become El Shaddai, who has denied you children? What more do you want of me?" The words were sharper than he intended, and he immediately regretted them.

"You have done everything that I could ask," Rachel said, repenting. "But you understand my anxiety, do you not?"

"I do," he replied, also repenting of his anger. He held out his arms, and she moved into his embrace. She placed her head on his chest, and they silently soaked in the healing contact for a moment.

"If you could do something more to give me children, would you?" she asked without looking up.

"You know that I would," he said, still savoring her closeness.

She waited a moment; then tilting her head back to look him in the eye, she said, "I have a way."

"What way?" Jacob said, puzzled.

"Bilhah!" Rachel called, and her young serving girl appeared. For some reason, she seemed ill at ease. Rachel gestured toward her.

"I do not understand," Jacob began. "What has Bilhah to do with giving you sons—"

But then Bilhah's blush cut his sentence short. He started to shake his head, but Rachel insisted. "It is the only way, Jacob. I cannot depend upon my sister's goodwill. You know that. If I adopt Bilhah's children as my own, both Bilhah's future and mine will be assured."

Jacob looked at the serving girl. At fifteen or sixteen, she was a picture of youth—and not unattractive. But his father's words rang in his ears. *"Your life will be simpler and happier with one wife rather than two. And that means handmaids and concubines too. Elohim gave Adam only one wife, and look at the trouble she caused him."* How well I understand those words, Jacob thought. *And I have enough trouble with two wives.* But Rachel's logic made sense.

"Is this acceptable to you?" Jacob said, addressing the serving girl.

"I do my mistress' bidding," said Bilhah.

"I understand that," Jacob said. "But we—my father, Isaac, and my father's father, Abraham—we do not treat our servants like cattle." *We do not breed them for pleasure or profit,* is what he meant.

"Thank you, master," Bilhah said, her eyes modestly averted. "But it would be an honor for me to serve Mistress Rachel in this way."

"And you are certain this is what you want, Rachel?"

"Perhaps the gods may smile on me some day in the future. In that case, I will have children from my own body to care for me. But by then, Leah may have so many sons that they would drive us out of the camp if you died. I cannot take that risk," Rachel said.

"You are right, my beloved," Jacob said, defeated. "Though I wish it otherwise, you are right."

And then he asked the question she dreaded to answer. "When shall we begin?"

Rachel started to speak, but she could not. She thought she had steeled herself for this moment, but now that it had come, she wavered. She buried her face in her hands for a moment and took a deep breath. Trembling, she took Jacob's hand and led him to Bilhah and placed his hand on the serving girl's. She pressed their hands together a moment, and then, turning quickly away, she stumbled out of the tent into the cold moonlight.

* * * * *

Bilhah lay wide awake on the bed she had just shared with Jacob, her mind racing. It had been one thing to agree to her mistress' request. Rachel treated Bilhah well, and the two women had genuine affection for each other. And Master Jacob was kind and considerate, all the servants said so. "You are lucky to be in Master Jacob's camp," the older servants said to her. "Master Laban does not treat servants with any dignity at all." For her part, Bilhah did not mind being a serving girl. Most of the people she knew had been born servants, as she and her sister had been. The gods blessed only a few with high birth.

"And you would not want to be a master anyway," one of the old, wise servants had often said when Bilhah was but a child.

"Why not?" the twins, Bilhah and Zilpah, had asked in unison. "Is it not good to be free?"

"To be free, ah!" the old man said, eyes dreamy. "To be free would be wonderful, but being free and being a master are not the same thing. Would you want to be an evil master, who beats his servants and makes their lives miserable?" the wrinkled old man asked. The twins shook their heads in unison.

"I did not think so," he said, chuckling drily at their wide eyes. "And the good ones have worries and responsibilities you would not want either," he said. "Masters are not free. They carry the burdens of the whole household. If a servant makes a mistake, he or she suffers for it. But if a master makes a mistake, everyone in the camp may suffer for it." He shook his head. "Better to know your place, do your work, and leave the decisions—and the worrying— to your betters."

Bilhah, as such a little girl then, had not appreciated the wisdom of the old man's advice. But her years of service to Rachel, putting her in close contact with Master Jacob, had brought her understanding. A serving woman without children might be sad, but a good master would take care of her all her life. And death would be welcome should she have a bad master. But seldom would a serving woman suffer the treachery and intrigue that seemed an everyday concern for Master Jacob and Mistress Rachel. Just being close to Mistress Rachel subjected Bilhah to more conflict than she knew how to handle.

Lying alone, after her first time being with a man, the complex physical sensations and tangled emotions overwhelmed her and drove sleep from her eyes. She felt at once pain and pleasure, fatigue and vigor, fear and delight, total submission and supreme mastery. As a servant, she might never have married nor had children. Master Jacob and Mistress Rachel had honored her by allowing her the status of bearing their children. And unlike her, her children would not be born into servitude. All these new thoughts and feelings chased through her mind. Eventually, fatigue overtook her, and as she drifted to sleep, one triumphant thought echoed in her brain: *My child will be free!*

* * * * *

"This is the fourth night I have seen her," Leah said, stepping back and letting the tent flap close. Zilpah said nothing as she lit the oil lamp to dispel the darkness. "I saw Jacob today, so I know he is not visiting the far pastures," Leah cupped her chin in her hand as she sat on her bed, her eyes peering into the unknown.

The boys had been put to bed long before by nurses and serving women. Jacob seldom visited Leah's tent, apparently believing that, by giving Leah four sons, he had fulfilled his husbandly obligations. With her status now secure, Leah told herself she did not care—at least not a great deal. *After all, it means more time for the servants to see to my needs,* she reasoned.

Then, many nights ago, Leah had glimpsed a figure walking away from Rachel's tent, silent and alone in the darkness. She had thought little of it at the time, but when she chanced to see the same thing twice again, and when she identified the figure as her sister, Rachel, curiosity consumed her. She raised the topic only with Zilpah, who seemed strangely incurious.

"Jacob is not with me," Leah said, puzzling it out. "And yet Rachel is alone in the dark." She looked at Zilpah, who sat silent, eyes averted. "Zilpah!" she said, causing the poor girl to start visibly. "You know something, do you not?"

Zilpah's eyes darted about. "I do not know—"

"Come now, girl," Leah purred. "What have you heard, then?"

"I have heard nothing."

"Do not play games with me, girl—"

"I am not, mistress," the terrified girl protested. "I do not know anything, and the servants do not speak of it," she said.

"Go on."

"My sister," Zilpah said, then hesitated.

"What about your sister?" Leah was pressing now. "What does she say?"

"Nothing, mistress," Zilpah said. "She behaves strangely. She speaks little to me. In fact, I see her little these days, and not at all after dark. Do you see her with Mistress Ra—with the second wife on these nightly walks?"

"I do not," Leah said, mind racing. "What are you telling me?"

"I cannot tell you anything, for I know nothing," Zilpah said, "I only know my sister is different." She held her hands up to signal her confusion. "I do not understand it."

Leah pondered. "Rachel walks alone in the night, when she should be with Jacob in her tent," she said, more to herself than to her handmaid.

"If she still wants children," Zilpah said.

"What was that?" Leah said.

"Nothing of importance, mistress," Zilpah said. "I was just thinking. She wants children so badly—it is strange that she should not, I mean, how can she . . ." Zilpah began perspiring. "I mean no impertinence, but her husband . . ." the girl gave up, flustered.

"Wait—something you said!" Leah stopped, mouth open wide. "I see it!" she shouted, startling Zilpah. "Rachel walks alone in the night when she should be with Jacob in her tent," Leah said. Then she pointed at Zilpah, saying, "*If* she wants children.

"Rachel walks alone, without Bilhah, her handmaid," Leah said. "So where are they?"

"Who, mistress?"

"The two of them. Jacob and Bilhah," Leah said. "Where are they if she, my sister, wants children?"

Zilpah looked at her, uncomprehending.

"Why, they are together!" Leah said, clapping her hands in finality. Next, she smiled cruelly and said, "And my poor spoiled little sister cannot stand the thought of Jacob in the arms of another woman." Her face darkened, her voice grew quiet. "Finally, she knows how it feels." Suddenly, she turned away, her head down. "Leave me, now," she said so softly it stunned Zilpah.

"Mistress?" Zilpah asked.

Without turning, Leah silently waved her servant away. When the girl still did not move, her voice still muted, Leah snapped, "Leave me!"

The puzzled Zilpah pondered Leah's unusual behavior. *Could Leah be crying?* she wondered, then shook her head. *Not Leah.*

In the following days and weeks, Leah demanded more of Jacob's attention, and at first he complied. But this time, Leah, who had conceived almost yearly like the sheep and goats her husband cared for, did not become pregnant. This time, Leah had to watch as another woman began to ripen and glow with childbearing. Rachel's gambit had worked; Bilhah carried her master's child. And this time the expectant mothers—for Rachel and Bilhah both accounted themselves mothers—soon monopolized Jacob's time, and Leah received almost none.

Outside the privacy of her own tent, Leah appeared uninterested. But her growing sons found her cross and distracted. She did not shout at the servants, but any who displeased her felt the sharp edge of her anger. And they looked with sympathy on her handmaid. For Zilpah seemed to be the focus of Leah's displeasure.

Inside her tent, Leah spent more and more time alone. Almost every evening, she sent Zilpah away, and the serving girl returned to find her mistress drawn and subdued. These actions at first puzzled Zilpah, then fueled a growing sense of concern. One evening, as she sat quietly outside Leah's tent, Zilpah felt certain she heard her mistress weeping. *No one will believe me,* she thought. *Leah seems so confident, so in command, but it is all a charade. Despite her brave talk, Master Jacob does not love her; he avoids her—as do all the rest. I almost feel sorry for her.* Shocked, Zilpah realized, *I do* feel *sorry for her.* She heard Leah's summons, and as she rose to answer, she thought, *She has alienated all the others. Perhaps I can be a comfort to her.* Entering the tent, she saw a devastated woman, eyes red, face drawn. Leah had never seemed so small, so fragile.

"The Kathirat have deserted me," Leah said, whimpering.

"You have four strong sons—" Zilpah began gently, searching for words of comfort.

Leah's eyebrows shot up, and she realized, *This slave girl pities me!* Other thoughts swarmed behind it: *Who are you to pity me? Presumptuous whelp! I will show you your place!* Her face hardened, her mouth twisted.

"Does it make you proud, girl?" Leah asked, "That your twin carries my husband's child?"

Zilpah started to shake her head, but Leah stopped her. "Do not deny it. I know your kind," Leah said. "All submission and compliance to my face, then ridicule me behind my back to the other servants. I should whip you," Leah paused, considering.

Zilpah did not know what to say. *Whip me? But I wanted to comfort you,* she thought.

"Oh, I know how proud you are," Leah said. "You think because your twin carries my husband's child, that makes you more than a lowborn slave. Well, it does not."

"Mistress, I do not think such things," Zilpah said, tears of shock streaming down her face.

"Do not think any child of a slave will be equal to my sons," Leah said. "Do not forget your place."

"As you say, mistress," Zilpah said, cowed, but her eyes blazed with indignation.

Leah saw the angry eyes and thought, *My moment of weakness emboldened her. First, she thought to pity me, and now that I remind her of her place, she thinks to defy me. Pity? Defiance? She will learn to fear me!* To Zilpah, she said, "Let me see what it is my husband diverts himself with these recent nights," and as she spoke, she made a lifting motion with an outstretched hand.

Zilpah stood mute, uncomprehending; her tears dried by the shock.

"Let me see you," Leah said, hands on hips.

"Mistress?"

"We are women in this tent. Take off your cloak." Another lifting gesture. "You and your sister are twins." Leah said the words calmly, as though contemplating the purchase of a fine ewe. "Let me see the sort of stock my husband is breeding."

Zilpah blanched, her head suddenly light. Not believing her ears, she remained still. So Leah stepped over and forcibly began removing the girl's outer clothing. Soon Zilpah stood exposed, shivering from fear and humiliation under Leah's measuring gaze.

"A little thin, perhaps," Leah said, as she circled the servant girl. "But you should be able to nurse well enough."

Zilpah's eyes burned with tears, but she squeezed them back, fearing what Leah might do if she let them flow.

"Your sister no doubt keeps Jacob well occupied at night," Leah said. "No wonder Rachel walks alone in the darkness." Just then, her lips quivered, but she set her mouth firmly. Then, with a snort, she continued, "With a little morsel like you, no doubt it gets noisy in that tent." But she choked on the last word and turned quickly away.

Serves her right, Leah thought. *Jacob fancies her and abandons me. Now he exerts himself with a pretty little serving girl.* And a small voice inside her said, *You may be first wife in name, but now you are third in his affections—and every one in the camp knows that, can see that.* For a moment, she surrendered to bitter tears, sobbing silently.

As the silence extended, the naked Zilpah clasped her elbows, chilled by humiliation and terror as much as from the cold. Finally, Leah turned to face her, took a deep breath and swallowed. "I see. So my sister thinks to gain favor by raising a slave girl's whelps as her own?" Zilpah recoiled at the words, but

Leah, lost in her own calculations, did not notice. "Well, we shall see." Again she paused for thought, fingering the bone amulet she wore around her neck and looking into the distance. "I can have more sons," she said, fixing her gaze on the forgotten Zilpah.

Zilpah did not know the meaning of Leah's intense gaze, but it sent another chill through her.

"One way or another," Leah said. Suddenly, she felt tired. "Get dressed, girl, and fetch me some water," Leah said. "Then prepare my bed. Do it right this time. My back hurts when you are careless."

Zilpah moved as quickly as her numbed limbs allowed.

"And make sure my chamber pot is available. I feel a bit of a chill tonight." Zilpah opened the tent flap to call the servant in charge of the chamber pots, but Leah stopped her. "You can take care of it, Zilpah. See to it yourself."

Zilpah thought, *I understand. You want me to know my place. Even though I hold the exalted station as your personal servant, I serve at your pleasure. You can force the most menial tasks on me.* She trembled as she retrieved the chamber pot and did not acknowledge the questioning look from the serving girl whose chore it was. *I know my place, all right. You would have done better to have whipped me. I came to comfort you, and you humiliated me, treated me like breeding stock. All because my sister bears Master Jacob's child.* Her breathing had slowed now, and she reminded herself, *I am a mere serving girl, like my sister, and have no power.* Then another thought, a pleasant thought, came to her. *That has changed for my sister.* And then she realized, for the first time, *My sister has power, and Leah fears that power! A power I might have as well. Leah said those mocking words, intending to shame me: "Your sister no doubt keeps Jacob well occupied at night." Clearly, she has. And we are twins.*

Zilpah would have to think about this. About its dangers, to be sure, for wounded creatures could be dangerous, and Leah was dangerous at all times. Wounded, she would be even more dangerous. *There are dangers,* Zilpah admitted, *and possibilities.*

נפתולי

naftulês

Wrestlings

He will not acknowledge the child, Leah thought, as she sat across from Jacob and Rachel. *He will not*, she thought, even as Bilhah stepped forward, holding the small bundle toward Jacob and Rachel, seated near the fire where all could see. *Even now, he will not accept the child of a slave as his own.* Leah's belief did not waver.

Beaming, Rachel took the bundle and placed it on her knees—symbolizing her adoption of the child—and then held the baby aloft for all to see. The crowd waited for her to speak. She smiled at Bilhah, who knelt before her, and placed a hand of blessing on the servant's head. "Adonai has heard my claim," Rachel said, "and this son is His judgment in my favor!" She used the legal term *dn'ni*, meaning "to grant my suit." "So his name is Dan!" With this, she turned and offered the child to Jacob.

He will not, Leah thought; but at that moment, Jacob, smiling broadly, dandled the infant on his knees, completing the act of adoption, acknowledging the child as his son and heir. The servants began chanting the boy's name, "Dan! Dan! Dan!" And this time, Leah almost fainted, but the vigilant Zilpah caught her before anyone noticed.

Later, in her tent, Rachel thanked Bilhah. "Dear friend, you have made me so very happy," Rachel said. "You and Jacob have given me what El Shaddai refused to—a child to call my own." Rachel beamed upon the nursing child and upon his happy mother. "Do not be afraid," Rachel said. "I will not allow anyone to take him from you. He will know you are his mother. But I will love him too."

"I trust you," Bilhah said. She paused, gazing at her child. "I know that this has been difficult for you," Bilhah said. "But you never took out your jealousy or anger on me."

Tears welled in Rachel's eyes and she held a hand to her mouth, not trusting herself to speak.

The baby finished nursing and after Bilhah covered herself, she held the child out to Rachel. "Would you like to hold him now?"

Rachel nodded and reached out to take the child. As she cradled him against her shoulder and patted his back to ease his full stomach, tears coursed down her face. Bilhah stood and embraced both Rachel and little Dan, and the women wept for joy.

* * * * *

"What does Leah want from me now?" Jacob asked, his voice sharp with impatience.

"Nothing, that is—that is not why I—" Zilpah's lip began trembling, and Jacob took pity on her.

"Forgive me, Zilpah," Jacob said, "It is not you I am annoyed with." Stooping slightly to look her in the eye, he said, "Why did Leah send you here?"

"She did not send me, master. That is what I have been trying to tell you," the girl said, regaining her composure.

"Then why are you here?" Jacob inquired.

"She has not eaten anything for several days."

"Is she ill, then?" Jacob inquired, suddenly concerned. When Zilpah shook her head, he pressed, "What is it, then?"

"I . . . I cannot say, master." Zilpah looked around quickly and then stepped closer to her master.

"Cannot? Or will not?"

"Please, master, she says she does not want you to know, but she is very distressed, and I do not know how to help her."

Jacob put his hand under the girl's chin and tipped her head up gently. "You can tell me, Zilpah. Are you afraid Leah will punish you if she finds out you told me?" The girl did not speak, but her lips trembled and silent tears ran down her cheeks as she slowly nodded.

Jacob caught her tears with his thumb. He put his arm protectively around the young girl's shoulders and led her to a bench, where they sat together.

"Tell me, Zilpah. What has you so upset?"

"Immediately after the naming ceremony for little Dan, she took to her bed. She sleeps little, speaks not at all, and has not eaten much," Zilpah said.

"Tell me truly. Your mistress is not above making a display of her discomfort in order to get what she wants." Jacob searched the girl's face for the truth. "Is she really ill?"

Zilpah did not answer, only shrugged her shoulders. "I cannot tell; that is why I am worried. If something happened to Leah because I failed—"

"Leah is blessed to have a friend who cares so much for her," Jacob said and gave her shoulders an affectionate squeeze.

Do I care so much for Leah? Zilpah wondered. *If something happened to Leah because I failed to care for her,* Zilpah thought, *I would surely be whipped.* But sitting there, with Jacob's arm around her shoulders, she realized two things. First, Jacob thought better of her than she deserved, for it was fear of punishment more than concern for her mistress that had brought her to speak to him. Second, Jacob's arm around her shoulders made her feel strange, unsettled. Not that it was unpleasant. Not at all. But it stirred something in her that she had not felt before. With these realizations fresh in her mind, she said, "I do not know what to do."

"Leave it to me, little one," he said, standing quickly. "I will see to Leah and make certain she does not know you spoke to me." With that, he patted her on the head and walked away.

Suddenly, Zilpah was furious with him. *Call me "little one" and pat me on the head as if I were a child! "Little one"? I am just as old as Bilhah! In fact, I am a little older! "Little one"? I am as much a woman as my sister!* Confused, she walked back toward the tent, where a despondent Leah still lay without speaking. *"Little one"!* Zilpah thought one last time. *Why does that bother me so?*

* * * * *

"Jacob? Here?" Leah sat up. "Delay him—just a moment," Leah hissed to Zilpah, "Give me a moment." She grabbed a comb from a small table near her bed and quickly ran it through her hair. She smoothed the front of her robe with her hands. Then, carefully arranging her cushions, she reclined on her bed. "All right, tell him to come in," she said to Zilpah. "Then leave us until I call for you."

The serving girl bowed and left without a word.

When Jacob entered, Leah held the back of her hand to her forehead, and said weakly, "Jacob, is that you?"

"It is," he replied.

"What brings you here?" she said, but she thought, *I knew that gossiping servant girl could not hold her tongue.*

"You have not been seen outside your tent for some time," Jacob said. "I was concerned."

"You were?" Leah said, sitting up.

Her sudden movement surprised him, and he said, "You have taken to your bed. Are you ill?"

"Ill?" Leah said, and she stood, seeming to notice the bed for the first time. "Not really—" she caught herself. "That is, I, uh, have been occupied."

" 'Occupied'?" Jacob repeated. "I must say, Leah, you do not seem to be yourself. I begin to think you may be ill. Shall I summon a healer?" He seemed genuinely concerned.

"Not myself?" Leah said, and left it hanging.

"Come now, woman," Jacob said. "If you are ill, let me summon a healer. I would not want anything to happen to you."

"You would not?" Leah said, reaching out to him. "Then you do love me?"

Jacob received her embrace, surprised. "Of course, I care for you."

"Oh, I knew it!" she said, holding him tightly. "After all this time, you know it too! I knew you really loved me and not my sister. All this time I knew it!"

"You knew what?" Jacob asked.

"It was obvious from the start. I was older, more mature," she said, smiling up at him.

Stunned, Jacob could only think to ask, "If I loved you, why did I ask for Rachel?"

Leah flared for an instant at the mention of her sister's name; but still reveling in his declaration of affection, she said, "You thought I did not know, you foolish man?" She laughed with delight and said, "That is why I knew you loved me so much!"

"It was?" said Jacob.

Seeing his confusion, she laughed again. "Of course. You thought me so valuable that seven years of your labor would never be enough to purchase me!"

"That is what I thought?"

"That is what you thought, and I knew it. So I convinced my father that someone who thought so highly of me deserved me, no matter the bride-price offered," she said, pressing her head into his chest.

"You convinced him of that?" When Leah nodded, he asked, "And I agreed to marry your sister because—"

"Because my scheming father deceived you," she said flatly.

"He deceived me; that is true," said Jacob. "And I spent so much time with her because?" The dialogue had taken a turn down a very strange road, and Jacob was concerned where it would end.

"I have wondered about that for a time," Leah said. "But now that you have come and declared your love for me, it is clear as living water."

"Now that I have declared my love it is clear?" he said. But by now, Leah needed no more encouragement.

"Once you . . . you mated with her slave girl, it became obvious," she declared.

"Obvious?"

"You were trying to make my barren little sister with child; you took pity on her," Leah said. Smiling slyly, she said, "It did not take so much time with me." And she nuzzled his chest again.

"Not so much. That is true," Jacob said, thankful she could not see his expression.

"Finally, you gave up on her—I would have told you to do it sooner—and found a more fertile field."

"I did. And you are not angry with me for, for sowing in other fields?" Jacob asked, feeling increasingly light-headed.

"I am not angry. You will be a wealthy man—I knew it from the first—with many flocks, many herds, many servants, and many sons. And as first wife, I shall be mistress of all. I have given you four strong sons," she said, looking up at him again. Reassured by his hesitant nod, she went on. "And now the slave girl has given you another. I will not be angry so long as you still care for me and do not neglect," she paused, "my field." She finished with a kiss. "Promise me?"

Jacob nodded, but he could not speak. Nor did he try, as she giggled and led him toward her bed.

* * * * *

They met, as women, especially servants, so often did, at the well, where they waited to draw water. "We must talk," Bilhah said, and her twin sister nodded her agreement. Weeks and months had passed since the naming ceremony of little Dan.

After filling their jugs, they walked together but separate from the other women. "Can you tell me," Bilhah asked, "what has happened to your mistress, Leah? Why has she been so . . . so *civil* to everyone?" Not letting her sister reply, she went on. "Everyone thought, at least, Mistress Rachel and I thought, she would be furious—Mistress Leah, I mean. Especially after the birth of little Dan."

"Where *is* your son?" Zilpah asked.

"Mistress Rachel has him now," Bilhah said. Seeing her sister's curious expression, she said, "I do not mind. I like getting away and outside for a while, even if it is to fetch water." Zilpah still seemed doubtful, so Bilhah continued, "It is almost like having my own serving girl to look after Dan for me, except that the one taking care of him for me is Mistress Rachel!" The girls laughed together.

"But about Mistress Leah?" Bilhah persisted.

The rest of the women had drawn their water and returned to the camp, leaving the sisters alone. "You must not tell *anyone*," Zilpah insisted, and her sister nodded. "She and Master Jacob had a talk—she does not know I heard—and they," she paused, searching for the word, "they came to . . . to an agreement." Bilhah looked confused, so Zilpah continued. "He spends more time with her now, and she believes she will have more sons."

"Perhaps *she* will," Bilhah said, diverting her eyes.

"Bilhah?" Her sister inquired, "What are you not telling me?"

"Now *you* must promise not to tell anyone, especially your mistress!" Bilhah said.

"I promise," Zilpah said.

"Mistress Rachel wants another son," Bilhah said.

Confused, Zilpah replied, "But everyone knows that—are you telling me Mistress Rachel is finally pregnant?"

"She wants another son . . . like the first," Bilhah said, her face glowing.

"Like the first?" Zilpah repeated, confused. Then it hit her. "Are *you* with child?"

"I am not *yet* with child," Bilhah said, eyes bright.

"You and Master Jacob? Again?"

Bilhah looked around before closing her eyes and nodding quickly. Then concerned, she looked up and said, "You must not tell anyone!"

No need to worry about that, thought Zilpah, remembering how Leah had humiliated her the last time she found out Bilhah was with child. "I will not, Sister," she said. Still, knowing this could be useful, *Another child for my sister,* Zilpah thought, *and there is no doubt that Jacob will acknowledge this one. Not after the ceremony with Dan.*

A strange world, Zilpah thought. A master, such as Master Jacob, ruled over everyone and everything in his camp. He could buy and sell women to be wives, just as servants were bought and sold. But some women could then rule over both male and female servants. Serving women occupied the lowest rung on society's ladder. *A strange world,* Zilpah thought, *that regards women as inferior to men, but those men need women to bear their sons.* Bearing the master's children, especially sons, moved a woman up the ladder, no matter where she had been before. "Even a serving girl," she said, unaware she had spoken that last thought.

"Sister?" Bilhah inquired. "You were silent for some time, and then you said, 'Even a serving girl.'"

"I did?" Zilpah shook her head to clear her thoughts. "I only—that is— you are honored to bear the master's children," she said. A declaration, not a question.

"I am," said Bilhah, smiling.

"What is it like?" Zilpah asked.

"Childbirth?" Bilhah answered. "Labor is painful, but birth itself is joyful. It is not so bad. After all, servants labor all the time, and usually with less reward."

Zilpah nodded, but she really wanted the answer to a different question. Finally, she could not restrain herself. "What I meant was . . . ," but she could not finish the sentence. The words would not come. Her cheeks burned, and she covered her face with her hands.

Bilhah suddenly laughed, "You mean *before?* Being with a man?"

Zilpah, still blushing, nodded her head.

"Master Jacob is considerate and gentle, Sister," Bilhah said.

And strong, Zilpah thought, remembering when he had squeezed her shoulders.

" 'And strong'?" Bilhah repeated.

Zilpah gasped, "Did I say that out loud?"

Bilhah nodded, laughing. "What have you been thinking about, Sister?"

Zilpah stood. "Nothing. I must get back. Mistress Leah will wonder where I am."

"You will say—"

"I will say nothing, Sister," Zilpah assured her thoughtfully. Then she looked up and said, "I must go now." She started walking, then turned back and said, "Do not be concerned. I will say nothing."

Bilhah shook her head. *I have never seen Zilpah like that,* she thought, as she picked up the water jug and made her way back to camp.

In the ensuing weeks, Jacob continued his attentions to Leah, but to her dismay, she did not conceive. And before long, it became clear that Bilhah once again carried her master's child. Rachel radiated happiness, and Leah became so sullen and morose that Jacob no longer came to her tent in the evenings. When the baby came, a son, Leah simply stayed in her tent, to the relief of most.

"With mighty wrestling I have wrestled with my sister, and I have indeed prevailed," Rachel said at the naming ceremony. The word for "wrestling" is *nphthuli,* so she named him Naphtali. "I have indeed prevailed," Rachel had said. And so it seemed, even to Leah, alone in her tent.

u • oluth

Offerings

"You must tell no one!" Leah said.

The raspy whisper of her words gave young Reuben a start. Already shivering in fear, every hair now bristled as her voice chilled him to the bone. *Tell no one?* The words failing to register, he looked blankly at her, so she took him by the shoulders and shook him.

"You must tell no one," she repeated.

Still stunned, he said the only words that came to mind, "Not even Father?"

"*Especially* not Father," she insisted. "Do you hear me?"

"I will tell no one," he said. "But what were you doing?"

"Do not trouble yourself with that, Reuben," she said. After a moment, she added, "This was something for women only." Then, considering, she said, "You should not be out so far from the tents in the dark. I will not punish you this time," she said, "so long as you do not speak of it." She made a shooing motion with her hand. "Now go off to bed where you belong."

The boy scurried off to the tent he shared with his brothers, watched over by serving women. Fortunately, they all remained asleep as they had been when the distant throbbing had wakened him. He made his way silently to his bed. But sleep did not come quickly to him. Even in the darkness, with his eyes squeezed shut, the strange sights of this night danced before him.

Aroused by a low thrumming, he had arisen and followed it to a small wadi some distance behind the tents. There he saw three women kneeling in the sand. One of the older serving women beat softly on a drum lying sideways on the ground before her, so that the skin-covered striking surface was on the side. Leah, his mother, rocked back and forth on her knees, chanting something over and over, then reaching up toward the crescent-shaped light in the night sky. And Zilpah, her serving girl, fanned a collection of smoldering embers arranged in a crescent in front of the women. Thick strands of smoke wove their way skyward from the embers, and even at some distance, Reuben detected in the smoke a sweet scent.

When the old woman stopped drumming and threw some powder on the fire, which softly blossomed into a cloud of flame, Reuben had gasped in surprise, alerting the women to his presence. That had led to his mother's strict warning. Whatever the three women had been doing, they wanted it kept secret. That frightened Reuben.

It seemed to the boy that something in his mother had broken with the birth of little Naphtali. Before then she always seemed certain of herself, certain of what she should do, sharp in her commands to servants and children; but now she seemed uncertain and tentative. Since Naphtali, she had very little time for her sons, for anyone, really. She walked about the camp, distracted, muttering in a voice no once could decipher. And now this. With the strange scenes of this night replaying themselves in his mind, Reuben drifted off to a troubled sleep.

* * * * *

"We must not meet in the night again," the old woman said. A week had passed since their previous session, and an anxious Leah sent Zilpah to entreat Donatiya, the aged priestess of the Kathirat. She sat, cross-legged, with a mortar and pestle, grinding grain into coarse flour.

"Our mistress will not be pleased," Zilpah said.

"You cannot threaten me," the old woman replied, pointing the pestle at Zilpah. "I risk too much already."

"Threaten you?" Zilpah demurred. "Mistress would never threaten you."

"Would she not?" Donatiya replied, clearly unconvinced. The pestle kept up its steady rhythm. "I do not trust the boy," she said.

"Reuben?" Zilpah said. "He will do as his mother tells him."

"And will he, now?" the old woman said. The grinding stopped as she looked up at Zilpah, raising a skeptical eyebrow. "I have seen him with his brothers. They outwit him all the time."

"I know what you mean. Simeon and Levi, those two rascals, little conspirators." Zilpah shook her head. "But Reuben will not disobey his mother."

"What about his father?" again the pestle jabbed at Zilpah.

"I do not understand," Zilpah said.

"Do you not, now?" the old woman said, eyes narrowing. "The boy would do anything to win Master Jacob's favor. Anyone can see that." She paused. "Mistress Leah wants him to take charge, but Master Jacob tells him he's nothing special. The poor boy's being pulled apart by his parents. It's cruel what they do."

"Oh, really now, Donatiya, you exaggerate," Zilpah said. "After all, the Kinnahu offer their children as sacrifices."

"There's more than one way to sacrifice a child," the old woman said, looking directly at Zilpah. "Depend on Reuben!" she snorted. "He does not trust himself. But it does not matter. Mistress Leah has offended the Kathirat," she said, and with that, the old woman took to grinding the grain again. "It will do no good to hold ceremonies anymore."

"Offended the Kathirat?"

"It must be so," the old woman said. "See how long she's gone without getting a child."

"What can be done?" Zilpah asked. "Mistress Leah will not accept that she will have no more sons."

The old woman paused her grinding and cupped her chin in her hand. Seeming to have reached a decision, she took up the grinding again. "There may be something, but I need something first."

"What?"

"I grow old," Donatiya said. Suddenly, the old woman stopped her grinding and looked off into the distance. "My mother did magic with a needle in her hands. Beautiful embroidery. Her nimble fingers flew. She brought much wealth to her master, who was paid well for her needlework. She held an honored place in his household." Donatiya's eyes misted over. "But time passed. Her fingers grew stiff; the joints swelled," she continued. "My *imma* could no longer even hold a needle. She could no longer sew."

"One day, a wealthy merchant came and asked her master to have *Imma* make some drapes for the new house he was building." The old woman's eyes grew hard. "Her master told the merchant she could no longer sew. So the merchant said, 'Maybe she can bless my dwelling in another way.' I did not understand his words." Donatiya paused. "He paid our master anyway."

Tears welled in her eyes; the old woman swallowed hard and looked off into the distance again. "I was too young, and the city too far away, but others told me what happened. On the building day, they gave my mother wine laced with milk of the sleeping flower—you call it *rosh*—to make her weak and drowsy. They paraded her through the streets, laughing, shouting, and clapping all around. When they reached the site of the merchant's new house, *Imma* realized what they had planned for her and began to struggle. But the poisoned wine made her too weak to resist." Bitter tears flowed freely down the old woman's face. "They threw her into the hollow foundation of the wealthy man's new house." The old woman wiped her eyes with the back of her hand. "They put a jug of water and a bowl of food with her. As she moaned and pleaded, reaching out with her crippled hands, they bricked her in." Now she fixed her searing gaze on Zilpah. "They buried her alive as a foundation sacrifice." She began pounding the grain with the stone pestle again. "That is what Ba'al worshipers do with old women slaves. And Ba'al rules the Kathirat."

"Is that what you fear? Mistress Leah would never do that!" Zilpah said, horrified.

"You think not?" Donatiya asked. "Leah is the firstborn sister, the first wife. She and Master Jacob treat their firstborn like a counter in *Aseb*, the game of twenty squares."

"I know the game," Zilpah said.

"If they treat him so poorly, how will they care for an old serving woman?"

"They will not sell you for a foundation sacrifice," Zilpah said.

"So *you* say," the old woman replied, clearly not convinced.

"How can I reassure you?" Zilpah asked.

"You," the old woman repeated, appraising Zilpah. "Perhaps that could be the answer." Another appraising look, then the old woman seemed to reach a decision. "There may be something."

"Anything," Zilpah said, knowing how desperate Leah had become.

"Anything?" Donatiya repeated. "Mistress Leah must make two offerings to the Kathirat, and you must make two offerings also."

"I make two? I am a servant. What offerings can I make to the Kathirat?" Zilpah asked.

"Mistress Leah first," the old woman said, and Zilpah nodded, knowing that Donatiya would do what she pleased anyway.

"The Kathirat must be deeply offended," Donatiya said. "To restore the favor of the Kathirat, she must make the same offering the second wife has made." Seeing that Zilpah did not understand, the old woman explained, "She offered her pride. By offering her serving girl, the second wife told the seven sisters it mattered more that she have a child to call her own, than whether it came from her own body." Zilpah's eyes grew wide, and the old woman acknowledged, "And that is part of the offering you must make—to offer your body to bear the child."

Zilpah blushed. "I serve Mistress Leah, if she—"

"I am no fool, girl!" the old woman fixed her with an offended gaze. "I know what Mistress Leah thinks about the children of slaves." Stunned, Zilpah shook her head slowly, but the old woman pressed on, "Do not deny it, child. I said she must offer her pride."

This will hurt her pride, all right, thought Zilpah. "You said there were *two* offerings?"

"There is a plant. A plant with legs like a man." She gave Zilpah a guarded glance. "They say it screams when harvested and kills the one who harvests it."

"Then how?" Zilpah asked, but the old woman interrupted her.

"If she makes the first offering, and you make yours, then I will reveal the secret of harvesting the plant safely," the old woman said.

"And *my* second offering?" Zilpah inquired.

"You promise to take care of me."

"I am only a servant myself," Zilpah protested.

"Not when you bear Master Jacob a son, like your sister," the old woman said.

Zilpah shook her head. "What if I cannot persuade Mistress Leah to . . . to set aside her pride and offer me," she flushed, then continued, "to bear a child for her?"

"Then you are not clever enough to protect an old serving woman," Donatiya said. She turned back to her grinding. Clearly, the conversation was over, and Zilpah slowly walked away.

"Zilpah! What did the old woman say?" Leah demanded, as soon as she saw her serving girl a few minutes later.

"She says it will do no good to hold more ceremonies," Zilpah said.

"No more ceremonies? But what can I do? Did she not say what I could— you look like you have seen a spirit. What is wrong?" Leah asked.

Zilpah moved her lips several times before any sound came out. "She said—oh mistress, please. I do not want to tell you. You will be angry."

"Angry? I will be angry if you do not tell me, girl." Leah raised her hand, and Zilpah cowered before her. "Silly girl, I will not strike you. What has frightened you so?" Seeing the fear in the girl's eyes, Leah's voice softened. "If the old woman has frightened you so, perhaps I should discipline—"

"Oh, mistress, please. Do not upset Donatiya. That would only make things worse," Zilpah begged.

"Donatiya? Does that old woman presume to threaten *me?*" That last word was almost a shout.

"She does not, mistress. But if you frighten her further, she will be of no use to you," Zilpah said.

"Then tell me what I can do," Leah insisted, exasperated.

"All right, mistress. But please remember, I only repeat what she told me," Zilpah said, her eyes entreating. Leah nodded, so the serving girl continued. "Donatiya says that you must make an offering."

"What sort of offering?" Leah asked, suspicious. "Does the old woman want gold?"

"Nothing like that," Zilpah said. "She says the Kathirat are deeply offended, that you must offer your pride to them."

"My pride?"

"She says that the second wife has found favor with the Kathirat by offering her pride."

"I do not understand," Leah replied.

"Oh, please. Please mistress, do not make me—please do not—" Zilpah begged.

"Tell me, this instant," Leah demanded.

"Oh, do not make me—" Zilpah repeated, but a warning look from Leah stopped her pleading. "The old woman says you must sacrifice your pride in being a mother and let another bear a child for you, as did the second wife." *Will she make the connection on her own,* Zilpah thought, *or should I bait her once more?*

"Sacrifice my pride, as Rachel did," Leah said softly to herself.

When Leah said, "Rachel," Zilpah nearly exclaimed aloud. *She must truly be troubled*, Zilpah thought, *to let that hated name slip out.* As the silence stretched on, Zilpah thought, *Time to set the hook.* "Please do not make me bear his child," Zilpah said.

Leah's eyes grew large, then horrified, then angry. Zilpah could scarcely hear her words, so softly she spoke. "*That* is what the old woman said?"

Zilpah only nodded. Weighing the moment, she swallowed once and said, "Please do not—"

"You are my servant," Leah's words cut her short. "You will serve me as *I* see fit. If the old woman says I must do this to win back the favor of the Kathirat," she looked haughtily at Zilpah, who remained silent, "then that is what we will do." Leah covered her eyes with her hands and sighed. After a moment, she folded her hands in her lap and spoke. "Well, go clean yourself up, girl, and present yourself to Master Jacob."

"What? Now?" the astonished Zilpah asked.

"Of course, now," said Leah. "We have wasted enough time already. But wash your face, girl. You have been crying, and your eyes are puffy. Jacob will not like that." But Zilpah didn't move. "Now, girl!" Leah said. "Stop wasting time."

So Zilpah stood up slowly, wiping her eyes, and went to wash herself. Leah, lost in her own troubled thoughts, did not see the sly smile on the serving girl's face as she left. *Oh, seven sisters, you exact a heavy price*, Leah thought. *If Jacob is to have sons by a slave, at least it will be* my *slave.* That night, and on the nights that followed as Leah sought sleep alone, knowing where Zilpah was, one fierce thought consoled her. *And how will it feel, little sister, when every woman who lies with Jacob can give him sons—except you? How will that feel?*

* * * * *

Later, Zilpah lay in the bed she had shared with Jacob. *It was all so easy*, she thought. *I knew Leah would not want to let me be with Jacob unless*—here she giggled quietly—*unless it became a matter of imposing her will. So all I had to do was make her think I was resisting.* Placing her hands on her belly, she wondered, *Has Jacob's seed already taken root in my womb?* Giggling again, she remembered, *Jacob looked so surprised when I came to him and offered myself to him. He had to go and ask Leah directly.* The thought gave her wicked pleasure.

Leah had to tell Jacob with her own lips, had to say aloud that she wanted her husband to lie with me. How that humbled her, Zilpah thought with satisfaction. In her thoughts, Zilpah addressed her mistress: *You humiliated me because my sister bore his child. Well, tonight was my turn to humble you. I, your lowly servant, now occupy your husband's attentions. I am the one who keeps him from your bed!*

Her energy and her anger spent, she stretched her arms and legs. Drifting off to sleep, a single thought remained. *I was right; Jacob is strong.*

gad

Fortune

"How fortunate I am," Leah said, as she took the infant from Zilpah, "to have this fine son. So I have named him *Gad*." Even as she said the words, Leah sounded melancholy. The servants repeated the name, "Gad! Gad!" but Leah seemed to hardly notice. Jacob beamed. In addition to his ability to build wealth through his management of the flocks and herds, in Gad, Zilpah had given Jacob a seventh son to help him. Lucky seven, named Gad, meaning "fortunate, or lucky." The servants knew that every son made Jacob more secure and that their security grew with his. Not many men could claim to have seven sturdy sons. Their cheers reflected a real sense of joy and greater security and a genuine affection for Zilpah, an affection they generally dared not show, lest a jealous Leah take it out on her hapless serving girl. Still, Leah's melancholy dampened everyone's enthusiasm, and the mood of celebration quickly dissipated.

* * * * *

"Does she understand that you are to have at least two children?" Donatiya asked. "The Kathirat demand Mistress Leah make the same offering as did Mistress Rachel."

"She understands that," said Zilpah, as she sat nursing little Gad. Leah had allowed Zilpah to claim the old woman as her helper. It was a small concession because Leah still expected Zilpah to be her personal servant, as well as care for her own newborn. Now, Donatiya stood behind Zilpah, massaging her weary neck and shoulders. "But she will not be put off forever. She wants more sons!"

"More sons? I think she wants more than that," the old woman said.

"She does want more than that. She really wants Master Jacob to love her," Zilpah said. "She wants him to love her as much as he loves Rachel."

"Foolish woman! All her life she has been so proud *not* to be like Mistress Rachel. Yet she wants to be loved like Rachel. She cannot be both." Gad stirred as Zilpah switched him to the other breast. Donatiya smiled. "He will be a good son for you, Zilpah," the old woman said. "And what about you? Does Master Jacob love you?"

Zilpah looked down at Gad, who had grasped her thumb with his little hand. She smiled sadly. "He is kind to me. When we are together, he treats me with gentleness, almost," she searched for the word, "almost a kind of reverence." She started to speak, but could not. A single tear ran down her cheek. "I did not, expect—Mistress Leah treats me like an ill-fitting sandal. Annoying but necessary." She swallowed once and wiped her eyes. "Master Jacob, he, when we are alone together, he treats me like a princess." Again the sad smile. "He treats me with kindness, but he does not love me, not as he loves Rachel."

Donatiya's voice interrupted Zilpah's reverie. "Then we cannot help Leah to get what she wants."

"We cannot," Zilpah admitted. "When she's not being mean, I almost feel sorry for her," Zilpah said. "She thinks he will love her if she gives him enough sons. But there must be something we can do to, to—"

"To keep her occupied," said Donatiya, her eyes narrowed. "If we cannot give Mistress Leah Master Jacob's love, and we cannot give her sons—"

"What can we give her, then?" Zilpah asked, puzzled.

"For now, we can give her hope." Coming to a decision, Donatiya said, "Later, maybe something more. Have you heard of the *duda'im*? The 'love plant'?"

Zilpah shook her head, " 'Love plant'? I have not. Is that the plant you told me of before?"

The old woman nodded. "Some call it *luffah* or even *beid al-jinn*."

"Jinni's eggs!" Zilpah cried, clutching Gad to her.

"So you know of them?" Donatiya asked.

Zilpah shook her head. "I know that the *jinn* are evil spirits."

Donatiya stroked Zilpah's shoulders. "They say some *jinn* are evil, some good. And these jinni's eggs are supposed to have great power. Power even to give a barren woman a child. That why they call it *duda'im*, 'love plant.'"

"You think this *duda'im* could give Leah another child?"

"Mistress Leah might be able to use *duda'im* that way. Only Nanna and the Kathirat can decide that. And the *duda'im* are very hard to find. Just to find it is a sign of good fortune, an indication of the gods' approval. If we find one, even if Mistress Leah doesn't have another child, she might use it to get what she wants even more."

"What? How—" Zilpah started to ask, but Donatiya cut her off.

"First off, we have to find one. Maybe we will be lucky."

* * * * *

"I do not believe it," Simeon said, and as usual, when Simeon spoke, Levi nodded agreement. "Who told you such a thing?"

Reuben grimaced. His two younger brothers always ganged up on him. *How much should I tell them?* he wondered. "It does not matter," Reuben said. "Mother has ordered us to look for these plants."

"Look for a plant that screams like a man when you pull it from the ground—" Simeon asked.

"And whoever hears the scream dies?" Levi finished Simeon's question.

"That is what Mother says," replied Reuben.

"Then how does anyone know about the sound?" Simeon asked, grinning at Levi.

"If they were dead, how can they tell us about the sound?" Levi said, and now both younger brothers laughed at Reuben.

I should've known better, Reuben thought in disgust. "If you're not going to help me, at least don't tell anyone else about it."

"Tell anyone?" Simeon and Levi said together.

"I mean it!" said Reuben. "Mother will be furious, and nobody wants that! If this gets out, and Mother asks me, I will tell her you two are the ones who told." Simeon and Levi looked at each other solemnly, then back at Reuben. "I intend to look for it," Reuben said, "and if you are not trying to help, at least keep quiet." Simeon and Levi nodded. "And if you should happen to find one, do not pull it up. Just in case the tales are true." Reuben looked from one to the other. Both boys nodded their heads solemnly. Then Simeon punched Levi on the shoulder and took off running. The younger boy squealed, more in outrage than in pain, and took off after his brother. Reuben, with all the wisdom of his eleven summers, thought, *Simeon and Levi, I wonder if those two will ever grow up. No matter. I shall look for these strange plants myself.*

* * * * *

"Why are you telling me this, Sister?" Bilhah asked.

"The old woman assures me that this *duda'im* will help even a barren woman to bear a child." Bilhah seemed not to understand, so Zilpah explained. "Leah believes it. She believes the Kathirat have given her the sons she has. And she believes that, with the aid of these plants, they will give her more. That's why Reuben for certain, and perhaps some of Leah's other sons, are looking for these 'love plants.'" Still, Bilhah showed no comprehension. "Everyone loves Mistress Rachel. This *duda'im* might help her to have the child she so dearly desires."

"Surely Master Jacob would not approve," Bilhah said.

"If he does not know, he will not disapprove."

"I do not think Mistress Rachel—" Bilhah said, but Zilpah cut her short.

"Even if it meant she could bear a child?" Zilpah asked. Bilhah did not speak, so Zilpah made one last appeal. "Will you at least tell her? After all I've risked to give you this information, at least let her choose."

"I will think about what you have said," Bilhah replied. "I will."

Later, when Zilpah returned to Leah's tent, Leah asked, "Did you tell your sister about the *duda'im?*"

"Of course not," Zilpah answered, but she thought, *Of course I did. It is part of Donatiya's plan. I hope the old woman knows what she is doing.*

* * * * *

"I do not care! I must have sons!" Rachel would not be comforted. "Leah has given Jacob sons. You have given him sons. Even your sister has given him a son! Every woman who shares his bed—*everyone but me*—has given him sons. But my womb," she placed her hands on her belly as if to tear the offending organ from her body, "my womb is as barren as the desert. Adonai," she spat out the name. "If He is the God of Jacob, then why does He deny Jacob a son through me? How can I be so cursed?"

Bilhah sat, miserable, listening as her mistress raged. "Cursed? But you are blessed, mistress. Master Jacob loves you, do you not know? My sister and I have spoken often of it. He was kind to us, gentle," she paused to search for the words. "But when he was with us, there was always a sadness. I did not understand it, but Zilpah saw it. He came to me only because he hoped it would make you happy. And Zilpah realized he came to her only to keep Mistress Leah distracted."

"Distracted? Ha! Zilpah schemed because she wanted Jacob's attention. She wanted what you had. Do not deny it!" Rachel's eyes blazed.

"She did scheme to gain Master Jacob's attentions. I see that, and she has admitted that to me. But it has been a bitter pill for her," Bilhah said.

"Bitter for *her*?" Rachel's smoldering temper began to ignite again.

"With respect, mistress," Bilhah insisted, "Mistress Leah resented Master Jacob's attentions to my sister as much as you did. I am sorry to say this, mistress, and I would not presume to speak so, except I know the kindness of your heart."

Bilhah's appeal calmed Rachel somewhat, so she said, "Very well, Bilhah. Speak your mind."

"With respect, mistress, my sister is not the cause of your sorrow. She may deserve some blame for her scheming, but between Leah's resentment and your own, you have made Zilpah's life unbearable."

Rachel, seeing the sad truth of it, seeing what her anger had made of her, began weeping softly. "I see that you are right," Rachel sobbed. "I am so sorry. But I must have a son!" she said, the last words broken by her weeping.

"I know," said Bilhah. "All the servants know you have a kind heart. We have trust in you. And that is why she wants to help. That is why she has told us of Leah's worship of the Kathirat and of her search for the *duda'im*."

"I told Jacob that Ba'al and Nanna and the Kathirat rule here. His precious Elohim may have shown Himself at Beth-El, but He has done nothing for me here. I do not care what Jacob thinks," Rachel stated. "I will do whatever I must to have a son, whether to worship the Kathirat or conjure with the 'love plant.' Tell me more of this *duda'im*!"

So Bilhah told her everything that she had learned. Then Rachel sat, pondering quietly for a time, until she reached a decision. "I must have this *duda'im*. Tell the servants you can trust to be discreet, to keep an eye on Leah's sons. Especially Reuben. I must have it."

But the *duda'im* was not so easily found. Months passed. "Lucky" Gad grew into a toddler. One growing season ended and another began. The celestial lights, Nanna and Utu, raced; the flocks grew and produced great mountains of wool, many lambs and kids, and an abundance of meat and milk. Women sang songs and shooed away mischievous boys while they ground meal, baked bread, and wove beautiful cloth. Jacob lay with Zilpah again, and again she swelled with child. Jacob and Laban experimented with growing wheat, and the results promised even more prosperity. Zilpah gave birth to another strong son.

At the naming ceremony, Leah hoisted the child high and declared with forced cheerfulness, "*Osher!* How happy am I! All of the women will call me happy!" No one dared comment on the irony of her words. "And so I will call him Asher!" She handed the child to Jacob and walked away from the assembly even before the chanting of the servants stopped.

* * * * *

Reuben wiped the sweat running in muddy rivulets down his face. Ahead of him in the wheat field, muscular servants and his father, Jacob, swung their sickles in a steady rhythm, mowing down the grain. Reuben, along with some other older boys and a few women, followed the reapers, bundling the fallen stalks into sheaves. It was hot, dusty work, which the boy did not much like. Reuben preferred working directly with the sheep. True, sheep could be stubborn and frustrating, but at least they were interesting. Reuben even enjoyed working with a particularly cantankerous old ram everyone called Old Stonehead.

Old Stonehead got his name when the herders attempted to move the goats from one area to another. The herders took the contrary goat to the new area first and tied him to a small tree. They hoped that once the others saw him there they would settle in. After the goat chewed through the rope they had used to tie him, bitten the top off the small tree, and eventually uprooted it, one of the senior herdsmen had had enough. Taking up a stout piece of wood, he cornered the goat, and when the ram had charged, he whacked the goat across the forehead with his club. The ram stopped in his tracks, shook his head and snorted, and then charged forward and leveled the herder. Sitting up painfully, the herder looked at the broken club next to him and said, "That old goat's head must be made of stone!"

Reuben smiled at the memory, but the heat of the afternoon sun brought him back to the task at hand. The wheat, turned golden and ready for harvest, was just so much dusty straw to Reuben. All afternoon the boy trudged forward, bending over, rolling up the stalks of wheat and bundling them into a sheaf. Step forward, roll up the stalks of wheat, bundle them into a sheaf, step forward, and repeat the process, each motion stirring up more dust. Just when the boy had come to think that his service in the wheat field would never come to an end, he spotted something. As he rolled up a bundle of wheat, he uncovered something green. A plant that did not belong in the wheat field. He started to rip the weed out of the ground with his free hand, but something about it stopped him. He examined it carefully, his interest and excitement growing. Could this be the *duda'im*? Carefully, he lifted the base leaves, exposing the top of the root. *This is it,* he thought. Realizing he had almost pulled it with his bare hands made him a little queasy. *I could be dead,* he thought. *I must tell Mother and find a way to harvest this dangerous plant safely.* He threw down his bundled wheat and took off running to his mother.

Noting the boy's swift departure, one of the servants cutting the wheat looked back to see what had sent the master's son running. He had just been at that location and doubted it was a snake, but took his sickle anyway, just in case. Instead of a snake, he found something Mistress Rachel would want to know about.

שכירים

sakiyrím

Hirelings

Zilpah helped Leah smooth her robes, and then she stepped back holding her hands out, palms down in a calming gesture. Leah took a deep breath and then nodded quickly twice. Zilpah pulled back the tent flap and bowed in courtesy. "Second wife has come to visit." Zilpah said the words casually, as if speaking of the weather, but her heart raced. *The sisters have not spoken since before the wedding, and now things move so rapidly.* The past few hours replayed themselves in her thoughts.

Not only had Reuben found the *duda'im* in the wheat field, he had harvested them safely. The ingenious lad had tied some twine around the base of the plant, and the other end to a particularly cantankerous old ram known as Old Stonehead.

Reuben knew that Old Stonehead wouldn't stay tied to anything for very long. The stubborn old goat pulled the *duda'im* plant from the ground without seeming to notice it. As a precaution, Reuben had stationed himself some distance away and had covered his ears with wool to protect himself from the reputedly lethal screams of the *duda'im*. He heard nothing, and thus survived. Old Stonehead stalked away, annoyed, but none the worse for wear.

He repeated this operation several times, Old Stonehead becoming slightly more difficult with each attempt, but eventually he had pulled out seven or eight of the *duda'im*. Some of the roots did indeed look like the legs of a man, so Reuben took care as he bundled them and carried them to his mother. *That's when events began to happen quickly.* Zilpah remembered.

"Go to Donatiya," Leah said to Zilpah. "Tell her that we have the love plants. Tell her that now she must find a way for me to have another son."

"I do not know if it is as simple as that," Zilpah said. She started to explain, but a sharp look from Leah stopped her.

"Simple. Not simple. I do not care," said Leah. "The old woman said, she promised—"

"Mistress! Please, mistress, calm yourself."

"Calm myself? You tell me to calm myself? But she promised—she promised. A son, another son. She promised. She promised me a son." Leah began weeping.

"I will go to her," said Zilpah, "but you must get ready, mistress." Zilpah placed her hands on Leah's trembling fingers and then bent down to look directly into Leah's eyes. "You do not want Jacob to see you red-eyed, your face tear-stained, do you?" Leah took a deep breath. "That's better," Zilpah said. "I will go to Donatiya now."

When she found the old woman, Zilpah asked, "What do we do now?"

Donatiya smiled a sly smile. "Go to your sister, and tell her that Mistress Rachel should come to Mistress Leah's tent and ask her for the *duda'im*."

"Ask Mistress Leah? Did you say 'ask Mistress Leah'? They have not spoken to one another for years—since before the wedding! Are you possessed, old woman?" Zilpah asked in horror.

Donatiya gave Zilpah a withering look. "Don't ask me that again!" She shook her finger in Zilpah's face. "If I am, what are you going to do? You think the fertility spell is the only conjure I know? Do you?"

Zilpah, terrified, shook her head. "I am sorry, Donatiya, please forgive me."

The old woman thought a moment. "Forgiven," the old woman said, "but don't call me 'possessed' again."

"I will remember," Zilpah said. "But is it really necessary for Mistress Rachel to ask Mistress Leah personally?"

"It is necessary," Donatiya said.

"But why? I do not understand."

"Because Mistress Leah needs more than *duda'im* if she wants a son," Donatiya said. Seeing only questions in Zilpah's expression, the old woman explained something so obvious that Zilpah did not know how she had failed to see it herself. Donatiya concluded, "So that's what you do now. Convince

Mistress Leah to give up some of the *duda'im*."

"I may be able to persuade her. But she will not be happy about it!" Zilpah started to say something more, but Donatiya leaned back and began laughing uncontrollably. Zilpah felt deeply unsettled. *Maybe we are both possessed,* she thought.

"What has possessed you, Sister?" Bilhah asked when Zilpah went to her. "They have not spoken to one another for years. You think Mistress Rachel will humble herself to ask her sister for some of the *duda'im*?"

"As for being possessed, I hope not," Zilpah said. "And as for Mistress Rachel, how much does she want to have a son?"

Bilhah shrugged. "I guess we will find out. And will your mistress, Leah, grant her sister's request?" Bilhah asked.

"Leave that up to me, Sister," Zilpah said. "Donatiya said something that may make all the difference, especially if your mistress Rachel accepts it as the price that must be paid for the *duda'im* and the opportunity of bearing a child."

"What the old woman said had better be powerful," Bilhah said.

"It is," said Zilpah. Bilhah's expression showed she did not share her sister's confidence, so Zilpah repeated, "Oh, it is."

"Give my sister some of *my duda'im? Give* her? Give *her*?" Leah demanded, once Zilpah had returned to her.

"I did not say 'give,' mistress. I said 'trade.'"

"What can my sister give me that is worth so much?" Leah demanded.

"Mistress, you might be able to conceive without the *duda'im*. You did before," Zilpah explained. "Even with the *duda'im*, you need something more."

"I do?" Leah looked puzzled for a moment, then asked, "And my sister can get this for me?"

"She can," Zilpah said. "When was the last time Master Jacob came to your tent at night?" Leah's eyes went wide. Zilpah wanted to say more, but at that moment, another servant stuck her head in the tent and signaled Mistress Rachel's arrival. "And here she is now." *You worked feverishly to put Donatiya's scheme into place,* Zilpah thought. *It was clever. Now we all find out if it was wise.*

Rachel came into the tent, followed by Bilhah. The two women bowed stiffly. Leah acknowledged their courtesy with a nod. "Welcome, second wife,"

Leah said. Zilpah glanced at Rachel, who flinched visibly. "To what do we owe this visit?" Leah inquired.

Rachel started to speak, her lips trembling. She paused to gain control, but all the years of her barrenness weighed down upon her. The reproach of being the only woman who could not give Jacob a child, of always being the nameless "second wife" crushed her spirit. Every expression of compassion for her plight pressed into her soul. She made to speak again, to bow in humility, but instead she toppled to the ground in front of Leah. Her words came out in sobs. "Please," she implored. "Please give me some of your son's love plants, the *duda'im* he found." Leah did not deign to speak, so Rachel asked again, "Please! I beg of you!"

Zilpah held her breath as Leah pondered a reply. Finally, she spoke, her tone indignant. "Was it not enough that you took *my husband*! Would you now take my son's *duda'im* also?" Leah waited silently, as if no reply was possible.

"Very well," said Rachel. "Let Jacob come to your tent in exchange for some of the *duda'im*." Now every eye focused on Leah. *Don't press any harder,* Zilpah thought. *You have humbled her, but do not push her too far. Even a slave has some pride.*

"So be it," Leah said, and she motioned for Zilpah to fetch the *duda'im*.

* * * * *

The sheaves of wheat stood like sentinels in the slanting rays of the afternoon sun. "This harvest is richer than last year," said Amos, grinning.

Jacob clapped Amos on the shoulder. "That's because you have done such a good job tending the crop." He liked young Amos. The lad had an intense gaze and an almost ferocious grin. He worked hard, he learned fast, and he didn't complain. So Jacob had come to depend on him more and more. And Amos had shown particular talent when it came to growing wheat. He did well enough with sheep and goats, but he loved to manage the crops.

Threshing would begin soon, but for now, they took satisfaction at the long rows of sheaves. The two walked along back toward the main camp in the glow of fatigue and achievement, looking forward to a leisurely bath and a long cool drink of water.

"Amos," Jacob said, "I would like to keep you with me."

"I do not understand, master," Amos replied.

"It has been more than seven years," Jacob said. "I have paid for both brides. Laban's flocks and herds have flourished under my care. I have given him full measure for my wives." Amos, still uncertain as to his master's meaning, simply nodded. Jacob continued, "Someday, Amos, probably soon, I shall return to my homeland. I have little to call my own, but I will need a good servant to help me. I would like you to be that servant."

"A servant goes where he is told," Amos said.

"A faithful servant does," Jacob agreed, "that is true. But I would not want to force you to leave if you wanted to stay."

"I would be glad to serve you, Master Jacob," Amos said, his infectious smile returning.

"I may have but little," Jacob said, "and in that case, the work will be hard, the rewards few."

"Master," Amos replied, "are you asking whether I would prefer to serve you, or stay and work for Master Laban?" The young man's eyebrows rose in amusement. "Do you really wonder?"

Jacob clapped the servant on the shoulder, and the two tired men laughed together. They were still laughing as they neared the camp, where they saw the serving girl Zilpah standing, rocking little Asher in her arms as she waited.

Once they drew near, Jacob, too weary to speak, simply nodded in acknowledgment. "Mistress Leah waits for you, master," Zilpah said. The formality of her words and her manner surprised him.

He stroked the infant's back. "Can I not say Hello to my little Asher?" Jacob inquired.

Zilpah's guarded expression concerned him, so he motioned for Amos to go on alone. "My mistress is eager to see you," Zilpah said. Jacob lifted his dusty, sweat-stained arms, and was about to speak, when Zilpah cut him off. "If she sees you took time to bathe first, she will think I did not take her commands seriously." Jacob nodded wearily. *Might as well get it over with*, he thought. He strode wearily toward Leah's tent. She emerged just as he arrived.

"You will come to my tent, tonight," Leah said. Jacob looked puzzled, but before he could speak, she said, "I have hired you with my son's love plants. So go and bathe yourself and come to my tent. You will lie with me tonight."

Jacob asked, " 'Love plants'? What are you speaking of?"

"Do not pretend you do not know of what I speak," said Leah. *"Duda'im,* the love plants." Jacob still seemed confused, so Leah pressed home the point. "Your precious little second wife has no children, and she has given up on Elohim! She's going to use the *duda'im* to conjure a spell, to curry favor with the Kathirat so that they will give her children. And since my Reuben found them, we made a trade, she and I. She got some of the love plants—and I got you."

Jacob felt numb. *Rachel, his precious Rachel, had she abandoned his God? Would she really seek the aid of the gods of the loathsome Kinnahu?* Fatigue, grief, and fear, slowed his steps. He moved toward Rachel's tent and saw Bilhah standing there, waiting for him. "Is it true then? Has Rachel *traded me* for some love plants?" He saw from her expression that it was true, but he needed her to say the words. "Is it true, girl? Tell me! Is it true?"

Tears welled in the girl's eyes. "She wants to give you a son so desperately, master," Bilhah said. "She can think of nothing else." They stood silently for a moment. "She will try anything."

"The Kathirat? Goddesses of the Kinnahu?" Jacob asked, knowing the answer, needing to hear the answer, yet not wanting to hear it. "Tell me, Bilhah," Jacob said, "tell me truly. Did I ever treat you or your sister like a woman I paid to share my bed?" Bilhah shook her head miserably. "Can you even imagine that I ever treated . . . ," now his voice failed him. He turned away.

As the water of his bath washed away the fatigue of the day and the dust of the harvest, Jacob pondered what had brought him to this sorry state. Suddenly, the realization came to him, hard and sharp as a flint knife. *It is true that I never treated any of the women who have shared my bed as though they were harlots whom I paid for their services. But it is also true that I came to view my nights with Leah as a chore, and I resented it. That resentment led me to neglect my husbandly duty. So now she has paid for me, and I have no excuse for resenting it. I have received what I deserved.*

As he finished bathing, a sense of resignation and a purpose settled on him. *She has hired me. It is only just that she receives fair value.*

Jacob was a man of his word, and Leah would receive what she had paid for. In time, Leah conceived again, and again she bore a son. She blessed Zilpah and Donatiya and vowed eternal loyalty to the Kathirat. They had rewarded her devotion, and she would not forget.

"Sakar! My payment, my reward! This son is my payment! *Is Sakar!* My

reward!" She held the infant high. "So I named him Issachar!" *Your payment?* Jacob wondered. *How many sons did those love plants pay for? How many of my nights did you purchase?* Jacob stared into the distance. He did not notice Rachel watching him. He did not realize she saw the pain in his eyes.

So Issachar is Leah's payment, thought Rachel. *She believes the Kathirat rewarded her. But what did I receive? And what has been the cost?*

Time passed and Issachar grew. The celestial lights continued their circuits. Jacob faithfully discharged his responsibilities—all of them. And so the flocks continued to prosper, the wheat grew in ever greater profusion. Laban's possessions, under Jacob's stewardship, had multiplied manyfold. Donatiya became Rachel's nurse, making potions from the *duda'im.* But it was Leah, not Rachel, who conceived once again. And once again, Leah gave birth to a son.

"What a marvelous gift, a *zebed,* I have received in this, another son!" This time, Leah truly beamed. "I have been exalted by this sixth son of my own body!" Fixing both Rachel and Jacob with her gaze, she continued, "My husband will exalt, will *zabal,* he will exalt me, for I have given him six sons! Therefore, I shall call this child *zebed, zabal*—Zebulun!"

The servants took up the chant, "Zebulun! Zebulun!" They were truly rejoicing, for Jacob now had ten sons. Ten! Surely the gods had blessed them. Surely prosperity would follow them into the future.

Ten sons, yet not one from my body, Rachel lamented. *I traded my Jacob's attentions for . . . for what? I still have no son, and Jacob has never been the same toward me. What a fool I have been!*

In the months and years that followed, Jacob remained constant in his attentions to Leah. She did have another child—a daughter she named Dinah—but no more sons. No matter how she petitioned the Kathirat, no matter how she conjured with the *duda'im,* she had no more sons. Slowly, slowly, she came to realize that Jacob had become a hireling husband, doing his duty. No amount of scheming, no divination, not even six sons from her own body, could purchase any more than that.

Even though she said nothing, in time Jacob sensed her resignation, her emotional retreat. More and more, when he came to her tent, he brought his roll of rawhide and a charcoal stick. Leah never bothered to inquire anymore about the marks on the rawhide. When she had, years before, Jacob went into a long explanation of how he chose which sheep and goats to breed.

"Have you ever wondered," Jacob asked, "why an almost totally black doe gives birth to some kids that are solid colored as she is, but to more that are spotted and speckled?" Leah started to say that, in fact, she had never given it even the slightest thought, but Jacob did not pause for a response. Pointing to rolls and rolls of rawhide he'd kept for many years, he said, "And yet I have never seen two spotted or speckled goats produce a solid-colored kid. With sheep," he said, warming to his topic, "it is a little different, but a similar type of thing happens." He kept going on and on, but Leah had little interest in kids or lambs of any coloration at any time. Clearly, it fascinated Jacob, but Leah could not understand it, and when she tried she got a headache.

Eventually, when he spoke of such things, Leah would reply, "Why do you work so hard to make my father rich? Have you not served your time? If you had not agreed to work an extra seven years for your barren second wife, you could have been making yourself wealthy. I have given you strong sons. You should be a man of great substance, but you keep working as my father's hireling."

At first, Jacob had tried to answer her, but as time went on and she asked the same question again and again, he realized that no answer would satisfy her. And then he realized that he was no longer satisfied. He realized that Leah had spoken a truth. *I have served my time, earned my pay,* Jacob thought. *I do not want to be a hireling my entire life. I need to think about providing for my own family.*

אימה

'eymah

Fright

"You promised to protect me!" Donatiya hissed in Zilpah's ear.

"Zilpah! What is that?" Leah asked in the darkness, not bothering to lift her head up from her pillow.

"I will see," Zilpah said, at the same time urgently signaling Donatiya to meet her outside the tent. Zilpah knew that Leah would not stir if not further disturbed.

"What has you so afraid that you come into Leah's tent in the middle of the night?"

"You promised to protect me," Donatiya said again.

"I will," said Zilpah, "but I must know what the problem is."

"She sent me away," Donatiya said. "Now she plans to sell me. I don't want to end up starving in the foundation of some rich man's house."

"Mistress Leah sent you away?" It didn't make any sense. "I have been with her constantly for weeks, and I have heard her say nothing about you at all."

"Not Mistress Leah," Donatiya said, "Mistress Rachel. She sent me away just now. She is going to sell me!" The old woman began sobbing.

"What did she say?" Zilpah asked.

"She said my spells are no good," Donatiya said. "She said that the Kathirat have not helped her conceive. She said that she has given up on my conjuring and on the potions made from the love plants."

"That does not mean she would sell you," Zilpah said. "Did actually she say that she would sell you?"

The old woman shook her head, "She did not say she would sell me. But she did say that she did not need my help anymore. I know what masters do when they don't need servants any longer." Donatiya looked at Zilpah with pleading eyes. "You promised to protect me."

Zilpah thought for a moment, then said, "Let me talk to my sister tomorrow. If there is any chance that Mistress Rachel is thinking of selling you, Bilhah will know. I doubt that Mistress Rachel would do such a thing. But I *will* protect you." Zilpah looked inquiringly at the old woman, and Donatiya nodded her assent. "Mistress Leah gave you to me, remember?" Once again, the little old woman nodded. "Mistress Rachel is not one to take revenge."

The two women parted in the night.

* * * * *

"Forgive me, my husband," Rachel said, when they were alone.

Jacob did not speak. He still loved Rachel desperately, but ever since she had sold his services to Leah for the love plants, there had been a distance between them. She had hurt him deeply, but he did not know how to speak of it. It pained him even more to think of her petitioning the Kathirat, so he did not speak of that, either. Silence had become a habit.

"Forgive me," Rachel said, "I realize that in my desire to give you children, I focused on my own needs. Blinded by my own pain, I did not see how much I hurt you."

Now Jacob felt he must speak, but he still did not know how to express himself. Her words had touched the wound in his spirit, and the emotions he had kept in check so long overwhelmed his tongue. Rachel spoke again, interrupting his thoughts.

"You never treated me, never treated Bilhah or Zilpah like paid bedmates." He looked at her with surprise. She nodded, and taking his face in her hands, she said, "Bilhah told me what you said that day—the day that I foolishly traded your attentions for those love plants." She touched her forehead to his, tears silently flowing. "Please, Jacob, forgive me. Tell me that I did not lose your love forever."

Now Jacob wept as well, tears of relief washing the pain from his soul. "Never," he said. "You could never lose my love." And he kissed her with a passion neither of them had felt for a long time. "Never."

Later, she explained, "When Leah declared Issachar her 'payment,' I saw the pain in your eyes," Rachel said. "And then I realized what I had traded away. Only later did I realize that in seeking the aid of the Kathirat, I had rejected you in another way by rejecting your God." She folded her hands. "I still want a son, but not at the price of losing your love. I do not pretend to understand the ways of your God or your devotion to Him. But at some point, I realized that your devotion to Him makes your devotion to me possible. So I will try—I am but a woman after all—I will try to be content with you and wait for Him to give me a son."

"My blessed Rachel," Jacob said, taking her hands in his. "I sometimes think the passing years have taught me little." He drew her hands to his lips and kissed them. "My God, the God of my father, Isaac, and his father, Abraham, is a strange God. Even though I still try sometimes, I have come to realize that I cannot buy His favor. And this painful breach between us has made me see again that some things cannot be bought." He pressed his cheek against her hands, his eyes searching the past, seeking for words. The silence broken, pent-up words came rushing out. "I thought I could buy the birthright from my brother," Jacob said. "I thought I could steal my father's blessing. So I tried. And when I came here, I bargained my labor for your bride-price. And when Laban and Leah tricked me into marrying her first, I learned that whatever could be bought could also be stolen."

He looked at Rachel with tenderness. "And now we both have learned that the most important things cannot be purchased, but neither can they be taken from us. At Beth-El, I discovered that El Shaddai has given me His favor. My mother—I have not told you this before—my mother had a dream before I was born, telling her that I, the second child, would rule over my brother. But I did not wait for El Elyon to honor His promise. First, I tried to purchase His favor from my brother, and then I tried to trick it from my father. That brought me only heartache and exile. And after all that, as I ran from home, El Elyon assured me at Beth-El that if I would serve Him, He would be with me. That is when I realized that I could not purchase His favor, but neither can anyone take it from me."

Rachel shook her head. "I have told you before, Jacob, this God of yours, this El Elyon, or El Shaddai, or whoever He is, this God of many names seems so strange. You cannot bargain with Him, as you can with other gods." She looked at Jacob, questioning.

"It seems so," Jacob agreed. "As you say, He is . . . He is mysterious. I do not understand Him either."

"But you serve Him faithfully—" Rachel began, but Jacob would not have it.

"I serve Him poorly," Jacob said. "I, I struggle with Him. I cannot seem to understand when I must do for myself and when I should wait for Him." They sat silently for a moment.

"I will, I will struggle with Him, too, then," Rachel said. "Bilhah tells me that Donatiya, the old woman who told us about the love plants, who helped us appeal to the Kathirat, she fears that she will be sold, now that I have abandoned my appeals to those seven sisters."

"Does her continued presence trouble you?" Jacob asked.

"It does not. May I assure her that you will not sell her?" Rachel asked.

"I see no reason to," Jacob said. "If my plans succeed, our need for help will increase, not decrease."

"Will He—will El Elyon grant me a son? Even after I spurned Him for the Kathirat?"

"I cannot say. He gave my mother twins after twenty years of waiting. He gave my grandmother a son after she was ninety years of age." He looked at her directly. "I do not know what He will do. I only know what He has done, what He can do."

Again, Rachel shook her head. "The other gods are greedy. Sometimes you can buy them off. They may be unreliable, like people, but at least I can understand them. But your God—"

"I may not understand El Shaddai, but unlike the others, He has made it plain *He knows me*." And as he said the words, Jacob realized the truth of it for the very first time.

"He *knows* you? That frightens me," Rachel said.

Jacob nodded. "It frightens me too." They sat silently for a time.

"Now, tell me about these plans of yours," Rachel said.

"You want to hear about sheep and goats?" Jacob asked, surprised.

"I do," Rachel said, her eyes aglow. But she thought, *I just want to hear your voice.*

He reached for a roll of rawhide and began telling her about the mysterious marks he had made there. Having reconciled, Jacob and Rachel behaved almost like young lovers again.

As for Leah, even with Zilpah's help, six sons occupied much of her time. Having resigned herself to her fate, she seldom troubled either Jacob or Rachel. Now she looked to her sons to meet her needs.

* * * * *

Rachel did not perceive the changes when they first came, and then she feared to credit them. The new moon came and went, then another. Before the third new moon came, Rachel knew for certain from the changes in her body that she was with child, yet she said nothing. She refused to risk disappointing Jacob. And, truthfully, she feared to speak of it, lest El Elyon change His mind and take the child from her. Rachel still struggled with Jacob's God.

Bilhah fussed over Rachel endlessly, and eventually everyone came to suspect that Rachel, the "second wife, but first in his heart," was finally with child.

* * * * *

"How long have you known?" Leah demanded. Zilpah started to shake her head, but Leah raised her voice. "Do not play with me, girl. *How long?*"

"I have suspected for some time," Zilpah replied. *Keep your eyes downcast,* she thought. *Give Leah no excuse to punish you.* In truth, Bilhah had suggested the possibility that Rachel might finally be with child weeks earlier, and the two servant sisters had prayed earnestly that it might be true and that the child would be the longed-for son. *But I did not know,* Zilpah reminded herself.

"You suspected. I see," Leah said. Zilpah could feel the force of her mistress' anger growing, so she kept her eyes focused on the floor. "Why, then, did you not tell me?"

"You do not like me to speak of her—of the second wife," Zilpah said.

Leah considered it for a moment and seemed pacified. For now. "Send for Donatiya. I must know if this child will be a son. The old conjurer should be able to tell me."

"I will summon her, mistress, but," Zilpah hesitated, "she has not been with Mistress—with the second wife for some time."

"Has she not? What of the Kathirat? The love plants?"

"Second wife gave up on them long ago and told Donatiya she had no more need of her help," Zilpah said, almost breathless, hoping to forestall an explosion from Leah.

"Then how?" Leah seemed totally baffled. Zilpah had no answer, so merely shrugged in a gesture of helplessness. In a moment, Leah regained her composure, and said, "Jacob will no doubt credit his God of many names." Leah pursed her lips, and Zilpah held her breath. But the storm of emotions seemed to leave, and Leah spoke calmly, talking to herself. "If it is a son, he will be number eleven. My Reuben is still firstborn. Nothing can change that." To Zilpah she said, "Summon Jacob's firstborn son, Zilpah. Summon my Reuben."

"You must assert yourself more, Reuben," said Leah, when the boy entered her tent. "As the firstborn, you are entitled to many privileges, but they also bring responsibilities." Leah kept talking, but Reuben no longer heard her.

I know, I know, thought Reuben. *You tell me this every day, Mother. "Be more assertive, Reuben. You are firstborn. Take charge." I have heard it all a hundred times, Mother.*

"Listen to me, Reuben," Leah said, raising her voice.

"I am listening, Mother," Reuben replied.

"It is more important now than ever before. My sister is with child. She may have a son," Leah said. "Do you understand now why you must be more assertive? Do you?"

The news took away what few words Reuben usually could muster in his mother's presence. He opened his mouth, but no reply emerged.

"You must continually remind everyone that you are the firstborn," Leah said. "By your words, by your actions. You must lead." She shook her finger in his face. "Can you get that through your head?"

But Reuben's thoughts were a jumble. *You want me to lead, to assert myself,* he thought. *But Father keeps telling me the opposite. He will not have his firstborn lording over the others, so he says. No matter what I do, I displease one of you.* He took a deep breath and immediately regretted it.

"And be respectful, young man!" Leah said. "Do not treat me as if I were one of your contrary animals. What are you laughing at, young man?"

Reuben started to say, "Nothing, Mother," but her words made him think of Old Stonehead, and he laughed in spite of his intentions. A stinging slap stopped his laughter.

"You will give me respect, Reuben. And do not look on me with angry eyes!" Leah said, hands on her hips now.

His mother's anger extinguished the sputtering flame of Reuben's will to resist. He bowed his head meekly. "I will respect you, Mother." Leah grasped his chin and made him look her in the eyes. Satisfied with the submission she saw there, she dismissed him.

* * * * *

"Did he really say that, mistress?" Bilhah asked, giggling.

"He did!" Rachel replied, laughing while caressing her expanding belly with her arm. She stood at her full height, stroking her chin as Jacob often stroked his beard when perplexed, and said, in her most masculine voice, " 'I do not wish to upset you, dear, but it seems to me like you have been putting on weight lately.' " And they leaned on each other, both giggling uncontrollably again. "And then I said, 'Upset me? I have waited years for this.' And he said, he said . . ." She covered her mouth with her hand, laughing silently as Bilhah waited, eyes alight. "And he said," here she used her deepest voice again, " 'Why have you waited? We have had plenty of food.' " Once again the two women dissolved in laughter.

"So what did you say, then?" Bilhah asked when she regained her breath.

"I said, 'My dear, it was not food that I lacked; although I shall need more food now.' That stumped him," Rachel said, "so much that he stopped stroking his beard, and he said, 'Why is that?' 'Because I will be eating for two,' I said."

Wide-eyed now, Bilhah asked, "What did he do then?"

"I could see his mind working, and when it hit him, he picked me up and began dancing around the tent, whooping and hollering."

"What did he say?" asked Bilhah.

Rachel hesitated. *His exact words had been,* "Praise El Shaddai. A son at last. A son of my own," *she remembered.* Seeing the happiness in Bilhah's face, she said, "He praised El Shaddai. And so do I."

Out with the flocks, Jacob told Amos the news. "A son at last, Amos. A son of my own."

"I am pleased for you. But one thing puzzles me, master," Amos replied. Jacob nodded his permission, so Amos continued. "Two things, really. First, how do you know it will be a son?"

"Because El Shaddai gave my mother two sons and my grandmother a son, after both had appeared barren for many years," Jacob explained. "I believe El Shaddai has done this for Rachel as well."

"But why did you say, 'A son at last, Amos. A son of my own'? Do you not count the other ten sons as your own?"

Shock filled Jacob's face. "Thank you for pointing that out, Amos. Promise me you will not tell anyone else."

"I will tell no one," Amos said, and Jacob knew that the young man could be trusted.

"Of course, the others are counted as my sons," Jacob said, but something in the sound of those words put him on edge, and his face darkened. "I must never say such a thing again," he said, musing to himself. Then louder, addressing Amos, "Favoritism tore my family apart, so I vowed never to let it affect my home. I must never say—must never think it again." And then his expression lightened again.

"A son, Amos! For my beautiful Rachel, a son. Now she can be happy; we can be contented," Jacob said, and Amos beamed.

יסף

yasaph

Increase

In her earlier years, at least, Leah had seemed to conceive effortlessly; but it had not been so for Rachel, and the pattern repeated itself for carrying the child and giving birth. Being with child confirmed Leah's sense of value to her husband and she thrived; but although Rachel had coveted the experience, each new day left her weak and weary. Giving birth left her looking so frail, Jacob feared for her. But the child—*a son!*—vigorous and strong, gave her courage. Jacob saw the pride in Rachel's eyes as she held the newborn.

"You were right, Jacob," Rachel said. "El Shaddai did remember me. He honored your trust in Him. He listened to me so that I could conceive and give birth to this precious son. Adonai Elohim has taken away my disgrace."

Jacob could barely speak. Jacob saw something different in this child even when he was but an infant. "He has your eyes," Jacob said to Rachel. "When I look upon him, I see your loving eyes."

"I see your faith," Rachel said. "This is a child of faith, and I know he will be a man like you. A man of steadfast faith."

"A child in your image," Jacob said. "I have everything I could have wished for."

"Oh, I shall give you another son," Rachel said, but faintly, her strength ebbing.

Seeing her, small and suffering, Jacob felt a twinge of concern. "You have given me a son, Rachel, but at great cost to yourself. Do you think it wise—"

"Remember when I said to you, 'Give me children or I shall die'?" Rachel asked.

"I remember."

"Well, I will hold El Shaddai to that. He will give me another son before I die," Rachel said.

"Hold El Shaddai? Nothing, no one can hold or constrain Him. Be careful what you say about—"

"He will," Rachel insisted. "He has removed, *asaph*, my reproach, and He will increase, will *Joseph* my house. The removal, *asaph*, and the increase, *Joseph*, go together."

"I am grateful to El Shaddai for you and for this son," Jacob said, but still focused on her apparent frailty, he continued, "but let us be satisfied with this one child."

"If Leah can give you six sons, why should I not give you the same?" Rachel inquired. Not waiting for a response, she said, "This child is the guarantee of your increase, your *Joseph*. So I name him Joseph, *increase*, to remind you every time you say his name that your God will *increase* your household."

Something about Rachel's words unsettled Jacob, but nothing he could identify. The birth of Joseph changed everything. *Increase*. For some time, Jacob had been formulating a plan to increase his personal wealth. With the birth of Joseph, of Increase, the time had come to *act*.

* * * * *

Laban returned to his camp, relieved. "How did it go?" Adinah asked him, as soon as she saw him. "Will he stay?"

Laban clapped his hands in delight and began to chuckle softly. "He will stay."

Adinah and Laban had worried for months that Jacob might be preparing to leave them. He had been with them for more than fourteen years, and therefore had fulfilled his obligation for both of his wives. But it was plain to both Laban and Adinah that Jacob possessed skills in handling flocks and herds that few could match. "Even the servants obey him willingly," Laban said.

Early on, Jacob's skill had surprised Laban, to the point where he consulted Adinah. "How can we find the source of Jacob's power with the animals?" he had asked his wife.

She had inquired among the servants, as to who might be able to help them discover their son-in-law's secret. That search led her to an old woman servant who currently attended to Zilpah, their daughter Leah's handmaid.

One day they summoned the old woman secretly to ask her. When she heard the question, Donatiya frowned. "His God is powerful," the old woman said. "My spells do not work in his camp. Even the love plants, the *duda'im*, do not work there." She leaned forward, confiding, "Master Jacob's God is not like other gods. He does not . . . ," the woman closed her eyes, searching for the right words. "He does not bargain. He does what He will do." She looked at Laban sharply. "Be careful. Jacob's God watches over him. Whatever Jacob does, his God prospers." She rose to her full height and looked Laban straight in the eyes, something that unnerved him, because servants rarely were so bold. "Watch how you deal with Jacob."

The interview left Laban unsettled. The old woman had convinced him that more than skill was involved in Jacob's prosperity. Perhaps the skill itself represented part of the blessing imparted by the One Jacob referred to as El Shaddai. In any case, the old woman left no doubt that Jacob's God, this El Shaddai, was not one to be trifled with. That revelation left Laban with the conflict between his desire to take advantage of Jacob's skills and his fear of what Jacob's God would do if he, Laban, tried to be too crafty.

As the months passed, Laban's and Adinah's anxiety grew. For Jacob had eleven sturdy sons that grew every day, and soon they would all be big enough to help their father. With a few livestock to start his own herds and flocks, Jacob would be self-sufficient and would no longer need Laban. On the other hand, Laban and Adinah still had great need for Jacob's skills. Their own sons lacked those abilities, as did Laban himself, in large part. So, Jacob's seemingly inevitable imminent departure greatly concerned his in-laws. Adinah wondered what could have happened, how the confrontation should have gone so well as to leave Laban so obviously in high spirits.

"Husband, I begin to suspect you have bested our son-in-law in bargaining. I cannot imagine what else would make you so cheerful."

Laban's eyes lit up; his face fairly glowed. "Are you suggesting I would try to take advantage of our son-in-law? Of course not. In fact, he suggested the compensation he desired for remaining here and managing our animals."

"If he suggested it, then how can you be so pleased?" And then she asked, "Can one so skilled at handling the flocks not be skilled at bargaining?"

"I cannot say about that. I can only say that the terms of his continued employment surely favor us more than they favor him."

"I do not understand, my husband. What are these terms, and how did they come to favor us?" Adinah's face showed her puzzlement.

"Here's what happened."

Jacob had walked all the way to Laban's camp. When he saw Jacob walking toward him that day, Laban knew what his son-in-law had come for. For all the times he and Adinah had discussed this possibility, he still had found no solution, nor even any approach he felt confident of.

"Send me on my way," Jacob began, "and let me return to my own homeland. Give me my children and my wives for whom I have served you these fourteen years, and I will go. You know how well I have served you."

So, the moment has come, Laban thought. Looking at Jacob, he realized, *He knows that I need him more than he needs me. No point in trying to deny it then.* Laban nodded. "If I have found favor in your sight," Laban began deferentially, "please," and here he looked directly into Jacob's eyes, "please, stay." He paused for a moment to judge Jacob's response. Seeing nothing negative, he hurried on. "I have learned—the priestess Donatiya affirmed it—that your God, the One you call El Shaddai, has blessed me because of you."

Another pause, but Jacob's expression remained noncommittal. *I am desperate,* thought Laban, *and he knows it. Since he knows it, it will gain me nothing to pretend otherwise.* Laban held his hands widely outstretched, a gesture of openness and helplessness. "Name your wages, and I will pay them."

Jacob cupped his chin in his hand, apparently calculating. Now he, too, spread his hands. "You know how I worked for you," he said, building his case. "You know how your livestock have fared under my care, and that my God, El Shaddai, has prospered you wherever you have put me in charge of your affairs." Jacob looked at Laban, who nodded. "But now, I ask myself—I ask you—may I do something for my own household?"

Nodding vigorously, Laban said, "What can I give you?" *What indeed,* he thought. *What can I give you to stay, and will there be anything left for me?*

Jacob waited, letting the suspense build. "You need give me nothing," Jacob said. *Here it comes,* thought Laban. Jacob continued, "But if you would do this one thing for me, I will go on watching your flocks and taking care of them.

"Let me go through the flocks," Jacob said, "and remove all the spotted and speckled sheep, the dark lambs, and the spotted and speckled goats. You can keep the handsome, solid-colored ones for yourself. The spotted and speckled goats and sheep and the dark lambs will be my wages. And you will always know which ones belong to you and which ones belong to me. You can check my flocks and herds at any time. Any goat or sheep that is not spotted or speckled, any lamb that is not dark, will be considered stolen."

The story finished, Laban looked at Adinah with delight. "We keep all the handsome, beautiful solid-colored animals, and he gets the ragtag remnants."

Adinah did not feel as confident as her husband did. "Are you certain this is a good idea?"

"Certain? I am! Especially after I went through and separated them. You should see how splendid our animals appear."

"You did this already? You agreed to this?" Adinah asked.

"Before he could have second thoughts," said Laban, "I separated the solid-colored from the others and sent his speckled and spotted lot to his sons to take care of."

"What will keep them separate?" Adinah asked, still concerned.

"We are moving camp. I have found another place, three days' journey from here." Adinah started to protest, but Laban cut her off. "You will like it. Fresh water, some trees."

"But how will Jacob take care of our flocks if it is so far from his camp?" Adinah asked.

"A man walking alone can make the journey much faster. But it would take three days to move a group of animals so far," Laban said, delight in his eyes.

"So we would know if he took any of our animals! You are so clever, husband!" Adinah said, her eyes showing admiration. Later, as she lay in bed, doubts filled her mind. *The way Laban explains it, we got the better part of the bargain, but we want to keep Jacob's services because he is so shrewd.* She shook her head in the darkness. *What is Jacob thinking?*

* * * * *

What is Master Jacob thinking? Amos wondered. Early in the day, Jacob had sent a group of servants down to a nearby stream with instructions to cut bundles of small branches and bring them to the area where they watered the sheep and goats. Once they had enough, he told them to peel off strips of bark, so that the remaining staves were striped and spotted. Finally, Jacob and Amos stuck them in the ground behind the watering troughs for the animals, so that the animals would face the striped and spotted wall of sticks when they drank. All the servants wondered but knew better than to ask if Master Jacob did not welcome questions. And other than giving instructions, he had spoken little today—none of the good-natured joking and chatter he usually engaged in with the working men, so they did not ask.

When the two were alone, out of the hearing of the others, Amos finally inquired the purpose of this strange-looking fence. "Have you heard that if a woman who is with child sees a man with a withered hand, it will cause her to give birth to a child with a withered hand?"

Amos, puzzled, said, "I have heard such notions."

"Do you think that those same people might believe that a pregnant goat, seeing the striped and spotted branches, might give birth to spotted and speckled kids?" Jacob asked.

"I suppose they might," Amos replied.

"And that might explain why there were more spotted and speckled kids than solid-colored ones?" Jacob asked again. And when Amos looked doubtful, he said, "That is, it would explain it to those same people."

Still troubled, Amos said, "I suppose it might." He paused, pondering, and asked, "Do you believe that this will cause more spotted and speckled kids to be born and increase your flocks?"

Jacob just smiled and said, "It does not matter what I think. Those striped and spotted sticks were not put there for me."

Whatever the cause, every year Jacob made sure that the strongest breeding does and ewes drank at the troughs with the striped and spotted sticks, and every year the flocks and herds produced more spotted and speckled kids and more dark lambs than the solid-colored ones. And, in accordance with the bargain he had struck with Laban, Jacob separated those spotted and speckled young for himself. As soon as they were able, he had them removed the three days' journey to his own camp.

And what Donatiya told Laban was true. Jacob's God, El Shaddai, did prosper him. Laban's herds and flocks of solid-colored animals grew large and strong. As quickly as Laban's herds and flocks grew, Jacob's increased faster. Caring for his burgeoning livestock required more servants, and they needed camels and donkeys, which, in turn, required yet more servants to care for them. So Jacob quietly accumulated animals, servants, and possessions, in the process, becoming one of the wealthiest men in the region. But because they were three days' journey distant from Laban's animals and because they started with far fewer animals, for a long time Laban and his household did not notice.

gez

Shearing

"Something is wrong," Jacob said.

Leah and Rachel eyed each other warily. Exactly why Jacob had called them together they did not know, but it must be important. Silently, they waited.

"Your brothers have been saying that I am stealing from your father," Jacob said. "They say I have stolen everything we have worked so hard for."

"Adnan and Jascher?" Leah sniffed. "They always complain about everything. Father never pays any attention."

"This is serious," Jacob countered, anger in his voice. "This time, I think he is listening to them. His behavior toward me lately has changed, and not for the better."

"Our flocks *have* grown rapidly. So strange," Leah said. "The spotted and speckled ones increase faster than the solid-colored ones. None of our flocks give birth to solid-colored young, but Father's solid-colored ones continue to bring forth spotted and speckled along with the solid-colored young."

Jacob and Rachel exchanged a glance. "You remember the rawhides with the marks on them?" Jacob asked, and Leah nodded. "While I studied those marks, El Shaddai showed me that would be true. Solid-colored parents give birth to some speckled and spotted young, but it never happens the other way around. And the strongest of the solid-colored ones will get spotted and speckled young, while the weaker ones will not. So El Shaddai has blessed me from your father's flocks, and from my own."

Jacob had told her of this before, but for the first time Leah understood. "Do not worry, husband," Leah said. "Father's anger—if he is angry—will pass."

"I do not think so," Jacob said, "not this time. And El Shaddai has told me it is time to return to my homeland."

"In that case, Father will have to give us," she gestured to herself and to Rachel, "the dowry he owes. The bride-price you earned rightly belongs to us, to care for us in our old age."

"That will not happen, Leah. Have I not told you that?" Jacob demanded, voice rising. "Your father has no intention of dealing fairly with us. He wants to change my wages. He checks the spotted and speckled livestock to see if we are using paint to change their coloring. He thinks I have cheated him!"

And then, anxiously, Leah inquired, "Do we still have *any* share in the inheritance of our father's estate?"

"He does not recognize your claim," Jacob told her.

Slowly, reality settled on Leah, and anger filled her eyes. "Does he regard us as foreigners?"

Rachel nodded, now prodding her older sister. "Not only has he sold us, but he has used up what was paid for us!" Sensing the moment, she looked at Jacob. "If that is the way he treats us, surely all the wealth that El Shaddai took away from our father belongs to us and our children. So do whatever your God has told you!" Rachel looked at Leah, and the sisters nodded in agreement.

"We must lay our plans and choose our time carefully," Jacob said. "Do not speak of this to anyone. Give your father no opportunity to block our plans." Again the wives nodded.

* * * * *

"He has made a fool of you, Laban." Adinah said the words flatly, without emotion.

"He has," replied Laban, voice dangerously quiet. "I know *why* he was named ʿaqob, 'crooked,' but I cannot discover *how* he does it. If I say, 'The spotted young shall be yours,' all the newborn lambs and goats are spotted. If I say, 'The streaked young shall be yours,' all the newborns are streaked."

"I thought I had seen some solid-colored yearlings—" Adinah started, but Laban cut her off.

"A few are born each year, enough to keep our flocks and herds growing slowly, while Jacob's holdings multiply."

"Your sons have noticed. It looks to them as though Jacob has enriched himself by taking from you, that all his wealth results from simple theft, and that everything Jacob possesses really belongs to you. They are angry with you because you do nothing to stop the plundering of what would be their inheritance," Adinah said.

"They have not been reluctant to share those views with me," Laban said bitterly. "But I cannot simply raid his camp and take everything back."

"Is that what Adnan and Jascher want you to do?" Adinah asked.

Laban nodded. "They do." Laban's face tightened. "My son-in-law makes me look the fool, and my sons mutiny against me! I wish Jacob had never come here. Raiding his camp and killing him would solve a lot of my problems. If it could be proven he stole from me, no one would question my actions."

"But remember what the old woman, Donatiya, said to us. She warned us to take care how we dealt with Jacob. She said his God, this El—El Shaddai is powerful and watches over him." Adinah's expression betrayed her fear.

Laban had been looking in the distance, but at Adinah's words his gaze shifted to her face. "I remember," he said. "And the way the young lambs and kids always are marked so that they favor Jacob gives me reason to believe she may be right. That is why I have not acted before now. That—and lack of proof!"

"What can you do?"

"Everyone makes mistakes. Sooner or later, Jacob will do something that will give me an excuse to act against him. Until then," he sighed as he ran his fingers through his hair, then he pursed his lips in an expression of resignation, "we wait."

"Your sons will not be happy," Adinah warned him.

"I am not happy either," Laban said so sharply that Adinah recoiled. His eyes glittered with hatred. "I will not tolerate mutiny, and I will not tolerate being made a fool of much longer. Jacob will make a mistake, and when he does—*I will strike.*"

* * * * *

"Shearing time," Rachel said. "I can hardly wait. It will be such fun watching little Joseph as he experiences the festivities. This will be the first time he is old enough to know what is happening! I want to see his reaction as they herd the sheep and goats to the village with the shearing shed."

"We move the flocks and herds," Jacob said, his eyes focused on something far away. "Everyone expects it. And that is our biggest operation of the entire year." Jacob said. "Moving the flocks and herds several days' journey to the shearing place. The shearers can shear only so many sheep at a time, so each owner must bring his animals in separately."

Tillers of the soil mark their years around the two great seasons of feverish activity—seed time and harvest. By contrast, shepherds mark the great events of shearing and lambing. Early in the spring, before the ewes drop their lambs, comes the great festival of shearing time. The fleeces have grown long and heavy for winter, but with the cold weather past, the dense wool would be an inconvenience at lambing time and a burden to the sheep in the warming days ahead. And so shearing time is the first great event after the winter. But it is a specialized task, and the herds and flocks must be moved to where the shearers had set up their shed and plied their trade.

"I love watching them wash the sheep," Bilhah said, laughing at the memory. "The way the young lads lead them into the stream, bleating and complaining."

"I know what you mean," Rachel said, seeing the events in memory. "The shepherds drive the sheep into those three-sided pens built in the shallow water."

"And they look so bewildered," Bilhah laughed at the thought, "as they mill around. Getting slower and slower as the water gradually saturates the fleece and weighs them down." Bilhah bent her elbows, as if swelling up herself.

Rachel nodded, raising her hand, "And then the sheep complain so much when the lads grab their legs and swing them back and forth in the stream, washing the wool." And Rachel swung her arms to demonstrate, and she chuckled again.

"And the poor sheep really do not like the strapping young fellow on the shore who wraps his arms all the way around them and presses the water out, drawing his arms along the body from head to tail. How they struggle!" Bilhah added merrily.

"The fleeces must be dried before shearing, but just think of how much strength that takes, to hold the struggling animal and then to press in and back hard enough to dry the wool!" Rachel said.

At this, Jacob roused, and said, "After a day of doing that, you ache all over," he said, "too tired to wonder what others might be doing."

"You used to do this?" Rachel said, amazed. At first, he did not answer. "Jacob?"

He looked at Rachel, slowly aware of her question. "Oh! When I was younger, I did."

"You never spoke of it before," Rachel said, exchanging glances with Bilhah.

"Did I not?" asked Jacob, whose attention wandered off, again.

Again the women exchanged glances, but Jacob, oblivious, did not notice. "And then there's all the feasting, singing, dancing," Rachel continued.

"Such joy at the great harvest of wool and anticipation of lambing soon to come!" Bilhah added, "And it is almost here. Only a few weeks now."

"It will be such a relief! Such a celebration!" Rachel said. "Do you not think so, Jacob?"

"What?" Jacob said, slowly focusing on Rachel again. "A celebration?" he said, and both women frowned in puzzlement. "A relief, certainly," he said. Seeing their concerned expressions, he said. "There are many things to be done . . . plans in the few weeks before . . . shearing time. They occupy my thoughts." Again he noted their concern, and smiling stiffly, he said, "Celebrate. Of course, *then* we will celebrate." He rose and said, "I must speak with Amos."

When he left, the two women looked at each other in puzzlement. "Did Master Jacob seem to act strangely to you?" Bilhah asked Rachel.

Rachel nodded her agreement. "Very strange," she said, and the two laughed at the shared secret.

A week passed, then a second week, and then Jacob summoned his two wives secretly in the night. "In four more weeks, we will depart," Jacob told them.

"Is that all?" Leah asked. "Why this secret meeting to tell us when the sheep are to be sheared?"

"You are not listening. In four weeks, less one day, your father, Laban, will take his flocks to be sheared," Jacob said. Leah started to interrupt, but a warning look from her husband silenced her. "On that day, we, too, will depart—all of us, all of our servants, all of our animals—for my homeland."

It was a shrewd plan, the women realized immediately. In the normal course of things, Laban would take his flocks to be sheared, and several days later, Jacob would follow, giving the shearers time to shear Laban's animals. While they sheared Jacob's flocks, Laban would return. This staggered schedule minimized waiting and wasted time for everyone.

"He will suspect nothing for several days," Rachel said, "all the while increasing the distance between us."

Jacob nodded. At first even Leah seemed to agree. But then her contrary nature asserted itself. "Why do you not go first and have your animals sheared? The way you have planned it, we will lose the income from the wool."

Jacob had expected this. "The journey to my homeland will be difficult for the animals as it is. To make them travel several days in the opposite direction, and then back again *before* we begin the main journey would be too hard on them. We would lose many animals, especially the lambs and kids who will be born on the way, not to mention the distress for their mothers."

"I can see that," Rachel said, causing Leah to nod in agreement.

"For Laban to be moving in one direction as we move in the other doubles the speed at which we leave him behind. If he moves three days in one direction, and we move three in the opposite direction, we would be six days' journey apart," Jacob explained, "even though we only traveled three days. If we went first and returned while Laban took his flocks for shearing, we would only be three days' journey apart, but we would have had to travel six days—three days there and three days back."

"But what about the wool?" Leah insisted.

"We will pluck what we can from the animals as we travel, as they used to in the old times," Jacob said. "We will lose some wool, but we will save the animals—and ourselves." This last statement sobered Leah. Many observers would consider them runaway servants, or worse, thieves. Few would question any actions Laban took against them, however extreme.

"Father *will* be angry," she said.

"Then better to keep him at a distance," Jacob said. "Or would you prefer to live here as his slaves?" That settled it.

"We will have to prepare carefully," Leah said, thinking on how to organize her servants.

"We will," said Jacob. "Carefully and secretly."

"But we must plan for shearing time, anyway!" Rachel said, catching the brilliance of her husband's plan. "Most of what we do can be explained as preparations for shearing!"

"Exactly," said Jacob. "Only your most trusted servants need to know what we are really planning. Servants cannot gossip about something they do not suspect. I have told only Amos and now the two of you. Bilhah and Zilpah must know, but other than that, I can think of no one." Both wives pondered his words. For once Leah agreed without argument. They nodded.

"If anyone gets curious at the extent of the preparations, just tell them we expect this to be a very special shearing time," Jacob said, and for the first time in the discussion, his eyes twinkled. "They do not need to know just how special an event we are planning." Jacob went on for a few minutes, discussing the plan and how to carry it out. Afterward, Leah slipped across the camp and into her own tent. Jacob watched her go and then glanced around at the quiet encampment. For a moment, he thought he saw a moving shadow among the tents. When he heard the call of an owl at the edge of camp, he sighed with relief. *That would explain the shadow and the silence,* he thought. Many nights sleeping in the open with the flocks had taught him that owls fly so quietly that a silent shadow is often the only evidence of their passage.

Donatiya had learned the same lesson. And as she gave the muted cry of the great owl once again, she pondered what use to make of what she had learned this night.

רבס

rekec

Rugged

"The *river*, Amos," Jacob said. "We must reach and cross the river before Laban catches up to us." This was in reply to Amos's question if Jacob still wanted to depart so late in the day.

The people of the region of Haran spoke of many streams, but of only one river—the mighty Euphrates. Jacob would begin to feel better only with the river Euphrates behind them. It would not be as imposing an obstacle to the force of fighting men Laban would no doubt bring with him. But with all his wives and children and livestock, the crossing would take Jacob a full day. Their greatest danger lay in the possibility Laban would trap them just before or during their crossing, in which case, Laban would have them at his mercy. Every day they could put the river farther behind them would increase their chances of escape. "Until we cross the river, there will be little rest for any of us."

Amos merely nodded and gave the servants their final orders. It had already been a long day.

Like every other year at shearing time, Jacob needed to know when Laban departed for the shearing location in order to coordinate their movements. Not one to be bothered with such details, Laban always insisted that Jacob send a servant to observe his departure and then inform Jacob of the time of Laban's leaving. This time, the arrangement had served Jacob's purposes quite well. And he made certain that Amos impressed the young boy chosen for the task that he should notify his master *quickly*. So it was that, on the morning of

Jacob's great exodus, a breathless young lad came to announce that Laban had begun his journey to the place of shearing. The lad's announcement triggered a whirlwind of activity, the culmination of weeks of preparation.

If I had fully realized the magnitude of the task, Jacob thought, *I might have been afraid to attempt it.* At first, everyone had taken the activities for granted as the usual preparations for shearing time. But as they progressed, it became increasingly evident a more significant movement might be in the offing. Jacob and Amos kept the men so busy they had little time or energy to speculate on the extensive preparations. The four mothers—Leah, Rachel, Bilhah, and Zilpah—talked endlessly of their relief at the end of winter and how their sons would revel in the shearing-time celebrations.

With Laban's clan likewise into feverish preparations for moving his flocks and herds, both camps were too busy to worry much about what the others might be doing.

But today, after receiving word that Laban had left with his flocks to go to the shearing, Amos and Jacob implemented their final plans. Under their direction, servants began striking tents, dousing fires, loading camels and donkeys with household items and long-term stores of grain and oil, and organizing servants and children into groups for travel. Soon everyone realized what was happening, and a new sense of urgency filled the air. Still, it took until past midday before they were ready to leave.

In the middle of all the commotion, Rachel came to Jacob. "I need two camels," she said to him, "to get some things from my father's camp."

"What? Now?" Jacob asked.

"I will be quick. There are items in my father's camp that belong to Leah and to me. I could not fetch them before without arousing his suspicions." When Jacob hesitated, she said, "I will only take one serving woman with me. With two fast camels, we can be there and back before you are ready to leave."

"All right," Jacob said. "Tell Amos to supply our two fastest camels." Seeing a serving woman standing idle, he said, "You there. Go with Mistress Rachel," he pointed to Rachel as she approached Amos, "to her father's camp and help her with whatever she needs." The old woman nodded and moved to follow Rachel. In the midst of the bustle, Amos still managed to quickly locate the needed camels. The women mounted the kneeling animals and were off.

With the swift mounts, they quickly reached Laban's nearly abandoned camp. Only a few servants remained, and they would never challenge the master's daughter. On the way, Rachel had explained their mission to the old woman, who nodded her understanding. Upon arrival, Rachel and Donatiya moved quickly through the tents, gathering Rachel's and Leah's keepsakes and small treasures.

"Are you angry with your father?" Donatiya asked.

"We are," Rachel admitted. "He has treated us like his livestock, only worse."

"You want to avenge yourselves?"

"We do," said Rachel.

"Then take his *teraphim*," Donatiya suggested. "Take a man's household gods right from under his nose." The old woman laughed noiselessly. "Hurt his pride." When Rachel hesitated, she added, "They are worth something."

Rachel thought for a moment. It would anger her father, no doubt about that. But after twenty years of labor, Laban still wanted to cheat her Jacob. *He insulted us, his own daughters,* she thought. *Serves him right! This will be part of our dowry he held back. Besides, he will be angry, anyway.* Quickly, Rachel grabbed the small talismans from their resting place on the family shrine; she wrapped them in cloth and placed them in the leather bag attached to her camel's saddle. "That is everything, then," she said. "Let us return."

Donatiya bowed in obedience. But she thought, *As soon as Master Laban sees that his* teraphim *are missing, he will know what happened! Same thing as leaving a sign.*

Rachel and Donatiya arrived in camp just in time to hear Amos's question about their time of departure and Jacob's answer. "Can we make it to the river and across before Father catches us?" Rachel asked.

"I hope so," said Jacob. "El Shaddai commanded me to return home and promised to be with me."

"Then all will be well," said Rachel, "is that not so?"

"He said He would be *with* me," Jacob replied. "He did not say where or whether your father might find us. And then," he paused. *And then, there is the reception my angry brother may have for us,* he thought. *But do not tell the others yet. One crisis at a time.* He sighed, the weight of anxiety pressing down on him.

"And then?" Rachel asked, concern revealed in her voice and on her face.

Jacob smiled. "And then we shall find out. For now, we move forward."

Amos had come to tell him all was ready. "I will take the lead," Jacob said. "Rachel's group will follow me. Then Leah. After them, Bilhah and Zilpah, in that order. You bring up the rear, Amos." He looked at his trusted steward. "Send some of your fastest lads scouting behind us. If Laban pursues us, we will need as much warning as possible." The servant nodded solemnly and re-treated to his designated position.

Jacob hoisted his pack on his back, slung his goatskin water carrier over his shoulder, and grasped his staff. He smiled to himself. *This is what I brought with me twenty years ago,* he thought. *My pack, goatskin with water, and my staff. Now I leave the same way.* Looking behind him, he saw the long twisting column of wives, sons, servants, livestock, and goods. *Well, not quite the same way.* He smiled again, set his face toward home, and took the first step.

* * * * *

It took Laban and his flocks three solid days of travel to arrive at the place of shearing. No sooner did they make camp for the night, than a runner from his tents arrived with news.

"The *teraphim* are gone?" Laban asked. "Who would dare do such a thing?"

"I cannot say," the servant said cautiously. "But Mistress Rachel and a serv-ing woman came to your camp the morning after you left."

"Are you saying that my daughter took the *teraphim?*" Laban said, anger rising. *If she did, her husband put her up to it,* he thought. *To taunt me.*

"I do not know," the servant said. "We sent a messenger to Jacob's camp to inquire, and they were gone."

"Gone? You mean Mistress Rachel and her serving woman?" Laban in-quired.

"Everyone was gone. Everyone and everything. The entire camp was gone," the servant replied. "We came here immediately to tell you."

Laban leaped to his feet, tearing at his robe and gnashing his teeth in rage. "Gone? Jacob has run off?" He clenched and unclenched his fists. "Summon Adnan and Jascher! Bring my sons to me, we must avenge this dishonor, ap-prehend this thief, this runaway servant!" The clamor had brought Adinah running. It took some time before Laban calmed enough to speak coherently to his wife and sons. Anger filled the air, talk of vengeance and punishment.

"We must go after him immediately," Adnan said.

Sobered but seething, Laban said, "That scheming *'aqob*, crooked Jacob! That clever ingrate! He planned this well. We *cannot* go immediately."

"But we must go!" Jascher said.

"We will go, but not now," Laban said. To answer his sons' incredulous expressions, he asked, "How many could we take, right now, to pursue him? How many?" The brothers began to speak at once, but Laban cut them off with a vicious look. "Here we are at the shearing place, with all our flocks. The washing and shearing will begin tomorrow. Nearly all of our servants will be necessary to assist in that. And who will bargain with the wool buyers and be certain we receive a fair price for our fleeces? It will take us three days just to finish our business here." The men could see his reasoning. He shook his head. Jacob had really put them in a difficult position, the clever scoundrel. "And it will take another three days' journey just to return home. After we return, it will take a day to situate the animals, and another two or three days to gather help from our neighbors, distribute our weapons, organize our forces, and prepare rations and water for ourselves and our animals for our pursuit. During that time, our camels and donkeys can rest so that they will be fresh. So, about ten days from now—then we can go after Jacob."

"But he must not be allowed to get away!" Jascher said.

"He will not get away," said Laban. "He is traveling with all his wives, his children, his livestock, his servants, and all his household goods. He cannot travel faster than the slowest animal can walk. And such a large group will leave a trail a blind man could follow at night. Even with a fifteen-day head start, we will catch him." He looked fiercely at his sons. "We will catch him, all right."

* * * * *

"I see now why they call this land *Gilead*, 'rugged,' " Amos said. He had been born in the highland plains of Padan Aram and never had traveled this far south before.

Jacob smiled wearily. "It is, indeed, rough country. But it is the shortest way home. And its rugged terrain, steep hills, and narrow valleys give us our best chance to defend ourselves." To Amos's questioning look, Jacob said, "On an open plain, Laban could come at us from any direction. But the narrow passages between the hills limit the avenues of attack, and thus help us know where to defend."

This had not occurred to Amos, who had little experience with fighting—or with running, for that matter. But hearing Jacob explain it, it made sense.

"And you notice that I never camp in the valley for the night," Jacob said.

"I did. And we—the servants—wondered why all the extra effort to scale a hill before pitching camp," Amos said.

"High ground, Amos. If your adversary chooses to attack, make him do it uphill," Jacob said. Taking Amos aside, he said in a quiet voice, "It is only a matter of time before Laban catches up to us, Amos. I want to select the terrain where we meet."

"Do you know where that will be?" Amos said.

"The place they call the Mount of Gilead, if we can get there. Every night I pick the most easily defended campsite available. If we make it to Mount Gilead, we will dig in and wait," Jacob said. He stood, arms folded, looking back toward the Euphrates. Back toward where Laban was surely in pursuit.

Jacob felt more confident every day the river Euphrates fell farther behind them. With all his wives, children, and livestock, the crossing had indeed taken Jacob a full day. So far, their journey through the narrow valleys of Gilead had been faster than he anticipated. Still, neither the river nor the rugged terrain would slow Laban's raiding force nearly so much as it had the families and the herds of animals with Jacob.

"Tomorrow or the next day," Jacob said, "we have to settle down and dig in. Even with our head start, Laban will catch us after that."

The next day, nearly three weeks into their journey, they came to the foot of Mount Gilead. Scouts quickly located a likely spot for the encampment, and by the middle of the afternoon, the rear guard reached the appointed place.

Jacob stood on a boulder, staff in hand, and addressed them. "I have driven you hard these many days, and you have cooperated well. For now, our running is done." He gestured to the area around him. "We will camp here for a while, fortify our position, rest, and wait. Laban will surely catch up to us sooner or later. I cannot choose *when*, but I can choose *where*." All eyes were on him. Even the weary animals stood quietly.

"I have chosen this place to make our stand. It will be easy to defend and hard to attack. Laban will find no allies nearby to aid him so far from his home, and will have to think carefully before risking an attack." Jacob still saw fear in some eyes, and so he said, "My God, El Shaddai, the Almighty One, the One who prospered our flocks," he looked again and saw nodding, heard murmurs of assent, "is in this place too. In fact, His house, Beth-El, the house of God, is not far from here." He pointed in the direction of Beth-El and saw his listeners' attention shift. "He commanded me to make this journey and declared He would be with me. So we need not fear. Tonight, we will make offerings to El Shaddai, and He will defend us. Sacrifice, feast, fortify, and then rest! Are you ready?"

"We are ready," rumbled the group in a rising chorus. "We are ready!"

The rest of that day they pitched camp, slaughtered the sacrificial animals, and feasted. Jacob and Amos kept watch on the trail behind them but saw nothing all day. After the weary travelers feasted, Amos sent two young scouts back up the trail to nearby hills to spend the night. If anyone approached, they would light a fire and warn the main camp.

The next day, Jacob and Amos directed the weary servants in fortifying their position. "I know you are tired," Jacob said. "But when we are ready, you can rest. Know that Laban's men and animals will be weary from their journey, and the prospect of storming these fortified heights will make him think twice before attacking us. Spend some sweat now to save blood later," he said. The tired men said nothing but worked with a will. Jacob himself took a bow and fired arrows down the facing slopes. Servants placed stone markers to indicate the range at which they could strike approaching attackers. By that evening, the work was done and the scouts called home. And before nightfall, a distant cloud of dust became visible to the north, back the way they had come.

"Laban," Jacob said, and Amos nodded. "We are ready for you." He and Amos organized the watch and went to bed.

They did not see a lone figure leave their ramparts and walk through the night toward the approaching foe. Donatiya had learned to move in the shadows, without a sound, and she put that skill to use now. She had a message for Laban.

mitspeh

Watchtower

"Seven days without rest. We finally catch up to that scoundrel Jacob, and look what awaits us!" Adnan's frustration only fueled his fury. For several hours, from first light until now, they had evaluated their situation. The more they surveyed Jacob's fortified camp on the heights above them, the more obvious it became that the wily Jacob had outwitted them again.

"A frontal assault would be suicidal," Laban admitted. "Jacob has several herdsman trained as archers to protect the flocks, as do we. We would face a storm of arrows long before we got close enough to shoot back. The only way for this band of fighters to take Jacob now would be through a lengthy siege."

"But it is *we* who lack the provisions for such a campaign," Jascher said, shaking his fist at the futility of the effort. "He sits up there with plenty of livestock to slaughter for food, plus water and grain for his lengthy journey, while we came on minimum rations to speed our pursuit. We will be in need long before he is," and he gave vent to a string of curses.

"And should we weaken our party by sending for more provisions, he can sweep down from those heights and destroy us," Laban said. "These are all ill omens, but even worse, I have been warned to be exceedingly careful in how I deal with Jacob."

"Warned?" Adnan asked. "How?"

"El Shaddai, Jacob's God, came to me in a dream," Laban said.

"But you do not believe in the God of Jacob, do you, Father?" Jascher could not believe his ears.

"I believe *something* prospered us and him under his stewardship," Laban explained. "*Something* came to me in my dream. And last night, that old woman, the conjurer, came from Jacob's camp with a message for me."

"What did she have to say?" Adnan asked.

"The same thing—that I must be very careful in my dealings with Jacob."

"So, have we come all this way for *nothing*?" Jascher asked, again bursting with fury and frustration.

"Perhaps not," said Laban. "There is still the matter of the *teraphim*. The old woman specifically mentioned them. Jacob has no claim on them. They could be proof of our claim of theft against him." Laban looked at his angry sons. "Up to this point, Jacob has outwitted us—outwitted *me*—at every turn. It is time we tried something unexpected on him."

"But what can that be? Clearly, we have come after him to punish him," Adnan said. "His preparations make it clear he has prepared for a full-scale attack."

"Then we shall have to try something else," Laban said.

"But what?" the sons asked in unison.

"Just we three shall go," Laban said. Adnan and Jascher looked from their father to each other, threw up their hands in frustration, and went to instruct the others what to do in their absence. Laban took up his staff and accompanied by his sons, began his ascent.

Moments later, Amos spoke to Jacob. "Master Laban comes, with only his two sons."

"We will greet them as visitors, then," Jacob said. "But make certain your watchmen keep an eye on the camp below." Amos nodded and went to inform the others.

Jacob walked to the point where the path entered the camp and waited for Laban's arrival. As soon as he was within shouting distance, Laban began his interrogation.

"What have you done? You've deceived me, and you've carried off my daughters like captives in war," Laban demanded.

Jacob refused to take the bait, thinking, *Much you cared about your daughters. First, you sold them and then used up their dowry. And I carried them off, all right. After fourteen years of labor. Make all of your arguments, Laban. If they are no stronger than that, they merit no reply.*

Nearer the camp, his voice was more normal now, "Why did you run off secretly and deceive me? Why didn't you tell me, so I could send you away with a celebration? Feasting and music! You didn't even let me kiss my grandchildren and my daughters goodbye."

Speaking just loudly enough so his own men could hear him, Jacob said, "Let me understand you. You wanted to have a festival in honor of my carrying off your daughters like captives in war? That would have been an interesting celebration." Laban had kept walking to the place where he could hear the men laughing in response to Jacob's words.

Having come almost face-to-face, Laban tried another tactic: being reasonable. "You have done a foolish thing. I have the power to harm you; but last night the God of your fathers said to me, 'Be careful not to say anything to Jacob, either good or bad.' Now you have gone off because you longed to return to your father's house. I can understand that." And then Laban sprung his trap. "But why did you steal my gods, my *teraphim*?"

The words stunned Jacob. *All my planning is now endangered by an accusation of petty theft?* Unnerved, he began speaking too rapidly, saying too much, but he could not stop. "I was afraid, because I thought you would take your daughters away from me by force." *Why am I saying this? We did not steal your* teraphim! *That is it. Prove him wrong!* "If you find anyone who has your gods, he shall not live." Laban made a gesture of helplessness, as if to say, "How can I tell?"

Jacob responded. "Your sons and my wives can be the judge. In the presence of our relatives, see for yourself whether there is anything of yours here with me; and if so, take it."

"Fine," said Laban, smiling his most charming smile. "Let me start with *your* tent." The three small images could be almost anywhere, and with a grim satisfaction, Laban began unpacking everything larger than a loaf of bread. He reduced bundle after bundle to heaps of clothing, implements, or small household items such as lamps and bowls. "Come here and help me," Laban called to Adnan and Jascher.

The moment Laban mentioned the theft of the *teraphim*, Rachel's mind began to race. She could not go to her tent without arousing the suspicion of her brothers. But when Laban called them to assist him, she seized the opportunity and walked casually back to her tent. Once inside, Rachel looked frantically about. The *teraphim* were still in the camel saddle, where she had originally put them. Other than a small chest containing such personal items as the *sappiyr* box with Isaac's thorn in it, there was nothing large enough to conceal the *teraphim*. While she had been thinking, Laban had finished with Leah's tent. *Will he be here next?* she wondered, on the verge of panic. But he went to the handmaids' tent next, and she could hear her father's and brothers' voices rising in frustration as they ransacked Zilpah's and then Bilhah's belongings.

Rachel could think of nothing to do, nowhere to put the *teraphim* to prevent her father from finding them. She had to think clearly, for more than just her life was at stake. If Laban's *teraphim* could be found in the camp, it would justify Laban's claim that Jacob was a thief. That could mean death or slavery for many. Once again, her gaze fell upon the camel's saddle where she had placed the *teraphim*. Hearing Laban headed in her direction, all she could think to do was sit on the saddle, arranging her skirts to hide it.

Laban stormed into her tent and began rummaging around. He had not found the *teraphim*, and he was becoming frustrated. Rachel knew she was flushed, both with her recent scurrying and the anxiety of knowing how close her father was to discovering her crime. Sensing her discomfort, Laban looked at her sharply. "Now I remember," he said. " 'Mistress Rachel and her serving woman'—you were the last ones to visit my tents before you ran away." Suspicion now focused on Rachel, he asked, "What is the matter, daughter? Why do you not rise in respect for your father?" He moved toward her menacingly.

Quickly, she placed an arm across her belly and said, "Do not be angry, my lord, that I cannot stand in your presence. The way of women is upon me."

That stopped Laban short, and with a disappointed grunt, he backed away from her. He gave the area another look and stormed out, angrier than he had entered.

He found nothing, so now is the time to strike, thought Jacob. "What is my crime?" he asked Laban. "What sin have I committed that you hunt me down? Now that you have searched through all my goods, what have you found that belongs to your household?" Laban held out his empty hands, so Jacob gestured to an open area of ground. "Put it here in front of everyone, and let them judge between the two of us."

Laban had nothing to offer and nothing to say. Adnan and Jascher looked increasingly embarrassed, so Jacob decided to turn a retreat into a rout. *Press him hard*, he thought. "I served you for twenty years. During that time your sheep and goats did not miscarry, nor did I eat rams from your flocks." Laban remained silent. Even his sons recognized the truth of his words.

"When wild beasts killed your animals, I did not bring the carcasses to you; I bore the loss myself. If thieves stole anything, by day or by night, you demanded I make up the loss." This, too, all knew to be accurate.

"And what did I get? For the twenty years I was in your household, the heat consumed me in the daytime and the cold at night, and sleep fled from my eyes. I worked for you fourteen years for your two daughters and six years for your flocks, and you changed my wages ten times." Laban and his sons were angrier than ever but now out of frustration. They had no case, and they knew it.

But Jacob was not done. "If El Shaddai, the God of my father, the Elohim of Abraham and the Terror of Isaac, had not been with me, you would surely have sent me away empty-handed. But El Shaddai has seen my hardship and the toil of my hands, and last night, He rebuked you."

Laban recognized that Jacob had outmaneuvered him; no defense remained for his actions. *Might as well put the best face on it*, he decided. Laban answered Jacob, "The way I see it, the women with you are my daughters, the children are my children, and the flocks are my flocks. All you see is mine." Adnan and Jascher backed behind their father, as Jacob and his servants inched forward, ready to repudiate the claim. Laban held his hand up to stop them, then held it out in surrender. "Yet what can I do today about these daughters of mine or about the children they have borne?" He smiled and shrugged, defusing the tension. *Time to make the best of a weak position.* "Come now, let's make a covenant, you and I, and let it serve as a witness between us."

Jacob nodded and strode toward a boulder at the edge of the encampment. He rolled it into a small cleared space and said, "Gather some stones, and we will make a monument to our covenant, beginning with this boulder." Jacob instructed Leah to prepare a meal of reconciliation, and then he and Amos, and Laban and his sons, gathered stones for the monument of remembrance. They placed a circle of stones for seats around the base of the monument; then they sat and ate the meal of reconciliation at the base of the monument. Around them, in ring after ring, Jacob's wives and children and servants also ate.

Both Laban and Jacob named it the "Monument of Remembrance." Laban used the Aramaic term, *Jegar Sahadutha*, and Jacob, the Hebrew, *Galeed;* but both signified the same thing.

After the meal, Laban arose and spoke so that all could hear. "This monument will remain a witness to our reconciliation. That is why we call it *Galeed.*" He surveyed the entire assembly. "And before you all I declare it a *mitspeh*, a watchtower. May your God, El Shaddai, watch between you and me when we cannot watch each other. If you mistreat my daughters or if you take any wives besides my daughters, even though no one is with us, remember that El Shaddai watches you and will hold you accountable to me." He walked slowly around the monument, stopping on its north side, the side toward his home in Haran. He motioned for his sons to stand with him. Reaching out, he touched the pile of stones. "Here is this monument, and here is this pillar I have set up as the boundary between you and me. This monument is a witness, and this pillar is a witness that I will not go past this monument to your side to harm you." A murmur of approval came from the assembly. Laban continued, "And that you will not go past this monument and pillar to my side to harm me. And may your God, El Shaddai, Elohim Abraham and the God of Nahor, the God of their father, judge between us should either of us violate this boundary or repudiate this covenant."

Jacob stood and walked to the south side of the monument, toward his homeland. "Let it be as you say," he said. "And let the God of my father, the Terror of Isaac, keep the watch and judge between us."

Then Jacob and Laban clasped hands and raised them to the sky. "There will be peace between us," they said. "Remember the *mitspeh;* remember the watchtower!"

Relief, joy, and gratitude flowed like waves through the assembly. There would be no fighting, no bloodshed. "*Mitspeh!*" the cry went up. They never wanted to forget the watchtower that marked this reconciliation. "*Mitspeh! Mitspeh!*"

Jacob raised his hands for quiet. "We will sacrifice tonight and give thanks to El Shaddai for the peace He has wrought today." Looking at Laban and his sons, he invited, "My father and my brothers, will you share our feast tonight and lodge with us?"

It will seal the peace, thought Laban. "We will!" he declared, and the assembly erupted in cheering, in more cries of "*Mitspeh!*" and laughter.

Jascher and one of Jacob's servants went to share the news with the remaining raiders in Laban's camp to the north. They were to lay down their weapons and come to share the feast.

After eight days of pursuit, they gladly accepted.

Even though the revels lasted far into the night, Laban and his men awoke at sunrise, were treated to a breakfast of camel cheese, dates, and almonds, and prepared to depart. Jacob's flocks had begun lambing here on Mount Gilead, and Laban and his sons knew their flocks would be lambing too. Duty called them home. Laban kissed his grandchildren and his daughters and blessed them. Then he left and returned home.

After Laban had gone, Amos came to Jacob and asked his plans.

"We will stay here a few days and rest. By then, many of the ewes will have dropped their lambs, and we can move forward after that. More slowly now, with the danger ahead rather than behind."

"Danger ahead? You mean bandits?" Amos asked.

"Bandits?" Jacob smiled. "Bandits are the least of my concerns. We are well prepared for them. A danger greater than Laban lies ahead of us."

"What danger, then?" Amos asked. "What could be worse than a man who claims you stole his daughters?"

"Laban knew his claims were groundless. Ahead waits a man who claims that I stole his birthright and his father's blessing and his place in the world," said Jacob.

"This man waits for you?" Amos asked. Jacob nodded. "That would be serious indeed, if his claims were true."

"That is just it, Amos," Jacob said. "His claims *are* true."

shním

Two

"The last of the ewes dropped their lambs last night," Amos informed Jacob at daybreak, five days after Laban's departure.

"Spread the word, then. After we eat this morning, we will depart. Strike camp, douse the fires, trail rations for the noon meal. We are still far from my homeland." Amos nodded, turned on his heel, and began notifying the chief servants for each function. Jacob himself informed his wives. After the morning meal, when all was in readiness, they formed up in their order of the march and resumed their southward journey.

"Because we no longer fear pursuit from Laban and because we have all the young animals, we will travel more slowly," Jacob announced.

One day, then two, eventually four days they traveled southward. On the fifth day, they came to a pleasant valley sloping down to a river, the Jabbok, running in a deep ravine at its foot. As he began the descent into the valley, Jacob suddenly stumbled, and went to one knee. He froze for a moment, and servants rushed forward to see if he was injured, but he waved them away. Rachel raced to his side, concern in every feature.

"I saw them," he said.

Rachel looked into the valley below, then along the path. "Saw who?" she said.

"The messengers," Jacob said, "from the tower."

By this time, Amos had come racing from the rear. "What messengers?" he asked, scanning the way ahead. "What tower?"

Jacob looked at Amos, then Rachel, as though they had not been there before. He smiled. "Twenty years ago, at Beth-El. I saw the messengers. Shimmering in light, ascending and descending a tower that reached to the sky. At Beth-El, when El Shaddai spoke to me. His messengers."

Amos looked at Rachel. "I do not understand." She could only smile and tilt her head toward Jacob. He, too, looked at his master. "What does it mean?"

"It means this is the place. *Mahanaim*," he said.

"Two camps?" Amos asked.

Jacob nodded. "We will camp here," he said. "And they will camp here."

"They?" Amos asked. Jacob only smiled in response.

After midday, when they reached a level area some eight hundred cubits above the steep banks of the stream, Jacob called a halt. "We will camp here," he said.

While they were pitching camp, he called two of his swiftest runners. "I want you to go, as quickly as possible, to the land of Seir, south of here. For some time now, traveling merchants bring tidings of a mighty hunter who has moved to Seir among the Horites. In fact, they now often refer to Seir as the 'land of Edom'—the land of my brother, Esau." Pointing to the river below, he said, "This is how they describe the journey." Then he knelt and drew a crude map in the dust, explaining directions and distances. "This is what you are to say to my master Esau: 'Your servant Jacob says, "I have been staying with Laban and have remained there till now. I have cattle and donkeys, sheep and goats, menservants and maidservants. Now I am sending this message to my lord, that I may find favor in your eyes."' " When they could repeat their directions and the message Jacob had given them, he summoned Amos.

"Give them fast mounts and provisions for a long journey," Jacob said, and Amos began preparations.

The next morning, the messengers departed. Amos asked, "What do we do now?"

"We wait," Jacob said. "We prepare for the worst, and we wait."

"We wait for the messengers to return?" Amos asked. Jacob nodded. "May I ask where they are going?"

"Remember the angry man who waits for me, the man with legitimate grievances?" Now Amos nodded. "They go to see him—to my brother." Amos raised his eyebrows and blew his breath through pursed lips, but said nothing.

Six days later, the envoys returned. "We found your brother, Esau, and we gave him your message," they said. "Now he is coming to meet you, and four hundred men are with him."

"Four hundred men? That is precisely the number of a war clan!" Jacob said. Turning to Amos, he said, "We must act without delay. We will divide the people and animals into two groups."

"Is that wise, master?" Amos asked.

"If Esau attacks one, the other may escape," Jacob replied.

"But is it wise to divide your forces in the face of the enemy?" Amos asked again.

"We have women, children, and many animals," Jacob said, "and not as many men fit to fight as Esau does. So we must take advantage of the terrain, as we did at Mount Gilead."

"You did not divide into groups there," Amos pointed out.

"Laban did not have a war clan, either. Nor did the terrain provide this opportunity." Jacob quickly drew a diagram of their current encampment in the dirt. "We will divide into two groups," he repeated, gesturing with a stick at his crude map, "one where we are, and the other on that slight rise over there." He pointed the stick to another flat area, on just the other side of a shallow ravine, and then drew the location of the second group. "That shallow ravine is between the two groups. We put half our archers in each group. Arrows from both groups can reach the riverbanks, and the attackers will have to deal with arrows from two directions, rather than one. If my brother decides to attack one group, the other will be behind him. And if he attacks both at once from the shallow ravine between our groups, he must attack uphill both ways, and each attacking force will be under attack from archers, front and rear. Have the second group move their camp before evening."

Amos looked for a long time at the marks in the soil. If he had doubts, he did not express them directly. "Let us hope he does not want to attack."

"That will be the subject of my prayers," said Jacob, "and the object of my diplomacy. Leave me now," said Jacob, as he gestured to the hollow between the two proposed camps. "I go there to seek Adonai Elohim."

Once alone, Jacob fell to his knees, look toward the heavens, and spread his arms wide. "Oh Adonai Elohim, God of my father Abraham, God of my father Isaac, Oh Adonai El Shaddai, who said to me, 'Go back to your country and your relatives, and I will make you prosper,' I am unworthy of all the kindness and faithfulness You have shown Your servant." He swept his arm toward the Jabbok River below and the Jordan beyond, and then at the two camps above and behind him. "I had only my staff when I crossed this river, but now I have become two groups. Save me, I pray, from the hand of my brother Esau, for I am afraid he will come and attack me, and also the mothers with their children. But You have said, 'I will surely make you prosper and will make your descendants like the sand of the sea, which cannot be counted.'"

Evening became night. The lights in the sky crossed the dome of the heavens, but Jacob still prayed. The watchmen who guarded the two camps during the night at Amos's direction paused during their rounds to look where their master had gone to pray, and each time they saw him still there. The light of dawn rinsed away the dark stain of night, and Jacob remained in the hollow between the two camps, communing with his God. Amos rose early, concerned for his master, only to find Jacob waiting for him.

"Did Adonai Elohim answer you?" Amos asked.

"Perhaps He did. Perhaps He did not," Jacob replied. And before Amos could inquire further, he added, "Last night was the time for seeking God's favor," Jacob explained, "and today we seek Esau's favor. We must send him a royal gift, for he has become royalty," Jacob said.

And with that, Jacob and Amos assembled nearly six hundred animals in five herds: two hundred female goats and twenty male goats, two hundred ewes and twenty rams, thirty female camels with their young, forty cows and ten bulls, and twenty female donkeys and ten male donkeys. He placed a chief servant in charge of each herd. "Go ahead of the two main groups here to my brother Esau. Keep enough space between the herds, so that each can see the one in front of it, but not well enough to determine how many or what kind of animals it contains." The serving men nodded their understanding. "Arrange yourselves so that as soon as my brother can take in one herd, the next is upon him.

"When my brother Esau meets you and asks, 'To whom do you belong and where are you going and who owns all these animals in front of you?' say to him, 'They belong to your servant Jacob, and they are a gift sent to my lord Esau. Your servant Jacob is coming behind us.'" After final instructions, he sent the herds and their tenders on their way. As soon as one herd traveled to where it became a smudge on the horizon, the next set out, until all five herds—goats, sheep, camels, cattle, and donkeys—had departed.

Amos marveled at the generosity of the gift. "A tribute worthy of royalty, indeed. Surely your brother will be satisfied?"

"That is my hope and my prayer. But do not be deceived," Jacob said, looking into the distant south, where the herds had disappeared. "Nothing can repay the wrong I did to him. If he does not find forgiveness in his heart, this gift might only whet his appetite. He might well reason that anyone who can afford such a tribute must possess much more."

"Forgiveness," Amos said, hesitating at the strange word. "I understand the meaning, but—pardon me for my poor understanding—it is like saying . . . ," he searched for a comparison and found one triumphantly, "it is like telling me of a blue goat!" he said. "I think I know what it would look like, but I have never seen it. Is this a custom in your homeland or in your clan?"

Jacob chuckled. "That," he said, "is what we are about to find out."

"Where did you learn of such a thing?" Amos asked. "In Haran, in Padan Aram, my homeland, people rarely forget an offense, and they take every opportunity for retribution, if they think they can get away with it."

"I learned it from my father and from Adonai Elohim, the Lord my God," Jacob said.

"This Adonai Elohim forgives?" Amos asked incredulously. "The gods I grew up with might overlook wrong done by their favorites, but they are relentless against their enemies. And they are fickle. We never know when we may lose their favor or when they may demand more sacrifice or when they may lash out in anger."

"Adonai Elohim, El Shaddai, forgives," Jacob said. "Soon, I may know how much." Amos shrugged; it was beyond him. "Now we must prepare to move. I want both camps on the other side of the Jabbok by nightfall." The two men supervised the now familiar task of striking camp and moving out for the day. The new campsites on the other side of the river took advantage of similar terrain as had the previous ones.

Jacob sent the others on their way. "I will remain here at the Jabbok for a while," he told Amos. "I must entreat Adonai Elohim again."

Amos could see his master was struggling to retain his courage in the face of tremendous uncertainty. He wanted to speak encouragement to his master but could not find the words, so he just nodded and helped move the final elements of the caravan across the river and up to the new campsites. Darkness fell, and Jacob remained alone to pray.

He felt, rather than heard, a solitary figure approach him in the darkness. The old woman, Donatiya, approached. "What do you want, old woman?" Jacob asked.

"I have come to warn you," she replied. She held up her hands, as if warding off some mortal threat. "Something powerful is here in the darkness tonight. Something will happen to you here!" she jabbed a finger at him. "You should not stay alone. I saw them, too, you know," she said.

"Whom did you see?" Jacob asked.

"The bright, powerful strangers that met you." She pointed back toward the spot on the trail where he had stumbled. "Something even stronger than the bright strangers awaits here. A great danger waits for you!"

"Thank you, Donatiya, but I will stay. Sometimes the danger is in staying," he said, "but sometimes the danger is greater in running away. For now, I am through running." Her eyes grew wide, as she saw his determination. She nodded and turned to make her way to the night camps. "I hope your God protects you," she said, and she was gone.

Sometime later, he never knew exactly when, he sensed another movement nearby. Suddenly, a form loomed in the darkness, as though pursuing Jacob's family across the Jabbok. Alarmed, Jacob moved to block him. When the silent figure continued toward the Jabbok and the tents on the other side, Jacob grabbed him around the waist and drove forward, bearing them both to the ground. Jacob's adversary repeatedly sought to escape, prying loose from Jacob's grip. And repeatedly Jacob blocked his escape, tackling or tripping him, and locking him in an iron hold. Time and again, the process repeated itself. Every muscle aching and out of breath, Jacob clung to the adversary, desperate to protect his family. Neither adversary seemed able to gain a permanent advantage.

Eventually, the struggle took on a life of its own. It seemed to Jacob as if his whole life had come down to this endless battle. Struggling with his brother Esau, struggling for his father's approval, struggling with Laban over his wages, struggling with Leah and Rachel over his attentions and their ability to bear children, struggling with Elohim over why so much of his life had been so difficult, why he, Jacob, had to work so hard for what others were simply given. The central riddles of his existence, every question that had ever perplexed him, everything that ever mattered to him—they all crystallized, concentrated, and focused in this one titanic effort. As darkness receded before the predawn light, he knew he could not prevail. And he knew he *would not relent*.

They grappled yet again, locking eyes as well as arms; and for the first time, Jacob saw, in the face of his opponent, recognition that Jacob would not be vanquished. Then, with a look that seemed to be compassion, his adversary released his grip with his right hand and reached down to touch Jacob's hip instead. For an instant, Jacob wondered that his opponent would waste effort on such an ineffectual move. But then fiery pain erupted in his hip joint, his leg collapsed, and Jacob began to fall. Despite the pain, he tightened his grip, clinging to his adversary, whom he now recognized.

"Let me go," the Figure said in a voice Jacob felt more than heard, "for the light has now come." And Jacob understood. Not just the light of day, but relief from the darkness of his years of struggle, his days of exile.

Let go? Jacob thought. *Let go of the Light that ends my darkness? Let go when the end of all my struggles is literally within my grasp. Let go? I will never let go of You.* And these thoughts burst forth in words, "I will not let go unless You bless me." As he said the words, they frightened him. *Who am I to make demands of the One I am wrestling?* Fear filled him, he dreaded the reply but did not loosen his group. The response, when it came, shocked him to his core.

"What is your name?" the penetrating voice of the Other inquired.

My name? He thought. *You know my name. Jacob. 'Aqob Jacob, the crooked cheater. That is my name.* He said, "Jacob."

"No longer," came the reply. "Your name will no longer be Jacob. From now on, your name is Israel because you have struggled with Elohim and with men," the Speaker paused, then smiled, "and have prevailed."

Relief, exultation, sheer joy flooded Jacob. *No, Israel! Finally, someone recognizes my struggles! And not just someone, but Adonai—but wait. Of all the names by which You are known, which name identifies You now?* Emboldened, he inquired, "Please, tell me Your name."

Another smile from the Other, as though laughing at a secret joke, "Why do you ask Me My name?" And then He uttered a blessing over Israel. A blessing whose words Israel could never recall, but which satisfied his soul. And so he let go, weeping in relief, burying his face in his hands. And when he looked up, the Other was gone. Daylight surrounded him, the two camps of his family waited on the slope above. He rose stiffly to his feet and limped toward home.

Peering down anxiously from the camps, Amos and Rachel saw a dirty limping figure walking toward them. They rushed out to him. "What happened? Are you injured?" they both asked at once. Smiling wearily, he told of the Other in the dark, of wrestling through the night, of the pain in his hip, and of his new name—everything that had happened.

"I have named the place *Penuw'el*—the 'Face of El,' " said Jacob. "Somehow, I cannot understand how, I have seen the face of Adonai Elohim and have survived."

"If you knew it was Adonai Elohim, why did you ask His name?" Rachel inquired.

"You have often remarked how my God has many names," Jacob said, and Rachel nodded her agreement. "Each name tells me something different about Him," Jacob explained. "I hoped to learn something new about Him through this experience."

"Did you not learn something new, Jacob?" Rachel asked, and he smiled.

"Of course. If nothing else, I learned that He will not tell me what I should understand through experience!" He smiled again, "And now *I* have more than one name." *Am I the crooked cheater or the one who struggles and prevails? Am I both? Perhaps only experience will tell that, as well.*

A servant ran and whispered in Amos's ear. Jacob looked at him, questioning, and Amos simply turned and pointed past the camp, toward the south, where a roiling cloud of dust moved rapidly toward them. "Esau," he said.

אחים

'achim

Brothers

Jacob limped through the camp to a high point at its southern edge. Already, a column of mounted men began to materialize out of the dust and rolling heat waves.

"Shall I deploy the archers?" Amos inquired.

"Quietly," Jacob said. "Tell them to be alert, but not arrayed for battle. We do not want to provoke a fight if we can avoid it. Send my wives and children to me as you go." Amos nodded and moved silently to fulfill his task.

With his family assembled, Jacob quickly organized them into groups. Zilpah, with her sons, Gad and Asher, in the front. Next came Bilhah, with Dan and Naphtali. Leah and her six sons, the four oldest—Reuben, Simeon, Levi, Judah—leading the way, while little Issachar and Zebulun held Leah's hands, and Dinah walked beside her mother. Last of all came Rachel with little Joseph.

"Follow me at a safe distance. I will do my obeisance to Esau. If he receives me, come forward and I will present you to him. If he does not, return to your two separate camps here." Jacob struggled for words of assurance and of comfort. He found a few. "Adonai Elohim, El Shaddai commanded me to return to my homeland and has promised to protect me and my household." He smiled, hoping to appear confident. "This last night," *What shall I tell them,* he wondered. *That I wrestled with my God? Will they believe it? Will they think me mad?* "Last night," he continued, "I implored El Shaddai to protect us, and He blessed me." They all looked intently at him. "You may have noticed my limp."

His statement was greeted with nods and murmurs of recognition. "That is the token of my blessing," he explained. "So as you watch me limping toward my brother, see each painful step as proof that El Shaddai will be with us, as He was at Mount Gilead." Kneeling, he held out his arms. "Come to me, my children."

And they came. The younger ones running and jostling, the older boys with careful dignity. He hugged them all, then each one, and kissed their foreheads. Then he embraced each of the mothers in turn: Zilpah, Bilhah, Leah, and Rachel. He gave them each a touch, looked into their eyes, and said a word of endearment. Then he turned and limped off toward the south and the approaching column of men.

The distance between them closed rapidly, despite Jacob's halting steps. In only moments, he could recognize his brother Red, Edom, riding at the front of the group. Esau held up his hand in the universal signal for the column to halt. His mount kneeled, and Esau swung off the saddle. He stood silently, watching his brother approach.

Jacob prostrated himself a little way off. Then he rose, took another step, and touched his forehead to the ground a second time. Four more times he repeated his obeisance. But as he was bowing the seventh time, Esau suddenly rushed toward him, fell to his knees, and embraced Jacob. Neither of them spoke as they wept in each other's embrace, washing away twenty years of bitterness, recrimination, and shame. Jacob had left. Israel had come home.

Jacob's wives and children, seeing Esau's acceptance, had come close. Esau put his hands on his brother's shoulders, looked him in the face, and nodded, smiling. Over Jacob's shoulder, he saw the women and children. Esau gestured toward them. "Tell me, who are these that have come with you?" he asked, eyes alight in anticipation. The brothers stood and faced the approaching group.

"They are the children El Shaddai has graciously given your servant," Jacob said. As he called their names, they each came forward and knelt before him; first the handmaids and their sons, then Leah and her sons, and finally Rachel and Joseph.

"Oh, you are a lucky man," Esau said. "So many fine sons!" Esau rubbed his chin a moment, seemingly puzzled over something. "Tell me, my brother," he said, placing a hand on Jacob's shoulder. "I keep meeting these herds of animals along my way. Why did you send them?"

Jacob bowed his head slightly, saying, "To find favor in your eyes, my lord."

Esau threw back his head, laughing, and clapped his hand on his brother's shoulder. "I thought as much. Brother, I have plenty. Keep them for yourself." He saw Jacob shaking his head, and said, "I mean it, Brother, you need not curry favor with me."

So Jacob turned facing him and grasped both of Esau's shoulders, eyes glowing. "Then all the more reason for you to keep them, not as an attempt to curry favor, but because I want to give you a gift celebrating our reconciliation. After all these years and all that has passed between us, for you to receive me as your brother—to see your face like this is like seeing the face of God! Please accept this as my blessing to you, for Adonai Elohim has been gracious to me, and I have all I need. And now I have my brother back!"

"All right, then," Esau said. "Not to gain my favor, but to celebrate our reconciliation, I accept!" The brothers embraced again, shouting, laughing, and weeping.

"I cannot keep my men waiting longer," Esau said, reluctant to end their time together. "We must be on our way soon. Why not travel together?"

"I would like nothing better, my brother," Jacob said. "But many of our ewes have lambs only a few days old, and as you see, there are children with us. If I drove them hard enough to keep up with you, even for one day, we would lose all the young ones, and many of the mothers too. There is no need for me to slow you down so. You and your men can move as you need to. I will travel slowly enough for the flocks and herds to prosper, and so as not to wear out the children. We will catch up to you later in Seir."

Esau considered for a moment, then suggested, "Let me leave some of my men with you for an armed escort."

Jacob smiled. "Thank you for the offer, Brother, but there is no need. Just let it be known that I am in favor with you; then no one will dare harm me."

"In favor with me? You are my *brother*!" Esau said.

"Exactly," said Jacob. "Who would risk Esau's anger by harming his brother?"

Esau chuckled. "My brother Jacob. Always thinking ahead. You are right, of course." Esau gave a short sigh and swung a leg over his kneeling camel. "I must be on my way, then; my men await."

Jacob nodded. "Go in peace, my brother," he said.

"And peace be with you, my brother," said Esau, before he returned to his waiting men.

Seeing there had been no conflict, Amos had quietly worked his way forward. As Esau rode away, Amos stepped up beside Jacob. "Master, may I speak freely?"

Jacob looked at him in surprise, "Of course, Amos. Always."

"Something about your brother—I do not trust him!" said Amos.

"Neither do I," Jacob said, "that is why I turned down his offer of an escort."

"Do you plan to follow him to Seir?" Amos asked.

Jacob shook his head and said, "A little distance often makes for happier neighbors, even when they are your relatives."

Amos protested, "But you said we would catch up with him later."

"I believe we will," said Jacob. "I did not say *when*."

"I see. So you do not wish to resume our journey right now?"

"I do, Amos. But we no longer need to hurry, do you think?" Jacob said, smiling.

"As you say, master," Amos replied and smiled in return. Amos started to go and inform the other servants, but then he paused. "Master?" he said.

"You want to say something?" Jacob asked.

"Just that it is good. For the first time on our journey to your home, there is no need to be anxious, no need to hurry. We have no pursuers. It is a relief for me," Amos concluded.

"A relief for me also," Jacob replied.

The next day's march brought them to a pleasant wooded area not far from the Jordan. "We will stop here," Jacob said. "With plenty of lumber, let us build *succoth*—sheds—to shelter our livestock and our goods while I scout for a place for us to settle permanently."

Even after his present to Esau, Jacob still possessed many, many sheep and goats, and large stores of grain and goods. Building sheds for so many required many days. More time for Esau to become occupied with other matters.

Jacob left Amos in charge of building the sheds. He took his oldest sons—Reuben, Simeon, and Levi—and several strong servants with him; they crossed the Jordan, looking for a place to pitch their tents and graze their flocks.

They had not traveled far when they came upon a major roadway winding through the hills. Though at first they did not meet anyone, the width of the road and the many foot- and hoofprints and rutted trails of wagons gave evidence of heavy usage. As they moved westward, they met caravans, long trains of camels laden with merchandise of all types; small family groups leading one or a few donkeys carrying heavy packs; even individuals with only a bundle and a staff. Reuben and his brothers watched in awed silence as they passed the strangers, then peppered Jacob and the older serving men with questions when they were alone or camped beside the trail in the evening.

On the third day, they sighted a settlement where the roadway passed between two mountains. From travelers they had met, they already knew this to be the city of Shechem.

"I see why they call it 'Shechem,' " said a delighted Reuben. "The way the houses nestle between the two mountains and flare out as they go up the slopes. It looks just like a *shechem*, or saddle!"

"It does," Jacob agreed. "Or maybe it was named for the many saddles they make and sell there."

Reuben pondered for a moment. "I had not thought of that."

"Maybe it was named because of all the roads that lead there," Simeon piped up.

Reuben looked confused, so Levi, as usual, finished Simeon's thought. "Because it took so many days in a saddle to get there!" Levi mimicked a saddle-sore traveler rubbing his backside. Simeon and Levi laughed. Reuben frowned. *Simeon and Levi are old enough to be considered young men now,* Reuben thought. *What will it take for them to get serious and stop acting like little boys?*

"Why not all three?" said Jacob, making peace. The boys shrugged agreement.

"We will look for our place near here," Jacob declared. "Near enough to see Shechem, but most of a day's travel distant. That way, we will benefit from the trade and commerce of the city and still have room for our flocks."

After a half-day's scouting, one of the servants, accompanied by Simeon and Levi, found a likely place. That night they camped there, and the next day they explored their surroundings, making certain there would be room for all their flocks and herds. "We will settle here," Jacob said, at the end of that day. "This site provides everything we need, even some cropland near a stream for Amos and his wheat and barley fields. A few trees in the main camp for shade. You have found a good place," he said. And Simeon and Levi beamed, as did the servant who had done the actual work.

"Tomorrow, you men stay here and prepare this camp for the arrival of my family. Dig a well and begin to build some pens. You know what we need." The men nodded. "My sons and I will go to Shechem and pay the sons of Hamor, the local chieftain, to stay here."

The next morning, as father and sons prepared for their journey, Reuben looked troubled. "Does Hamor own this land, Father?" Reuben wanted to know. "Why is it abandoned if it belongs to him?"

"Whether Hamor owns it or not," Jacob said, "it is in his power to make our stay here pleasant or unpleasant. If we pay him for the land and send him meat, milk, and grain from time to time, he will see our presence as an advantage to him. He will let it be known that raiding our livestock is an injury to himself. That knowledge alone will discourage many from bothering us."

"So we are paying him to protect us?" Reuben wondered.

"It is not that simple, nor that direct," Jacob said. "Let us just say that we are being courteous, showing our goodwill, so that he will be inclined to show us his goodwill."

"Why are we walking, instead of riding your best camels, arrayed in their finest saddles and trappings? It would be faster, and it would impress him," said Reuben.

"It would also make him think we are wealthy," said Jacob.

"Are we not?" Reuben said.

"Let me ask you a question, my son. From whom do you think Hamor would ask more, a wealthy man or a poor one?" Jacob said.

"That is easy. He could not expect too much from a poor man, so he would ask him for less," Reuben said.

"And do we want to pay more or less?" asked Jacob.

"Everyone knows that," said Simeon, and Levi said, "Less!" And the two laughed at Reuben, much to his displeasure.

Reuben said no more, but he asked himself, *How will deceiving Hamor help secure his goodwill?* But his father had started walking to Shechem, and the boys raced to catch up. They knew to be quiet on this trip, lest anything slip out that would work to their disadvantage.

At the city gate, Jacob approached the dignitaries seated nearby. "Where may I find Hamor or his sons?"

"We are his sons," said a strapping young fellow, dressed in beautifully striped robes, as he gestured to another. "What do you seek?"

"I am Jacob, son of Isaac, brother of Esau." The men nodded; they knew the reputation of Esau and of Isaac. "I sought my fortune in Padan Aram for the last twenty years, and now I am returned with my few possessions. I seek to live in peace on a small site near Shechem."

"You seek to live near me?" the strapping fellow asked, and he and his brother laughed. Then he explained, "My name is Shechem. My father, Hamor, liked this place so well that he named his eldest son after it." He looked slightly repentant. "I apologize for the crude joke. Where is this parcel of land you wish to settle on?"

Jacob carefully described the site, the setting, and the boundaries of the land he had in mind. Shechem grinned and nodded. "Quite a bit of space in this 'small site' for one with a 'few possessions.'"

"It seems small compared to the vast empty areas around it, where no one lives, which generate little or no tribute. Your servant hopes to develop the site and prosper there, in time. And as your servant prospers, he will be more able to demonstrate his gratitude," Jacob said, eyes down.

Shechem slapped his thigh and laughed again. "You are a shrewd one, are you not, now? What do you offer for this 'small site'?"

"I am a traveler, as you see. Most of my wealth is in flocks and herds. The little silver I have must be preserved for necessities. However, I can offer fifty silver *kesitahs* for the land," Jacob said. Everyone, including the crowd that had gathered to watch the negotiations, knew it was only an opening bid, a signal to begin the serious bargaining.

"Fifty? My father would not consider less than two hundred *kesitahs* for that site. It has a stream, trees, and large grazing areas."

"And it is wild now. It will take much labor and investment of money to make it fully usable. If I pay more than seventy-five *kesitahs*, not enough would remain to do the place justice," Jacob said.

"My father understands the need for a reserve fund. I will intercede with him, but he will need at least one hundred fifty *kesitahs*," Shechem countered. The crowd drew nearer, leaning in to hear the words and read the expressions. This bargaining would be the talk of the town for days to come.

Jacob clapped his hands to his head. "One hundred fifty! Oh, my poor wives and children. I thank you for your courtesy, but I must regretfully tell them," he pointed to his sons, "their mothers and their brothers, that we must continue our journey. I cannot pay such a sum!" He began backing away, and a gasp of disappointment ran through the watching crowd.

Shechem's brother made a show of whispering in Shechem's ear. The crowd leaned in even farther, hoping to catch a word or phrase. Shechem raised his hand and spoke. "Wait a moment, my friend." Jacob paused. "My brother properly reminds me that our father is a man of compassion. He would not want us to turn away so promising a man as yourself over a few *kesitahs*. I can persuade him, I think, to accept one hundred twenty-five silver *kesitahs*." And Shechem held his hand out as if to ask, "What about it?"

Jacob held up his hand, signaling that they should wait a moment. He pulled a leather purse from beneath his robes and began pulling out silver *kesitahs*, counting them aloud as he did so. "Fifty, fifty-five, sixty, sixty-five," the crowd held its breath as he counted, "eighty-five, ninety." He held the purse upside down, but nothing fell out, and a collective sigh of disappointment filled the air. Jacob's face showed his deep sorrow, as he dropped the empty purse to the ground. He started to turn away, when, suddenly, his face lit up, and he pointed straight up with his empty hand. Clearly, he had thought of something. He reached under the sash securing his robes, and his hand emerged with two more coins. "Ninety-five, one hundred," he said, as he placed those two with the other coins in his left hand. Then reaching forward with the coins in both hands toward Shechem, he asked hopefully, "One hundred?"

Shechem slapped his thighs and roared with laughter, nodding his head as the crowd erupted with cheers and applause. "One hundred," Shechem agreed, between fits of laughter. Jacob winked at the crowd as he poured the coins into Shechem's open hands. Shechem gave them to his brother, who placed them in a small chest chained to the bench where they sat, and the two bargainers clasped hands to seal the agreement. Still laughing, Shechem said, "Welcome to Shechem. May you prosper and live in peace with your neighbors."

Jacob bowed and responded. "May Shechem and your father, Hamor, always remember with joy the day they welcomed Jacob the traveler. May we always live in peace, as neighbors."

The crowd cheered, clapped, and danced their delight; and Jacob said to them, "When my flocks and herds arrive, I will send some choice rams to Shechem for the city to feast upon, as the first token of my gratitude." More cheering and clapping erupted.

Jacob and his sons made the appropriate courtesies to Shechem and the other elders at the gate and made their way back to their new home. Along the way, Jacob and Reuben walked quietly, alone with their thoughts. Simeon and Levi, on the other hand, were almost giddy. They could not stop talking about the wonders of the city, the marvels of Shechem.

nevalah

Disgrace

Jacob sent a runner back to the sheds, or *succoth,* as they now referred to the collection of simple shelters for his livestock and goods, telling Amos to bring the rest of the people, the flocks, and the herds, to the new settlement overlooking Shechem. A few weeks found everyone and everything ready and in place at the new camp. Weeks turned into months. The flocks flourished, wheat and barley stood tall in the rich soil near the stream, and Jacob's children grew toward adulthood. The occasional trading party went to Shechem, but for the most part, Jacob and his family kept to themselves.

Still the ever present mud-brick mass of Shechem loomed on the horizon like a slumbering giant nestled between the two mountains, Gerizim and Ebal. By day, dust and smoke smudged the sky above the city, and the occasional sound or scent drifted into camp on a capricious wind. At night, the moving lights of watchmen's lanterns and the glow of lamp-lit dwellings illumined its streets. Most in Jacob's camp regarded Shechem as a convenient place to buy and sell, but too crowded with animals and people for their comfort. But for Jacob's lone and lonely daughter, Dinah, Shechem became a place of mystery—all the more intriguing for being so near, yet rarely seen.

Simeon and Levi saw her interest and delighted in spinning romantic tales about their initial visit to the city. About the wonders there, about the rugged and dashing fellow, who not only helped run the city, but shared its name. And Dinah continually asked for more stories. But even Reuben, the eldest, rarely made it to the city. Still the stories seemed to delight their sister, so when they ran out of real experiences to relate, Simeon and Levi, never ones to take life too seriously, simply began making up stories. The walls of Shechem grew taller, its markets abundant with more exotic goods, its rulers more distinguished and wealthy. It all dazzled the young girl.

"I am concerned for your only daughter," Leah said to Jacob one day.

"Is she ill?" Jacob asked. "I have noticed she seems a little, perhaps, listless?"

"She is not ill, you silly man. She is a young woman, stuck here in a camp full of men. She needs the company of other young women."

"She has you and Rachel and the serving women. Even a few young serving girls," Jacob said.

"Men!" Leah said. "None of you understand that a girl, a young woman needs friends her own age."

"Did you have friends when you were young?" Jacob asked.

"I had my sister," Leah said, "and though not exactly friends, we could at least talk about our feelings with each other."

"Talking about her feelings with another young woman? This is necessary?" Jacob asked.

Leah put both of her hands up in the air, as if pushing Jacob away. "Men!" she said, shaking her head. "Sometimes!"

Jacob shrugged. He felt he knew little enough about raising boys. Until little Joseph came along, Jacob handled his sons like trusted servants. Joseph changed all that, or more accurately, Joseph changed Jacob. *Joseph, what an outstanding lad,* Jacob thought. *The image of his mother, yet masculine, a little boy through and through. Very thoughtful for his age. None of the others are anything like him!* The boys puzzled him. But Dinah totally mystified him.

Leah interrupted his musings. "It *is* necessary, Jacob. Your daughter needs young women, friends, her age." Jacob did not feel fully at ease with the notion, but Dinah's unhappiness and Leah's pleading eventually took their toll. He reluctantly gave his consent, and so it was that periodic visits to the young women of Shechem became part of Dinah's routine. At first, Jacob felt anxious during her absences, but over time, even his concerns subsided.

* * * * *

"Let us go to the marketplace," Nachalah said. "I hear they have some fine silks there today. Oh, I love to see the colorful, shimmery, dreamy silks." Dinah enjoyed her visits with Nachalah more than time spent with any of the other Shechemite girls she had met. Her family's wealth and connections—they were distantly related to Hamor, the founder of the city—gave her knowledge that impressed the country girl Dinah. And her name, *Nachalah*, meant "brook"; in her case, definitely a "babbling brook," as Simeon and Levi liked to say. Dinah found her friend's incessant chatter charming.

"Silk?" said Dinah. "I have heard of it, but I do not remember whether I have actually seen it. Herdsmen's daughters have little occasion to buy silk."

"You have not touched silk?" Nachalah fairly squealed, and Dinah shook her head. "Oh, my poor girl, you do not know luxury until you feel silk against your skin." Nachalah shivered. "It is unlike any other kind of cloth." Gesturing toward the door, she said, "We have to go to the market now. You *must* have something made of silk." Nachalah took Dinah's hand and began leading her out the door and down to the marketplace.

"But is not silk expensive?" Dinah asked. She had but little money in her purse.

"Once you see it shimmer and experience that delicious feeling, you will not care how much it costs," Nachalah assured her.

Truly, the silks in the market dazzled Dinah. And when Nachalah ran the fabric across her cheek, Dinah nearly swooned from the sensation. But it *was* expensive. Far too expensive for what little Dinah carried with her. Still she clutched it to her face with both hands, eyes closed, just for another instant.

"You must have it," a male voice said.

Both girls turned to see the speaker, and Dinah froze while Nachalah fairly burst with excitement. "That is Shechem!" she whispered in Dinah's ear. "Son of the town ruler! What a lucky girl that he should take notice of you!"

Dinah could not even nod as the man paid the merchant and held out the exquisite silk scarf to her. She recognized Shechem from Simeon and Levi's oft-repeated descriptions of the "strapping fellow they met at the gate" when they first entered the town. "And who is this exquisite desert flower?" Shechem asked, still holding the scarf toward her. Dinah reached forward, took hold of the scarf and, inadvertently, his hand. She wanted to speak, but no words came as she looked into his smiling dark eyes.

"Her name is Dinah," said Nachalah, giving Dinah a little nudge to break the spell. "Her father is Jacob, the wealthy herdsman who lives up the valley."

"Jacob has a beautiful daughter then," Shechem said, still looking directly at Dinah.

Nachalah nudged her again, hissing, "Say something."

Dinah felt her face flushing. In an attempt to shield her face, she suddenly pulled the scarf from his hand, seeming to snatch it away. Realizing what she had done, she said, "Oh, please forgive me . . . I . . . I . . ." More embarrassed than ever, she blushed again.

"You need not be sorry for being beautiful," Shechem said. Looking at the eager Nachalah, Shechem said, "I would love to treat you two young women to a meal at my home."

"The palace?" said Nachalah. Looking at Dinah, she said, "I have seen the palace only from the outside. It would be a dream to eat there! We would love to," Nachalah said, looking from Dinah to Shechem and back again. "Is that not so?" she said, prompting Dinah and nodding at the same time.

"I . . . I do not know," Dinah said. Actually, she knew her father would not approve. But Simeon and Levi would be so envious when they found out she had dined with Shechem—*in the palace*. She looked at Nachalah, who was still nodding eagerly. "Both of us?" she asked.

"Why, certainly," Shechem assured her. Dinah nodded her assent, and Shechem gestured toward his home. "Then follow me, ladies," he said.

The meal went beautifully. Servants attended their every need. Shechem offered them wine, as he would to proper ladies. Nachalah talked on and on, commenting on the palace, its furniture, the servants' livery—anything and everything. Shechem had eyes only for Dinah, asking her questions, complimenting her on her beauty, her attire, and her manners. She ate little, drank the delicious wine, and listened to his soothing voice. Looked into his mesmerizing eyes. At some point, she never really knew when, Shechem suggested Nachalah might like to tour the palace grounds, while he and Dinah continued to talk. It seemed harmless, and she did not see the gestures Shechem made to his chief steward. In any case, Nachalah did not return, but dazzled by the wine and attention, Dinah did not notice as evening fell. She saw only his eyes, tasted only the wine, and, as he reached for her, felt his gentle touch.

* * * * *

Awareness stole slowly over a weary Dinah. At first she sensed only a dull ache behind her eyes, aggravated by a glow that resolved itself into bright light. Inhaling deeply, she stretched her arms above her head, then outward.

Her right arm struck something, something that moved and groaned. Groaned! Suddenly reality hit her. She was in a strange bed, apparently without clothing, and not alone! She opened her eyes—and began to scream.

Out at Jacob's encampment, a concerned Jacob had sent his sons into the fields with his livestock, while he prepared to journey to Shechem in search of Dinah. "Do not do anything rash," Leah said, as he prepared a camel and a donkey for his expedition. "There may be a perfectly good explanation why Dinah did not return last night." Looking over his shoulder, she said, "Look, there she comes now."

Looking toward the road to Shechem, he saw a small group approaching, so he waited in hopes that Dinah might be among them. When they reached Jacob's tents, a teary-eyed Nachalah and her father presented themselves.

"Where is my daughter?" Jacob asked.

"Oh, my lord, Jacob," Nachalah's father began, "forgive your servant."

Alarmed, Jacob demanded, "Spare me the elaborate courtesies! Tell me of my daughter!"

"We . . . we went to the market," a sniffling Nachalah said. "I wanted to show her the fine silks there."

"Out with it, girl; where is Dinah?" Jacob said, his voice low, so as not to overwhelm the skittish girl, but insistent.

"With Shechem," Nachalah said, eyes downcast.

"I know she is still in the city," Jacob said, frustrated with the girl's evasion.

"My lord," Nachalah's father said, eyes pleading, "not the city, the *man*."

Jacob's blood turned cold. *With Shechem.* The girl's sad words echoed in his mind. "How long?" was all he could say.

"I am sorry to say this, my lord," Nachalah's father said. "Since yesterday afternoon."

* * * * *

Shechem took the screaming Dinah in his arms. "Do not cry, little flower," Shechem said. Dinah pushed him, and the sheet that had covered her fell away. She hugged herself in embarrassment and shame. Shechem pulled the sheet around her shoulders, and said, "I am sorry you feel badly, little flower. I did not mean you any harm."

"Harm! I am disgraced!" Dinah wailed. "Who will want me for a wife, now?"

"Is that what worries you, little flower?" Shechem said, tracing the path of a tear down her cheek with his finger. "I want you for my wife."

Dinah looked at him in disbelief. "Truly?" she said.

"Truly," he replied. "And to prove it—" he picked up a small mallet and struck a chime hanging at the head of the bed. A servant quickly answered. "Go to my father, Hamor. Tell him," he smiled at Dinah, "tell him to send to Jacob, the herdsman who lives out by the main road. Tell my father to pay whatever Jacob asks for his daughter, Dinah. Tell my father to do whatever it takes to get me this girl for my wife." The servant nodded and hurried away.

* * * * *

Jacob sat quietly after Nachalah and her father had departed. The sun had not reached its highest point in the sky yet; all his sons remained in the fields and with the flocks and herds. *It will profit nothing to disturb them at this time,* Jacob thought. *And I need time to think.* Leah had overheard the news, but she kept her distance. She had nothing helpful to say, and her role in urging Jacob to let Dinah visit the city made her less than eager to hear what Jacob might be thinking.

Despite Jacob's reticence, the news spread rapidly throughout his settlement. Before long, his sons returned, in ones and twos, from their work in the fields. They knew better than to address their father without invitation, and so they spoke of their grief, their anger, and their outrage to one another. Simeon and Levi hung back slightly, speaking in hushed tones.

"We should never have told her all those stories," said Levi. "We made Shechem sound irresistible."

"Our stories did not defile our sister!" Simeon countered. "Shechem did that!"

"I know. But our stories did make the city more enticing to Dinah. You know that is true! And we wanted her to think that way," Levi said.

"We did, that is true," Simeon agreed, "but Shechem, the man, did this terrible thing. Not our stories, not her dreams."

"We still bear some responsibility for this," Levi said, "and we both know it!"

"All right, I agree. What are we going to do about it?"

"This is an outrage," said Judah. "We must avenge our father's honor. We cannot tolerate this offence against Jacob's name."

"It is his name and his decision," said Reuben, loud enough to be heard by all the brothers. Judah gave a disgusted growl like a displeased lion. "Wait until he decides."

But Jacob felt numb with grief, guilt, and anger. He appeared oblivious to his sons' concerns, but from the aggressive rumblings of the conversation, Jacob could tell their blood was up. When runners came to announce Hamor's soon arrival from Shechem, the tone turned from angry to sullen as they watched a small party of men mounted on camels approach.

A grizzled and stocky man dismounted from his camel a respectful distance away and walked to Jacob. "I am Hamor," he said. "My son Shechem has his heart set on your daughter. Please give her to him as his wife." Jacob said nothing. Hamor surveyed the angry men around him and went on. "We welcome your settlement here. We invite your fine sons here," he said, with a sweeping gesture, "to intermarry with us; give us your daughters and take our daughters for yourselves. You can settle among us; the land is open to you. Live in it, trade in it, and acquire property in it." Still Jacob did not speak.

A second figure left his camel and walked up to Jacob. "I am Shechem," the young man said. Jacob merely nodded, while hostile sounds came from the brothers. Shechem surveyed the hostile group, and, entreaty in his tone, said, "Let me find favor in your eyes." As the angry rumbling increased, Shechem raised his voice, making his appeal, "I will give you whatever you ask." This silenced his audience, so he elaborated on his offer. "Make the price for the bride and the gift I am to bring as great as you like, and I will pay whatever you ask me." He scanned the faces again, and said, "Only give me the girl as my wife."

Judah spoke up. "We cannot do that," he said in a quiet voice. Jacob looked at Judah questioningly, so despite a warning glance from Reuben, Judah went on. "We cannot give our sister to a man who is not circumcised. That would be a disgrace to us." The brothers murmured their agreement, further emboldening Judah.

"We will give our consent to you," he said, eliciting shocked looks and grunts of disbelief from his brothers, "on one condition only: that you become like us by circumcising all your males." Simeon and Levi started to protest, but Judah silenced them with an imperious gesture. Judah, after all, had been the one insisting on vengeance earlier, so each brother's face registered the same question: *What are you up to, Judah?*

"If you will do this, *then* we will give you our daughters and take your daughters for ourselves. We'll settle among you and become one people with you." He looked at Hamor and Shechem. To Shechem, he said, "*That is our price.* If you will not agree to be circumcised, we take our sister and go," and he underlined the last word with a sweeping gesture of his hand.

Hamor and Shechem exchanged glances. "It is agreed," Hamor said. "All of the men of Shechem, including myself and my sons, will be circumcised."

"Soon," said Judah, pressing his advantage. "Our sister cannot remain long in her present situation. We will not tolerate a continuing disgrace."

"Right away," Shechem said. "I will return to the city and begin persuading the rest of our clan this very day.

"By your leave, then," Shechem said, looking at Jacob, who gestured a dismissal. Hamor and Shechem returned to their camels and the rest of their waiting party, and soon were a smudge of dust above the road into the city.

As soon as they were out of range and away from their father, the brothers all turned to Judah. "What are you up to?" they asked. And he laid out his plan.

ba'ash

Stench

It was not a battle; it was slaughter. Simeon and Levi, eager to avenge their sister's disgrace, struck at dawn on the third day after the mass circumcision of all the males in Shechem.

Totally smitten with Dinah, Hamor's son Shechem lived up to his part of the bargain, convincing the men of the city to be circumcised.

"These men, Jacob and his sons, are friendly toward us," Shechem had told them. "It is in our interest to let them live in our land and trade in it; the land has plenty of room for them. We can marry their daughters, and they can marry ours." He surveyed the crowd. "But the men will consent to live with us as one people only on the condition that our males be circumcised, as they themselves are." Everyone began speaking at once, so Shechem raised his hands, and then his voice. "Where will they sell their livestock and wool? Why to us, do you not see? So eventually their livestock, their property, and all their other possessions will be a great benefit to us. So let us do this small thing for them, and they will settle among us." It had taken some doing, but eventually Shechem convinced them all that this would be to their advantage.

And so all the men of Shechem were circumcised in one day. Simeon and Levi had mentioned that wine and *rosh*, the milk of the bright red "sleeping flower," would help with the pain. So the drinking of wine and *rosh* began even before the circumcisions. After three days of wine and *rosh*, no effective resistance remained. Weakness brought on by blood loss, aggravated by drinking large quantities of wine to deal with the pain, left them inebriated, uncoordinated, and confused. Very few of the Shechemite men could even lift a weapon. A few of the more wealthy, such as Hamor and his sons, could afford larger amounts of *rosh* in their wine. They were the lucky ones, struck down in their drugged sleep.

When Judah explained his cunning plan, Simeon and Levi eagerly volunteered to be the vanguard, to serve as the executioners. So on that fatal morning, Simeon and Levi waded into their work in a fury of revenge and bloodlust, cutting down every male they found. When the rest of the grown brothers followed up their attack, they found no male alive to impede their orgy of plunder. The bodies of the dead lay everywhere—at the city gate, in the streets, in doorways to houses, on their sickbeds. Only the sickening smell of blood slowed their progress as they swept up every item of any worth: silver, gold, precious stones, bronze weapons, and armor. Then they began rounding up the livestock and the shocked, grieving women and children for removal.

"What are you doing here?" Dinah demanded, as Simeon and Levi burst into her bedchamber. A glance at their stained hands, clothing, and bloody swords sent a thrill of horror through her. "Shechem?" she called. "Shechem!"

"He cannot answer you," Simeon said, as he reached for her with his free hand.

"What have you done to him?" Dinah screamed. "What have you done to my Shechem?" She writhed, screamed, sobbed, and flailed, grabbing at a silk scarf by her pillow, so her brothers wrapped her in a cloak, then wound a fallen drape around and around her, and carried her over a shoulder, like an animal trussed for slaughter. They tried to shield her eyes, but she caught sight of Shechem's crumpled form, a pool of congealing blood spreading from his body, and Dinah began screaming hysterically.

Once outside, they placed her across the saddle of a donkey and joined the wailing and bleating column of women, children, and animals leaving the burning ruins of Shechem. Simeon and Levi led the donkey carrying their sister down the road, guarded by their brothers and the menservants who had accompanied them on this raid. They nodded and waved in grim satisfaction as their fellow raiders cheered and clapped at their accomplishment.

Jacob watched with growing agitation as the column of people, goods, and livestock approached his camp. Looking beyond them to the smoke arising from the pillaged city, he realized what his sons must have done. When at long last Simeon and Levi walked into camp to the cheers of their brothers and the others of the raiding party, he could remain silent no longer.

Simeon and Levi, expecting his approval as well, took their sister down from the donkey and unraveled the cloth that had bound her. But the sobbing girl simply fell to the ground and curled up. "Our sister is avenged," Simeon said.

"And we have brought you all these spoils from those who offended you," Levi added.

Jacob regarded the bleating animals and the wailing women and children with disgust. He looked at the still-weeping Dinah on the ground, and he could no longer restrain himself.

"Avenged your sister, have you? Brought me spoils?" He shook his head and spat out the words, "You ignorant boys! You have brought me nothing but trouble. Can you smell the stench of blood, the reek of death, the vile odor of treachery you bring into my camp?" The boys stood in stunned silence. "Can you smell the smoke of betrayal?" He gestured at the dark cloud above Shechem.

"You have taken something sacred to our family—circumcision, the sign that we belong to El Shaddai—and have turned it into an instrument of treachery! You think you have made the inhabitants of this land *respect* the name of Jacob? Do you?"

Simeon felt deeply offended and spoke up in their defense. "I think they will fear to offend you in the future!" he said, to the general assent from his brothers.

"I am not the only one with a nose," Jacob said. "The Kinnahu and the Perizzites who live around here, they can smell the blood, the death, the treachery, and the betrayal as well as I can. And they will call that stench 'Jacob.' You have made *me* a stench in this land." Jacob paused, his anger giving way to fatigue.

"The Kinnahu and the Perizzites who live here may take it into their heads to rid themselves of this malodorous camp. You think you had a raiding party? If the Kinnahu and the Perizzites nearby banded together, they could destroy us, all of us. And then the column of wailing women and children and bleating sheep and goats would be our women and children, our sheep and goats. The smoke that darkened the sky would be the smoke from our tents and belongings, and it would be our blood soaking into the ground and adorning the hands and weapons of our enemies."

Still defiant, Levi said, "Should they have treated our sister like a prostitute?"

Jacob grabbed Levi and forced him to look on Dinah, still weeping on the ground. "Look at your sister, Levi. Look at her! Does she look like someone who has been rescued? Does she?" Dinah looked up at Levi's face, pure hatred in her eyes. Jacob thrust the lad away from him. "Has your vengeance made her happy? Has your anger," he said, pointing at Simeon, "healed her injuries? Do not speak to me of your sister."

Exhausted from rage, futility, and grief, Jacob turned away from the scene, covering his face with his hands. "How have you benefited your sister? You killed the man who wanted her as his wife. What do you offer her in his place?"

The brothers said nothing, mumbling again something about treating Dinah as a prostitute, but they knew better than to speak aloud. Jacob waved his hands again. "Take all this," he looked at the sorrowing wives and devastated children, the flocks and herds, "all this plunder and put it out of my sight. Amos! Leah! Rachel!" he summoned his wives and number one servant. "Take care of the people and the animals. See to it that none are abused. Now I must be alone. I must commune with Adonai Elohim, if He will hear me after what was done to His name this day."

Through the night hours, Jacob once again searched the dome of the heavens, seeing in his mind's eye the shimmering tower of light he had seen so many years before. His face upturned, he spread his arms wide. "Oh Adonai Elohim, God of my father Isaac and of his father Abraham, my household has done great evil this day. We have made Your name, and our own, to stink among our neighbors. Forgive us, Adonai. We ask for mercy." He petitioned El Shaddai all night, pleading for guidance. This night he heard no voice, met no shimmering messengers. The lights in the sky moved but did not speak. Despite that, as dawn broke and dew anointed his robes, he felt a strong sense of purpose. Though he heard no voice, the message seemed clear: *Go up to Beth-El and settle there and build an altar there to God, who appeared to you when you were fleeing from your brother Esau.*

Beth-El. The house of God. If Jacob could find peace and guidance anywhere, he would find it there. But he had something else to take care of first. When he returned, he would disclose his plans to his sons.

מרפא

marpe'

Healing

"Who is this that comes to my tent?" Isaac asked. The years had not been kind to him. One son thought dead for twenty years, the other blamed for that supposed death. His beloved wife, Rebekah, had passed to her rest without hearing that Jacob still lived. Loyal servants still cared for him and his possessions, and Esau visited now and then. But for the most part, the sightless old man sat alone in darkness, waiting for death. Usually a servant informed him of anyone visiting the camp, but the rustling of the tent flap and the sounds of at least two pairs of sandals prompted his question.

"It is I, your firstborn, Esau," a voice replied.

"Why did you come in unannounced, and who is with you?" Isaac asked.

"It is I, Jacob," another voice said. For a moment, no one spoke.

"Jacob! Truly, is it you?" Isaac's reedy voice revealed his excitement.

"Truly, Father," Jacob replied.

Isaac held out his arms, "I have longed for this day. Come and embrace me." Jacob did so, and the two men wept unashamed on each other's shoulders. "Why? Why did you wait so long to return?" Isaac asked.

"I feared . . . I feared you would still be angry with me. For deceiving you," the words came slowly from Jacob's reluctant tongue. "Since you never tried to contact me during all the twenty years I lived in Haran, I feared you had disinherited me. Never wanted to see me again. Surely," here he gave a meaningful look to Esau, "I gave you reason enough."

"Never contacted?" Isaac could not comprehend what he had heard.

245

"I have not told him, Father," Esau said.

Jacob looked at him. "Told me? Told me what?"

"We sent a courier to inquire after you. We were told you were dead," said Isaac.

"Not exactly," said Esau. "They showed Mother and Father some stained rags that someone said belonged to you."

"And they told us of a *sappiyr* box, like the one I gave your mother, the one I received from my father. We believed you must be dead."

"Who did this cruel thing?" Jacob demanded. "Who deceived—who spoke of my supposed death?"

"Your uncle Laban," said Isaac. "He told our servant you had never arrived there."

"Never arrived there!" said Jacob. "That lying, cheating—I labored for him twenty years. Twenty years, Father. And then I had to escape from him simply to take what I had earned!" Suddenly Jacob turned on Esau. "After my return, why did you not tell our parents that I still lived?"

Esau looked grim but did not speak.

Isaac broke the silence. "Probably because he feared we—I—would not believe him. And with good reason."

"Why would you not believe him?" Jacob asked. "Esau and I have had our differences, but I cannot remember any time that he deceived me." It was Jacob's turn to look grim. "I deceived you both, for which I am deeply grieved," Jacob paused. "But why would you not have believed him?"

"When you left for Haran, I pursued you," Esau admitted, "with—forgive me, Brother—with murder in my heart and vengeance on my mind. I pursued you for four days."

"I know," Jacob said.

"It was no secret," Esau admitted.

"I meant, I know you pursued me for four days," said Jacob. "Until you went to sleep under a twisted myrtle tree." Esau turned a shocked stare to Jacob. "It was far too exposed a position for sleeping. A prudent hunter would not have made that mistake."

"How do you—" Esau began, but Jacob had not finished.

"Of course, a prudent quarry would not have startled you awake the next morning, either," said Jacob.

Astonishment spread on Esau's face like morning light on a mountain.

"You circled around behind me?" When Jacob nodded, Esau searched his memory. "That gazelle that the hyenas devoured. That's where you lost me!" He began smiling.

"That's where I lost you," Jacob said. "I left a faint false trail, thinking the very faintness of it would convince you it was real."

Esau gave a rueful laugh. "Clever, Brother."

Isaac's face clearly revealed that he could not follow the conversation, so the brothers took turns describing the spoor left by the quarreling hyenas and how Jacob had used that to conceal his trail.

"But wait," Jacob said suddenly. "That still does not explain why Father would not believe you," Jacob said. Once again, the tent fell silent.

"When Laban presented the blood-stained rags to our servant," Isaac said, the words heavy on his tongue, "it seemed almost certain that Esau had either killed you or had driven you so hard that wild animals had devoured you."

"I told them I had not seen you after you left here," Esau said, then shrugged.

"Your mother did not—we did not believe him," said Isaac, silent tears flowing down his weathered face. "It is no secret," Isaac said, "Rebekah favored Jacob. And believing you had killed him," he said, waving a hand in Esau's direction, "she could never forgive you. She would not hear your name spoken," he said, the words now pouring out in a torrent. "She kept muttering about the older serving the younger and laughing bitterly. She ate little, spoke little. In a few short months, she grieved herself into nothing, and she died." Now his sightless eyes sought out Esau. "I blamed you for her death," Isaac said. "And it was pointless. Pointless. Jacob was not dead, and she died in vain. She let her grief cost her both of her sons, and I nearly did the same. I am sorry, Esau, my son. So sorry."

"We all have much to be sorry for," said Esau, looking into Jacob's eyes.

Jacob nodded. "We do, indeed. But that is behind us now," he said, as he embraced them both. "We have many tales to share."

They talked long into the night. Jacob told of the tower of blazing brightness he saw at Beth-El, of his bargain with Laban, of the substituted sister at his wedding. He told of his flight at shearing time and the encounter with Laban at Mount Gilead. As the comfort level grew among the three men, Jacob spoke of the recent events in Shechem, his regrets and anger.

"That is why I cannot stay," Jacob said, as dawn drew near. "I must return and move my household back to Beth-El."

"That is wise," said Isaac. "And although I would wish you near, my heart can rest knowing you live and prosper."

"Thank you, Father," Jacob said. "After I rest, I will return to my household."

"With my blessing," said Isaac. "But I have one servant that I think you should take with you." He motioned to Esau, who was smiling strangely. "Fetch her, Esau."

"I need no more servants," Jacob replied.

"Whether you realize it or not, you need this one." Isaac said. "She can give you something no one else can."

"She?" said Jacob, incredulous. "The last thing I need is another serving woman."

"Oh, she is too old to serve," said Isaac. "Truly, she is of little use here."

"Then why would I want—" Jacob started to say, but just then Esau returned with a very frail old woman Jacob did not recognize.

"I have grown so thin that he does not recognize me," the woman said, smiling. "Old Deborah is only half the woman she was when I swatted your backside when you were a little boy."

"Deborah?" Jacob said, smiling in spite of himself.

She walked up and grabbed his earlobe. "Any doubts now, little fellow?"

"None at all," he said, sweeping her tiny form up in his arms. "Your master is sending you back with me," said Jacob. "Is that all right with you?"

"All right? When I heard you were here, I told him he better send me back with you!" Deborah said, laughing her old hearty laugh, a sound too big for such a small body.

"What is happening when serving women tell their masters what to do?" Jacob said.

"Even a master can grow wise enough to know what is good for him," Deborah replied.

Jacob set her down and said, "All right, Father. I'll take her with me, but you owe me for doing it." Deborah howled indignantly, and the men laughed.

Isaac sent an oxcart and a driver with Jacob to carry Deborah on his return journey. The old woman's excitement at his return had energized her, but it became plain that though her spirit remained strong, her body was failing. It made the journey back slow, but Jacob did not mind. During the days, he walked beside the oxcart, talking to Deborah when she was awake, thinking quietly when she nodded off.

"I loved her, you know," Deborah said, as they sat around a warming fire one evening on the trip to Shechem. "Your mother," she added.

"You did love her, I know that," said Jacob. "Why do you mention it now?"

"Because I must tell you . . . other things about her," Deborah replied.

"You must?" Jacob said, his chest tightening. He had avoided thinking about his mother, her last years and her death.

Deborah nodded slowly. "And you must listen." Jacob nodded. "When Rebekah came to Hebron to wed your father, Isaac, Rebekah's father, Bethuel, sent me with her." She looked in Jacob's eyes to see if he understood. He nodded, so she continued. "I saw them when they were young—Laban and Rebekah," Deborah said, looking past Jacob as if viewing things at a great distance. "They lacked the talent for happiness," she said, looking sharply at Jacob.

"I . . . do not know what you mean," Jacob said.

"Do you not?" Deborah said. "When do you remember your mother happy?"

"I . . . I . . . ," Jacob could not find words. "I suppose I did not think about it," he said.

"And now that you have?"

The tightness in Jacob's chest had intensified. "She was not—I do not—I have no memories of her happy. Only a few of her smiling."

"It is painful, I know," said Deborah, "to realize this about someone you love." She paused, seeing the tears welling in Jacob's eyes. "But it is the only way to truly love them."

Jacob wiped his eyes. "What do you mean, 'The only way to truly love'?"

Deborah sighed. "Because otherwise, whatever affection you feel is not for the person who lived and breathed, but for the one who exists only in your thoughts." She placed a hand on Jacob's shoulder. "That's why I told you I loved her, Jacob. I saw her faults, and still I loved her." Jacob nodded his understanding.

"Your mother and her brother Laban always found reasons to be unhappy. Someone was trying to take advantage of them, or what they attained did not live up to their expectations. Bethuel, their father, took a hands-off approach to child rearing. 'Let them fight it out,' he used to say. The effect of all this was to teach them to trust no one, to take what they could."

"That sounds like the Laban I know," said Jacob, "but I never thought—"

"Of course, you did not," Deborah said. "No one wants to think of his mother as . . . anything other than perfectly loving and kind." The old woman paused, watching Jacob's face carefully. "Your mother blossomed under Isaac's love," she said, her own eyes sparkling at the thought. "I could see that his love gave her a happiness she had never known. I thought for a time that she might leave her old feelings of distrust behind."

Her voice grew quiet, "But when she could not conceive for twenty years, the old habits came back, and she found unhappiness despite Isaac's devotion. And then when she finally conceived, I thought that might finally bring her peace. But her pregnancy was so difficult. And then," she waited until Jacob lifted his head and looked into her eyes, "the 'Voice in the light'—she always called it that—gave her the Promise."

"Were you there? When she saw the light?" Jacob asked.

"I . . . was . . . nearby," Deborah said.

"What happened? Can you tell me about it?"

Deborah put her hands to her face, shaking her head. "I only saw its effects on Rebekah, and that was enough for me. But when she spoke of it, her face shone, just as yours does when you speak of Beth-El."

"Thank you for telling me that," Jacob said. "It must have been the same Voice that I heard."

"Perhaps," Deborah said, "but she turned that Promise into a curse." Jacob started to protest, but the old woman shook her head. "You know it, Jacob," she said. "That Promise, and Isaac's resistance to it, took her back to her old ways. Did you suggest deceiving your father, or did she?"

Jacob did not want to believe her words. "But, but she always told me to be patient, to wait—"

"And to be alert? Always looking for an edge, an advantage?" Deborah asked, eyebrows raised. Jacob could only nod in agreement. "That was her way. Hers and Laban's. And I always thought she was the cleverer of the two. From what you told me of your experience with Laban, it sounds like you got your mother's cleverness."

Jacob smiled, despite the ache in his chest. "I did get the better of him, more often than not," he said.

"But cleverness can never make you happy. And a lifetime of guarding against being taken advantage of only makes you bitter. I am sorry to say your mother never learned that. She could rarely trust anyone, not even El Shaddai." Old Deborah closed her eyes. "And that made her untrustworthy, that's why she schemed and deceived."

"She told me we had to be worthy of El Shaddai's promise, to be alert to make His word come true," Jacob said.

"And when you deceived your father and gained the birthright El Shaddai had promised, did that make you feel worthy?" Deborah asked.

Jacob looked into her face and saw, not condemnation or even pity, but empathy, and it broke his heart. "I did not," he said, sobbing. "I never felt more ashamed in my life," and placing his head on her shoulder, he wept freely. Those healing tears washed away the years of guilt, the endless regrets, the betrayal of his father and brother, the sorrow at the loss of his mother, and the grief for her life of unhappiness.

אמתם בנים

amthim, benim

Mothers, Sons

"We can no longer stay here," Jacob announced on his return from Hebron. "Our neighbors no longer trust us. It is only a matter of time until violence erupts. For our own safety's sake, we must leave."

Everyone agreed. All the brothers and most of the servants had encountered hostility and suspicion, which were increasing both in frequency and
intensity. The raid on Shechem had generated anger and distrust among all
their neighbors. Dinah had never recovered. She sat, day after day, looking
into the distance, rocking back and forth, clutching her piece of silk, and never
speaking, never seeming to hear. Upon their return from Hebron, Deborah
saw Dinah's grief and immediately went to comfort her. And when she met
Donatiya, the two aged serving women formed an instant bond.

"Where will we go?" asked Reuben. "We cannot return to Padan Aram.
We are pledged not to return past the *mitspeh*, the watchtower."

"We will go to Beth-El, where I encountered El Shaddai so many years
ago," Jacob replied. "El Shaddai will protect us there."

A buzz of discussion broke out, everyone registering his or her opinion.
"But we cannot go without preparation to Beth-El. El Shaddai will not accept
the presence of other gods. Before we set out for Beth-El, you must get rid of
the foreign gods you have with you and purify yourselves and change your
clothes. Then we shall go up to Beth-El, where I will build an altar to El
Shaddai, who answered me in the day of my distress and who has been with
me wherever I have gone."

One by one, they brought their *teraphim*, their amulets, and their talismans, representations of bulls and sparrows and rams and many other things. Rachel brought the *teraphim* she had hidden from her father, shocking Jacob, who until now had not realized the danger they had all been in because of her theft. Last of all, and anticipated by most, came the old woman, Donatiya, carrying a small bag filled with items of many types, accompanied by Deborah.

"Do you have things to dispose of?" Jacob asked Deborah.

The old woman smiled. "I do not. When I left the house of Laban with your mother, I still worshiped the gods of old Akkad," she said. "But when I saw how your father's faith in El Shaddai helped him to love your mother, my mistress, I gave up the old ways. I am here, now, to stand by my new friend."

Turning to Donatiya, Jacob asked, "Are you certain you want to do this, old woman? You have depended on these for a long time now. If you want to keep your gods and not accompany us to Beth-El, I am willing to give you your freedom and enough silver *kesitahs* to sustain you."

Donatiya bowed her head in respect, then looked Jacob square in the eye. "Thank you, Master Jacob. But this old woman has learned her lesson." Throwing down her bag, she said, "These gods have not taken care of Donatiya, not the way El Shaddai has watched over you!" She paused, appraising Jacob as a mother does an errant child. "Remember," she said, "I saw those shimmering messengers at Mahanaim." Her gaze grew distant. "I sensed, but did not see, the stranger that you wrestled with at Jabbok." She gave Jacob a penetrating look. "You have not been the same since that night."

"I am not," said Jacob. "That is why He gave me the name *Israel*," he said.

"*Israel.* 'Struggle with God.'" Her eyes grew wide at the realization. Then she folded her arms, delivering a verdict. "If any god is willing to take care of an old woman, it must be your Adonai Elohim. I will stay with you and with Deborah. I will go with you to Beth-El." And, side-by-side with Deborah, she walked away from her lifetime's accumulation of talismans, amulets, and charms. With the collecting completed, Jacob and his sons dug a deep pit at the base of a terebinth tree and buried everything there.

That evening they all, from Jacob and his wives and sons to the lowliest servant, bathed in the stream that ran through the camp and put on clean clothes. The next morning, they struck camp and headed south toward Beth-El, leaving the ruins of Shechem—and the life they had hoped to build there—behind them.

They began their journey with great concern, but no inhabitants from the towns they passed challenged them. Whether they feared Jacob and his God, El Shaddai, or were simply happy to rid their environs of those who destroyed Shechem, no one knew. Whatever their reasons, they let Jacob and his entire company pass without hindrance.

At Beth-El, Jacob found the stone he had erected two decades earlier. He made offerings to El Shaddai and worshiped there. One night as Jacob kept vigil, El Shaddai made His Presence known, renewing His promises to Jacob and once again naming him Israel.

A distraught Donatiya came to him early one morning. "She's gone," Donatiya said, tears in her eyes.

"Who is?" Jacob asked. "And where did she go?"

"Deborah," Donatiya said. "She did not wake this morning."

Jacob could not speak for a moment. He bit his lip and nodded silently. "Did she . . . ," he finally began to ask but could not finish the question.

"She just went to sleep," Donatiya said, her voice calm, "and didn't wake up." She saw Jacob's sorrow and added, "She was ready to rest." She paused a moment and then continued, "I miss her. We were like sisters these last few weeks. But she was tired. Now she rests."

Jacob could only nod. "I will miss her too. She . . . she helped me too."

And so they buried Deborah at Beth-El. Although Jacob never spoke of it, Deborah's death and burial at Beth-El both strengthened his connection to the place and released him from the need to remain there. After a few months, he let the grazing patterns of the flocks lead them slowly southward. When asked, he would say that he hoped to settle in Ephrath, but he made no effort to move decisively in that direction. Instead, they drifted southward only as they needed fresh pasture.

Early in their journey, a delighted Rachel informed Jacob that she was once again with child. "I told you El Shaddai would give me another son before I die!"

Remembering how she appeared after Joseph's birth, small and suffering, Jacob felt a twinge of fear. "I was satisfied with one son. I worry that you are too weak to—"

"Too weak! If Leah can give you six sons—"

"Leah was much younger when—"

"Are you telling me I am too old?" She said, smiling that she had him trapped.

He embraced her fiercely and said, "I care only for you."

"I know," she said, leaning back and brushing the hair back from his fore-head. "So be happy with me. I will bear you another son. I just know it is a boy!"

He buried his head in her shoulder and said no more. Even though he could see that carrying the child made her suffer, he did not speak of it again. She refused to be discouraged. All the same, concern for her reinforced Jacob's decision to move slowly. With her pregnancy not going easily, Jacob did not want to stress Rachel further with continual travel.

Before they reached Ephrath, Rachel went into labor. Jacob's concerns proved well founded, as labor was long and difficult for her. She delivered the infant with the last of her strength. Hoping to encourage her, the midwives said to her, "Do not despair, for you have another son!" But Rachel could tell that the effort had cost her too much. *"Ben,"* she said, "a son." Her face covered with perspiration, she gave a brave smile, and said, *"Ben, oni."* And with a final sigh, she lay still in death.

Rachel looked so frail when he saw her last that anxiety filled Jacob as he waited some distance away. When he heard the wailing and distress of the midwives, the mournful sounds chilled his heart. He ran to Rachel's tent. What he saw confirmed his worst fears. Rachel, his beloved, was gone from him forever. His knees collapsed, and he sank to the ground. But his grief was so great he could not weep. One of the midwives handed him a bundle. He looked, and there he saw his infant son. Joseph had Rachel's eyes. But this child had the rest of her features—nose, mouth, and ears.

"Ben, oni," the midwife said to him. "Son, sorrow. Rachel named him 'Son of sorrow' with her dying breath."

Jacob shook his head. "You misunderstood her." The midwives looked at him in wonder. "My Rachel would never," and, realizing she would never do anything again, the finality of her death hit him, and he began weeping. "She would never have named a child after sorrow." The words came in between sobs. "She . . . was so pleased . . . to be . . . with child . . . after so many years . . . of disappointment."

"But she said, '*Ben, oni,*' master," the midwife said. Gesturing to the others, she added, "We all heard her."

Breathing deeply now while looking at the infant's face, his jaw trembling as he spoke, Jacob said, "I know Rachel. She was saying, 'Son, I am sorry.'" He paused to let the hot tears dissolve the lump in his throat. His voice firming, he addressed the infant, "We are sorry, little one, that you must grow up without your mother." He paused once again to calm the trembling of his jaw. "But there is nothing sorry about this little jewel," he said, handing the child back so that he could be nursed. "His name is *Ben-jamin*," he declared. "He will be my right-hand little man," he said. "Do not forget his name! What is his name?"

And the women replied, "Benjamin. Son of the right hand. His father's right hand."

They buried Rachel right there at the campsite, not in some city, but just a place along their way to Ephrath. Jacob erected a monument over her grave. He anointed the monument with oil and prayed to El Shaddai. Then he prepared to leave.

Jacob now had twelve sons. Twelve. But two of them had no mother, and he no longer had the comfort of the only woman he had ever loved. Jacob did not want to stay where he had lost Rachel, so they struck camp and moved on, away from Beth-El, southward toward Jacob's homeland.

They resumed their slow drift southward at the speed at which their animals exhausted the grazing lands. As the days and weeks wore on, Jacob worked more and spoke less and less. Only Amos enjoyed his confidence. Jacob moved about the camp silently, almost like a ghost. Sometimes, it seemed as though they had left him in the tomb with his beloved Rachel.

By this time, the collection of people and animals that made up Jacob's household had grown so large that it became impractical for them all to camp together. So, leaving Leah and the rest behind, Jacob took half the animals and servants to care for them, along with his trusted Amos and his Rachel's two sons, and moved farther south to Migdal Eder, that is, to the tower of Eder.

In Jacob's absence, things did not go smoothly in the first camp. So Leah decided to act, summoning Reuben to her tent.

"Now is the time for you to assert yourself," Leah said when they were alone.

"Father did not leave me in charge; he did not assign anyone to run things," Reuben said. "And he always cautions me against throwing my weight around."

"You are Jacob's firstborn! It is your right by law and custom to take over when your father is gone," Leah declared, frustrated with Reuben's reluctance.

"My brothers do not see him as being gone," Reuben protested. "They say he is just in a different part of the camp."

"Then you must convince them otherwise," Leah said, fairly shouting. "Do something that unmistakably demonstrates that you are the master of this encampment."

"And what would that be?" Reuben asked. "I know you have something in mind, Mother. Just tell me." Reuben said, a feeling of unbearable weariness stealing over him. What Leah told him shocked him to his core. "I-I do not know. I—"

"Oh, stop stammering like a little boy," Leah said, disgusted. "If you want to show them you are in charge, you must act the man. Act the man!"

Reuben swallowed hard. Swallowed his pride, his fear, and his anxiety. "All right, I will!"

"Really?" Leah said, voicing her doubt and her contempt. "When?" she demanded, startling Reuben.

He glanced across the darkened encampment and took a deep breath. "Now!" he said, and turning on his heel he marched toward the tent sheltering an unsuspecting occupant.

The next morning, the news of Reuben's action spread through the camp before the midday meal. Within a week, it reached Jacob's camp.

Amos heard it first and immediately took it to his master. Jacob took the news stoically, as he did most things since Rachel's passing.

"So Reuben is spending his nights with Bilhah?" Jacob said, confirming that he had heard correctly. Amos merely nodded, not wanting to inflame the situation. "Claiming my concubine as his own and thereby asserting that he is now the head of the family. Is that what people are saying?" Once again, Amos nodded silently. "I have told that boy that he must earn respect, not demand it," Jacob said. "If I have learned one thing in life, it is that anything worth having cannot be taken by force from another." Although he spoke softly, the force of his words left Amos in no doubt of his anger. Jacob pondered a moment. "Leah is behind this, Amos," the words came out slowly, as if bitter to the taste. "She always pushes Reuben forward. She made much of being born first, believed she had the right to be married before her sister, and so felt justified in tricking me into marrying her." Jacob shook his head, "And now this. More treachery. Treating me as if I were dead."

The silence went on so long that Amos thought it time for him to leave his master alone, so he moved to leave, but Jacob stopped him with an upraised hand.

"I want you to go to the other camp, Amos. You, not someone else," Jacob said.

"As you direct, master," he said.

"Take this message to Leah. Tell her, 'Your lord Jacob says, "I have two sons with me. Joseph, the firstborn, and Benjamin, the younger." ' Tell her, 'Your lord Jacob says, "I know your son Reuben. I know he would not do this on his own. I am not dead, and I will avenge myself on those who act as if I am." ' " Amos nodded, then repeated the message.

"Take this message to Reuben. Tell him, 'Your lord Jacob says, "Sons inherit when their father dies. Thieves take what they can when the master is absent. Jacob lives. Your actions from this day forward will tell whether he is your father or only your master. Choose wisely, remembering that while fathers may forgive, masters must rule." ' " Once again, Amos repeated the message. "Take what you need, and go without delay," Jacob told him.

I am not dead, not yet, thought Jacob. And then it occurred to him, *Neither is my father. It is time for me to return once more before my father dies.*

כתנת פסים

kᵉtonet passím

Tunic of Distinction

"You would think Joseph was his only son," Issachar said. "Father talks of no one else." A series of grunts acknowledged his statement. The ten older brothers rarely had the opportunity to meet together. But they had been sent to move a large number of sheep and goats from one grazing area to another. As usual, Jacob kept Joseph close by, so the brothers could speak freely.

"I do not think he will ever forgive Simeon and Levi for the raid on Shechem," Reuben said.

"We all were involved in that raid, Reuben," Judah reminded him.

"Reuben is right, though," Simeon said.

Levi agreed, "Father blames us more than the rest of you."

"He seems to be especially angry with we four, the four oldest," Judah said, gesturing toward Reuben, Simeon, Levi, and himself.

"Reuben should never have gone into our mother's tent!" said Dan, jabbing his finger at the oldest brother, eliciting an angry response.

Issachar rarely spoke, but now he did. "Fighting among ourselves will not do any of us any good." Dan bristled, but backed down, and Issachar continued, "It will not win favor with our father, and it will only make Joseph look better."

Judah nodded. "Issachar speaks wisely."

"Besides," said Reuben, "whatever we have against each other, Joseph is a threat to us all."

"That is true," said Asher. "He can do no wrong in Father's eyes. He is only seventeen, and yet, when he was with the four of us," here Asher indicated Bilhah and Zilpah's sons, "tending the sheep, he ran back to Father, tattling on everything he could. He caused no end of trouble for us."

"Our mother, Bilhah, explained it to me one day." This from Naphtali. All the brothers looked at him. "He is Rachel's son." Several grimaced, as if to say, "We know that. So what?" Naphtali shrugged. "Rachel is the only woman he ever loved."

"Rachel, Rachel!" said Reuben, with real venom. "Enough of Rachel! She is dead, finally, and that is the end of her."

"Not really. She left Benjamin and Joseph. They remain, and they remind Father of her." Angry rumblings greeted this remark. "It does no good to be angry on our mothers' behalf," Naphtali said. "Indeed, my mother, as you know, was Rachel's body servant. She says she understands how he feels. She does not resent it; in fact, she told me this," Naphtali struggled for the word, "wistfully," he said.

"We all know there was rivalry between Leah and Rachel," this from Asher. "Why keep bringing it up? We ten brothers have three different mothers, but we usually find ways to get along. We have the same father, is that not enough?"

"But do we have the same father?" Judah asked. "Do we have the same father as Joseph does? Does he treat us all the same?"

Asher grasped the point. "I see. He does treat the ten of us more or less the same. Even little Benjamin does not get the kind favor Joseph does." He pondered a moment. "But what can we do about it? We cannot change our father. That has been tried and failed. Joseph is the problem." Asher looked up sharply, aware of the implications of what he had just said. And he saw nine other faces nodding grimly. *Joseph is the problem*, their faces said.

And the problem only got worse.

Jacob had moved back to his homeland, close to his aged father, Isaac, and his brother, Esau. The sheer size and number of each of their households dictated that they live some distance apart. Sufficient pastureland alone would necessitate significant distance. And unlike at Shechem, no city stood near their camp. So they depended upon itinerant merchants to supply certain of their needs: metal implements, tools, and some types of cloth.

Usually the frugal Jacob limited his purchases to a few necessities. He might purchase a few trinkets for his wives or simple toys for the children, but he had built his wealth by shunning luxuries. Still, the merchants never gave up hope that the wealthy herdsman might open his purse more liberally, and accordingly made a full display of their finest wares.

It was Jacob's custom to entrust one of the younger sons with his list of needed goods and the opportunity to bargain for them. The young men enjoyed the challenge, the responsibility, and the opportunity to see what the world had to offer, even if they could not buy it. "They must learn how to bargain sometime," Jacob told Amos. "How much better to do it here, with a limited list of goods, than later, when much more is at stake." Amos could see the wisdom in that. Once finished, the chosen bargainer would present the final results to Jacob for his evaluation and approval. Jacob never upbraided the son chosen to negotiate, only asked questions and made suggestions. This approach had proven itself, as each of the brothers became skilled bargainers. This day it was Joseph's turn. He looked at Joseph. *A tall lad*, he thought. *He is no longer a boy, but a young man. In fact, it looks like he has outgrown his cloak. I must have the women weave a nice new one for him.*

One by one, Joseph acquired the items on his list. He could pay in silver *kesitahs* or barter some of their own fine wool, grain, or even cheese. He presented the final tally to his father.

"Excellent job, Joseph." Jacob beamed at his son. And truly, Joseph had traded shrewdly. Excellent grazing and grain harvests had yielded an unusual surplus of high quality goat milk, which, in turn, provided an abundance of cheese. The merchant, as it turned out, had an eager market for the cheese and gladly accepted that instead of silver for his goods. Silver might have value, but did not itself yield further profit. Whatever silver he received would be worth exactly the same wherever he went. But a city hungry for quality cheese would pay a premium. So Joseph had struck bargains that made the most of the camp's resources. Jacob rewarded Joseph's diligence with a silver *kesitah*. "Buy something for yourself," Jacob said.

Jacob was surprised and not pleased when he saw Joseph purchasing an expensive silk scarf with his reward. *A strange thing for a young man to buy*, he thought, but he held his peace. And when he saw Joseph take the scarf to the still-grieving Dinah, he was glad he had.

"Here is a new scarf for you," Joseph said. Dinah looked at the scarf. She reached out and fingered it for a moment, a look of wonder temporarily replacing her usually pained expression, but then she shook her head, clutched the original piece of silk, now much worn, all the closer, and looked away. "I will keep it for you," Joseph said. "Perhaps you will change your mind."

A moved Jacob decided to take a look himself before the merchant packed up his goods to depart.

He had no intention of buying anything. Joseph had obtained everything on the list, all the necessities. All the sons were beyond the desire for toys. Even Benjamin, the youngest, looked more and more the young man every day. *Benjamin,* thought Jacob, smiling to himself, as he absentmindedly looked at some bolts of cloth. *"Son of my right hand." And he is left-handed! But Joseph is really the one I depend on. And what a compassionate lad, to think of his sister.*

He focused on the cloth again, and there he saw a tightly woven fabric, bright with the reds and purples for which the Kinnahu were famous, and from which they got their name, but including blues and greens in a repeating leaflike pattern. It was, in a word, exquisite. Behind him, he heard Joseph gasp at the beauty of the fabric. And he noticed again that Joseph's cloak was too small for him. Jacob reached a decision. Joseph needed a cloak fit for a man, a man of property and responsibility. And here was a fabric that shouted substance and prosperity.

"What do you call this weaving pattern?" Jacob asked.

"My lord has excellent taste," the merchant said, bowing repeatedly. "They call that pattern 'fruitful bough,' my lord. You can see the vigorous grapevine."

Jacob spoke to Amos, who fetched a seamstress.

"I want you to make a cloak for Joseph out of this fabric," he told her. "I do not want one of those short ones that barely reaches the knee. He needs one that goes down nearly to his ankles." She nodded and began measuring Joseph on the spot. Casting about, Jacob spotted what else he wanted. "I want it edged with that golden fringe, over there."

The merchant smiled and said, "Excellent taste, my lord. It will be a robe fit for a king!" The seamstress told the merchant how much cloth and fringe she required, and Jacob settled on a price fair to them both. His business completed, the merchant packed and left.

The seamstress, the best in the camp, had the cloak ready in three days. Joseph put it on and looked at his image in the seamstress' polished brass mirror. His breath fled, taking the power of speech with it. Jacob could neither contain nor express his delight. "Your reward for a job well done, my son." *He does look like a king!* Jacob thought. *His mother's eyes and a strong, manly bearing.*

Not everyone had the same reaction.

"I cannot believe Father bought Joseph that cloak," Simeon said.

"He struts around like he is royalty and the rest of us his slaves," Levi snorted in return.

"Joseph looks ridiculous in that new robe of his," Asher said, "like a goat in silk!"

Joseph's expensive and ostentatious new cloak soured his relationship with the ten older brothers even further. In front of their father, they behaved civilly, but in private, especially with each other, their comments were vicious. The spectacle of him strutting around in his "royal" robe exacerbated his brothers' long-term resentment to the point where they literally hated the sight of him. Jacob, seeing only what he wanted to see, remained oblivious to the older brothers' molten rage intensifying beneath the surface of meticulous courtesy.

Bilhah could see this. She had been Rachel's closest confidant in life, and she understood Jacob's devotion to Joseph and Benjamin as the heritage of his beloved. But she could not find the way to explain to Jacob what he was doing to all his sons.

"My sons hate him as much as their brothers do," Bilhah said to Donatiya. She found the old woman to be a patient listener, a close observer, and an experienced counselor. "I wish Jacob had more sense than to buy him that ridiculous robe! It stirs up his brothers beyond reason."

"It is not the cloak itself that matters," Donatiya said.

"What do you mean?"

"From birth, Master Israel surrounded Joseph and everything he said or did in a mantle of unwavering preference," Donatiya explained. "Joseph, the golden child; he can do no wrong. This cloak of favoritism isolates both Israel and Joseph. They cannot see the brothers' hatred."

"How can I help them see this cloak of favoritism you speak of?" Bilhah asked.

"What makes you think they want to see it?" Donatiya asked. "They will not see it until they have no choice!" the old woman said, sadness in her eyes and voice.

"What will that take?" Bilhah asked.

"Nothing good," Donatiya said. "Something bad is going to happen, I reckon. Really bad."

"What can we do to stop it?"

" 'We'?" Donatiya gave a bitter laugh. "*We* cannot stop it. Even the gods—maybe even Israel's El Shaddai, I think—sometimes cannot stop what evil men are determined to do. Maybe El Shaddai can turn things—I do not know how to explain—not stop bad things, but twist them for good." The old woman shrugged her shoulders. "Maybe. I don't know." She thought for a moment. "Pray," she said, "pray to Israel's God. That is all I know to do."

After the initial rancor provoked by the extravagant robe, on the surface it appeared that emotions calmed a bit. With the approach of the wheat harvest, if not peace, at least a truce between the older brothers and Joseph began to settle in. With the warm weather, Joseph had no reason to wear his ostentatious cloak except at night, and then its bright colors were not so conspicuous. The prospect of a bountiful wheat crop raised everyone's spirits, further easing the tension.

The immense but joyful task of harvesting wheat commanded everyone's attention and increased their labor. Those who remained watching the flocks and herds worked twice as hard, taking on the duties of their fellow herders whose labor was needed in the wheat fields. Even those accustomed to strenuous labor viewed the wheat harvest as arduous. The strongest workers went first, bending and swinging their sickles in a steady rhythm, each swath carving a great arc from the standing grain. Following them, workers stooped to gather the grain into bundles, which they then tied into standing sheaves. At the end of the day, after a good meal and a bath, the weary harvesters slipped into a deep and untroubled slumber.

One morning during harvest, as all the workers moved into the fields to continue their work, Joseph looked at the ranks of sheaves and suddenly exclaimed, "I saw this in my dream last night!"

Reuben heard him and said, "We all have the same problem—swing the sickle all day in the field, then go to bed and swing the sickle in our dreams!" Several of the older brothers laughed in recognition. "I know what you mean," Asher said, "I cut down twice as much grain in my dreams at night as I do in the daylight."

"This was different," Joseph said. "In my dream, we were all—even little Benjamin—binding sheaves of grain out in the field when suddenly my sheaf rose and stood upright, while your sheaves gathered around mine and bowed down to it."

"Are you serious?" Judah asked. "Do you intend to reign over us? Do you think you will actually rule us? Dream on, dreamer," Judah said, and everyone began laughing. But it was bitter laughter, and the story of Joseph's harvest dream stirred up anger that had begun to fade.

Summer gave way to autumn and cooler weather. Everyone dressed more warmly, Joseph in the fringed and multicolored cloak that so annoyed his brothers. To make matters worse, he announced another dream.

"Listen," he said. "I had another dream, and this time the sun and moon and eleven stars bowed down to me."

After Jacob heard this, he shook his head and said, "What is this dream you had? Will your mother and I and your brothers actually come and bow down to the ground before you?" Seeing Joseph's crestfallen expression, Jacob asked, "Joseph, why do you say such things? It only inflames your brothers against you."

"Father, these are not ordinary dreams," Joseph said. "They are powerful. I do not know what they may portend. I hoped others might be able to help me understand them. I am sorry."

"Can anyone understand someone else's dreams?" Jacob said. "I do not understand my own." Softening, he said, "I have had frightening dreams sometimes, too, Joseph. Everyone does."

"These dreams do not exactly frighten me—neither are they like common dreams," Joseph said.

"You are still young," Jacob said. "They may be more common than you think."

But Joseph only shook his head. *They do not believe me*, he realized. *But these dreams are anything but common.*

בעל החלמות

ba'al hacholomot

Lord of the Dreams

A difficult winter stressed the nearby grazing lands. Jacob's flocks and herds had become so numerous that finding enough pasture became a continuing challenge. This forced the servants to scout out suitable grazing areas farther and farther from Jacob's base near Hebron. Eventually, one did return with a favorable report.

"Amos tells me that one of his scouts located a grazing area large enough for most of our animals," Jacob reported to his assembled sons.

"Good news!" said Issachar, "I will reward that servant personally." The other brothers murmured their approval.

"There are two concerns, however," Jacob said. The brothers looked at him expectantly.

"This grazing area is some distance away—"

"Come, Father, we knew that would be the case, since our animals are so numerous. And the winter has stressed all the grazing areas nearby," said Judah.

"That may be, but this area is a significant distance and may not be welcoming to us," said Jacob.

"If it is empty grazing land, who would be there to welcome us or not?" said Simeon.

"It is near Shechem," Jacob said. The town's name settled on the air like smoke from a distant fire.

"I see," said Judah. He thought for a moment, then said, "We are not going there to trade, anyway." He looked at his brothers and saw them nodding. "If we stay clear of the city and away from the main road, perhaps, they will not be troubled by our presence."

"My thoughts too," said Jacob. "We will divide the animals into three equal groups. One group will remain here, with me, Amos, and Joseph and Benjamin. The rest of you, my sons, will take the other two groups and all the servants and camels and donkeys you need, and journey toward Shechem."

"I do not like it," Dan said. "Being separated by so great a distance makes us vulnerable. And if we do not go into Shechem, how will we obtain the foods and supplies we cannot provide for ourselves?"

"I will send messengers on a regular basis," Jacob said. "You can send me word of your progress and lists of goods and things that you need from merchants. I will purchase them," said Jacob, "and send them with the next courier. If an emergency arises and you have to send someone to Shechem, have him wear dusty and worn clothing, as though he has traveled a great distance."

After discussion, the brothers agreed to the plan and began preparing for the massive relocation.

"It is a good plan," Amos said, hoping to reassure his master. "We urgently need more pastureland after this difficult winter. It will be good to have more space."

"Not only for the animals," said Jacob.

"Master?"

"I am sending the ten older sons," said Jacob.

"I know this," said Amos.

"I am keeping Joseph and Benjamin with me," Jacob added. Amos shrugged, his face revealed puzzlement. "I think my sons might benefit from space every bit as much as the animals. Separation may reduce the rancor between the older sons and Joseph. Do you not think so?"

Comprehension spread across Amos's face. "Very wise, master."

"Am I?" Jacob asked. "Let us hope so."

The plan seemed to work well. Returning couriers reported abundant grazing land near Shechem, and no incidents with the residents of the city. The brothers' camp included so many artisans that they could supply most of their own needs. And with planning, Jacob's return couriers could take with them what few items they needed from traveling merchants.

After some time, communication broke down. Jacob had sent several couriers but had received none in return.

"Should we be concerned?" Amos asked.

"I am not alarmed," Jacob said. "The last courier said they needed all the servants they had to manage their flocks and herds. Perhaps they simply could not spare anyone for courier duty."

"Should I go and see what has happened?" Amos inquired.

"I have the same problem," Jacob said. "I cannot spare you right now." He thought for a moment. "I will send Joseph. I can spare him, and it will be good for him to make this journey on his own."

"Will his brothers not still be angry with him?" Amos asked.

"I have considered that," Jacob said. "I think enough time has passed so that tempers will have cooled. They should be glad for any assistance we can render them, no matter who brings it. In any case, he need not be there long enough to annoy them further. They can send him back quickly with a list of their needs." Again he paused for contemplation. "Joseph it will be."

Amos knew that Jacob welcomed advice, but not after he had reached a decision. A good servant had to know when to question and when to obey. From the tone of Jacob's voice, Amos knew that this time was a time to obey.

For his part, the prospect of a long journey on his own excited Joseph. He had been younger during the sojourn from Haran to Shechem, but the memories of some of those distant places called to him.

"Find out where your brothers are, if they have moved, and what supplies they require. Bring back news of how they fare," Jacob had told him.

"I will, Father," Joseph said. "You can rely on me."

"I know that I can," Jacob said, beaming at him. Jacob put his hands on Joseph's shoulders and looked him up and down. "Quite the splendid young man," he said. Jacob looked over his son one more time, sighed, and said, "Off with you then. The sooner you go, the sooner you will be back with me. Remember whose son you are. Let your conduct bring honor to my name." *I will miss you, my Joseph*, he thought. *Protect him, El Shaddai. Bring him back to me.*

Three days' journey brought Joseph to a small rise overlooking the road to Shechem. From this vantage, he had an unimpeded view of the broad plain below Ebal and Gerizim, the two mountains between which Shechem nestled. He could make out the dark masses of some sheep and goats, but in nothing like the numbers his brothers would have with them. He decided to leave the road and move toward one of the flocks. Before long, a herdsman spotted him and came over to ask his business.

"What are you looking for?" the man asked.

Joseph replied, "I'm looking for my brothers. Ten men with a great number of sheep and goats, many servants, donkeys, and camels. They came from near Hebron, looking for grazing lands. Have you seen them?"

"I have seen them," the man answered.

"Can you tell me where they are?"

The man leaned on his staff and made a sweeping gesture toward the north. "They have moved on from here," the man answered. "I heard them say, 'Let's go to Dothan.' Cross over that wadi, there," he said, pointing. When Joseph nodded his recognition, the man went on, "You will find their trail on the other side. Just follow the trail they left. With so many animals, it will be easy to follow."

Joseph found the trail leading through the center of the vast plain. Traveling alone, it would not be difficult to overtake the slow-moving mass of animals and people. Eventually, he caught sight of a group of men near some sort of abandoned settlement. Even without the flocks and herds, Joseph felt certain he had found his brothers. With a sense of accomplishment, he quickened his pace. *Will they not be surprised to see me!* Joseph thought.

The ten older brothers had sent the flocks on ahead to graze while they considered the merits of settling in to the remains of a long-abandoned encampment.

"I think we should make this our base camp," Judah said. "With a little work, a few relatively simple repairs to the remnants of livestock pens, grain storage areas, and an empty cistern for storing water, we could have a fully equipped camp up and running in short order."

"I see that," said Issachar. "But even here, the grazing is not so rich. There is a reason whoever built this camp abandoned it. We might put in that work and still have to move on before we reaped the full advantages."

"Look, my brothers," Dan said. "Here comes the lord of the dreams!"

"You mean he dreams that he is lord!" said Asher.

"I am so sick of his superior attitude," said Simeon.

"I thought at least way out here, we were rid of him," added Levi.

"Why not?" said Dan.

"Why not what?" asked Reuben.

"Why not get rid of him for good?" Dan said. "We could throw his body in that abandoned cistern. No one would find him for years." The import of Dan's words struck the brothers silent for a moment.

"We could take that fancy robe of his, rip it up, and put some goat's blood on it," said, Simeon, warming to the idea.

"And we could tell Father some wild animal killed him," said Levi. "See what comes of his dreams then!"

"Let's do it!" The words came from several directions at once.

Joseph was drawing closer to the brothers. Soon he would be within earshot. Reuben said, quietly, "No matter what we say now, we do not really want to be guilty of shedding our brother's blood. Do we want the sin of Cain on our heads?" These words seemed to sober the brothers a little. "Why not just throw him into the cistern? That would give us time to think about this." *And maybe I can talk you out of this or rescue him before we do something we cannot undo*, he thought to himself. "If we decide to kill him, he will still be in the cistern."

The brothers looked at one another and each gave assent. They waited in silence for Joseph's approach.

"Our father sends his greetings," Joseph said, when he reached the brothers. "He was concerned when he did not hear from you."

The brothers gathered around Joseph. Dan put an arm around Joseph's shoulder. "We are so glad he sent you to express his concern," Dan said.

The greeting seemed a little to strange to Joseph, but, eager for acceptance, he ignored the alarms in his mind. "I was glad to be the one selected," said Joseph. He sensed a flicker of movement behind him. "What—" a sudden blow stunned him. Another sent him into darkness.

When he awoke, it seemed that night had fallen. Aching all over and slightly chilled, Joseph found himself in some sort of circular enclosure. A shaft of moonlight illuminated the far side. But no, it was far too bright for moonlight. The darkness told him he must be in a cave or somewhere deep within the earth. Rising stiffly, he looked up to see an opening overhead, to blue sky far above him. He was in some kind of dry well, maybe an empty cistern. In any case, the walls rose straight up, rendering it impossible to climb out. *I will just have to wait*, Joseph thought. *My brothers enjoy tormenting me. They will tire of the sport and let me out.*

The aroma of roasting kid filtered down into the cistern, helping Joseph distinguish one of the pains he felt as hunger. *It must be time for the evening meal,* he thought. He felt chilled again and realized that he no longer had his outer cloak for warmth. *If I complain about hunger or cold, it will only give them reason to abuse me more.*

On the surface, the brothers settled into their evening meal, calling out to Joseph about how good it tasted and how tender, accompanied by the raucous laughter of the others. As they ate, they caught sight of a trader's caravan coming their way. A train of camels led by a few weary men. Judah called out to them. "Come share our humble meal, brothers."

The traders thanked them, secured their camels, which promptly knelt to rest, and eagerly partook of the roast kid. "So tell me, friends, who are you? What is your business, and where are you going?"

The traders shared guarded glances. A tall one, with dark eyes and crooked teeth, spoke for them. "We are sons of Kedemah, the son of Ishmael. We are merchants, come in peace, just passing through this plain with goods from the East, bound for Egypt."

"My brothers and I," Judah gestured to the rest, "are grazing substantial flocks. You may have passed by them just to the north."

"We did. Many sheep, many goats. But we passed by another man who claimed to be the owner," said Crooked Teeth.

"That would be Reuben, our brother," said Judah. "Strapping fellow with a blue stripe on his cloak. He was going to—" the other brothers leaned forward, wondering what he was going to say, because Reuben had gone to check in with the servants watching the flocks, so that no messengers would suddenly come upon the brothers and ask why Joseph was in the cistern, "inform our herdsmen that we would be with them in the morning."

"Now that you tell me, I can see that he resembles several of you," the trader said.

"What goods do you take to Egypt?" Judah asked.

"On this trip, we have mainly balm and myrrh."

"Do you buy other kinds of merchandise?"

"Anything with profit in it." The trader gave him a sly look. "You have something to sell?"

"We might. Let me talk to my brothers in private," he said, arising. The others followed him a safe distance away from the traders, still attacking their food with enthusiasm. Judah said to his brothers, "What will we gain if we kill our brother and cover up his blood? Come, why not sell him to the Ishmael-ites instead; after all, he is our brother, our own flesh and blood."

"If we kill him, we might get a little satisfaction, but he will not suffer very long," said Simeon.

To this, Levi added, "As a slave, he might live in misery for years."

Dan added his thoughts. "This way we have something to show for our trouble! We split up the money, and every time we think of it, we will see our obnoxious little brother clothed as a slave, instead of in his ridiculous robe." The brothers agreed.

Judah went back to the traders. "We happen to have a strong young slave, if you are interested."

"Male or female?" asked Crooked Teeth.

"Male," said Judah, and seeing what appeared to be disappointment on the trader's face, he added, "but young and strong." He clenched his fists and flexed his arms to demonstrate, "Very strong."

"Twenty silver *kesitahs*," the trader said. "If he is as good as you say."

"Done!" said Judah. The transaction completed, Judah took Crooked Teeth over to the cistern. They lowered a rope, and Joseph climbed out. He started to speak, but a single sharp stroke from the trader's camel whip silenced him. Before the stunned boy could protest, Crooked Teeth bound his wrists behind his back with a leather thong while Judah held him. The trader lifted Joseph's hands, causing excruciating pain. Then, using Joseph's bound hands like a tiller, Crooked Teeth steered him over to the camels. There another trader fixed a leather collar with a long cord attached around Joseph's neck. Joseph twisted away from him briefly, but Crooked Teeth struck him repeatedly with the whip until the lad lay quietly sobbing. Hoisting him up painfully by his bound hands, the trader tied the free end of the cord attached to his neck to the aft pommel of a camel's saddle.

Crooked Teeth showed Joseph the whip in his hand, raised his eyebrows, and said, "If you cause any trouble, I will whip you. Do you understand?" Joseph's head dropped, and the trader, placing the handle of the whip under the lad's chin, jerked his head upward. "Do you understand?"

Joseph said quietly, "I understand."

Crooked Teeth ran his hands over Joseph's body, testing his muscles. Once again flourishing his whip for emphasis, he forced Joseph's mouth open, examining his teeth. Satisfied, he nodded at Judah. "Twenty *kesitahs*," he said again, holding out his hand. Another trader placed a small leather pouch there, which Crooked Teeth offered to Judah.

"May I speak to my brothers?" Joseph asked both Judah and Crooked Teeth.

The trader raised his eyebrows in alarm. "Your brothers?" he asked.

Judah did not answer the trader's question, simply saying, "Let him speak."

Looking at his brothers, Joseph said, "I would rather die than be a slave. Will none of you help me?" In desperation, he asked, "What have I done that you should hate me so much?"

Judah looked at the miserable Joseph. Then he looked at the rest of the brothers, wordlessly asking, "Do we really want to do this?" He saw eight pairs of troubled eyes: some angry, eager for revenge; others wavering and fearful. As he looked into each face in turn, several gave sharp nods, while others seemed to ponder an instant before signaling assent. They all agreed. So Judah nodded to Crooked Teeth and accepted the silver.

Joseph, too, had searched the faces of his brothers, seeking a single gleam of sympathy. He saw anger, reproach, fear—but no sympathy. He continued to look at them as the traders roused the rest of the camels, took their places, and with clucks and whistles, cajoled the beasts forward, but, except for Judah, all his brothers averted their eyes. The camel he was tethered to moved forward, forcing Joseph to turn and walk away.

Watching him walk with head down, all the brothers shared the same thought, *He strode into this camp like a prince; he trudges out a slave. So ends the lord of the dreams!*

'evel

Mourning

Nearly out of breath, Reuben kept up the pace nevertheless. *I must get back before they harm Joseph,* he thought. *Simeon and Levi are agitating for blood, but everyone's blood is up. What was Father thinking, sending Joseph here in that ridiculous robe?* As he approached, the others seemed not to notice him, apparently caught up in animated discussion. *Just as well,* he thought. *This way I can go to the cistern and assure Joseph I am on his side, before the rest notice me.*

Accordingly, he moved silently to the edge of the old cistern. "Joseph?" he said, in an urgent but quiet voice. No answer. "Joseph!" Still no reply. Gingerly, he peered over the edge into the darkness. *Joseph is gone!* Dread and nausea struck Reuben. *Have I failed after all? Did they kill Joseph in my absence?* Reuben groaned in mourning and tore at his clothing. The others heard the commotion and came to him. "Joseph is not here!" he said. "What can I do, whom shall I turn to?"

"It is not what you think," Judah said, eager to comfort his brother. "Joseph is alive."

Relief flooded Reuben's face. "Where is he?"

"On his way to Egypt—as a slave," said Issachar.

Shock purged the relief from Reuben's features. "As a slave? To Egypt?"

Judah locked eyes with Reuben. "We decided it was better to make a little profit, selling him, *alive,* than to commit the sin of Cain and have him dead." Reuben heaved a great sigh and then nodded, indicating that he understood what Judah was saying.

"What do we tell Father?" Reuben asked.

"What we said earlier," Simeon explained. "We take that fancy robe, rip it up, and put some goat's blood on it."

"And we tell Father some wild animal killed him," said Levi.

"Better than that," said Issachar, "we tell Father we found this robe, torn and blood spattered, and we ask him if he knows whose it might be."

Judah agreed. "If we tell him too much, he might become suspicious. But if we ask him, and he comes to the conclusion on his own—"

"He will believe it," Dan finished the thought. Looking at Issachar, he said, "That is very devious, Brother. Remind me not to match wits with you." Issachar shrugged in modesty. Several of the brothers laughed. Short, grim, grunting chuckles: derision without joy.

Judah spoke again. "And the less we say, the less chance to be tripped up." Grim nods all around. "That will be our watchword; say as little as possible about this whole sorry episode." More nods. "Then let us get to it. We have work to do. The robe must be torn and a goat slaughtered. Servants informed that we will be traveling back to Father's camp, and duties assigned while we are gone, and—most important—kept away until we have prepared the bloody robe."

"I will go and instruct the servants," Reuben said. "I was just there. My return will not arouse any curiosity."

"I will gladly tear the robe," Simeon said, with Levi nodding at his elbow.

"I will slaughter the goat," Judah said. He did not add, *I want nothing to do with tearing the fabric of Joseph's robe. I still see his pleading eyes.*

The next morning, they set off on their melancholy journey to Hebron, to inform a father of his favorite son's apparent death. They dragged the now ragged remnants of Joseph's princely robe along the trail behind them. Before long, it looked as if wild animals had killed its wearer, shredded it, and left it to fade in the sun. Reuben picked it up and carried it the rest of the way.

As they approached their father's camp, Israel hurried out to meet them, anxiously searching their faces. "Where is your brother?" he asked. "Where is your brother?" When none answered, he asked, "Did not any of you see your brother Joseph? I sent him to find you." Still no replies, but the grim expressions he saw on their faces filled his heart with dread. "Why have you come, then?"

The brothers all looked at Reuben, who took a halting step toward his father, a dirty bundle in his hands. "We found this," he said. "It may be your son's robe."

Jacob reached for the bundle with nerveless fingers. He let the cloth unroll and recognized it at once. "It is my son's robe!" he said. He scanned its surface: the deep tears that rent the repeating leaf pattern, the dirt and dark brown stains that dulled its bright colors. Then he clutched it to himself, and said, almost in a whisper, "Some ferocious animal has devoured him. Joseph." Shaking his head from side to side in misery, he stated, "Joseph has surely been torn to pieces."

Suddenly Dinah ceased her endless rocking. She jumped to her feet and walked from one brother to the other, poison in her eyes. Dinah clenched her fists, one holding her worn scrap of silk and began to wail aloud. As each brother, in turn, averted his gaze, her keening grew louder and more intense. When the last brother, Zebulun, cast his eyes down in shame, she began pummeling him, until Judah came and pulled her away. When he released her, she darted to the tent where Joseph had slept and emerged with the fine silk scarf he had bought for her months earlier. Clutching both pieces of silk to her face, she sobbed until she finally fell asleep.

Stunned into inaction until now, Jacob dropped the blood-stained cloth that had been Joseph's cloak on the sand and began tearing his own garments. Raising his hands heavenward, he dropped to his knees, imploring El Shaddai for mercy. But he made no sound and heard no answer.

After a time, Reuben and Judah stepped forward and helped their father to his feet. He walked to his tent, throwing off garments as he walked. Clad only in his loincloth, he sat before his tent, called for sackcloth to cover his nakedness, and smeared himself with ashes.

He sat there for many days, not speaking, seemingly unaware of anyone or anything. He ate little. The weight of his grief bore down on everyone in the camp. Faithful Amos noted that the brothers often exchanged guarded looks. They were sons and he but a servant, so he held his peace, for the most part.

Despite the lack of nearby pasture, the sons dispatched messengers to the camp near Shechem, arranging to return everyone and everything to Hebron. Concern for Jacob's welfare brought all the sons and their growing families near to the old patriarch. They made his favorite foods, told stories designed to make him laugh, all to no avail. "Leave me alone," he told them. "I will mourn until I go down to the grave with my Joseph."

He said little, but his thoughts cried out. *El Shaddai, Adonai Elohim, You named me Israel. Am I Israel indeed? I struggle, but is this what it means to prevail? I have lost the ones I loved! How can I go on?* But he saw no shining messengers, no towers to the sky, heard no voices. He longed for the stranger to come, so they could grapple through the long nights. But none came. He struggled but in vain.

Days became weeks, weeks became months. The grieving Jacob did not die, but he refused to participate in life. Without Rachel and without Joseph, he felt his own life had little purpose. He gazed fondly at Benjamin, his left-handed right-hand man, but he rarely spoke to him and almost never to anyone else. He slept long and rose late. Although he might trudge about the camp, head down, leaning on his staff, he took no interest in the affairs of running the household. The camp celebrated shearing and lambing time. Jacob mourned. His sons celebrated the birth and growth of their own children. Jacob mourned. Amos and the brothers planted wheat and harvested it. Jacob mourned.

With eleven grown sons, and eventually their grown sons and daughters, a thousand little dramas played themselves out around Jacob, but he took no notice. Judah became embroiled in a scandalous situation regarding his sons and his daughter-in-law Tamar. Jacob did not comment and appeared not to notice.

"What can I do to help my master?" Amos asked Donatiya. Amos's concern for his master made him alert to the reactions of those around Jacob. He quickly discerned that Bilhah cared more for Jacob than did the other wives. He had first approached her with his requests for help, and she had directed him to Donatiya, now very old and nearly blind.

The old woman stared wide-eyed beyond Amos, focused on nothing in this world. "He is lost," she said.

"I do not understand," Amos replied.

"He loved Rachel; Rachel died. She left Joseph and Benjamin," the old woman said, her rasping voice barely more than a whisper. "Joseph is gone now," she went on, "and Benjamin reminds him of Rachel's death."

"I see that," Amos said.

"Your master is lost," she said.

"What do you mean?"

"He worked many years for riches," she said. "Now he has eleven strong sons and their families; he has many, many sheep and goats, servants, camels, and donkeys. He is a rich man," she said. Then making a fist and placing it over her heart, she said, "But he is poor in here. Without the woman he loved, the son he loved, he thinks that his own life has no purpose. No reason to live."

"What can I do about that?" Amos asked.

"There is nothing you can do," she said. "Master Israel is no more. He has given up. He no longer will fight."

"Fight? I do not understand?"

Donatiya smiled. Even her vacant eyes lit up. "Israel. He struggles with God." When Amos did not respond, she reached out for his hand. "Some men go through life like this," she said, holding his hand open, palm up. "They go through life with open hands. They give freely, receive freely. Things come easy to them. Other men," she folded his hand into a fist, "go through life like this. Hand clenched, grasping for what they can get, shaking their fists at the world."

"I think I understand you," said Amos.

"Master Jacob was born a fist man," Donatiya said. "Grasping, striving, and struggling. He even wrestled with God. After that, his hand became open. He learned to give to Joseph. But Joseph is gone. Jacob's hand now is neither open nor clenched," she said, pushing Amos's hand away. "Now he is not even holding on to life. Right now he is not Jacob, not the grasping cheater; and he is not Israel, not wrestling with God. He is nobody."

"Is there anything I can do, anything at all?"

"Make him clench his fist and wrestle again," the old woman said. "He is not mourning. He is angry with God. He needs to wrestle with his God about this."

"What will that change? Can it bring Joseph back?" Amos asked, daunted by the challenge she had given him.

"Change? It would change Jacob into Israel again! It would make the master into what El Shaddai intended him to be." She paused to take a deep breath. "As for bringing Joseph back, it all depends on where he is."

"What does that mean?" Amos asked.

"I don't know," Donatiya said. "But I think we have not heard the last of Joseph." She sighed deeply. "I'm tired now."

Amos thanked the old woman and left her to get her needed rest. She had given him much to think about.

* * * * *

Time passed. Year followed year, and as Benjamin grew and married, Jacob found himself thinking, *If I had not sent him to find his brothers, Joseph would be a father now. Joseph would be the head of a large household.* Benjamin looked something like his mother, but quite different from Joseph. Jacob tried hard to summon the images of Rachel and Joseph in his mind, but the years had faded his memories—had all but erased their faces. Still, Jacob clung to his grief. *If only I had kept him close, Joseph would be an important man now. A man of wealth and power. If only.*

One bounteous harvest followed another, and the flocks multiplied almost beyond imagination, but Amos and Jacob's sons no longer needed his help in managing the affairs of the household. The more his possessions multiplied and his household prospered, the less Jacob felt needed or connected to the world beyond his own grief. So he wandered through his days without goals, without purpose, and without hope.

And then something changed. The years continued to roll, the seasons came and went. But the rains stopped. Flocks and herds that had swelled during the recent years of abundance quickly depleted the drought-stressed pasturelands. Grazing became sparse, then disappeared. Sleek animals became gaunt. Wheat and barley sprouted in fields near streams, but blazing heat and dry winds scorched the young stalks. Soon the streams ran dry. Cisterns emptied and wells failed. Herdsmen slaughtered scores of animals to preserve the meat and to save what little grazing and grain remained for the breeding animals. Men like Jacob and his sons, who counted their wealth in livestock, watched the animals starve and die, and watched their riches evaporate before their eyes. Soon hunger spread from the animals to their human keepers. Even the wealthiest men, those who had saved the most through selective slaughter early in the drought, found themselves facing not merely poverty, but uncertain survival.

None living remembered such a famine.

Jacob's neighbors turned to Ba'al, the lord of the rains, to bring them relief. But no relief came. Traveling merchants reported drought all along their routes. Drought everywhere, including the great empire of Egypt. Even the mighty Nile, they reported, ran low. But though the drought haunted Egypt, famine did not. They told of an extraordinary ruler, called Zaphenath-Paneah, who had somehow foreseen the coming famine and had stored up grain during the years of abundance that had preceded the drought. So despite a lack of rain in Egypt, pharaoh had plenty of grain: enough for the needs of his household, enough for his nation, and enough to sell even to foreigners.

Donatiya, now too frail to leave her bed, asked for Bilhah to visit her. "How are you doing, Imma?" Of course, Donatiya was not Bilhah's mother, but Bilhah had grown to love the old woman and used the title *Imma* out of affection and respect.

The old woman laughed soundlessly. "Less and less," she said. "Soon I will be done, altogether."

Bilhah started to reassure her, but Donatiya would have none of it. "I have lived a long time now. Long enough, thanks to El Shaddai. Most of my life, I looked for power. Born a slave, I thought that learning to conjure, to please the gods, might give me power and make my masters treat me right." She paused, gaining her breath. "Then I learned that Master Jacob's God takes care of him and that Master Jacob is kind to the servants. I learned that I did not need power. I needed Master Jacob's God."

Donatiya reached out, and Bilhah took her hand. "I have one last thing to do," she said. "Tell Master Jacob, 'Go get grain from Egypt.'"

Silence followed. Bilhah wondered if the old woman had fallen asleep, so she asked, "Is that all?"

Donatiya squeezed her hand. "The great man of Egypt, the one they call Zaphenath-Paneah?"

Bilhah replied, "That is the name, they say. Strange Egyptian name."

"When I was a little girl, my best friend was a little Egyptian servant girl. She taught me her language. We used to share our little girl secrets in Egyptian. None of the chief servants or the master knew what we were saying." She smiled at the memory. "*Zaphenath-Paneah* means 'God speaks. He lives.' Remember that."

"'God speaks. He lives,'" Bilhah repeated. "Is that important?"

"Tell Master Jacob, 'Buy grain in Egypt from the man named "God speaks. He lives."'" Donatiya paused once again. "Will you tell him?"

"I will tell him," Bilhah replied.

Donatiya squeezed her hand so hard it hurt. Bilhah wondered that the frail old woman had so much strength left. "God speaks. He lives. God speaks. He lives." Her voice trailed off, her breathing grew shallow, and Donatiya drifted gently to her final rest.

The weeping Bilhah pulled a blanket over the old woman's body and went to call others to prepare Donatiya for burial. Bilhah would have done it herself, but she had a message to deliver.

מְרַגְלִים

m^eraglím

Spies

As far as the eye could see, a living ribbon of people and animals moved south and then west, toward the land of the pharaohs, the land of the mighty Nile. The stores of grain in Egypt irresistibly drew the survivors of those drought- and famine-decimated lands for many days' journey in every direction. The grunts and whinnies of animals, mingled with chatter in dozens of languages and scores of dialects, assaulted the ear in a wave of noise. Periodically, a ripple in the living ribbon revealed the approach of a party returning from the land of the Nile. Up and down the moving ribbon, calls rang out in one tongue after another asking those headed back home, "Do they still have grain available in Egypt?" Some answered by chattering happily; others simply pointed to the bulging bags of grain, smiled, and nodded. Whether anyone understood or even heard their words, everyone recognized the reply as the affirmative, "There is still grain in Egypt!"

Grain. Next to water, the stuff of life itself. Whole, it could be planted to grow more grain or be fed to livestock. Mashed and fermented, it could be made into beer, a beverage that withstood long-term storage, provided a source of nourishment, and remained safe to drink when water might carry pestilence. Ground into flour, it could be made into bread, the stuff of life. And for many, many days' and weeks' journey in every direction, only Egypt, the land of the pharaohs, possessed an abundance of grain.

At Jacob's camp near Hebron, his sons soon ran out of ideas and out of energy, so that they simply stared at one another, hoping someone else could see a way back to prosperity. But, exhausted from the effort to combat the progressive devastation of drought and famine, the focus of the brothers narrowed until they saw only disaster and ruin ahead.

When he heard that grain could be purchased in Egypt, Jacob roused from his grief to confront his sons. "Why do you just keep looking at each other?" he demanded. "I have heard that there is grain in Egypt. Grain for sale! Go down there and buy some for us, so that we may live and not die." His words broke through their exhaustion and apathy, and they quickly assembled enough healthy pack animals and an accumulation of silver to purchase and transport enough grain for their remaining livestock and all their people.

At first, they traveled alone. But day by day, as they drew nearer to their destination, the number of fellow travelers grew. Although they spoke different languages, wore different styles of clothing, and worshiped different gods, they all shared the same story. Driven by drought and famine from their homelands, and drawn to the promise of grain in Egypt, eventually they all found themselves a part of this living ribbon moving toward the Nile. Like the Nile, the throng traveling to Egypt swelled as it grew nearer its destination.

Only a small army outpost marked their entry into Egypt. The entire procession moved under the watchful eyes of the local military. Here and there, soldiers stopped individuals or small groups of travelers, questioned them, and inspected their belongings. But for the most part, the dusty travelers passed unchallenged. Egypt's monopoly on grain gave her more power than could be exercised by any army. An army can be fought by another army, but only grain could combat famine.

Not long after their entry into Egypt, the road curved south toward the city of On, just above the place where the mighty Nile fanned out like a giant hand reaching for the sea. Once near the city walls, representatives of pharaoh took their names and told them where to pitch camp and await their turn to buy grain, and at what time they would be allowed into the city.

"Someone has done an excellent job of organizing all this," Issachar said their first night outside the city walls. "Despite the massive numbers seeking grain, everything and everyone is moving in an orderly fashion."

"It is impressive," said Judah, "and the name on everyone's lips is 'Zaphenath-Paneah.' Apparently, he is the royal official in charge of all this."

"Probably some relative of the pharaoh," said Reuben.

"They say he is of foreign birth," Judah answered, gesturing to their neighbors in the campground. "Our friends over there know something about Egyptian customs. Apparently, high-ranking Egyptians carry a sort of ornamental tool. Pharaoh carries a miniature shepherd's crook and a flail. The crook represents his role as protector of his people, the flail as the provider of food. This Zaphenath-Paneah fellow should carry a ceremonial flail, since he is in charge of grain, but he doesn't."

"What does he carry?" asked Reuben.

"They tell me," again he nodded at the neighbors, "that he carries something called a 'throwing stick,' a straight stick with a bend near the top."

"And that symbolizes?" prompted Issachar.

"Foreign birth," said Judah. And, seeing a richly dressed royal official approaching, he added, "Looks like we may find out tomorrow."

The following day at midday, their turn came. Following a military guide, they led their pack animals laden with empty grain sacks into the city. The brothers looked in wonder at the tops of two pillars of red granite towering over the mud-brick buildings within the walls of On. Their military guide could not speak their language, but after considerable gesturing, Judah returned with the news that these pillars were called *tejen* by the locals.

Much to their surprise, they turned a corner onto a broad avenue leading to an impressive building, before which the two red granite needles stood. Off to the left of this building, they saw their destination: a small raised platform where royal officials accepted payment for grain. They took their place in line, which put them almost at the base of the granite pillars. Close up, they could see the hieroglyphics carved into the granite surfaces on all four sides, from top to bottom. "They must be more than forty cubits high," Issachar said. The others merely gazed and nodded.

One group after another went to the raised platform, where a scribe waited for them to make their requests. Nearby, an official seated on an elevated chair, spoke in low tones to a seemingly endless stream of other officials seeking his advice, counsel, permission—something. Periodically, he punctuated his words by gesturing with a ceremonial miniature staff.

At the table, the scribe told them the price, which they paid in silver. He noted their purchase on a roll of papyrus in front of him, and then he counted out some wooden tokens, representing the amount of grain they had purchased. The buyers then took these tokens to the nearby granaries, where they exchanged them for grain, which waiting servants fetched to fill their containers. Finally came the turn of Jacob's sons.

Reuben stepped up to the scribe and started to speak. Before he could say anything, the official on the elevated chair came down to the table. All the Egyptians froze. The official said several words in Egyptian, which an interpreter translated, complete with tone of voice and gestures. "You," he said, pointing to Reuben and then at his brothers, "where do you come from? What is your business here?"

"From the land of the Kinnahu, my lord," Reuben said, bowing. "We have come to buy grain." As the translator relayed his words, Reuben looked intently at the Egyptian official.

The official stroked his chin for a moment, then began shaking his head slowly. Once again, he bit off a few Egyptian words, which the translator repeated in their language. "My master, Lord Zaphenath-Paneah, says, 'I have been watching you. I think you are spies, scouting out our defenses, looking for places where we can be attacked.' " Two soldiers carrying spears stepped forward, but Zaphenath-Paneah held out his hand to stop them.

"That is not so, my lord," Reuben said. "Your servants have come, like the rest, to buy food. We are all," here he made a sweeping gesture that took in all the brothers, "sons of one man. Your servants are honest men, not spies."

Still shaking his head, Zaphenath-Paneah said, "I do not believe you. You have come to see where our outposts are far apart and our lands unprotected. There are many who would like to conquer Egypt, take our grain for themselves. They would send just such a group of men as you to spy on us."

"My lord, we were twelve brothers," Reuben said, "the sons of a man who lives in the land of the Kinnahu." Reuben could see Zaphenath-Paneah counting the men, so he quickly added, "The youngest brother remains at home with our father. And the other—is no more."

Zaphenath-Paneah flicked his ceremonial staff toward the soldiers, who quickly seized Reuben. At the same time, other soldiers materialized and surrounded the rest of the brothers. "You say you are brothers. I say you are spies. Very well. This should be easy to test. Here is what we will do; as surely as pharaoh lives, you will not leave this place unless your youngest brother comes here. Send one of your number to get your brother; the rest of you will be kept in prison, so that your words may be tested to see if you are telling the truth. But if there is no younger brother, then as surely as pharaoh lives, you are spies!"

Reuben was about to protest, but a sharp gesture from Zaphenath-Paneah, and the soldiers began moving the brothers away. The Egyptian then folded his arms and returned to his elevated seat, while the guards marched the brothers straight to prison. There prison officials confiscated and catalogued their remaining silver, their pack animals, and all their belongings.

Jacob's sons had much to think about and much to talk about. "Did you notice the ceremonial miniature staff he carried?" asked Judah. "A small gilded stick about a cubit long, with the top portion, about a span in length, bent forward?"

"Now that you mention it, I did see that," Dan said. "And you said that the staff indicates he is of foreign birth?"

"That is what I was told," Judah said.

"Must be a very intelligent fellow," Issachar added, "a foreigner risen to such a powerful position."

"I noticed how the other officials hold him in awe," said Dan. "We had better be careful with this fellow."

"If," Judah said, "we ever see him again." Pressing his hands against the unyielding stone walls, he added, "He will have to come to us. Because we cannot go to him."

"Puts me in mind of Joseph," Reuben said. "We sold him into slavery. I wonder if he was ever in this prison."

And silence settled over the brothers again.

On the third day, the foreigner, the clever alien who had risen to the heights of Egyptian power, came to their cells, dressed as regally as before and accompanied by his interpreter. "I have been thinking," he said. "I will give you another chance to verify your words, because I have heard of your God, El . . . El . . . ," he looked hopefully at the brothers, and Judah supplied the name, "El Shaddai." The official nodded. "I respect this El Shaddai, and so I will give you another opportunity. If you are honest men, let one of your brothers stay here in prison, while the rest of you go and take grain back for your starving households. I am a reasonable man." He let them ponder this for a moment, before adding, "But you must bring your youngest brother to me, so that your words may be verified and that you may not die. Consider your answer well."

Zaphenath-Paneah stepped away to let them decide, and it seemed as if all the brothers spoke at once. Issachar summed it up, "I have been thinking about what Reuben said yesterday. He was right. Surely we are being punished because of our brother, Joseph. We saw how anguished he was when he pleaded with us for his life, but we would not listen; that's why this distress has come upon us."

Outside the cell, the foreigner turned away for a moment, head lowered. Reuben replied, "Oh, brothers, did I not warn you and tell you not to sin against the boy? But you would not listen! Now we must give an accounting for his blood."

"I gave an accounting for it every time I looked at Dinah, for as long as she lived," Judah said. Many solemn eyes met his.

Issachar went on, "We cannot atone for that now. We must give this man an answer," he said, pointing to the foreigner.

"What choice do we have?" Judah asked, and they all gave their assent. He moved toward the door of the cell and said to Zaphenath-Paneah, "We agree."

Immediately, the foreigner stepped forward and pointed his ceremonial staff at Simeon. Two guards entered the cell, bound Simeon hand and foot, and took him deeper into the prison complex.

"In the morning," he said to them, "you leave for your return journey. Bring your younger brother!" It was a command, not a reminder.

At dawn the next morning, the jailer came and rousted them out of their cells. They looked for Simeon on their way out of the prison, but no one caught even a glimpse of him. Outside, they found their pack animals loaded with sacks full of grain, water, and provisions for their journey, and all of their belongings. The soldiers who led them to their animals made it clear through emphatic gestures that the brothers were to go directly to the city gates and back out the main road they had come in on.

Blinking in bewilderment at one another, they set out on the journey. Now they were the contrary ripple running through the moving ribbon of travelers seeking grain. Strangers smiled and pointed to the bulging sacks on their pack animals, but the brothers felt no elation, and they simply nodded grimly in reply. "There is still grain in Egypt." *And Simeon is still in prison,* they thought. *And we are suspected as spies. If we do not persuade Father to let Benjamin come back with us, Simeon may die there.*

With their sacks full of grain, they should have been buoyant, bringing sustenance back to their father's struggling camp. Instead, they came to the end of the first day of their return travel in low spirits. When they stopped for the night, Dan opened the sack of grain to feed his donkey. When he saw what was in the sack, his blood froze. "Look," he said, holding out enough silver to pay for the grain in the sack. "My silver was returned. They put it in my sack of grain."

The frightened brothers quickly opened every sack and found their silver also returned. A grim Dan said what they were all thinking, "Now he can charge us with theft too."

"Stealing food in a famine," said Issachar. "That is a crime punishable by death. He could have us all executed."

The brothers looked from one to another. The color had drained from every face. *Why has El Shaddai done this to us?* everyone wondered. But no one could find the strength to speak.

גְּבִיעַ הַכֶּסֶף

gᵉviya' hacheset

The Silver Cup

Jacob counted them more than once, and when they came close enough to be recognized, he knew for certain who was missing. "Where is your brother?" he asked. "Where is Simeon?"

As soon as the traveling party had broached the horizon, word had spread quickly through Jacob's camp. "They have returned, and they bring much food."

Jacob had roused himself and walked to the edge of the camp, eager to greet them. His eyes moved from one figure to the next. And that had led to his question. "Where is your brother?"

And so the brothers recounted all the details of the trip, including the imperious foreigner's accusations of spying and the test of their denial. Simeon had been imprisoned, where he would stay until they returned with their youngest brother, Benjamin.

Jacob refused to hear of it. "You have taken my sons from me," he lamented. "First Joseph, now Simeon, and you would take Benjamin? I forbid it." He rocked back and forth. "Only Benjamin remains to me," he said. "If you take him, too, it will kill me. I would go down to the grave in despair."

From then onward, Jacob refused to speak of the matter. The brothers knew nothing they could say would convince him otherwise. For Jacob, Joseph and Simeon were dead, and he would not risk losing another son, especially Benjamin, the only remaining son of his beloved Rachel.

But famine had the last word. The rains still did not fall. The drought continued, and starvation loomed once again as the grain supply brought from Egypt dwindled. Still, Reuben, Judah, Issachar—all the brothers—waited.

When the situation became critical, Jacob roused himself again. "Go down to Egypt again, and buy some more grain for us."

"We cannot—" Reuben began, but Issachar put a hand on Reuben's arm and then nodded toward Judah.

"We can do as you say, Father, but Zaphenath-Paneah, the great ruler of Egypt who sells the grain, made it very clear that we will be treated as spies unless we bring our youngest brother with us."

Jacob began moaning and tearing at his clothing. "My son will not go down there with you; his brother is dead, and he is the only one left. If harm comes to him on the journey you are taking, you will bring my gray head down to the grave in sorrow."

Issachar spoke sharply. "You will lose us all, Father, and get no grain to save the rest, if you do not let us take Benjamin with us."

"Issachar is right, Father," Judah said. "Zaphenath-Paneah, the man in charge of the grain, warned us solemnly, 'You will not see my face again unless your brother is with you.' If you will send our brother along with us, we will go down and buy food for you. But if you will not send him, there is no point in our going, because the man said to us, 'You will not see my face again unless your brother is with you.' He will not sell us grain unless Benjamin goes with us."

"If anything happens to Benjamin, you may put my two sons to death," Reuben said. "Trust him to my care, and I will bring him back."

"Bring him back? Did you bring back Simeon? How will killing your sons bring him back?" Jacob asked.

Jacob looked at his sons and saw unity there. But Jacob was not ready to yield, and so he asked Judah, "Why did you bring this trouble on me by telling the man you had another brother?"

Judah replied, "The man questioned us closely about ourselves and our family. 'Is your father still living?' he asked us. 'Do you have another brother?' We simply answered his questions. How were we to know he would say, 'Bring your brother down here'?"

Jacob seemed to waver a moment, and Judah said quietly to him, "Send the boy along with me, and we will go at once so that we and you and our children may live and not die. I myself will guarantee his safety; you can hold me personally responsible for him. If I do not bring him back to you and set him here before you, I will bear the blame before you all my life."

"I need time to consider this," Jacob said.

"We have no time, Father," Judah replied. "Our supply of grain will not last much longer. As it is, if we had not delayed, we could have gone and returned twice."

"Very well. If it must be, it must be." He thought for a moment. "Take some of the choicest products of our land as gifts," he said. "Some honey, some balm, some myrrh." More thought. "Take twice the amount of silver. Perhaps it was put in your sacks by mistake. Demonstrate our honesty by taking enough silver to pay the grain we received last time and for that we hope to purchase this time as well. And may El Shaddai grant you mercy before the man so that he will let your other brother and Benjamin come back with you." Jacob's countenance darkened, and he added, "As for me, if I am bereaved, I am bereaved."

Once again they joined the movement of hungry people toward Egypt. If not for Benjamin's continual questions, the trip would have been unbearably grim. But he peppered them with questions about Egypt, about On, about the great red granite pillars covered with Egyptian glyphs. Perhaps he felt no fear; perhaps the questions concealed his anxiety. In any case, it made the trip seem shorter to the brothers. And urgency caused them to travel more rapidly. Soon they approached the walls of On once again. Once again, a royal official approached, but this time he did not tell them where to wait. Instead, he brought several soldiers armed with spears. "These men will escort you to Zaphenath-Paneah's palace. He has been waiting for you."

The escort formed around the brothers and began the march to the ruler's house.

"We are going to a palace?" Benjamin asked.

"That is what he said," Judah replied. Quietly to Reuben, he said, "The last time we saw this man, he threw us in prison."

Dan replied in a soft voice, "It is because of the silver. He wants to attack us and overpower us and seize us as slaves and take our donkeys." He looked from one brother to the next and saw grim expressions. Except for Benjamin, who appeared not to hear, preoccupied with the exotic sights of this great city.

Their escort led them to a vast brick building with sandstone footings. The whitewashed walls had been painted with agricultural scenes of grain being planted, growing, and being harvested. A very tall Nubian, his dark skin contrasting with the white linen he wore, stood at the door. "I am Nebibi, chief steward of Zaphenath-Paneah—" he began, but Judah stepped forward and knelt in front of him. The other brothers knelt where they were.

"Please, sir," Judah said, "we came down here the first time to buy food. But at the place where we stopped for the night, we opened our sacks and each of us found his silver—the exact weight—in the mouth of his sack." Here he gestured to their pack animals, "We brought it back with us. We also brought additional silver with us to buy more food. We don't know who put our silver in our sacks."

Nebibi laughed gently and motioned for them to rise. "Do not be concerned," he said. "Your God, the God of your father, has given you treasure in your sacks; I received your silver." The brothers looked at each other uncertainly. Seeing this, Nebibi turned and clapped his hands, and another servant appeared from inside the house—with Simeon! "If you still doubt, here is your brother, safe and sound!"

Suddenly, cries of joy and relief filled the air. Simeon embraced each of his brothers in turn, assuring them of his health and his good spirits.

Nebibi watched all this, arms folded, smiling. When the commotion faded, he said, "Come, we have water for washing your feet and fodder for your animals. We will take care of all your needs. My master says, 'Be comforted.' You will be dining with him this noonday."

Judah approached Nebibi, and said, "Please, sir. We have brought gifts for your master. We would like to present them to him when he comes."

Nebibi nodded, and replied, "Tell me how the gifts are wrapped. Servants will bring them to you."

When Zaphenath-Paneah arrived, the brothers had the gifts ready. They presented the gifts they had brought and bowed before him, touching their foreheads to the ground. "How are you? Have my servants taken care of your needs?" he asked.

"They have, my lord," Judah replied without rising.

"How is your aged father you told me about? Does he still live?"

"Your servant, our father, still lives and is well." The brothers remained prostrate before him.

"Rise," he said to them, and he looked them over. Coming to Benjamin, he asked, "Is this your youngest brother, the one you told me about?" They assured him he was. He simply stood and looked at Benjamin, until the youngest brother became uneasy. Zaphenath-Paneah seemed to have difficulty speaking. He cleared his throat several times before saying to Benjamin in a low voice, "El Shaddai be gracious to you, my son." Without another word, he turned suddenly and walked away. The brothers looked at one another with baffled expressions.

After an unexplained departure, he returned and escorted the brothers to another spacious room with three large tables. The table at the far end spanned the room; it held the food and a place setting of a silver bowl and cup. The two other tables, stood at right angles to the main table, parallel to each other. The walls had been painted with scenes of an oasis garden: tall palm trees, beautiful flowers, and even brightly colored birds. Their host sat at the main table, while a group of what looked like Egyptian nobles occupied one of the parallel tables. A servant directed the brothers, one by one, to be seated at the third.

Reuben, the first seated at the brothers' table, looked at the others. They had seen the same thing he had. They were seated in order, from the oldest to the youngest. "Did you tell them about our ages?" Reuben asked Simeon.

Simeon shook his head. "I am as surprised as the rest of you!"

"How did they know to seat us this way?" asked Judah. The all looked to the head table for some indication from their host. But Zaphenath-Paneah appeared not to notice. The food was at his table; he had been served first, and he was busy eating. One by one, servants brought food for each of the brothers in bright copper bowls. But when it came to Benjamin, they brought five large bowls of food, not just one. No one said anything about the difference. With some misgivings, the brothers did their best to enjoy the meal.

When they had finished, their host announced, "These brothers have passed the test. They are not spies. To make up for their distress, they will spend the night in my house." The Egyptian nobles looked at the brothers in awe. "In the morning, they will all be free," he said, gesturing to Simeon, "to return to their father." Then he left the room.

On the road home the next morning, Reuben said, "He said we were free to go. What could go wrong?" They had been awakened the next morning to find their animals already packed with brimming sacks of grain. By dawn they were on the way home.

"He said that," Dan agreed, "but I will not feel at ease until we leave Egypt."

"The man all but apologized to us," Simeon said. "And they treated me better than most prisoners. I am just happy to be out of On."

Before they had gone very far, they saw a man on a speedy camel followed by several similarly mounted soldiers racing after them. Soon, it became apparent that Nebibi, Zaphenath-Paneah's chief steward, pursued them. With their loaded pack animals, they could not outrun him, so they waited for his approach.

At the last moment, he reined in his camel, showering those nearest with sand. "Why have you repaid good with evil?" Nebibi's voice boomed. "You have the cup my master drinks from and also uses for divination. This is a wicked thing you have done."

The brothers exchanged shocked looks. "Why does my lord say such things?" Reuben replied. "Far be it from your servants to do anything like that! We even brought back to you from the land of the Kinnahu the silver we found inside the mouths of our sacks. So why would we steal silver or gold from your master's house?" Nebibi's face did not soften, so Reuben added, "If any of your servants is found to have it, he will die, and the rest of us will become my lord's slaves."

"Very well, then," Nebibi replied, "let it be as you say." And so the brothers took their sacks down from the animals, and Nebibi inspected them, one by one, beginning with Reuben, the oldest, and taking each in order. In each sack, they again found their silver, but Nebibi had not come for that. In the last sack, in Benjamin's, he found his quarry—the silver cup.

He motioned to the soldiers, "We found our thief. Bind him."

The brothers tore their clothing in grief and frustration. *The very thing Father feared has happened,* they thought. *How will we ever show our faces in his camp again?* They all returned to On.

At Zaphenath-Paneah's house, they threw themselves at his feet. "What is this you have done?" the Egyptian demanded. "Do you not know I can interpret dreams and foretell the future? Did you think I would not find out?"

"What can we say to my lord?" Judah replied. "What can we say? How can we prove our innocence? El Shaddai has uncovered your servants' guilt. We are now my lord's slaves—we ourselves and the one who was found to have the cup."

But Zaphenath-Paneah said, "Far be it from me to do such a thing! Only the man who stole the cup will become my slave. The rest of you, go back to your father in peace." And with this, he made a gesture of dismissal. Guards began herding the brothers, except for Benjamin, toward the street.

But Judah went up to him, prostrated himself, and said, "Please, my lord, let your servant speak a word to my lord. Do not be angry with your servant, though you are equal to pharaoh himself."

Zaphenath-Paneah paused a moment, and then said, "You may speak."

"When we came here before, my lord asked his servants, 'Do you have a father or a brother?' And we answered, 'We have an aged father, and there is a young son born to him in his old age. His brother is dead, and he is the only one of his mother's sons left, and his father loves him.' "

"I remember."

"Then you said to your servants, 'Bring him down to me so I can see him for myself.' And we said to my lord, 'The boy cannot leave his father; if he leaves him, his father will die.' But you insisted that unless our youngest brother returned with us, we would not see your face again."

"I did insist."

"But the drought continued. Our crops did not grow. The grain we bought before began to run out. So our father said, 'Go back and buy a little more food.' But we reminded him that we could not come again without our youngest brother."

"As you should."

"Your servant, my father, said to us, 'You know that my wife bore me two sons. One of them disappeared, torn to pieces by a wild animal, and I have not seen him since. If you take this one from me, too, and harm comes to him, you will bring my gray head down to the grave in misery.'

"So now, if the boy is not with us when I go back, my father will die, so closely bound up with the boy's life is his own."

"What do you propose? Someone must be punished for stealing my cup."

"Your servant guaranteed the boy's safety to my father," said Judah.

"That was not wise."

"Now then, please let me take the lad's place. Let me remain here as my lord's slave in place of the boy, and let the boy return with his brothers. I cannot go back to my father if the boy is not with me. I could not bear to see the misery that would come upon my father."

Zaphenath-Paneah covered his face with his hands for a moment; then he commanded, "Leave me alone with these men!" Nebibi searched his master's face and found certainty there. So he motioned to all the others, and when they had left, he followed them out of the room.

As soon as the servants departed, Zaphenath-Paneah began to sob, loudly enough so that servants in the rest of the house could hear him. The stunned brothers could only watch. Then, in a barely audible voice, he said, "I am Joseph! Does my father still live?"

If they had been stunned at his weeping, his announcement froze every nerve. It seemed they ceased even to breathe. *Joseph?* The thought raced through every brother's head. *What does he mean, "I am Joseph"?*

The man who claimed to be Joseph broke the spell. "Come close to me," he said. "I am your brother Joseph." When he still received no reply, he looked from face to face, "Joseph, the one you sold into Egypt!" Horror still filled their faces.

They looked at the face beneath the ornate gilded headdress. They searched the eyes, outlined in black in the Egyptian manner. *Zaphenath-Paneah, the foreigner who had risen to influence in Egypt. Their brother?*

He hastened to reassure them. "Do not be distressed and do not be angry with yourselves for selling me here, because El Shaddai sent me ahead of you to save lives. For two years now, there has been famine in the land. The drought will last five more years, the famine somewhat longer. But El Shaddai sent me ahead of you." Still they remained frozen in shock.

"Do you not see, El Shaddai purposed to preserve you and to save your lives by a great deliverance? So then, it was not you who sent me here, but God. He made me a father to pharaoh, lord of his entire household, and ruler of all Egypt."

Suddenly he stood, pacing, the ruler making decisions. "Now hurry back to my father and say to him, 'This is what your son Joseph says, "El Shaddai has made me lord of all Egypt. Come down to me; don't delay." ' " He looked at his brothers, who had begun to move, nodding slowly.

"You shall live," he paused for a moment, then pointed a finger at them, "in the region of Goshen and be near me!" He nodded and smiled at the thought. "You, your children, and grandchildren, your flocks and herds, and all you have. I will provide for you there, because five years of famine still remain. Otherwise, you and your household and all who belong to you will become destitute."

The brothers began murmuring to each other, trying to take it all in, still uncertain. "You can see for yourselves, and so can my brother Benjamin, that it is really I who am speaking to you. Tell my father," here he gestured to his fine linen robe and then at his great house, "about all the honor accorded me in Egypt—about everything you have seen. And bring him here quickly."

The spell broke. Everyone spoke at once. Joseph—for now they knew it was him—threw his arms around his brother Benjamin and wept, and Benjamin embraced him, weeping. One by one, he embraced all his brothers and wept over them. They talked until late into the night.

גֹּשֶׁן

goshen

Goshen

"The orders came from pharaoh himself," Joseph told his brothers. The news that Joseph's brothers had come and that his father still lived so delighted pharaoh that he insisted on moving Jacob and all his family and flocks to Egypt. Pharaoh himself would provide all the wagons and carts needed to transport them all. The royal proclamation read, in part:

> To the brothers and family of the honorable Zaphenath-Paneah, viceroy, lord of dreams, and chief provisioner of Egypt:
> Return to the land of Kyn'n, and bring your father, the honorable Jacob Israel, and all his household back to me. I will give you the best of the land of Egypt, and you can enjoy the fat of the land. Take some carts from Egypt for your children and your wives, and get your father and come. Never mind about your belongings because the best of all Egypt will be yours.

"He is willing to welcome so many foreigners to his land?" Dan asked, suspicion written on his face.

Joseph laughed. "Have you not heard that the most powerful man in Egypt, save for pharaoh himself, is a foreigner? It is a scandal among the Egyptian nobility! Besides, it is not so many. A general in the Egyptian army commands more soldiers than the number of all our family. And that general might well be a foreigner, as well as many of his soldiers."

"Does that not trouble the Egyptians?" Dan asked, unconvinced.

"Perhaps," said Joseph, "but wealthy Egyptians are happy to have someone fight for them, just as they are happy to buy grain from me."

Dan still looked concerned, but Joseph clapped him on the shoulder, and said, "Good old Dan, always thinking about security. I will share with you later—after you bring Father and your families here."

Joseph continued, "Do not be concerned. I have plans for dealing with my foes and for keeping my family—secure. But for now," his face brightened, "we must move quickly to bring your families and animals here. Pharaoh expects speedy obedience!"

Joseph requisitioned the carts and provisions for their journey from pharaoh's household, as the proclamation provided for. From his own considerable resources, Joseph presented each of his brothers with splendid new garments, as befit the family of the viceroy; but to Benjamin, he gave three hundred pieces of silver and five sets of clothes. To his father, Joseph sent ten donkeys loaded with the finest goods Egypt had to offer, and ten female donkeys loaded with grain and bread and other provisions for his journey.

Altogether, it made an impressive company. Many carts and their Egyptian drivers, the pack animals laden with gifts and provisions, and a sizable military escort. Joseph himself saw them off. After embracing each brother one more time, he said, "May El Shaddai watch over you as you travel. Bring my father to me quickly." With a twinkle in his eye, he added, "And please, do not quarrel along the way." The brothers chuckled ruefully at first, then more and more in relief and delight. Joseph gave a hand signal, the Egyptian officer in command barked an order, and the column began to move off. Joseph stood a long time watching them recede into the distance.

* * * * *

The sheer size of the approaching column paralyzed everyone in Jacob's camp. The rising cloud of dust and the strange banners riveted everyone's attention. Servants stopped and stared, children abandoned their games, even Jacob and Amos remained still and strained their eyes. More than a score of carts and wagons, a large group of soldiers, and donkeys laden with grain and other goods. And among them—was it possible?—walked Reuben and Judah, Dan and Issachar, all the rest, including Benjamin, and even Simeon! But dressed in finery such as few in Jacob's camp had ever seen. And, even at a distance, he heard his sons shouting, "Zaphenath-Paneah! God speaks. He lives! God speaks. He lives!"

Finally, they reached camp. Shaking his head in amazement, his eyes going from soldier to cart to sons, Jacob said, "I do not understand. Why do you keep saying 'Zaphenath-Paneah! God speaks. He lives'?"

"Because, Father," Judah said, grabbing Jacob by the shoulders and shaking him in his excitement, "Zaphenath-Paneah, the foreigner who rose to become the ruler of Egypt?"

"I remember his name," Jacob said.

"Zaphenath-Paneah, whose name in Egyptian means, 'God speaks. He lives,'" Judah said.

"I said that I remember," replied Jacob, slightly annoyed.

"He is Joseph! Joseph lives!"

The old man stumbled to one of the carts, where he sat down, leaning against the side to steady himself. "I am growing old," Jacob said. "For a moment I thought you said, 'Joseph lives!'"

"Joseph lives!" Judah repeated. "He is Zaphenath-Paneah!"

The cataract of images and information left him nearly breathless, but the revelation of Joseph's survival stunned him to silence.

Benjamin was beside himself with excitement. "He lives in a palace, with many servants, in the heart of this beautiful city with a great temple, and two giant needles of red granite covered with Egyptian glyphs, and pharaoh himself sent all these carts and wagons and soldiers, and—"

Issachar stepped between them and said, "I think Father has had enough for right now, Benjamin." Jacob could only nod slowly.

Finally, he found his voice. "Joseph lives! Can it be true?" Jacob asked.

"Joseph lives! In fact, he is ruler of all Egypt." Issachar said the words, as he did everything, plain and direct. Gesturing to the soldiers, the carts, the fine gifts they had begun unpacking from the donkeys, he said, "How else could we return with all this? We took enough silver for grain, not for any of this. And why would pharaoh send his army as an escort?" He waited for his words to sink in. "Joseph lives, and he rules Egypt."

Jacob stood, looked from one face to another, a spark of hope bursting into flame within him. "It must be so. Joseph lives!" His mind repeated the words over and over until he knew them to be true. Finally, his tongue revealed what his thoughts had told him. "Joseph lives!" Then, turning to his sons, Israel said, "I am convinced! My son Joseph is still alive." Then, for the first time in many years, he acted decisively. "I will go and see him before I die."

The soldiers moved with practiced efficiency, organizing people and animals into groups sized to be easily accommodated on a single wagon. A spindly Egyptian named Adjo with a shaved head came to Jacob with a piece of papyrus covered with marks and symbols. He questioned the patriarch closely, sometimes stopping to make corrections on the papyrus. He then went from one loaded wagon to another, confirming the contents or passengers in each wagon. When he finished, he returned to Jacob.

"My lord Jacob, your servant Adjo, finds that your household consists of some fifty-seven freeborn families with one hundred nineteen adult men and women, three hundred fifteen children, and one hundred eighty servants of all ages."

"So many?" said Jacob. "I never realized there were so many."

"If you please, my lord, is that an accurate accounting?" Adjo asked.

"I am sure it is," Jacob said, chuckling to himself.

This did not satisfy the slight Egyptian. "My lord Zaphenath-Paneah is very exacting in these matters, and I—"

Jacob held up his hand, and Adjo paused, obviously displeased. "I am sure your accounting is accurate. If there is any problem, I will speak personally to Jos—to your master on your behalf."

Adjo considered this a moment, one eyebrow raised in disapproval. "Very well." He pointed to the wagons of livestock. "We generally do not make such a strict accounting of animals. They are subject to accidents, predation, they even get lost—"

Once again, Jacob cut the Egyptian short. Clearly Adjo was not experienced in the care of livestock. "It is all right, uh, Adjo, was it?" The Egyptian nodded curtly at the sound of his name. Jacob continued, "We are accustomed to the problems of moving livestock. I assure you, we will not hold you responsible for every lamb and kid. Does that take care of your concerns?"

Adjo thought for a moment, opened his mouth, and then thought better of it. His mouth set in a grim line, he nodded and walked to the head of the column, where he gave the officer in charge the signal to commence the march.

With everyone and everything either mounted or on wagons or carts, the procession moved rapidly. At the end of the second day's journey, they reached the well at Beersheba.

"From here we leave the land of my father, Isaac," Jacob announced. "This night we will make sacrifices to Adonai Elohim, El Shaddai, the God of my father. I shall not return in life to these lands, so I must make my sacrifices now." Jacob assured Adjo that the animals slaughtered would not be forgotten, nor would he request restitution for them when they reached Egypt, and so the scribe did not object—verbally, though his facial expressions said otherwise. But Jacob refused to let an Egyptian functionary dictate his actions. After the feast, Jacob went outside the camp to pray.

His thoughts reached out to the windows of heaven. *El Shaddai*, he prayed silently. *My heart is torn. After all these years, for Joseph to be restored to me gives me great joy. But I am loathe to leave the land You promised to Isaac, my father, and to Abraham, my father's father. My heart is torn between longing for my son and wanting to honor my father and to remain true to the Promise You gave Abraham. I can see no other way. The famine makes survival impossible. But I do not trust pharaoh. Without the promise of seeing Joseph, I still would resist going to Egypt. But I am advanced in years and my strength has gone. I can wrestle no longer. Tomorrow, I leave the land of my fathers forever. Have mercy on Your servant, Adonai.*

And with that, he limped to his bed. He slept soundly. And yet, in the middle of the night, a Voice, gentle yet powerful, like the current of a mighty river, resonated in his mind. *"Jacob! Jacob!"*

"Here I am," he replied.

"I am El Shaddai, Adonai Elohim of your father." As a gentle ocean swell lifts a great ship, so the mighty current of sound lifted his mind to understanding. *"Do not be afraid to go down to Egypt, for I will make you into a great nation there. I will go down to Egypt with you, and I will surely bring you back again. And Joseph's own hand will close your eyes."*

The mighty current of sound moved on, leaving only stillness in the tent. Jacob's thoughts reached out again, *Thank You, Adonai Elohim. Oh, thank You.* Tears of joy filled his eyes, and he wept himself to sleep.

The next morning, Jacob spoke to the officer in charge of their journey. "Please give my son, Judah, one of your fastest mounts and provisions for the journey. Let me send him ahead of us to Zaphenath-Paneah, so that he may meet us and guide us to our final destination."

The soldier nodded sharply, as though saluting, and said, "My lord Zaphenath-Paneah, and pharaoh himself, charged me directly that I should grant you everything in my power. It shall be as you wish." And so Judah went out ahead of them to Egypt.

Not long after the procession entered Egypt, the road to On turned southward, but their military escort took the road straight west to Goshen. The next day, they spotted a chariot, accompanied by a squadron of mounted men, speeding toward them. Jacob's military escort halted their column, the men assuming an attitude of attention. When the chariot reached them, a regal figure in richly adorned white linen leaped out and ran straight to Jacob, stopping an arm's length away.

For the first time in more than twenty years, father Jacob and son Joseph looked into each other's eyes, time standing still. Then Joseph took his father in a fierce embrace, the two wept and laughed without speaking. Finally, Israel said to Joseph, "Now I am content. I am ready to die, since I have seen for myself that you still live."

For the rest of the day, Joseph and Jacob talked of the lost years, of trials, and the leading of El Shaddai. Before nightfall, they reached a new mud-brick house, whitewashed and painted with scenes that looked remarkably like the hill country near Hebron. "Your house, Father," Joseph said. Jacob went from room to room with sparkling eyes while Joseph directed the disposition of the people and animals from the wagons.

Later, all but his personal guard departed, Joseph spoke to his father and brothers in private. "This is some of the choicest land in Lower Egypt," Joseph told them, and the brothers murmured their agreement. "When the drought ends, some five years from now, many will desire it. But if you have been settled here all that time, no one will be able to question your claim. Indeed, if you keep your sheep and goats here, no one will want to challenge you."

"I do not understand," Issachar said. "With even a little rain, this valley could be a wonderful pastureland. Why would they not challenge us? Does not pharaoh himself carry a ceremonial shepherd's crook?"

"Oh, they like mutton, well enough, and wool and cheese," said Joseph. "But the nobility of Egypt left the farming to their servants long ago. They no longer want to dirty their hands. Especially with sheep." This led to much grumbling and shaking of heads among the brothers. Joseph raised his hand and said, "I will go up and speak to pharaoh and will say to him, 'My brothers and my father's household, who were living in the land of Kyn'n, have come to me. The men are shepherds; they tend livestock, and they have brought along their flocks and herds and everything they own.' "

"This is true," said Judah.

Joseph raised his hand again. "Sooner or later, pharaoh himself will want to speak with you. When pharaoh calls you in and asks, 'What is your occupation?' you should answer, 'Your servants have tended livestock from our boyhood on, just as our fathers did.' "

"All right," said Dan, "but why do you tell us this?"

"Because," said Joseph, "then you will be allowed to settle in Goshen, for all shepherds are detestable to the Egyptians." Seeing they still had questions, Joseph continued. "Goshen is far enough from On so that the nobles will not have to see or smell the sheep, but close enough so that we can visit often."

Everyone seemed satisfied, except for Dan, who said, "Is there something you are not telling us?"

Joseph smiled a weary smile. "Dan, Dan. All right. You asked me before if pharaoh is willing to welcome so many foreigners to his land, do you remember?"

"I remember," Dan said.

"Pharaoh is happy to welcome my family because through me, El Shaddai has saved the land of Egypt from the famine. But even though he may appear all powerful, even pharaoh has challengers," Joseph said.

"Challengers?" Dan said.

"Other families, whose noble birth and great wealth fuel their ambition," Joseph said. Seeing the puzzled looks on his brothers' faces, he chuckled, "Anyone who occupies a position such as mine soon discovers he has rivals," Joseph confided, "and so does pharaoh, even if they must remain undeclared rivals."

"Of course," said Dan. "And you being a foreigner gives them something with which to stir up opposition."

Joseph nodded. "And giving choice land to foreigners, even if the nobles do not currently desire it, only gives them more fuel for their fires of resentment."

"But since they dislike sheep so much, they will be pleased we are not closer, is that it?" asked Issachar.

Joseph nodded. "It gives pharaoh an excuse. If they complain, he can say,

'Did you want these shepherds closer?' And that will leave his critics with nothing to say."

Jacob finally spoke. "Very clever, my son. Devious, but very clever." The old man thought a minute, and then said, "Experience tells me that this explanation will quiet the critics only for a time. Eventually, when memories fade, they will use it against pharaoh, against you, again."

Joseph nodded grimly. "My experience tells me the same thing. I designed this 'shepherd defense' for the short term, as a way to silence the critics for now and get you settled safely into the land around Goshen."

"And do you have a long-term plan?" Jacob asked.

Joseph broke into a broad smile and laughed out loud. "I do, Father. I certainly do."

'erets

Land

Joseph bowed before pharaoh. "My father and brothers, with their flocks and herds and everything they own, have come from the land of Kyn'n and are now in Goshen," he said, making a sweeping gesture to the five brothers behind him. Judah, Issachar, Asher, Dan, and Benjamin, all arrayed in their finest apparel, also bowed before pharaoh.

The great ruler sat on a raised stone platform in his golden lion's head throne. A long, narrow carpet led between rows of stone columns painted with bright green, blue, and red horizontal stripes in the main hall of his palace. Courtiers, nobles, and royal officials in their finery lined the aisle the brothers had passed along to the throne, where they knelt in respect. Pharaoh smiled in pleasure at the sight of his trusted viceroy and motioned for the brothers to rise.

Pharaoh asked the brothers, "What is your occupation?"

"Your servants are shepherds," they replied to pharaoh, "just as our fathers were."

"And why do you come before pharaoh this day?"

"We have come to live here a while because the famine is severe in Kyn'n and your servants' flocks have no pasture. So now, your servants respectfully request permission to settle in Goshen." A sudden buzz erupted behind them, but pharaoh raised his hand, and the silence returned.

Pharaoh addressed Joseph. "Zaphenath-Paneah, your father and your brothers have come to you. By the decree of pharaoh, ruler of Upper and

Lower Egypt, all the land of Egypt is before you; settle your father and your brothers in the best part of the land. Let them live in Goshen." The buzz began again, and this time pharaoh ignored it. Leaning forward, he smiled and said, "And if any of them possess special ability, put them in charge of my own livestock."

"My brother Asher, my lord. We all envy his skill," Joseph said in confidential tones, and the other brothers signaled their assent.

Then pharaoh silenced the hall once more. "Have you more business before pharaoh this day?"

"My lord," Joseph said, "if it pleases pharaoh, my father is here to see you."

"It pleases pharaoh very much," the ruler said, "to meet the father of the man who has saved all Egypt from the famine." He said these words with a flourish of his ceremonial flail, and the assembled audience recognized their cue and applauded.

The aged Jacob stepped forward, also arrayed in the finest clothing Joseph could obtain. Joseph said simply, "My father, Jacob Israel."

Jacob knelt before pharaoh, and said, "May Adonai Elohim grant pharaoh a long life, a peaceful reign, and a fruitful harvest."

The words touched pharaoh's heart, and he asked, "Blessed father of Zaphenath-Paneah, him you call Joseph, how old are you?"

And Jacob said to pharaoh, "My pilgrimage has occupied a hundred and thirty years. My years have been few and difficult, and not equal to the years of the pilgrimage of my fathers."

"One hundred and thirty?" said pharaoh. "That does not sound like few. But I am sorry they have been difficult. May your Adonai Elohim, the great God who gave your son the ability to interpret dreams and protect the prosperity of my kingdom, grant that your years here may be times of plenty and peace."

"Thank you, my lord," Jacob said. "And may pharaoh's years not be few, and may they not be difficult. Blessed be pharaoh for the kindness he has shown to me and my household."

Joseph then addressed the throne. "My father is not young anymore, and his strength is not great. If it pleases pharaoh, dismiss us now and let me take my father home where he can rest."

Pharaoh nodded. "It pleases pharaoh. Let it be as you say."

So Joseph took his father's arm, and he and his brothers walked down the long aisle and out of the great hall. Outside, a sedan chair waited for Joseph, but he placed his father in the chair and walked beside him to Goshen.

"I noticed one Egyptian in particular did not seem to like us," Judah said. "He stood on the right side of the aisle, quite near the raised platform, dressed in beautiful white linen trimmed in green and gold."

"You noticed him, did you?" Joseph said. "That was Hetshepsu, one of the wealthiest and most influential nobles."

"And one of pharaoh's rivals?" asked Issachar.

"Probably his greatest rival," Joseph said. "And no doubt he will question pharaoh's giving you the land of Goshen. Not openly, of course, but in subtle ways he will question pharaoh's judgment in this matter."

"What can you do to counter his subtle attacks?" asked Dan. "I know about swords and bows, but what weapons can you use against slander and innuendo?"

The procession passed an open square with a sundial in its center. Joseph said, "In this case, I will use that," pointing to the sundial. "That and grain." The brothers looked at him, their eyes full of questions, but he just smiled.

After that, in accordance with pharaoh's decree, Joseph settled his father and his brothers in Egypt and gave them property in the best part of the land, the district of Rameses, as pharaoh had directed. Joseph also provided his father and his brothers and all of his father's household with food.

As Joseph had predicted, however, the drought did not end, and the famine grew worse. Hungry people throughout Egypt and Kyn'n brought their silver to Joseph to buy the grain he had stored away during the years of abundant harvests. Eventually, the silver ran out. Even among the wealthiest Egyptians, the famine outlasted their stockpiles of silver.

One day, Itennu, eldest son of Hetshepsu, dressed in his family's livery of green, gold, and white, came before Joseph to buy grain. "My lord, my father, Hetshepsu of royal blood says, 'We have no more silver to buy food,'" Itennu said. "It will profit you nothing if we simply die before you."

"Pharaoh would be grieved to lose such loyal subjects as yourself and your father," Joseph replied.

"Thank you, my lord," Itennu said, "We have heard that you were willing to exchange livestock for grain." Joseph did not respond. Clearly, Itennu found this difficult. "We have livestock, my lord, but we cannot feed them without grain." Itennu's eyes darted up and down, but still Joseph did not speak. "My father Hetshepsu requests—will you accept our livestock in exchange for grain?"

"Just so," said Joseph, nodding. "Bring in your livestock, and we will trade you grain for them at the posted exchange rates in grain for horses and camels, sheep and goats, and cattle and donkeys. You can trade enough livestock to feed yourselves and your remaining livestock, or bring in all your animals to assure enough grain for you and your families."

"Thank you, my lord," Itennu said.

Hetshepsu did what everyone with livestock did that year—brought them in and exchanged them for grain to keep them through another dry year. But the famine still did not end. And just as the silver had run out, so did the livestock. The next year found the Egyptians with neither silver nor livestock. Itennu came before Joseph again, hoping for grain.

"My lord, last year I came before you without silver, and my lord graciously accepted our livestock in exchange for grain to keep us alive. I return this year, and my father Hetshepsu says, 'We cannot hide from our lord the fact that since our money is gone and our livestock belongs to you, there is nothing left for our lord except our bodies and our land.' " Itennu paused, then asked, "Why should we perish before your eyes—we and our land as well? Buy us and our land in exchange for food, and we with our land will be in bondage to pharaoh. Give us seed so that we may live and not die, and that the land may not become desolate."

Joseph thought for a long time before replying. "Pharaoh's heart is torn to see your suffering. He does not want to see his subjects die and the land become desolate. It shall be as you say. From now on, you and your land will belong to pharaoh. But pharaoh cares for his own property, so he will see to it that you have grain to eat; and when the rains come again, you will have seed to plant, so that you may live and the land will be fruitful again."

Continuing, Joseph said, "Once I have bought you and your land for pharaoh, and supplied seed for you so you can plant the ground when the crop comes in, give a fifth of it to pharaoh. The other four-fifths you may keep as seed for the fields and as food for yourselves and your households and your children."

Itennu bowed low before Joseph and said, "You have saved our lives. May we find favor in the eyes of our lord; we will be in bondage to pharaoh."

With Hetshepsu's surrender, Joseph completed the subjugation of the nobility. They could never again challenge pharaoh's authority. Pharaoh now owned every bit of land and everyone on the land. Except for the priests, whom pharaoh already supported, including a grant of food. And except for Jacob and his family, who lived unchallenged in the land of Goshen. That land, watered by the reduced but still flowing Nile, provided pasture so that the flocks and herds of Jacob and his sons survived, even as the nobility of Egypt sold off their livestock, and then themselves, for grain.

For seventeen years, long beyond the end of the famine and the return of normal rains and harvests, Jacob and his sons prospered.

Then one day, Jacob called Joseph to his house. "The years here in Goshen have been good years," the old man said, "but the years lie heavy upon my shoulders. The time draws near for me to die, to lie down with my fathers." Joseph started to protest, but Jacob would not permit it. "We both know this," Jacob said, and Joseph silently acknowledged it as the truth. "If I have found favor in your eyes, put your hand under my thigh and promise that you will show me kindness and faithfulness. Do not bury me in Egypt, but when I rest with my fathers, carry me out of Egypt and bury me where they are buried." And Joseph promised Jacob that he would be buried with his fathers.

Jacob lived on, but became increasingly frail. One day, Amos sent word that Jacob had fallen ill. Joseph decided that he could no longer delay, that the time had come to present his sons to Jacob for his blessing. So he set off for Goshen, taking Manasseh and Ephraim with him. They arrived just after midday.

Amos saw them coming and went into Jacob's bedchamber. He gently touched the old man's shoulder, and Jacob opened his eyes. "Your son Joseph is here with his sons, Manasseh and Ephraim."

"Joseph? Here?" The old man started to rise.

"Easy, master, easy," said Amos.

But Jacob said, "I am not dead yet, Amos." Jacob sat up and slapped his thighs. "Bring my children to me."

Outside, Amos motioned for Joseph and his sons to enter. "How is he today?" Joseph asked.

"More difficult than usual," Amos said, smiling. "Thinks he is young again."

"I will try not to tire him too much," Joseph said, and Amos gestured for him to enter the old man's room.

"Joseph?" Jacob asked, for the years had finally begun to dim his eyes.

"Father," Joseph said.

"I have been thinking of you," Jacob said. "El Shaddai appeared to me at Luz in the land of the Kinnahu, and there He blessed me and said to me, 'I am going to make you fruitful and will increase your numbers. I will make you a community of peoples, and I will give this land as an everlasting possession to your descendants after you.'"

"You have spoken of this before, Father," Joseph said. "Why do you mention it now?"

Jacob seemed not to have heard the question. "Now then," he said, "your two sons born to you in Egypt before I came to you here will be reckoned as mine; when El Shaddai keeps His promise and gives to my children the land of the Kinnahu, Ephraim and Manasseh will have equal status with Reuben and Simeon; they will receive an equal share of land."

A stunned Joseph did not know what to say. His sons would be reckoned equals with his brothers? Jacob had just announced the bestowal of a priceless gift.

But Jacob had not finished. "Any children born to you after them," he said, "will be yours; the territory they inherit will be reckoned under the names of their brothers."

"This is a great gift," Joseph said, as much to his sons and himself as to his father.

But Jacob had moved on, his dimmed eyes welling with tears. "As I was returning from Haran, to my sorrow Rachel died in the land of the Kinnahu while we were still on the way, a little distance from Ephrath. So I buried her there beside the road to Ephrath." He paused, then, for the first time, seemed to notice Joseph's sons. "Now, who are these?"

"They are the sons God has given me here," Joseph replied.

Israel said, "Bring them to me so I may bless them."

So Joseph brought his sons close to Israel. And the old man kissed them and embraced them, and placed them on his knees, thus adopting them as his own. His face radiant, Israel said to Joseph, "For many years, I never expected to see your face again, and now El Shaddai has allowed me to see your children too."

Joseph removed his sons from Israel's knees, prostrated himself, touching his forehead to the ground. Then he took both sons, Ephraim on his right toward Israel's left hand and Manasseh on his left toward Israel's right hand, and brought them close to Israel. But Israel reached out his right hand and put it on Ephraim's head, though he was the younger, and crossing his arms, he put his left hand on Manasseh's head, even though Manasseh was the firstborn.

Joseph saw this so he took hold of his father's hand to move it from Ephraim's head to Manasseh's head, saying, "My father, this one is the firstborn; put your right hand on his head."

But Israel refused. "I know, my son, I know," he said. "He, too, will become a people, and he, too, will become great. Nevertheless, his younger brother will be greater than he, and his descendants will become a group of nations."

Then he blessed Joseph, "May El Shaddai, before whom my fathers Abraham and Isaac walked, the God who has been my Shepherd all my life to this day, the Angel who has delivered me from all harm—may He bless these boys. May they be called by my name and the names of my fathers Abraham and Isaac, and may they increase greatly upon the earth."

Then he spoke to the Joseph's sons. "In your name will Israel pronounce this blessing:

" 'May Adonai Elohim make you like Ephraim and Manasseh.' " Thus, he declared Ephraim ahead of Manasseh.

Joseph asked, "Is it not the custom that the firstborn should be given preference?"

"That is man's reckoning," Israel agreed.

"Is there some other reckoning?"

"Whom has El Shaddai chosen?" Israel replied.

Joseph shook his head. "I do not follow—"

"Was Abraham firstborn?" Israel inquired.

"You told us as children that Haran was born first."

"So I did. Was my father Isaac firstborn?" Joseph seemed about to confirm that statement, when Israel interjected, "Or was Ishmael born first?"

Joseph's eyes went wide. "And your brother Esau was born before you!"

"It is so," Israel agreed. "But El Shaddai told my mother in a dream, before our birth, that I would receive His favor. Adonai Elohim does not reckon as we do."

Joseph thought for a moment. "It seems so—so contrary," he said. "I am struggling to understand it."

Israel laughed. "Struggling? I have been struggling with El Shaddai ever since I was born—*born second*," he said.

"I first realized the night before I met Esau again, twenty years after I had wronged him, when I struggled all night with the same One I had always been struggling with."

"Struggled? But you did not let Him go until He blessed you," Joseph said.

"Let Him go?" said Israel. "What makes you think I let Him go?" He laughed again, a crackling sound like ancient papyrus shattering. "Let Him go? Nothing can hold Him."

"But, you said—did He not bless you?"

"That is the secret," the old man said. "You think you are wrestling with Adonai over what should be done, and you are," he paused, suddenly fixing his eyes on his listener. "Without realizing it, it is you trying to escape, not Him."

"You escape? I do not understand," Joseph said.

"Escape from the path He has placed you on." They sat silently for a moment. "When you stop trying to escape His plan for your life, there is nothing else to struggle over."

"And how do you stop trying to escape?" Joseph asked.

The dry laugh again. "You never do, at least I never did. So you just hold on to Adonai Elohim, and He holds on to you."

Again they sat in silence, then Israel said to Joseph, "I will soon die, but El Shaddai will be with you and take you back to the land of your fathers. To you, as one who is over your brothers, I give you the double portion, the portion of the firstborn. Reuben may have been born before you were, but as El Shaddai made clear in your dreams, He chose you."

שלום

shalom

Peace

Israel lay silent for a moment, breathing softly. He had talked of the past for what seemed like hours—and yet, the time had passed so quickly that the crowing of a rooster startled them. Amos looked up with alarm. Israel's story had lasted through the night. "We must let your father rest," he said to the brothers, but Israel raised his hand.

"At my age, sleep comes when it will. And soon enough, it will come to stay." Israel moved his hand about. "Are all my sons still here?" he asked.

"We are here," came from a dozen voices.

"I have told you of my years of struggle," Israel said. "And I near the end of my greatest struggle."

"What struggle can be so great?" asked Issachar. "Even greater than your struggle with the Divine Stranger at the Jabbok?"

"The struggle of a parent to help his grown children make peace with each other," Jacob said. "Do not look shocked. I know of your conflicts, of your fears," he said, his eyes bright. "My parting gift to you is to help you recognize how my struggles became the root of your own," Jacob said.

"I do not understand," Reuben said.

"You suffered as much as any of your brothers," Jacob said. "Because my father always favored my older brother, and would have given him the birth-right no matter how outrageously he behaved, I vowed not to play favorites with my firstborn."

All the brothers began to protest, but Jacob silenced them with a wave of his hand. "And in so doing, I made your life impossible, Reuben. I demanded more from you as a child, than most men could live up to.

"My father was distant to me," Jacob said, "and I vowed not to be." Here, he closed his eyes as if in pain and shook his head slowly. "But because Leah deceived me, and I loved only Rachel—I am sorry, my sons, but you know it, do you not?" He looked around the room, and saw his sons looking down and nodding sadly. "Because of that, I became close only with Joseph and Benjamin." Tears coursed down the old man's face. "And that is how I broke my vow to avoid favoritism. And in so doing, I made everyone's life miserable."

The old man wept silently for a moment. Then he continued, "As much as possible, I want to save you from my mistakes, to lessen your struggles. That is why I told my story. Now let me share what I learned from those struggles, as it applies to each one of you." Israel motioned to Amos, who helped him to sit up.

"We are ready," they said.

"Reuben," he said, and Reuben came and knelt beside his bed. Placing one hand on his son's shoulder and one on his head, he said, "Reuben, you are my firstborn, my might, the first sign of my strength, excelling in honor and excelling in power." Israel paused, shaking his head sadly, "But your spirit is turbulent as the waters, driven this way and that by your desire to please others. So long as you do this, you cannot excel. Trying to prove yourself, you went up on to your father's bed, on to my couch and defiled it, and in the process discredited yourself. You must learn not to need to seek anyone's approval, except Adonai Elohim who made you."

Reuben fought back anger for a moment, and then replied, "You are right, my father. But how do I achieve the approval of Elohim?"

"It took me years to discover the answer to that," Israel said. "Years of trying to be the firstborn, to earn the approval of my father."

"Please, what did you discover?" Reuben asked.

"That I could not earn the approval of Elohim. He made me. Before I was born, He knew me. In my struggles to overtake the firstborn, to take the blessing by stratagem, I was 'aqob Jacob, the crooked cheater. But when I ceased my attempts to take what I wanted and took my concerns to Adonai Elohim, I became who He made me to be—Israel, the one who struggles with God."

"Who does Adonai Elohim want me to be?" Reuben asked.

"That is for you to take up with Him," Israel said. Releasing Reuben, he called out, "Simeon and Levi."

The two men knelt before their father, and Israel placed a hand on each one's head. "Simeon and Levi, from the very first, inseparable brothers. But each of you ignites the other's passion, until you cannot contain your anger, and your swords wreak terrible violence." Looking at the other brothers, Israel said, "Do not get involved in their disputes, the times when they increase each other's anger. Do not become their followers, for they have killed men in their anger and hamstrung oxen as they pleased. But this fierce anger of theirs brings them only grief." Now focusing on the two brothers, he said, "As much as you desire each other's company, for your own good, you should be separated. Brothers," he said, "keep them apart for their own sakes—and yours."

Judah came forward next. "Judah, you have grown into a natural leader, whom your brothers praise, and your enemies fear. All your brothers wisely follow your leadership." A murmur of assent ran through the room. "You are a lion's cub, Oh Judah; when you hunt, you find your prey, and when you rest—none cares to disturb you!" Subdued laughter greeted this remark.

"Because of this, you and your children will continue to rule and receive tribute, not only among us but others as well. Your lands will prosper, yielding abundant wine and milk."

"Zebulun," Israel said, and that son assumed his place before his father. "You love your independence, to rule your own world like a ship's captain, so you will live by the seashore and become a haven for ships, even as far as Sidon."

Next came Issachar. "You are like a sturdy, big-boned donkey." Good-natured laughter of recognition filled the room. Even Israel and Amos smiled. When the sound died down, Israel continued. "When you recognize good land, a good place to settle down, you put your shoulder to the load. You see what needs to be done, and you do it!"

Dan followed, and Israel declared, "Dan has a wandering spirit, but a keen eye for tactics. Anyone facing an enemy will want Dan on their side. He strikes with lethal speed, like a serpent in the path."

Gad took his place at Israel's feet. "Gad, like his brother Dan, may sometimes place himself in danger, and like his brother, he strikes with speed and deadliness, making him a dangerous adversary and a welcome ally."

"Asher," Israel said when his turn came. "Asher, whose name means 'happy,' how happy you will be. Pay attention to how he cares for crops and livestock: Asher's food will be rich; he will provide delicacies fit for a king." This brought laughter, since Asher had taken over the management of pharaoh's flocks at the ruler's request.

Next, Naphtali. "Naphtali," Israel said. "You, too, like your independence. You like to be alone with the flocks, and you show special skill with newborn lambs."

Everyone held their breath as the viceroy of Egypt knelt before his father. "Joseph," the old man said, his voice trembling. "Joseph, you are like a fruitful vine, a fruitful vine near a spring, growing so vigorously its branches climb over a wall.

"You are like a warrior whom bitter archers attacked; shooting at you with hostility. But your bow remained steady, your strong arms remained nimble because of the hand of the Mighty One of Jacob, because of the Shepherd, the Rock of Israel, because of your father's God, who helps you, because of El Shaddai, who blesses you with blessings of the heavens above, blessings of the deep that lies below, blessings of the breast and womb.

"Your father's blessings are greater than the blessings of the ancient mountains, than the bounty of the age-old hills. Let all these rest on the head of Joseph, on the brow of the prince among his brothers."

Finally, Benjamin. "Benjamin, young though he is, has the heart of a ravenous wolf; he and his descendants will be great warriors. In the morning, he devours the prey; in the evening, he divides the plunder."

Then Israel addressed them all. His strength consumed with much speaking, his voice began to fade. "My sons. Find your peace with each other. El Shaddai has placed you together as brothers. Your differences can contribute to your collective strength, or they may cause you to quarrel among yourselves and divide you." He looked from one to another without seeing. "Tell me that you will seek peace with each other. I spent so many years in conflict—conflict with my brother Esau; conflict with my father-in-law Laban. I have seen much strife and would hope that you might live in peace."

"We will, Father," Joseph spoke first. Then Judah, Reuben, and the rest, all saying, "We will seek peace with each other."

Israel sighed and laid his head on his pillow. "I am about to be gathered to my people. Bury me with my fathers in the cave in the field of Ephron the Hittite, the cave in the field of Machpelah, near Mamre in the land of the Kinnahu, which Abraham bought as a burial place from Ephron the Hittite, along with the field. There Abraham and his wife Sarah were buried, there Isaac and his wife Rebekah were buried, and there I buried Leah."

"We will, Father," Joseph said again. Then Israel smiled, folded his arms, and went to his rest. Joseph threw himself upon his father's lifeless body, weeping. Then he kissed his father one last time, and said, "He is gone."

* * * * *

Joseph commanded that his personal physicians oversee the embalming of his father's remains. Pharaoh declared a national time of mourning of seventy days. The embalming rituals took forty days, and the mourning extended a full cycle of the moon beyond that.

When the days of mourning had passed, Joseph sent a message to pharaoh's court. "My father made me swear an oath and said, 'I am about to die; bury me in the tomb I dug for myself in the land of Kyn'n.' If I have found favor in your eyes, now let me go up and bury my father; then I will return."

Pharaoh replied, "Go up and bury your father, as you swore to do."

So Joseph went up to bury his father, but not alone. All the officials and dignitaries of pharaoh's court—indeed, all the dignitaries of Egypt accompanied Joseph and his brothers. A vast procession, complete with royal chariots and horsemen also went up with him. The babe who had come into the world clutching at his brother's heel now went to his burial with all the pomp and power of the great Egyptian Empire at his heels.

Such a large retinue required a large open area for the necessary ceremonies. They found one at the threshing floor of Atad, near the Jordan, and there Joseph observed the official seven-day mourning ceremony for his father. And the whole assembly lamented loudly and bitterly. When the Kinnahu who lived nearby observed the mourning Egyptians, they named the area *Abel Mizraim*, "the brook of the Egyptians."

So Jacob's sons did as he had commanded them. From Abel Mizraim, they carried him to the cave in the field of Machpelah, near Mamre, which Abraham had bought as a burial place from Ephron the Hittite, and there they buried him.

After burying his father, Joseph, together with his brothers and all the vast assembly who had gone with him to bury his father, returned to Egypt.

One thing remained to fulfill the legacy of Israel, the one who struggled with God. Joseph's brothers still worried. *Joseph holds great power. Could it be that he refrained from taking revenge on us so that Father would not have to witness it?* they wondered.

So the brothers sought an audience with Joseph. Judah stepped forward to speak on behalf of the others. "We ask you to forgive us the sins and the wrongs we committed in treating you so badly. Now please forgive the sins of the servants of the God of your father."

Then Judah and all the others threw themselves down before him. "We are your slaves," they said.

Joseph wept. And then he bade them rise. "Do not be afraid. Am I in the place of God? It is true," he said, "you intended to harm me, but El Shaddai intended it for good. Look what has come of it, how many lives have been saved from famine."

He smiled. "You are my brothers, you have nothing to fear from me. Indeed, as pharaoh's viceroy, I will provide for you and your children."

The brothers questioned him closely, but his every word reassured them and evinced his genuine affection for them. Joseph lived on many years in the land of Egypt. Lived in peace with his brothers and their children, all the days of his life. The man named Jacob, or "cheater," at birth, who struggled his whole life, through those trials had become *Israel*, the one who struggles with God. Now that his children, the children of Israel, lived in peace, Jacob's struggles had truly come to an end. And for the time being, Israel struggled no more.